INTO THE STORM

EVIDENCE: UNDER FIRE

RACHEL GRANT

Books By Rachel Grant

Evidence: Under Fire

Into the Storm

Trust Me

Evidence

Concrete Evidence

Body of Evidence

Withholding Evidence

Night Owl

Incriminating Evidence

Covert Evidence

Cold Evidence

Poison Evidence

Silent Evidence

Winter Hawk

Tainted Evidence

Broken Falcon

Fiona Carver

Dangerous Ground

Crash Site

This one is for Jenn Stark,
Amazing author and dear friend. From Golden Hearts to Twelve Shades
of Midnight to the Hot Sexy Six you have been a guide and companion
on this journey. With your friendship, every year is the Year of the
Unicorn.

Chapter One

Olympic National Park, Washington
January

Adrenaline flooded Audrey Kendrick's system as the SUV slid toward the edge of the road. *Black ice.* The invisible, treacherous patches were the reason this winding road through the Olympic foothills was closed to park visitors in winter. For long stretches of roadway, there was no shoulder, just a steep drop dotted with evergreens that clung to the slope. If she went over the edge, thick, old-growth trunks would break her fall, but the damage could still be deadly.

She turned into the skid. Tires gripped pavement, and the vehicle veered back into the center of the road, saving her from slipping off the side.

She tapped the brakes as shaking hands held the steering wheel in a white-knuckled grip. Her heart pounded at a rate that couldn't be healthy. The SUV slowed, and she took a deep breath to calm herself. She needed to focus on the pavement ahead and not what she'd find at the end of it.

At least with the road closed to all but park employees and inholding landowners, she didn't have to worry about other cars. She could take this calming break without fear she'd cause an accident if a vehicle careened around the curves in either direction.

A roadside mile marker sank her already dark mood even deeper. She was only eight miles from the gate that closed the road in winter months. She had ten more slick and twisty miles to go before she would reach Lake Olympus Lodge.

She wished she could have waited at the gate for law enforcement park ranger Jae-jin Son, but according to the dispatcher, Jae was stuck at Mora Campground, dealing with visitors who thought park rules were for other people. She didn't have time to wait. As it was, she'd be lucky to have thirty minutes of daylight to inspect the site before nightfall and the predicted storm rolled in.

Her belly was cramped tight with fear, an unpleasant accompaniment to her racing heart. Had the site been looted again? Why hadn't George called her back?

A little more than an hour ago, she'd been at the Forks Ranger Station, planning a spring break archaeology camp for tweens and teens with an interpretation park ranger, when she got a call from headquarters informing her the cameras she'd set up to protect the archaeological site had stopped transmitting.

She'd installed the cameras herself in November, after the site had been looted and tribal elder George Shaw had looked at her with such disappointment. The memory of his words still cut straight to her heart. *"I recommended you as Roy's replacement when he retired as park archaeologist. I trusted you to protect our sacred sites. Maybe this time the looting isn't your fault, but if it happens again, it will be."*

George took the desecration personally, and she, as the person entrusted to protect all cultural resources within

Olympic National Park, had failed him and the tribe. She'd installed the cameras within days. They couldn't stop looting, but they could alert her department when it happened.

And now the cameras weren't working.

According to headquarters, the lodge had electricity. This wasn't a simple power outage. Meaning this could be her worst-case scenario: looters had cut the line before digging up the site.

Her first call had been to George, who had an inholding cabin near the ancestral village. George was one of the few people who wintered near the lodge, and with the forecasted storm, he'd be settled in for the next few days, ready to ride out the wind and rain, the worst of which would hit this evening. But the elder hadn't answered her call or responded to her messages.

From the moment she couldn't reach George, her fear had shifted from the archaeological site to George himself. What if he'd seen the looters and confronted them? Looters sometimes turned violent when caught in the act. She couldn't simply wait by the gate for Jae as the dispatcher had instructed. She had to check on the site and George.

She picked up her phone from the center console to check for messages. No bars. Expected, but no less frustrating. This was one of the park's many dead zones for cellular coverage. She wouldn't be in call range until she reached the lodge complex, which, in addition to having cellular antennas for two providers, also had the latest, greatest satellite Wi-Fi.

Jae might be angry when he learned she hadn't waited for him to make this trek, but with a winter storm rolling in tonight, the heavy rain would freeze on the pavement. Tomorrow, this road would be an endless slick of black ice, far worse than it was today. It would be days before she made it back out here, and by the time she did, the storm could have washed away evidence that might identify the looters. If she found anything at the site, she had all the tools she needed to photograph, map, record, and collect it like a forensic investigator. CSI and archaeologists shared a lot of the same methodology.

She put the SUV in Drive again and inched forward, skittish about finding more black ice. The headlights cut through the dark curves, but ice remained impossible to see. She touched her hand to her belly, then returned it to the wheel. She dropped her speed by five miles per hour. Slow and cautious.

Her fingers ached from their tight grip on the steering wheel, but the SUV remained steady on the shadowed, winding road. In the summer, this road would be dappled with sunshine and flowers. She touched her belly again, thinking about what the road would look like in late July. The wind would ease in from the ocean, keeping the air fresh and cool even on the hottest of days.

In July, the days would be long. The sun would shine. And everything about her life would change.

At last, thirty minutes after nearly sliding off the road, she rounded the bend and the magnificent old Lake Olympus Lodge spread out before her. Built in the 1920s, the hotel embraced the lake with wide arms. In the summer, it would be full of guests, all enjoying the most magnificent of US National Parks. Today, however, the entire complex— store, museum, gas station, maintenance shops, annex guest cabins, and of course, the massive main lodge—was cold and silent. Abandoned and forlorn.

Even after the stressful drive, Audrey couldn't look at the lodge without thinking of Xavier. It was a mixed bag of emotions. Part of her was glad she would never forget the surprising, intense, hot night spent in this very lodge. There'd been a magic she wanted to hold on to. But now that perfect night was tainted with betrayal.

Xavier had been an old friend of Jae's, which should have made him trustworthy. Attraction had flared, hot and bright, probably blinding her.

He'd been handsome, sure, but it was his energy that spoke to her. Like her, he was an avid outdoor enthusiast. Plus, he'd been charming and funny and made her feel desirable after a breakup a year before that had left her questioning her choices.

Still, she'd accepted the no-strings fling for what it was, even if she did want more. There was no real future for them. She lived on the Olympic Peninsula and was only a year into her tenure at the job she'd wanted since she was eleven, and he lived…she didn't even know where he lived. At the time, she'd assumed he was still in the Bay Area, near where he'd grown up with Jae.

They hadn't exchanged phone numbers. He'd made it clear from the start that one night was all they'd have. As they said goodbye, it had stung, but she'd accepted it.

But then the home test stick indicated she was pregnant.

She'd been shocked. And elated. At thirty-eight, she was all too aware her biological clock was winding down. She hadn't planned this pregnancy, and they'd used condoms to prevent it—apparently, expiration dates mattered—but she was glad neither of them had bothered to check the wrapper in the heat of the moment. She was thankful for the wild, impulsive night with Xavier.

She wanted this baby with every fiber of her being.

In December, she'd been nervously excited to tell him the news. She'd planned what to say. She was having his baby, but she wouldn't force him to be a father. He could make his own decisions about what role he wanted to have in their child's life. She didn't want her child to be fatherless, but neither did she want her baby to have a dad who resented the responsibility.

She'd called Jae and left him a message, asking him to tell Xavier to call her. It was the only way she had to get ahold of him. She then spent the rest of the day waiting with her cell phone in hand.

Nothing could have prepared her for the shock she felt the following morning when she stepped into park headquarters and came face-to-face with Xavier. For a moment, she'd thought he was there because he'd guessed why she needed to speak with him and wanted to hear the news in person.

She'd felt a rush of wild joy.

The feeling lasted less than sixty seconds. Her happy fantasy flamed out when he opened his mouth and told her what he'd just done: he'd filed a complaint with the park superintendent. The subject of the complaint was none other than Audrey herself for refusing to sign off on a Navy SEAL training slated for Lake Olympus Lodge and the surrounding forest.

A proposal for the training had crossed her desk just days after the site was looted. Upset by the damage to the site, she would admit she'd viewed the proposed exercise with a jaundiced eye. What if she approved it, and then the SEALs harmed the historic or prehistoric sites that dotted the lakeshore? Sites were everywhere around the lake. For thousands of years, Lake Olympus had been an important gathering place for Indigenous people. If SEALs playing war games hurt those sites after she'd given them the green light, it would be her fault.

She'd never be able to look George in the eye again.

She sent the proposal back, asking the Navy to resubmit in the spring after they did a proper assessment of potential impacts to cultural and historical resources. Perhaps with more information and after extensive consultation with local tribes, they'd be approved for the following year.

It was standard procedure for a substandard—and clearly rushed—proposal.

It turned out Xavier didn't take rejection well, so he turned to the park superintendent to override Audrey's finding. When Jim refused to ignore the finding of his subject matter expert, Xavier insisted on bringing it before the Advisory Council on Historic Preservation—the ultimate governing body for her profession—to put pressure on the superintendent. But Xavier's complaint wasn't a simple objection to her findings. No. That she could understand and even forgive. He had his job; she had hers.

But that wasn't what he did.

When he couldn't win with the facts, he smeared her, claiming she wouldn't agree to sign the Finding of No Significant Impact because of their personal involvement. Because he'd slept with her and then rejected her.

The accusation was ridiculous—she hadn't even known Xavier was in the Navy until she saw him in uniform at park headquarters—and she certainly hadn't known he had anything to do with the proposed training. But the truth hadn't mattered to ACHP. They'd believed him.

His accusations nearly got her fired. She was still a little surprised she hadn't been. Her boss, at least, had believed her, which was why Xavier had to turn to ACHP in the first place. But that didn't mean her job wasn't hanging by a thread in the fallout of the success of his ploy. And that this had all happened on the heels of the looting? Not a great month for ONP's park archaeologist. A month later, her job remained on shaky ground.

That day at park headquarters, she'd been too angry to tell Xavier their big news, and she still hadn't told him. She wanted to. And she would. Soon. But every time she reached for the phone, anger would rise and steal her ability to speak. This was joyful news. For the rest of her life, she would remember telling the father of her child about her pregnancy. Did she really want that memory tainted by anger?

She imagined telling him dozens of different ways, but they always ended up tinged with bitterness. *"Hey, funny thing, remember how you tried to get me fired two weeks before Christmas? Yeah, well, I'm pregnant with your child. Good thing I kept my job and didn't lose my health insurance."*

Or sometimes she went a different route. *"Guess what? I'm having your baby, so you might want to recant what you said so I don't lose my job and the maternity leave I've accrued."*

She didn't want to be bitter. She wanted to share the joy in her heart. But she didn't know how to get into that mental space with Xavier.

Now she stopped in the circular drive that fronted the lodge and stared at the façade as memories of that night flooded her. His touch. His smile. His warm laugh and deep, husky voice as he told her exactly what he wanted to do to her. The heat in his gaze during the intense stare down before that first incredible kiss.

Facing the lodge, she realized this was the first time she'd been able to think of Xavier without anger since mid-December. Maybe she should call him right now. She shook her head, irritated with the distraction of it all. She had work to do. She needed to check on the site. Check on George. Then head home before the storm hit.

She parked in the spot next to the blue-painted accessible spaces at the far end of the loop. Even in the middle of winter when the lodge was closed, she couldn't bring herself to park in a blue spot. She hit the lock button on the SUV as she walked away, knowing that too was unnecessary. Some habits were too ingrained.

Before hiking to the site, she would check the fuse boxes

to see if the outbuildings had power. This might not be about looting. A surge could have caused an outage at the blacksmith shop. She'd braced herself for the worst-case scenario, but there was a whole continuum of possibilities. This could be nothing.

She rounded the lodge, heading for the exterior basement door on the lake side of the building. Wind swept along the roof, whipping water from the gutter and dropping it straight down the back of her neck.

She squealed at the frigid shower and pulled the hood of her raincoat up, protecting her neck too late to do any good. The temperature hovered at forty degrees, and the wind had a cold bite. She wished she'd grabbed her gloves from her pack in the back of the SUV.

She reached the basement door, which was at the base of a set of stone steps cut into the earth. She inserted her key into the lock, but it wouldn't turn. She checked the key. Gray plastic ring around the top. It was the right key.

She inserted it again. It refused to budge.

Frustration won over, and like a petulant child, she kicked the thick door. "Dammit! I do not have time for this."

A chill ran down her neck, but it wasn't raindrops that triggered it. Someone was behind her. She didn't know *how* she knew this, because she hadn't heard a sound except for the incessant wind. Before she could turn, she heard the distinctive clicks of a slide being racked to chamber a bullet.

"Do you have time for this?" The words were a soft, malevolent whisper.

Cold fear swamped her, as if a cascade of icy rain had drenched her neck and slid under her clothes down her back.

Her breath left her in a whoosh. She couldn't speak. Couldn't draw in air. Couldn't scream.

Was this a looter? But why would they be here and not up at the site? Plus, looters only turned violent when confronted—yet this person was confronting her, not the other way around.

A hand snaked around her side, pulling her back against a hard body. From the size and feel, she guessed it was a man. He dragged her backward, up the stone steps. She released her muscles, becoming an instant deadweight, but the man didn't falter. His grip merely tightened. When he reached the top, he swung her around and tripped her. She landed face-first in the wet peat that capped the lawn. She finally regained breath and voice and screamed in pain and panic.

Instinct told her to protect her belly, but her arms were yanked behind her. Her stomach was still flat, at least, the fetus too small to be harmed by this violence. She bucked as he grappled with her hands and pinned her down with a knee on her back. She screamed for help, but it was useless. There was no one around for miles.

Metal cuffs even colder than her chilled skin cinched her wrists together. The man couldn't be a law enforcement ranger. She knew them all and knew which ones were on duty right now. Jae was closest. Anyone not in law enforcement who carried around handcuffs must've planned this.

Am I being abducted?

Since when do looters abduct people?

Panic swamped her. She needed to escape. She tried to get leverage with her knees, to throw him off, but he was too strong. Too heavy. "Why are you doing this?" she choked out.

Hands ran down her body, checking pockets.

She could barely breathe. "Are you a looter?" she rasped in a low, breathless voice.

The man above her froze, hands stopping mid-pat down. "What?"

"Why are you doing this?" she repeated.

The man placed a hand on her shoulder and flipped her to her back. She lay there, her arms trapped beneath her, digging into her spine.

He straddled her with his gun pointed to the clouds. He wore a military combat uniform, which included a tactical vest and helmet with night vision goggles mounted to the crown. His face was coated in forest-colored paint. But his eyes weren't hidden or disguised.

Tears and panic ceased, replaced by shock. It was like the wind had been knocked out of her. Again, she couldn't speak or breathe.

She was staring into the eyes of Xavier Rivera, the father of her unborn child.

Chapter Two

*X*avier stared down at the woman he couldn't get out of his head, the woman he'd ruthlessly wronged, and saw shock and terror in her eyes.

He wanted to rear back, pull her to her feet, and apologize for being rough with her, but through his earpiece, he heard Cohen say, "What's the deal, Rivera? Is she here to stop the training?"

His focus snapped into place. He holstered the gun, which only fired paint-tipped rounds. She'd never been in any real danger from him, but he'd wanted to scare whoever was attempting to break into the basement.

From the look in her eyes, he'd succeeded. But Audrey Kendrick wasn't a threat. He knew that much at least. He responded, "Gimme a minute."

"We don't have a minute. What's going on?"

"Subject is in custody. I need to question her."

He ignored Cohen's reply.

He needed answers, fast. He met Audrey's gaze again. Her fear had faded, replaced by anger. He deserved her anger, but if she'd come here to stop the training, then she'd earned his.

When he'd seen the woman in a thick raincoat skulking around the building, it hadn't occurred to him it could be Audrey. He'd assumed she was an antimilitary activist who'd gotten wind of the exercise and shown up to cause trouble. Then he saw her go for the basement and figured she was there to do damage.

It had been a dick move to go around Audrey to get approval for the training, but he'd had no choice. She, however, did have a choice, and if she'd come here today to stop the trial run for the op, she'd find herself more than out of a job. He'd see to it she landed in jail. "What are you doing here?" he asked. "This place is restricted during the trainings. You know that."

She startled. "Training? What?"

"If you're here to stop the op—" He caught himself and added, "Exercise, then I can—and will—have you arrested."

"I didn't know one of your trainings was happening now." She glanced around as if she expected to see a platoon of SEALs watching. Perhaps hoping for rescue. No such luck. The team wouldn't arrive until after dark. They were on Whidbey Island right now, being briefed on their mission.

He'd been planning this op since October, and he'd be damned if he'd let Audrey ruin it because her ego was in a twist. He stood and pulled her to her feet. "Bull. Why else would you be here? Everyone who was involved in the permitting process was notified the lodge complex and surrounding parklands are off-limits this week."

She glared at him. "You had me cut out of the permitting process. I wasn't notified. I'm here because my cameras went out all at once and I'm afraid looters have hit the site again."

He frowned. "You have cameras? Here?"

"They're looking over the village site about a mile from here. Not far from Kaxo Falls."

"Then what the hell were you doing trying to break into the basement?"

Her pretty hazel eyes narrowed, and her bottom lip overlapped the top in a classic glare that had him suppressing a smile. He had a flash of memory of a very different view of those eyes and that mouth. Damn, it had been a night to remember. She'd had a libido to match his and a joyful energy that had made their one night together nothing short of amazing.

In the weeks following that first, memorable meeting, he'd planned to ask her out again. But he had to wait until after she signed off on the Finding of No Significant Impact for the Environmental Assessment that had been a required part of the proposal. He'd known that to prevent any perceived bias, there could be no visible relationship between them while the proposal was under review. He'd hoped she'd never learn he'd been part of the proposed training at all. But then she'd refused to sign off on the FONSI, leaving him no choice but to find another way to get approval. Unfortunately, *another way* had meant throwing her under the bus.

"I wasn't breaking in," she said. "I have a key. You see, in spite of your best efforts, I am still park archaeologist for Olympic National Park." She said the last with a bitter edge, triggering all the guilt she wanted him to feel.

He said nothing. What could he say? She was right. What he'd done to her was the worst thing he'd ever intentionally done to another person—outside an op, that is.

There were rules for one-night stands and rules for engaging with an enemy. Audrey was the former, but not the latter, and with her, ROE had been turned upside down. Because of Xavier, she'd become collateral damage in a war she didn't even know the US military was fighting.

"The line that powers my cameras runs from the old blacksmith shop," she said when he didn't respond. "Shop power is controlled by an auxiliary panel in the basement of the lodge. There's no point in hiking all the way out to the site if all I've got is a power problem, not a looting problem."

Her excuse was reasonable. Even plausible. But he still had a hard time believing she didn't know the training was starting today. Even though she'd objected to the project, she should have been notified along with inholding property owners.

Cohen interrupted before he could respond. "We need an update, Rivera. The team is on the jet and preparing for takeoff. Over."

The SEALs were being flown in from NAS Whidbey. It was a short flight, but they needed altitude, so they still had time. Into the radio, he said, "She's an NPS employee. The park archaeologist. Dr. Audrey Kendrick. Over."

Audrey continued to glare. She couldn't hear Cohen's side of the conversation, and that probably made her uneasy.

"The one who objected? What the fuck is she doing in the restricted zone?"

"There's a problem with some of her cameras losing power. I'm going to check it out, see if she's lying."

Audrey's eyes narrowed. "There is only one known liar standing on this lawn, and it's not me."

She was a hundred-percent correct, but he didn't have time to deal with her anger right now. The team was on the jet. To Cohen, he said, "It's going to take several minutes to confirm."

"We don't—"

Again, he ignored his partner in running this exercise and faced Audrey. "We need to hurry."

"*I'm* lying? Why the hell else would I be here?" she demanded, her voice tight with fury.

"I don't know. Maybe you just couldn't stand the idea of me being in town and not seeing me. Bad news for you"—he flashed a fierce grin—"I'm here to work."

"Oh, screw you. You're the last person in the world I want to see." At least the fire in her eyes was better than the devastation of their last meeting in her office. With a final glare, she turned and offered him her bound wrists. "Unlock the damn cuffs."

He stepped behind her and turned the cuffs to access the keyhole. "If I remember correctly, you like being bound—"

"I swear I will kick you in the balls if you keep talking."

He deserved it, which was probably why he'd baited her. If they weren't in a time crunch, he'd let her tear him to shreds. But the training he'd sacrificed her for was about to start, and it was paramount.

Still, he felt a strange joy at seeing her. He got a whiff of shampoo and rain and had a flash of memory. Her hair had been freshly washed—still damp—when he'd kissed her for the first time. Audrey was probably the only person on the planet who could distract him in this way, on today of all days.

He unlocked the cuffs and tucked them away in one of his tactical vest's pockets. He'd been lucky he carried them. He wasn't fully tricked out for combat—he was just an observer, after all—and only had the basics he'd need for monitoring the training. He wore the helmet with attached night vision goggles—he'd need the NVGs once darkness fell, which was rapidly approaching—but had skipped the heavy body armor and didn't have his HK416 assault rifle or breaching charges, or even extra Simunition magazines for his Glock.

He'd grabbed the cuffs just in case one of the locals tried

to mess with the training. He'd never once considered he might use them on Audrey Kendrick. She wasn't the enemy, even if he wanted her to be.

She faced him, rubbing her wrists. "I can't believe you pulled a gun on me."

"Not a real gun. It only fires Simunition—as you demanded in your response to the Environmental Assessment you refused to sign."

She pursed her lips. Oh damn. Those lips. He remembered their feel on his skin. "I'm well aware Simunition is standard practice for these trainings. What I found strange was that you didn't propose it in the first round."

"That wasn't my call. My guess is the brass wanted to hold it back for negotiation purposes."

"A crappy tactic if they expected me to sign off quickly."

He shrugged. "I don't get to tell a captain in the Navy what to do. I could only make recommendations."

"So now you're going to claim a captain made you lie about me?"

"No. The blame for that is all on me." He took a deep breath. "But we don't have time to discuss that now. You wanted to check the basement?"

She turned and marched back to the stairs inset in the earth. "Why didn't my key work?"

"It's not the original door. We had replacements made, special design so the team can simulate blowing locks without damaging your precious historic structure." He was baiting her again and wanted to bash his head against the nonhistoric door for being an ass. The doors had been changed to match very specific parameters, and there wouldn't be explosives used at all.

Plus, the lodge was old, and it was cool. He didn't want to see it harmed any more than she did. After all, he'd spent one of the most entertaining nights of his life here with an incredibly sexy woman who now glared at him with earned loathing in those beautiful hazel eyes. "Listen, you've got about ten minutes to show me your cameras are down, and then you need to get the hell out of this area."

"Jae's meeting me at the site. I need to wait for him," she said.

Jae had introduced Xavier to Audrey that fateful night. He'd known Jae-jin Son forever; the Korean-American park ranger was one of his oldest and closest friends. And his old friend knew the training was starting today, which meant Audrey was, in fact, lying. Was she here to stop the training after all?

"No way is Jae coming. I spoke to him this morning. About the training."

"He told the dispatcher he'd meet me at the gate."

Relief settled in. So she might not be lying. He didn't want her to be a liar. "Yeah, probably because he planned to tell you that you couldn't come up this way. Meeting at the gate and meeting at the site are two different things. He couldn't exactly tell the dispatcher to announce on the radio to stay away from this area because a top-secret training is starting at sunset."

Her lips formed a regretful O. "Shit."

"Why didn't you wait for him at the gate like a good girl?"

"I can't believe I didn't realize what a condescending ass you are the first time we met."

That was fair. He *was* trying to make her feel in the wrong. Because right now that real estate was all his, and he didn't like it. "I'll rephrase. Why didn't you wait for Jae at the gate as he requested?"

"He was out at Mora dealing with unruly campers. The nearest law enforcement ranger after Jae is even farther away —out at Shi Shi Beach. Daylight is dwindling, and a storm is forecast for tonight. If the site's been looted again, I have a narrow window to collect evidence before the rain washes everything away. And I need to check on George."

"George?"

"George Shaw. The tribal elder who lives in a cabin not far from the site, on the other side of Kaxo Creek." She gave him an exasperated look. "He was in the lodge that night. Remember?"

With that nudge, he remembered. Jae had pointed him out too.

"George has a wood carving shop on lodge grounds, next to the blacksmith shop. What if he saw the looters and confronted them? His whole reason for wintering here this year was to protect the site after it was looted in November. I tried calling and texting him after the cameras cut off, but I wasn't able to reach him." Her eyes turned fierce. "I'm worried about George and the site. I won't leave until I know they're both safe."

Xavier glanced up at the gray sky. She was right about the storm. She was right about everything. And as much as he didn't want her to be a liar, he was also a little disappointed her excuse was reasonable. Part of him wanted this to be on her. He wanted her to be guilty of something too, because otherwise, he was the only asshole standing on these stone steps.

He'd screwed her over, and it would hurt a lot less if he didn't like her so much. If she didn't invade his dreams every night. If he didn't wonder every day what he'd thrown away.

He rolled his shoulders, centering himself with the dull ache in the joint that was a souvenir from his last mission. The team would be wheels up in a matter of minutes. He needed information, fast. Focus on the job and forget Audrey was the messenger.

Later, he'd check her story with Jae, but for now, he could

at least confirm her cameras were down. He pulled her key from the lock on the basement door and inserted his own. He handed her the ridiculously endowed key chain.

Who carried that many keys? He didn't even have real metal keys to his car or house anymore. It was all proximity locks and four-digit code numbers.

She took his flashlight from his belt without waiting for permission. If anyone else did that, he'd have them pinned to the ground for making a move that looked like they were going for his gun. It wasn't good that she'd taken the item without him even flinching. She threw off his reflexes.

She was kryptonite.

The light beam bounced along the rear wall, landing on the row of breaker boxes. She crouched down and entered the dank space, heading straight for the panel with "black-smith shop" written in reflective letters on the cover. A green light glowed brightly. She opened the cover to reveal the main circuit breaker firmly in the ON position. "The shop has power," she said.

They left the basement, and Xavier locked the door again. "Let's check out the shop." He radioed Cohen, updating him on the situation, giving more details about the archaeological site, cameras, and why it mattered as they walked toward her vehicle.

The clock was ticking on the op countdown. If there was something odd going on at the blacksmith shop or the archaeological site, he had precious few minutes to call off the training.

"You think something's wrong?" Cohen asked.

"I'm not sure," he said as they rounded the building to the road- and mountain-facing side. The blacksmith shop was the farthest from the lodge down a gravel track that continued after the paved road dead-ended at the lodge. "We'll take your SUV to the shop. It'll save time."

He reached out a hand when they reached her vehicle. "Keys." It was not a request.

She glared at him. At this point, it was pretty much her permanent expression when looking at him, but she handed him her heavy key chain.

The road was pitted with potholes filled with gray water. He dodged as best he could at speed. Audrey held on to the bar above the passenger window and cursed at his driving as she bounced in the seat, but they reached the blacksmith shop in what had to be record time.

The building had wide double barn doors at the front that were chained closed for winter. Audrey led him to the rear door. He flipped through her key chain. "Which one? I don't have keys to this building." It had been specifically deemed off-limits for the training, which was fine because it didn't belong in their planned simulation anyway.

"Black," she said, indicating a key that had a black band around the top. "For blacksmith."

He looked at the key she'd used for the basement of the lodge. "Why is the basement key gray?"

"Dark. Dank. Full of gray-panel breaker boxes."

"What's the front door of the lodge?" he asked as he slipped the black-tagged key in the lock.

"Purple."

"Why?"

"It's my favorite color. My favorite building in the park."

All at once, he remembered her purple sports bra. He'd met her after a long day of fieldwork, and her bra and panties had been all business, no play, but the color—and the woman who filled them—had been sexy as hell and plenty playful.

This was *not* the time to remember those sorts of details.

He shoved open the door and groped for the light, but old buildings like these didn't always have switches next to the door. Audrey unerringly crossed the dark room and flicked the switch. Flame-shaped sconce lights mounted to vertical log posts filled the room with a warm yellow glow.

She nodded toward a door to his left. "The electrical relay station is in there. It powers this building, George's shop next door, landscaping lights, and everything else at this end of the lodge complex."

He opened the door and flicked on the light. A bare bulb illuminated a small utility room with high tech wiring not in keeping with the old blacksmith shop.

He studied the panel. A row of lights glowed green, but the last one on the end was yellow.

"The yellow light is the line for my cameras," Audrey said. "Yellow means there's power, but there's a break in the circuit."

He snapped a photo and texted it to the five SEALs overseeing this training. They'd all have cellular service for the next thirty minutes, then the van they'd set up to act as signal jammer would kill all radio, satellite, and cellular communication within the lake basin. Given that there were no cellular antennas in this part of the park except for the ones close to the lodge, a large swath of the forest would be effectively cut off from all wireless communication. This was one of the hurdles the SEALs would have to overcome for a successful mission.

It was a good simulation for real-world ops. Teams were often dropped into parts of the world that lacked infrastructure, and satellite phones could get shot, dropped, be jammed, or just plain fail. But it also meant the trainers themselves would be without radios and cell phones and would face their own challenges.

He radioed his team. "That photo I just sent means we've got a problem. I'm going to accompany Dr. Kendrick to the archaeological site to see what's up with her cameras."

"Do we need to delay the op, Rivera?" Reichmann asked.

"That's what I'm trying to determine." He paused. He could be blowing this out of proportion. The cameras were guarding an archaeological site and had nothing to do with the lodge. Nothing to do with the training. "It's probably nothing. But it needs to be checked out just the same."

"Roger. How long will it take you to get to the site?"

He turned to Audrey, who could only hear his side of the conversation. "How long will it take to get to the site, Aud?"

"It's only a half mile from here, but it's uphill, and steep in places—up the first leg of the cliffside trail that dead-ends at the falls. With wet, muddy ground, it could take fifteen minutes."

For a civilian maybe. "We don't have fifteen minutes. Seven or eight, tops."

"Then we'd better get moving."

He relayed the information to his team, then closed and locked the blacksmith shop. She turned to the SUV. "Unlock my car. I need to grab my pack."

"It'll be faster if we leave it."

"I don't hike without supplies, ever. There are bears in these woods, it's getting dark, and the ground is slippery. Things can go wrong."

"The bears are hibernating, and you've got a SEAL with you."

She cocked her head. "You're a SEAL?"

Her question startled him. "Yes. I thought you figured that out when I was in your office."

He hit the button to unlock the back of the SUV so she could grab her pack. Arguing would only waste more precious minutes. She grabbed the pack, then pulled gloves from a side pocket.

He hadn't realized she was cold, but then, he wasn't

exactly focused on her comfort. After donning the gloves, she settled her pack on her hips, adjusting the straps with practiced ease. There was a grace and competence to her movements that he found all too appealing.

But then, that had been the problem from the start. He'd been utterly charmed from the moment she'd interrupted his conversation with Jae. He remembered the first words he'd ever heard her say: *"Jae, my dearest, bestest friend, I will name my firstborn child after you if you have a room and will let me use your shower."*

Her reservation had been inadvertently canceled. Exhausted and grubby after a day in the field, she'd hoped to shower before sleeping in her car.

Jae didn't have a room, as he returned to his home in Port Angeles that night. Luckily, Xavier had a room and shower, which he'd been happy to let Audrey use. What happened after that had been unexpected…and incredible.

"I never considered you might be a SEAL," she said. "I was too busy stewing over the fact that you'd lied when you said you worked in security. You never mentioned the Navy. That seemed like a big omission. Especially considering I asked about your job."

There wasn't much he could say to that. He'd lied, plain and simple. He wasn't proud of it, and she had every right to be angry.

She set out for the trail. He grabbed her arm. "I lead."

"This is my park. I think I can handle this."

"This is America's park and I'm a Navy CW5—Chief Warrant Officer 5. During this op, it's my job to protect this park and people in it. Your job is to dig up old garbage." He probably shouldn't have said the last part in such a condescending tone—he knew what her job meant to her, how seriously she took her role in protecting cultural resources.

But she'd never understand how in this instance, national security trumped old bones and tools.

That had been the underlying truth that had gotten them here in the first place.

Still, saying it like that proved he really was a first-class prick. It made his skin itch, like he'd rolled in poison oak. He couldn't escape his entirely deserved case of karmic eczema.

She rolled her eyes. "By all means, Chief Warrant Officer Rivera, lead the way and protect poor little me from the big bad coyote. Forget that I spend about three hundred days a year in this park. I know these trails better than you know a woman's body."

Ouch. Still, he was glad she was getting her digs in. "That's not what you said in November."

"I was faking," she said in a singsong voice.

He chuckled. They both knew which one of them was lying now.

As they walked upslope in silence, he felt her behind him as much as heard her. Smelled her. It was strange to think he'd been inside her. He knew the taste and texture of every curve and slope. They'd shared a night that had been wild. Special.

He hadn't been scheming when he'd taken Audrey to his room. He'd just reacted to an intense, primal attraction that grabbed him from the moment they met. It didn't help that Jae had introduced them. He'd known Jae since childhood. They'd fought with lightsabers and dreamed of being Jedi. She knew Jae as a coworker and friend. They both trusted the park ranger without hesitation.

Before the introduction, Jae had warned Xavier that Dr. Audrey Kendrick would likely be the deciding factor in the environmental approval process. Knowing that, he should have kept his hands to himself, but the wrong head had been doing all his thinking.

Later, any hope he'd harbored for a repeat encounter once the project was approved had been crushed under her worn hiking boots. Sure, she'd just been doing her job, but he, in turn, had to do his.

He glanced at his watch as they climbed the slippery, steep slope. Darkness was crowding in. The platoon was in the air now. He needed to get this boondoggle over with so he could get her back on the road before she screwed up the training. He should be in the control room with Cohen this very minute.

The first phase of this training was a hostage rescue scenario focusing on the lodge. The conditions were just right, coming in under the cover of a storm. Ideally, the team would arrive later in the night, but the storm was hitting early, so they'd moved up the timeline by two hours.

They'd have to work with the weather when the real mission was a go, so this abrupt change in timing was also excellent practice for everyone.

In the coming days, the platoon would run multiple rescue missions on the lodge, refining the plan once the SEALs knew the details, but the first run would be cold—the team knew very little about what to expect.

"To the right," Audrey said when the path forked.

He took the high trail and continued upward. The path was wide with a low grade that required several switchbacks through the woods. If they could go straight up, they'd reach the flat in less than half the time. "Why run a power line from the blacksmith shop? That couldn't have been easy when you could use satellite links with solar panels to power the cameras."

"No budget and no time. The burials were looted in November. We needed a quick fix. I put in a request for solar and satellite, but that would take months—possibly years—to get approved. As it was, I spent days laying and burying PVC pipe so I could run power and Cat 5 cables for the video feed."

That would have been just a week or two after they'd met. It must have been difficult, digging a trench up the hillside in the November rain. He rolled his shoulder, thinking of the work involved as he stretched injured muscles that stiffened with the cold rain. A year and eight months ago, he'd been shot during what became his final op. That injury was why he was here and not with the SEALs in the jet heading their way.

Recovery had been a bitch. He'd been gutted at the prospect of no longer being an active member of the teams. He no longer had full range of motion in his left rotator cuff, and never would. But after several surgeries and physical therapy, he'd finally been able to return to work, this time as a trainer. This job had saved him. Gave him purpose again. He didn't even know who he was without his SEAL identity. He'd thought it had been lost forever. But as a trainer, he was still connected to the teams.

Rainforest shadows deepened as they ascended the hill. Finally, the ground leveled out beneath their feet, and they faced a wide, open meadow as it caught the last light of the gray day. It was overcast and dreary even without the shadows of the trees.

The Pacific Northwest in January. How did Audrey and Jae deal with the dark, gray winters?

"Where's the site—a village, you said?" All he saw was an open marshy meadow bordered by trees all around. The rush of flowing water carried across the flat, hinting at the presence of a large stream that poured down the rocky hillside above the meadow. The stream, he knew, cut a shallow swath across a corner of the meadow, then disappeared again into the rainforest, winding another half mile before it would reach the cliffs above the lake. The heavy flow cascaded from there, dropping forty feet into the large, glacier-carved lake bed, filling the basin with crisp, fresh water that flowed from high on the slopes of Mt. Olympus.

Kaxo Falls was one of the most photographed features of Lake Olympus, usually captured from boats on the lake in the summer, but there was a cliffside trail for the adventurous hiker eager to stand at the top of the falls. From reading up on the history and prehistory of the area in preparing the Environmental Assessment, he knew that "kaxo" meant *dog* in the local dialect of the Coast Salish language. But he didn't know much beyond that.

His gaze returned to the immediate area. He knew prehistoric sites were in the ground, but still, he was disappointed there weren't any structures that proclaimed "Prehistoric Native American Village Site." No ancient longhouse. No totem pole. He figured totem poles must be in the Pacific Northwest because the lodge was decorated with a large one as part of the front façade.

Audrey spread her arms to indicate the wide meadow. "The site is all around us, with the most notable concentrations by the creek on the far edge. The area that's been looted—where the burials are—is in the woods not far from here." She nodded toward the forest they stood on the edge of, but then shifted her focus and pointed north to a footbridge that crossed Kaxo Creek. "The fastest route to George's cabin is that way. It's deep in the woods on the other side of the creek. After we check on the cameras, I'm going to check on him."

"George isn't here. All inholding landowners were paid to vacate during the trainings. They all signed the agreement and accepted payment."

She shook her head. "Your scope of work only included the property owners with inholdings on the lakeshore. George's cabin is nowhere near the lake thanks to the cliffs.

It was outside your Area of Potential Effect and this meadow was expressly excluded from being operational territory because of the site, burials, and proximity to the falls. Because of this, George was left out of the environmental process and ignored. You'd know that if you read my rebuttal when you went around me to ACHP."

He *had* read her rebuttal, and he remembered something about a tribal member being vocal in his dissent, but an officer much higher in the chain of command than Xavier —who occupied a tiny realm that sat between enlisted and officers—had said the Navy would negotiate a deal with him. The permit had gone through, and inholding landowners had been paid. That was all he knew, and frankly, all he'd cared about. "I was told he was paid," Xavier said.

"You were told wrong, because if George had received— and accepted—payment from the Navy, he would have told me. Not to mention his family would have gleefully moved him out of the cabin to winter with them on the reservation on the coast. But as far as I know, George isn't on the reservation."

"As far as you *know*."

"Yes." She pulled out her cell phone and showed him the screen. "I've left him—and his family members—several frantic messages in the last hour and a half. No one has called back."

Xavier frowned. "Does George get cell coverage out here?"

She nodded. "Not so much in his cabin, but the meadow is within range of the antennas. There's also a landline in the woodshop. He has voicemail on that line."

In about ten minutes, all signals—radio, cellular, and satellite—would be jammed. George would be as hampered as the SEAL team. Worse, no civilians were allowed in the lodge complex for the duration of the training, so he couldn't access his woodshop at all.

"Does he have electricity in his cabin?" If not, the next several days would be very uncomfortable for the man, if he were truly here. Unless he planned to do a very long hike up and out of the lake basin, he wouldn't be able to reach the road without crossing the lodge complex or lake, effectively trapping him in the rainforest until the training was over.

"He lives mostly off the grid, but he has a generator to keep his phone and other electronics in power, and before winter set in, we hauled enough fuel to see him through the worst of it. Plus, he's got power in the woodshop, which is right next to the blacksmith shop. He can always charge his phone there in a pinch."

"But not this week. He's alone out here?"

She nodded. "No one tells George how to live his life. His family tries, but they'd rather he respond to their calls than cut them off completely, so they've stopped fighting what he wants."

"Cameras first, George second," he said. But damn, checking on the elder would eat precious minutes.

Audrey led him to a tall tree on the edge of the meadow and pointed to the lowest branches, which were at least ten feet above Xavier's head. "Three cameras are up there, two looking over the meadow, the third into the woods. It's not a full three-sixty view from the tree, but close. There's another camera in the woods, directed at the area that was looted in November."

He scanned the moss-covered trunk, looking for the power line and not seeing it. "Where's the cable?"

She circled the tree and pointed to a camouflaged line. It was well concealed under moss and paint. It wasn't hard to figure out what happened when his gaze followed the cable to the base of the tree.

Audrey had seen it too. She cursed and pressed her palm to the trunk, as if thrown off-balance. "Well, there it is. Fresh cut."

Xavier squatted to take a closer look and added a few mental curses of his own. From the gouge in the root, it looked like someone had taken an axe to it. He scanned the ground and spotted footprints in the marshy surface in an area where neither he nor Audrey had stepped.

If Audrey was right about having a close-to-three-sixty view, they'd have footage of the person approaching the tree. Maybe they'd have a face. "I need you to call your office and have them send me everything the cameras captured before they were cut off. What time did this happen?" he asked, pointing to the hacked root.

"Just before three o'clock."

He checked his watch. Just over two hours ago. Thankfully, Audrey had gotten here in time to show him this, because while the team was in the air, it wasn't too late to turn them back. He tapped the mic button on his radio and said, "Someone cut the camera line. We need to delay the training at least twenty-four hours. Abort the jump."

The radio didn't make a sound. Dead air.

When was the last time he'd heard chatter between the team? They'd been running through the checklist when he and Audrey reached the meadow. The last update had come from Cohen two or three minutes ago, when he'd given the countdown: ten minutes until the signal jammer would go online.

"I need to check the other camera," Audrey said, turning for the woods.

Xavier followed, trying to raise Cohen and the others as they wove through the fern-and-moss-covered ground, winding around trees and stumps and dodging moss draping from low branches. "Send the team back to Whidbey. Abort the jump." He checked his watch. According to the op clock, they had seven minutes before all communication would be shut down. Cohen wouldn't have activated the jammer early, not without announcing it on the radio, and not when he was waiting for Xavier's report.

He pulled out his phone. This close to the meadow, it should work, but it didn't have a signal.

Somehow, some way, the signal jammer had switched on early.

He followed Audrey around a thick old-growth tree. She stopped short in front of him. "Well, now we know why they disabled the cameras." Her voice was low. Pained.

Five feet away a large, uneven hole gaped open.

"But—it doesn't look like a looter pit," she said. "It's too narrow and too deep—it goes past the cultural layers into sterile glacial till."

Archaeology was her specialty, but this was Xavier's. He'd seen pits like this before. Caught on a root, he saw evidence that told him everything he needed to know.

"This hole wasn't dug by looters." He jumped into the pit and grabbed the scrap of stray black plastic. "Something was wrapped in plastic and stored here. Whoever cut the cameras was here to claim their stash."

Chapter Three

*Q*udrey took a step back as she stared at the plastic in Xavier's hand. He stood hip-deep in the pit. The walls had collapsed after whatever had been stored in plastic had been retrieved, and loose brown soil littered the hard-packed gray till beneath his feet. She spotted the distal end of a long bone sticking out of the sloped wall and thought she might be sick.

This area had been looted in November. They'd seen evidence of the digging on the surface, but, because it was a burial ground, they didn't excavate or probe to assess the extent of the damage, as that would only further disturb and desecrate the remains.

"So what was done here in November wasn't looting..." Her words trailed off as her mind raced. She pressed a hand to her belly, thinking of all that had happened since the loot-ing. She'd denied the permit in part because of the looting. Xavier had savaged her reputation because she'd denied the permit. And George had insisted on wintering in the old cabin near the ancestral village because of the looting.

"It was storage," Xavier finished for her. He spoke into

his radio again. "Abort the training. We've got company in the woods. And they're armed." He tapped his earpiece and cursed. "These are the best field radios the military has. They're designed for this range and terrain. No way would Cohen have jumped the gun on the signal jammer."

"Signal jammer?" she asked.

"Yeah. Part of the training. No radios. No cell or sat phones. No communication with the outside world."

She pulled out her own phone. No bars. Uneasiness trickled down her spine. "We need to check on George."

He climbed from the pit, the loose wall collapsing under his foot, making her wince as she spotted rib bones in the soil where he'd stepped. "I've got to get to the command center. We need to call off the jump. Once the SEALs are in free fall, there's no turning back."

"I understand, but George is seventy-two and he's out here alone. He might've seen who cut the lines to the camera. He could be injured, or worse. You go back to your command center and do what you need to do to abort the training, but I need to check on George."

Xavier closed his eyes and nodded. "You're right. I'm sorry." He met her gaze. "But George isn't supposed to be here. All inholding landowners signed the contract."

"But George wasn't in your APE. Do you know for a *fact* he signed?"

Xavier's entire body radiated with tension. He glanced toward the meadow and said, "Is there any way to get to his cabin without crossing the meadow and footbridge? It's too exposed. The bridge is an obvious target."

Her relief was tempered by the answer she had to give. "It's not much better. It's part of a loop from here to the falls. We'd have to go back downhill and take the other side of the loop. When we reach the fork we came across on the way here, we'd take the other path, the one that goes up to the falls along the cliffside trail. It's not very wide in places and has a steep drop, and we'll be visible from the lake on the switchbacks along the cliff. Once we reach the top, we'll be in the forest again, where there's another bridge, but it's in the trees and not so exposed."

He studied the meadow, then gave a reluctant nod. "We'll take the cliff trail." He ran a hand over his face. "Odds are, weapons were stored in this pit. Whoever is out there is armed and ready to mess up the training. We need to hurry."

She stared into the pit, her gaze caught on the exposed ribs as she shivered. "Why do you think they stored weapons here?"

"The road was still open in November. It would've been easy to hike up here from the lodge in the middle of the night and stage supplies. Once the road closed, anyone planning to disrupt the training would have to hike in from the main road outside the park, carrying all their gear uphill, what, ten to fifteen miles without a trail?"

"As the crow flies from the west, yes. In truth, it would be a lot longer given the terrain and river crossings." She considered other routes. From the north, there was a trail that would get them within five miles of the lodge, but it was on the other side of the eastern ridge of the lake basin, up the slopes of Mt. Olympus. An easier hike given the maintained trail, but still five miles of overland schlepping down a steep, wet hillside from there to the lodge.

Xavier nodded. "That's why weapons would be staged here, within easy range of the lodge. A team hiking in would only need camping gear."

She swallowed hard and told herself George was fine. He had to be. "But how could anyone have known about the training in November? Your proposal landed on my desk days *after* the looting."

His jaw set in a hard line. "We informed inholding landowners of the proposed action a little more than a week before we finalized the proposal and submitted it to the park. We needed to start the thirty-day public comment period right away to make our timeline, so the landowners received priority notification."

That explained how Jeb McCutcheon had known about the proposal before she did. He'd mentioned it when she, Jeb, and George had stood in this very spot, looking at the desecration to the burial ground. She hadn't believed him at the time, figuring it was another of Jeb's conspiracy theories. His concerns about the lake community ran the gamut from other inholding landowners running illegal Airbnbs to the federal government seizing his cabin through eminent domain. A secret government training ground fit nicely in between, so she'd dismissed the comment.

He'd gloated after she discovered he'd been right. She had to admit, she'd then wondered if the Baldwins really were renting out their cabin on a dark web vacation rental site.

"It was the day the comment period closed that you came to my office." And lied in an attempt to get her fired from the job she'd wanted since she was eleven years old.

And he'd done it knowing what her job meant to her.

Xavier gave a sharp nod. Between the face paint and the shadows of the forest, she couldn't read his expression. Did he regret what he'd done?

Foolish of her to hold on to that pathetic hope. Of course he didn't. He was here right now thanks to his lie.

But none of that was important in this moment. She needed to focus on what mattered. "You think one of the inholding owners revealed your plans?"

"Right now, it's the most likely scenario."

She was having trouble grasping this turn of events.

She'd been rattled at meeting Xavier at the lodge. After all, the father of her unborn child had tackled and handcuffed her. And even as she'd reeled from that, she was distracted by the need to tell him about the baby. It wasn't the sort of thing one blurted while hiking up a hillside to check on potential damage to an archaeological site. Plus, she was worried about George.

Her brain had been stuck on everything except what this could mean for Xavier and his training. Only now did it sink in how serious this was.

She'd been trying to figure out how to tell him he was going to be a father, while he was worried about security for the training. "You think the SEAL team is going to be ambushed"—she pointed to the pit—"with weapons that were stored there?"

He nodded. "The platoon is in the air right now, armed only with Simunition, and I can't raise anyone on the radio to stop it." His nostrils flared. "To be honest, I'm scared of what this means. It's unprecedented."

Xavier Rivera was scared. She'd been wrapping her mind around the fact he was a SEAL, and now he'd admitted to being scared. The math on that really only had one solution: they were in deep trouble. Plus, it solidly answered the question of whether or not tonight would be a good time to tell him he was going to be a daddy in late July. He needed to focus on this disastrous turn of events without distraction.

They could fight about the rest later. "Let's hurry and check on George, then. We can skip the path up here, cut across the forest, and catch the cliffside trail with less zigzagging. You want to lead?"

He nodded. "Step where I step. Try not to make noise."

She nodded. "I'll do my best."

He lifted a hand as if he intended to cup her cheek, but dropped it without touching her. "I know you will."

He was fast and silent as he moved through the rainforest, heading downhill at a rapid pace. She kept up as best she could, trampling over ferns and dodging roots.

These woods were familiar territory. Four years ago, she'd run an eight-week archaeological field school excavation of the village, and they'd done plenty of test pits to find the extent of the site in areas where the ground leveled out.

During the day, the rainforest glowed brightly in shades that ranged from pale greenish yellow to deep dark green due to an abundance of mosses and lichens, which covered the ground, rocks, and trees. High and low limbs of Sitka spruces, western red cedars, and Douglas firs were draped with mosses and lichens, creating yellowy veils they had to duck under.

In addition, bright yellow and orange fungi sprouted from fallen logs and branches. Large green ferns covered the forest floor. In summer, the ferns were perky, knee-high, and shrub-like, but tonight, the plants lay flat, having been tamped down by several inches of snow that had melted a week ago. Both fern and moss ground cover softened the sound of their steps as they slipped through the ever-darkening forest.

The cold air smelled of moss, fungi, pine, and saturated soil. The scents all familiar to her in the darkening shadows. She knew this place, winter and summer, night and day. But for the first time, the smell—even the very feel of the rainforest around her—wasn't comforting.

They passed a lichen-coated rocky outcrop where she'd escaped on field school afternoons to write up her site notes for the day, uninterrupted by her students. When George discovered her hiding place, he'd taken to joining her. He'd bring a thriller novel and a snack—often biscuits with elderberry or salal jam made by a cousin, or smoked salmon and crackers—while she provided a thermos of herbal tea. He'd sit in the shade and read while she worked. Sometimes, he'd take a look at her notes and quiz her on what she thought they'd learn about the village that he didn't know already about his ancestors.

George enjoyed consulting with archaeologists and liked working for the park as an on-site master carver, demonstrating his skills for visitors from all cultures, but he was disdainful of her profession at times, and with good reason. Archaeologists had spent decades yanking other cultures' ancestors from their sacred resting places and putting them in museums without any regard for the beliefs and cultural practices of their living descendants.

Anthropologists in all disciplines had a lot to make up for.

As she passed the area where they shared their daily tea together, she found herself holding her breath, as if the superstitious act would protect him and they'd find him safe and undisturbed in his cabin.

"Audrey?" Xavier asked in a whisper.

She realized she'd stopped walking in addition to breathing. She shook her head. "Sorry. George and I—"

"You can explain later. We need to hurry."

Xavier didn't wait for an answer. He turned and resumed walking. She followed, placing a hand on her abdomen. There were so many things she needed to explain to him later. Teatime with George was the least of it.

Minutes later, they were back on the path and reached the fork. They turned and headed down the trail that some visitors claimed was more suited to the park's mountain goat population than it was to humans. This was an exaggeration —it was a safe trail for hikers if they were mentally prepared for the steep drop and pinch points along the switchbacks

once they began to ascend the cliff. Signs were posted all
over the lodge grounds and trail maps, directing the casual
hiker and visitors with a fear of heights who just wanted to
see the top of the falls from a safe vantage point to take the
easier path across the meadow.

But the truth remained: this wasn't a trail for casual
tourists even in good weather.

They began their ascent up the first switchback, no
longer sheltered by the forest canopy, the basalt ground bare
of moss and ferns. From his sure stride, she could tell Xavier
was undaunted by the drop-off. And usually she was fine
with it, but she'd never hiked this trail in January before,
when the ground was saturated and what little soil had
collected on the rocky path was slippery. It didn't help that
she wore only lightweight cloth hiking boots not suited to the
trail or conditions.

They'd turned the corner on the first switchback, and her
tension began to ease. She could do this. She knew this trail.
This was her park. It was home to her as much as her rental
house in Port Angeles.

Xavier was a few strides ahead—showing no signs of
being winded from the steep climb—and she had taken
several quick steps to catch up to him when she planted a
foot on a loose rock. She let out a yelp as she scrambled to
regain her footing, and her other foot landed on more loose
rocks.

She reached for him as he turned. Her reaching fingers
missed his arm, but he caught her. He gripped the lapel of
her winter raincoat and anchored her to the path.

Her heart beat frantically as her belly did somersaults.
This was worse than the icy roadway. If she'd gone off the
edge on the drive to the lodge, the SUV would have
slammed into some trees. She could've been injured, maybe

killed, but also might have survived with nothing more than a few scrapes.

But this cliff?

Right here, it was a thirty-foot drop down a seventy-five-degree rock face. She'd land in icy-cold shallow water filled with jagged basalt boulders that had broken from the face over the centuries. If she somehow survived the fall, she'd probably be knocked unconscious and drown before Xavier could climb down and save her.

"You okay?" he asked.

No. But she didn't voice the response. She was the one who'd insisted on checking on George. And she was the one who'd taken an incautious step. They needed to keep going.

Still, she was frozen with fear, which wasn't like her. She hiked trails like this all the time. But never in this weather and never in the wrong boots.

The sound of her heartbeat and ragged breathing drowned out all other sounds. She had to get her shit together.

He pulled her close, wrapping his arms around her. "I'm sorry," he whispered, just loud enough for her to hear over her pounding heart.

She didn't know what he was apologizing for, but she was rattled enough to accept his comfort and tucked her head against his chest. The various objects stored in the pockets of his vest poked at her as she took a deep breath. She could do this. She had to.

She leaned away, and the arms that held her loosened. "Let's go," she said.

He smiled, and the warmth in his eyes triggered a flutter. Or maybe a memory. She wasn't sure, but his smile somehow made her feel good. Like north was still north and he somehow wasn't the man who'd set fire to her career.

Temporary insanity triggered by fear.

He turned and faced the steep path ahead. "I'll go slower."

"Thank you."

Fortunately, the narrowest part of the trail only lasted until the next switchback, where the natural grade became less sheer cliff face and more sloped hillside.

They reached the turn, and she let out a deep sigh of relief. The worst was over. Now the lake was on her right side and the trail widened out. Two more legs and they'd reach the top of the cliff.

Thanks to the wider, gentler path, they quickly reached the next turn, which was a large open flat—a great spot for picnicking in the summertime with a spectacular view of the lake. They'd reached the final, widest stretch of trail, which would take them to the top of the cliff and back into the forest.

Once upon a time, there'd been railings along the edge of the flat, but barriers, the park service had learned, only made park guests more fearless. Foolish. Tourists would ignore the warning signs and climb over the fence, taking chances they wouldn't if there wasn't a rail to hold on to.

The railings were gone, but the signs remained, warning hikers of the fifty-foot drop. Darkness was descending rapidly, and the signs were two-legged silhouettes. Alien looking in the natural landscape.

Deep shadows swallowed the rocky outcrop where the flat transitioned into sloped hillside. Audrey couldn't put her finger on it, but the boulders dotting the slope didn't look right. It had been at least three months since she'd last stepped on this flat. A winter storm could have pushed more rocks down from above.

Still, the back of her neck prickled, and she paused as Xavier rounded the bend and started up the last switchback. "Xavi—"

She sucked in a sharp breath, swallowing his name as a shadow shifted. A specter rising from stone and earth. She'd never believed in ghosts or spirits but in that moment, belief had nothing to do with it.

Then the shadow charged forward, and she wasn't seeing anything remotely supernatural. It was a man, rushing for her with a long knife that glinted in the waning light.

Chapter Four

*A*udrey screamed as she took a step back, then stopped short. She was only steps away from the edge of the cliff. Unable to retreat, she planted her boots and raised her arms to somehow fend off the coming knife attack.

Xavier was a blur as he launched himself at the man, catching the assailant around the waist and slamming him to the ground. The two men rolled, bumping into Audrey and knocking her down, close to the edge. She scrambled to the side to get out of the way, then gasped as Xavier rolled toward the brink, gripping the other man's knife-wielding arm by the wrist to stop the blade from plunging downward into Xavier's throat.

She'd seen the scars on his left shoulder. She knew the arm that held the knife at bay was the weaker one. He lacked full range of motion with his left arm.

She crawled to the side, looking for something, anything that would help, and spotted a jagged cobble the size of a grapefruit, a meter away at the base of one of the warning signs. She scrambled toward it as Xavier and the dark shadow of a man grappled at the edge of the cliff.

She hadn't thrown a softball since middle school, but she chucked the rock with all her strength.

It hit the man in the neck and thumped down onto Xavier's chest, but it was the distraction her SEAL needed. He shoved upward, pitching the specter back and reversing their positions. The knife disappeared into the void beyond the cliff edge, and Xavier straddled the assailant, landing blows with both fists on the man's face.

"Who are you?" Xavier asked between blows. "Who do you work for?"

The man said nothing and managed to land a few punches of his own.

They grappled and rolled, and again, Xavier was at the edge, on his back.

She searched for another rock, but before she could lay her hands on one, Xavier kicked upward. The man launched into the air, but his hand caught the night vision goggles mounted to the top of Xavier's helmet.

Panic surged in Audrey's chest as momentum from the kick sent the man over the cliff, his hands grasping equipment strapped to Xavier's head. The moment seemed to freeze as the SEAL was jerked toward the edge.

Audrey dove forward to grab Xavier at the same time he punched at the man's hand and twisted his head.

In a blink, the specter disappeared over the edge, taking Xavier's goggles with him. A chilling wail echoed across the lake.

Xavier still teetered on the edge. Audrey grabbed him, centering his weight firmly on the wide flat.

He rolled toward her, adding more distance between himself and the edge, then flopped to his back. His breath came out in ragged pants.

Audrey collapsed beside him, her heart still pounding. "You almost went over."

He rapped on his helmet, then dropped his hand and threaded his fingers through hers. "I could've worn full gear for this exercise. But I'm just a trainer—not participating, just observing—so I passed on body armor and chose this cheap, lighter helmet. I only needed it to mount the NVGs so I can monitor the team in the dark. And the cheap-ass mounting clip on this helmet just saved my life."

She took that in. Breathed it, like his words were air. A mounting bracket on a helmet was such a minor thing to be the difference between life and death. She squeezed his hand, feeling so thankful for the cheap helmet's crappy mount.

She rolled to her side, facing him. "Thank you for saving my life," she whispered. "When he charged me, all I could do was freeze."

"There was nothing else you could do, given where you were standing." He rolled toward her, bringing them chest to chest. He brought their joined hands to his lips, pressing a kiss to her glove. "Thank you for saving mine too."

"I didn't—"

"My shoulder was a hairsbreadth away from giving out. If you hadn't thrown that rock, I don't know what would have happened." He shifted, rolling the joint. "Fuck, that hurts."

She wanted to reach out and touch him, to try to soothe his pain, but getting too familiar with Xavier Rivera was certain to only bring her more agony.

She rolled to her back again. "Who was he?" It was a silly question. Xavier couldn't possibly know more than she did, but they were the first words that came to mind.

"No clue."

"Why come at me with a knife? Wasn't that a rifle strapped to his back?" It had all happened so fast, she hadn't registered the rifle she'd seen until just now.

"He might simply prefer knives. Or he wanted to avoid the noise. Gunshots would have echoed across the lake."

She rose to her feet. "We need to find George."

"Audrey," he said as he too stood.

She looked at him, and even in the dark, with grease-paint covering his face, she could read him. "You agreed," she insisted.

"That was before we were attacked by a man with a knife and an AK who was guarding the path we were headed up. I lost my NVGs. I'm not taking you up into those dark woods where more men could be waiting. Not without night vision. Not without a gun."

"I have a gun. A real one. If you want it."

"You're carrying?" She could hear the edge of hope in his voice.

She nodded. "A Glock 19. Last spring, some hikers harassed me when I was working alone. It was pretty scary, and they still haven't been identified. So I got a permit to carry concealed. Jae taught me how to shoot."

"I'm sorry that happened, but thankful you have a weapon."

She slipped off her pack and pulled out the gun. She handed it to him, holding the barrel. "It's loaded, but not chambered. The magazine is a standard fifteen shot. I don't have any more bullets."

He took the weapon and racked the slide, chambering the first bullet. "I'll never complain about you insisting on grabbing your pack again."

In spite of everything, she managed a smile. She wouldn't park in an accessible space in front of a shuttered lodge, and she never hiked out of sight of her vehicle in bad weather without taking her pack.

"You still won't take me to George, though, will you?"

"We need to get to the command center. The SEALs are

in the air, on their way here now. They're doing a High Altitude Low Opening jump. I *need* to get to a phone and call it off. We just saw proof there are armed men here. He tried to kill us without hesitation. The team only has paint pellets, and they won't know the tangos in these woods are real."

The horror of the situation sank in. The SEALs would be facing real enemies, but believe they were fake. Part of an exercise.

Xavier had known the man with the knife was a real attacker. One of the SEALs, in the same situation, wouldn't know it wasn't a simulation. They'd fire their paint pellets and expect to tally it as a success. But the tango—as Xavier had called him—would fight to the death. And they had real guns.

She took a deep breath as her heart cracked in two. She wasn't in the military, but she understood triage. They weren't even certain George was here and in danger, but the specter with the knife had made it clear the SEALs were. Not to mention she and Xavier both could have been killed. "Where is your command center? I might know a faster—or safer route."

"It's the yurt on the other side of the lodge complex from here."

She bit her lip, mentally going over the trail map. It made sense that the yurt was their command center. The seventies-era home was not in keeping with the historic lodge and not yet old enough to fall under her domain with historic properties, so Xavier's team didn't need her approval for its use. Plus, being round and situated on a point as it was, it had an amazing view of the lake.

There was a trail that ran through the woods above the blacksmith shop and lodge. It intersected with the forest behind the yurt. If they hiked up the hill from the burial ground, they'd reach that trail in about a mile.

She described the route to Xavier. "We'll have to go back to the meadow and burial ground, but we can bypass the road behind the blacksmith shop and lodge. Except for the switchbacks here, the entire route is in the forest."

"For safety, we'll have to do most of the hike without light, and I don't have my NVGs. You up for it?"

She'd always said she could navigate these woods blind-folded. Time to put that bravado to the test. "My watch has a compass and Indiglo. As long as we can stop to check our bearing, yes."

"Let's go."

He led the way back down the switchback, moving as fast as the terrain allowed. They reached the narrow trail where she'd slipped before, but he didn't slow. She shifted her center of gravity toward the hillside and kept pace with him. When they reached the corner of the switchback, he stopped abruptly. She caught herself right before she stepped on his heels.

"What's wrong?"

"Blood. I think." He pulled out his flashlight and shined it on the rocky edge, and she saw the red streaks.

He glanced up, and she followed his gaze. "We're below the ledge where you tossed him," she said. She looked back at the bloody rocks. It hadn't been a straight fall. He'd tumbled down the slope and hit this ledge. Had he continued down, falling to his death? Or had he managed to scramble onto the path here or on one of the lower switchbacks? "If he survived, he could tell others where we are," she said.

He nodded. "And he now has military-grade NVGs." He studied the streaks on the rocks and shook his head. "We need to hurry." He tucked away the flashlight again, and they resumed at a brisk pace.

They reached the intersection for the trail that led to the archaeological site and jogged up the hill into the forest. Full darkness had descended. Storm clouds cloaked the sky, leaving them without moon or stars to light the path or provide direction. Audrey could barely see the ground beneath her feet, but she kept up with Xavier just the same. She couldn't let him down.

They reached the top of the slope and continued to follow a game trail, just as narrow as the cliffside trail, but without the sheer drop-off. She used the glowing dial on her watch to check their bearing when it was time to leave one trail and cut a path to the other.

During the pause, Xavier tried his cell again. They were close to the cell tower up here, but it didn't matter. Whatever had been used to jam all radio and cellular signals had been effective.

She could just make out his eyes in the shadows. Handsome and focused, he reminded her of another time, when he'd stared at her with similar intensity, but without the accompanying tension. Darkness made it easier to see the man she'd met in November. She didn't see CW5 Rivera. He was Xavier, Jae's friend, a man she'd been drawn to as if caught in a charismatic tractor beam.

Having sex with him had been both incredible and inevitable and was something she'd never regret, no matter how awful he'd been weeks later. She touched her belly. At a little over eleven weeks, she wasn't showing, but her uterus was firmer. She couldn't feel that firmness under the padded raincoat, but the reflexive touch comforted just the same. Later, she'd tell him she was pregnant, and maybe, just maybe, it would be joyous news, shared with excitement.

They were a long way from anything close to settled, but at least she had a respite from the seething anger. She used the hope she and Xavier could salvage a workable relationship for the sake of their child to tamp down her fear.

Because fear threatened to swallow her whole. Her worry

for George had expanded to include the SEAL team that was en route along with Xavier and his team of trainers.

Strange that the fear for herself was more focused on the baby she carried, even though it had only just transitioned from embryo to fetus. According to the week-by-week pregnancy guide, her fetus was the size of a fig.

She followed Xavier as they cut a path through the woods, focusing on the little fig that would change her life and the man before her who might play a huge role in that new reality.

As she followed him, she made every effort to move with the same degree of stealth he'd mastered. She'd never aimed for silence in the woods. The opposite, in fact. This was bear country, after all. With bears and cougars in the woods, silence was the enemy. It was better to warn animals of her presence than to stumble into their path, startling them both.

But she'd do as Xavier commanded, because at this point, it was clear anything they came across in these woods was far more dangerous than a hibernating bear.

*avier wanted to break into a full run, but Audrey wouldn't be able to keep up and be silent. There were people in these woods. He could feel them. They might not have eyes on him and Audrey, but they were nearby.

They reached the maintained path, wide enough for tourists to walk side by side, but in need of maintenance now that it was winter. But the trail was clear enough that he and Audrey could move faster without making noise.

He checked his watch. Dread ran down his spine.

If everything had gone according to plan with Naval

Special Warfare Command, the team would be jumping any time now.

There was nothing like the adrenaline rush of a HALO jump. Nothing like landing in enemy territory, loaded with gear and ready for battle. But this was meant to be an exercise. The team didn't know they were jumping into enemy-held territory for real. SEALs were the best of the best, but they'd be fighting real bullets with fucking paint pellets.

He needed to get to the landline phone in the yurt. *Now.*

He broke into a run. Forget stealth, it took too much time. He could hear Audrey behind him, keeping pace on the smooth trail. He saw the spire of the yurt through the trees and turned, leading her downslope, off the path.

He came to an abrupt halt when he reached the road. Shit. The nearest culvert to cross under the road was at least a half a klick away. The fastest route to the yurt and a working landline phone was across the two-lane forest road that dead-ended at the lodge complex.

They'd be exposed, but he was out of time.

He turned to Audrey and whispered, "I want you to stay here. Tuck down in the well of a tree. Hide. I need to cross, and I don't want you exposed."

She shook her head. "No. I don't want to be alone out here. There's a culvert—"

"I know. But it's too far. We're out of time."

"Then let's go."

Without further argument, he did. Every second mattered.

He crouched low and darted across the street, diving for a thicket of trees that hugged the opposite side. Audrey kept pace with him, and together, they wove through the small cluster and made their way to the back of the yurt.

He slowed as he approached the command center. He couldn't screw up now. This wasn't a training anymore; this was an op. He had to scope out the yurt before stepping inside.

The round house looked quiet on its perch above the lake. A light rain had begun as they trod the path, and he could see the dark mass of the lake as raindrops littered the surface. The forecast had indicated the wind would pick up after nineteen hundred hours, which was another reason they'd bumped up the time for the jump.

The team would have to deal with cold rain and cold lake, but wouldn't face a fierce wind from the get-go.

For their part, the SEALs would be pumped, at the peak of their game. Even armed only with Simunition, they'd be hard to take down.

Xavier felt a fierce pride. He was one of them. The old man now with a bum shoulder, but still one of them.

The man he'd fought on the ledge had been trained. Well. He knew how to fight. Xavier's loss of range of motion in his shoulder had given the tango the advantage. That didn't bode well for his team. He had to assume they were all equally trained.

Who were they? What was their goal here?

Beyond destroying a platoon of SEALs, that is. He assumed there was a bigger objective, although the humiliation of destroying a team on American soil might be enough.

If a SEAL encountered an ambush similar to what he'd faced on the cliffside trail, he'd assume the attack was part of the training. He wouldn't fight to the death as Xavier had— or at least hoped he had. The blood on the trail worried him.

He should have called a halt to this exercise the moment he recognized Audrey, should have gone with the instinct that told him something was off. But he'd spent the last three months working toward today.

This was a thousands-of-lives-hang-in-the-balance test run for an op. When it was time for the real mission, they'd only have one shot. This exercise was their best shot at refining the plan before they went wheels up. And after what had happened on Xavier's last op, he was determined his team would be prepared.

He'd thrown away something special with Audrey to make this day happen. This exercise was crucial, in ways that not even the SEALs about to jump into a frigid lake in winter knew.

He studied the darkened yurt. Everything looked as it should. It was bathed in darkness, no lights to give the SEALs anything to fix on to. They were in full blackout mode for this op.

He circled the structure to the daylight basement door on the side. A few feet from the door, a large power meter was affixed to the exterior. The darkened shape was all wrong, however, and it took a moment for his eyes to register what the dark lump over the meter could be.

Next to him, Audrey let out a sharp gasp, then slapped a hand over her mouth.

He wrapped an arm around her waist and pulled her deeper into the cover of the woods. He acted on autopilot as his brain reeled. Only one action made sense in the moment: get Audrey to safety.

Once she was safe, he'd check the body that was slumped over the power meter.

Chapter Five

*L*ieutenant Chris Flyte needed to get his shit together. He took several deep breaths. There was no room for distraction here.

The sadistic trainers who'd come up with this exercise deserved a special place in hell. HALO jumps were risky enough, but executing them right before a storm, with their target being a thirty-five-degree lake, was a special treat.

No way was this a "generic" training as laid out by command. HALO jumps usually weren't even allowed in this area, but they'd gotten special permission for this one exercise. They were practicing for a specific op that required a frigid lake HALO jump right before a storm.

And damn, but he couldn't think of any mission that was worth that risk. Bin Laden had been dead for over a decade.

He stood in the open back of the plane and checked his gear with the rest of the team. Oxygen mask secured. Gear he'd need for the next five days packed in a heavy, watertight pack. Every inch of his skin was covered—protection from the balls of ice he'd meet when he dropped through the cloud layer that was between the plane and Lake Olympus.

As he went through the vital, lifesaving checklist, he also tried to box away Pam's betrayal to a dark corner of his mind. He couldn't afford to give her any of his headspace until after the training was behind him.

He should have withdrawn from this exercise, but that wasn't exactly an option. He'd only learned his wife was having an affair two days ago and had zero time to process the utter destruction of his life before flying north to Whidbey.

For the last forty-eight hours, he'd been on autopilot, doing his job and trying not to think about the end of his eight-year marriage. And now here he was, ready to jump from twenty thousand feet into a frigid lake, all to rescue a fake hostage.

The only easy day was yesterday.

Yesterday was the day he'd learned *who* his wife had been fucking for the last eighteen months.

Yesterday had been total and utter shit.

The signal came. Go time.

Deep breath. Get centered. Time to lead his team.

He pitched and rolled forward off the ramp. Wind buffeted him, roaring in his ears, blocking all other sound. He turned to face upward. The plane grew smaller as the last of the platoon rolled off the ramp, dots above in the night sky.

Satisfied his team was in free fall, he rolled to face the cloud cover below him. The plane would return to Whidbey. They were on their own and would treat this as a real op until the first task was complete and the trainers called a halt to debrief on their successes and failures.

There was an exhilaration to free fall that didn't go away, even when he had hundreds of jumps under his belt. But today, the feeling was muted.

He dialed in, checking his altitude. There was no room

for a wandering mind here. Even with every patch of skin covered, it was damn cold as he plummeted toward earth. The lake would be even worse.

He hit the cloud layer and felt the sting of ice pellets as they pummeled his thick wet suit.

Thankfully, the storm hadn't quite started yet, and beneath the cloud canopy, his chute opened without a hitch and the wind wasn't so wild as to throw him off course.

All around him, chutes bloomed as the others pulled their cords.

The quiet that came after the chute opening always brought a sense of peace, but in a low-opening jump, there wasn't a moment to enjoy it. This was an op, and he was about to go into battle.

He released the chute as his feet touched frigid water. The water was hellishly cold, but the insulating layers of wet suit did their job, keeping the worst of the cold at bay, and his body heated the trapped liquid.

He made his way toward shore, weighed down by the heavy gear bag. He was going to kick Rivera's ass for coming up with this nightmarish scenario. Didn't matter that they'd been friends for years. The paces the team was being put through were bullshit.

Without warning, a memory surfaced. A barbecue on the beach two years ago. He'd been there with Pam. Rivera had Lynn at his side. Everyone on the team had been there, including Brock.

Had that been when the affair started? Or had it been later, after the op that had sent Rivera to the hospital and Forsythe and Adams to the morgue?

Do I even want to know?

Not really.

He'd told no one on the team about Pam's affair, and apart from the SEALs, he had no other friends. No family.

No life beyond his marriage and his work. He'd been alone in his miserable thoughts as he prepped for the training.

Betrayed by his wife and a man he'd considered a brother.

Shit.

Focus. Swim. Kick. Breathe.

Before the jump, he'd thought this exercise would be good for him. He'd be forced to get out of his head. Solve problems. Lead his team. How could he think about betrayal when swimming in thirty-five-degree water?

He turned his mind to the cold. Leaned into the pain of it as he swam, fast and hard, carrying a watertight bag filled with the gear he'd need to survive the coming days. He focused on that.

Old friend or not, Rivera wouldn't let mistakes slide. If he failed this training, Rivera would be right to flag him as unfit for ops. He could be a danger to his team.

Now that his marriage was ending, if he lost his spot on the team, he'd have nothing. No one.

The thought added power to his stroke as he swam toward shore. For this first exercise, they'd divided the sixteen-man platoon into four Fire Teams. Each team knew their extraction point from the lake and mission once they were on land. If they didn't free the hostages in the first few hours, they'd rendezvous in the forest to the northeast of the lodge at oh four hundred and hatch a new plan.

Chris's team had selected an extraction point near a campground on the west side of the lake. They'd have to hike a fair distance around the north end to get around Kaxo Falls, but they'd be able to approach the lodge complex from an unexpected angle, taking the tangos from behind. Two Fire Teams would have the direct approach, flanking the lodge compound from the north and south, while the fourth would extract from the water directly opposite the lake from Chris's team.

If he knew Rivera and Cohen, they'd have set up some nasty surprises in the woods for all four teams—but the trainers didn't know where each Fire Team had chosen to extract from the water. They were as in the dark as to the planning done by the platoon this afternoon on Whidbey as the team was clueless as to what was in store for them.

Rivera was a big fan of expecting the unexpected and could be diabolical when coming up with ways a mission could go FUBAR. But then, he and Rivera had survived some messed-up operations together, and they both understood the need to put the team through extreme tests.

Rivera had barely survived the last op. Memories of that night, hauling his wounded teammate from the building, would haunt Chris for the rest of his days.

At least in training, if the op went FUBAR, no one would die. That was sort of the whole point.

Chris reached the shoreline. He could see the dark outlines of NPS campground signs on the beach. He chose a spot to the east, where trees abutted the water, and slipped from the lake directly into the cover of the forest.

Raindrops dotted the lake surface, the patter growing more rapid in the moments it took for his teammates to follow him into the woods. They'd barely beaten the predicted storm.

The thick forest camouflage wet suit kept him warm, but they'd be here for days, so they'd take turns changing in one of the campground shelters while the other three acted as guards.

Chris had wanted to parachute onto the meadow above the lodge and skip the hassle of swimming, but the sadists in charge had wanted the frigid swim to be part of their ordeal.

What the hell is Rivera preparing us for?

Grimly, it occurred to him that he'd managed to forget Pam for several minutes. Nothing like freezing his balls to change his perspective.

Jonas, Huang, and Phelps followed him into the woods like silent shadows. They located a pit toilet and took turns changing. Huang and Phelps used the break to touch up the dark greasepaint on their faces, to hide their pale skin. Jonas and Chris were both Black with skin on the darker end of the spectrum and didn't bother with face paint.

As he waited for his turn, icy raindrops pelted him and wind whipped through the branches of the trees. The storm was coming, but he cursed the wind and rain only in his mind. Why would anyone attempt a hostage rescue in these conditions? This training was full of obstacles for obstacles' sake. He couldn't imagine a good enough reason to infiltrate an enemy stronghold in such piss-poor conditions. The odds of failure were too high.

Once he was changed and dry—but still fricking cold— he tucked away his wet suit in his pack, then tapped his earpiece to check in with the other Fire Teams' progress.

The receiver didn't make a sound.

He clicked the mic button and hailed the other teams again. Nothing.

"Shit," he said softly to his team. "Signal jammer."

Huang pulled out a cell phone and checked the screen. "Cell's out too."

Chris pulled their Fire Team's only satellite phone from his pack. It too couldn't get a signal. Could be due to forest and cloud cover, but he didn't think so.

Jonas cursed and tapped his mic button. "Looks like we've found the first hurdle."

Chris didn't pick up anything from Jonas's headset, meaning the radios didn't even work when a mere three feet apart. Yet his NVGs worked. If he still had night vision, then their electronics hadn't been wiped out by an electromagnetic pulse. An EMP wasn't selective. It took out all or nothing. So this wasn't your average signal jammer, and it wasn't an EMP.

Fucking great.

Phelps, who was usually the glass-half-full type, also swore. "Assholes. It's not bad enough that we're dealing with a freezing monsoon? They had to cut out communication too?"

Chris tucked the sat phone away. This little wrinkle meant that after they secured the hostages and identified an extraction point, they'd have to use a landline to call in the helicopter. And they'd have to find their teammates to coordinate without revealing themselves to the trainer/tangos.

The degree of difficulty had gone up exponentially.

Odds were they were going to need that preset oh-four-hundred meet point.

That's it. Rivera wasn't invited to the divorce party. Cohen was out too.

Any hope they'd complete the first task and start the second phase of the training in a matter of hours was shot to hell. It was going to be a long cold-ass night.

Usually, he lived for this shit. He'd be pumped, full of adrenaline, ready to take on the world, but today, he just wanted to get it over with so he could go home, confront his wife, and begin divorce proceedings.

At least for a few minutes, Pam had slipped from his mind. He ruthlessly shoved her to the dark space at the back. He needed to take this training seriously, as if it were the real deal. Anything less could put him and others at risk of injury and get him kicked off this team, which, thanks to her, was all he had left.

*A*udrey was going to be sick. She buried her face against Xavier's tactical vest, trying to hold herself together. Everything was surreal. Grotesque. This couldn't be her park. Her lodge. Her life.

She'd felt ownership of these mountains and this forest since she was a kid. The park belonged to everyone, but the eleven-year-old girl who'd just moved to Forks had desperately needed to belong somewhere, to feel something was *hers*. She'd adopted the park, which had, in the form of ONP Archaeologist Roy Heller, adopted her right back.

The park was a haven, her escape from classmates who'd rejected the awkward new girl, and also from her hostile mother, who'd resented the move to Forks even more than Audrey had.

But this, right now, was straight out of a horror movie, and ONP and Lake Olympus Lodge didn't belong in this reality.

This was all a bad dream. It was probably three a.m. this morning, and she was deep asleep in her home in Port Angeles. Today hadn't happened yet. Her subconscious had served up Xavier because they had massive unfinished business, and George was a concern in sleep because she was worried about him weathering the predicted storm. Perhaps she'd eaten something to trigger the stomach upset that led to this nightmare.

Scrooge's words in *A Christmas Carol* came to mind: *"You may be an undigested bit of beef, a blot of mustard, a crumb of cheese, a fragment of underdone potato. There's more of gravy than of grave about you, whatever you are!"*

Like Scrooge, she needed to look to her other senses for the truth in the moment. Xavier's arms that held her tight to his chest. The scent of damp woods, the feel of cold rain filtering through the branches. The tapping of raindrops on evergreens increasing in tempo as the storm gathered and settled in.

This *was* her park. Her forest. Her lodge. She wasn't dreaming, and no matter how much she wished to, she wouldn't wake from this living nightmare.

The only way out of this situation was to face it head-on. She lifted her head and tried to see Xavier, but could only make out his outline in the dark woods. Full darkness had settled like a cold, wet blanket. "Was that…one of your men?"

"No." His voice was gruff. "I was going to ask if it was George."

She shook her head, then realized he probably couldn't see the motion. She swallowed and found her voice again. "No. George is smaller, wiry." From her limited glimpse, the dead man had been large, with thick shoulders. Classic mountain man physique.

"I need to go back," he said. "Check on the body. Enter the yurt. But first, I need to get you somewhere safe."

The idea of being in these woods without Xavier scared the hell out of her. "Nowhere is safe."

"True. But checking the body will be dangerous. I'll be exposed."

"Don't leave me. Please."

He paused, then said, "Fine. One of us will have the gun, the other will examine the body. See if he's alive. We should take pictures too. Which job do you want?"

Now was not the time to be squeamish. Her stomach was first-trimester sensitive, but she'd do her best to keep her lunch down. Xavier was more skilled with weapons, and she knew how to look for a pulse. "I'll check the body."

She squared her shoulders and stepped back from Xavier's embrace. The wind picked up and a chill ran through her body, but she figured the blast of cold had more to do with leaving his warmth than from the wind. It was damn cold out here, and it would only get worse as the storm strengthened.

As if to punctuate her thoughts, the rain increased from steady patter to faster staccato. And this was still only the front edge of the squall. She followed Xavier through the trees to the body she'd have to search. Her gag reflex had been triggered, but she held it down.

He covered her as she stood over the body. She snapped a picture with her cell phone before turning him over. If TV and books had taught her anything, it was that she was messing with forensic evidence, but she didn't have the luxury of worrying about that now. Rain would wash evidence away even if she did nothing, and if there was even a miniscule chance this person was alive, that overrode evidence preservation.

She grabbed a thick shoulder to turn him, and the body slid from its perch on the meter box and slumped to the ground. She gasped and jumped back, unable to control her reaction as she took in the man's face. She snapped another picture. The camera lit the gruesome scene in a bright white light.

"Holy shit," Xavier said.

Her hands shook as she checked the photo on her phone. "They must've used an axe to cut his throat. Just like they cut the power line to the cameras. His head is attached, but barely."

No point in checking a severed carotid for a pulse. He was dead.

Xavier shined a red flashlight over the face and gaping neck wound. "Do you know him?"

"Yes." She stared at the familiar blank eyes and bloody chin. Rain splattered down, mixing with blood and washing it away in thin channels that cut lines in the packed soil. "Jeb McCutcheon. He owns one of the inholding cabins."

"He was in the lodge that night. With George."

"Yes."

"He a friend?" Xavier asked, concern in his voice.

"Not like George. More of an associate. He often tried to use environmental and historic preservation laws to stop government action and development in the park, so he contacted my office frequently." He'd been an irritant at times, but also a decent man. He'd been true to his convictions, and she respected that.

"He opposed the training," Xavier said. "But in the end, he took the payment and signed the contract agreeing to vacate this week."

"I assume you changed the lock on the inholding access gate?" she asked. Inholding landowners had a separate gate with their own keys.

"The lock was changed two days ago, per our contract. Plus, we checked the cabins on the lake and all were vacant, as agreed. Which one is Jeb's?"

"It's the one closest to the Civilian Conservation Corps campground. 'No trespassing' signs everywhere. He must've hidden during your inspection." Audrey's teeth started to chatter—but it wasn't cold that triggered it. She took more photos of the dead man, shielding the flash as much as she could with a cupped hand. "I wonder if he's part of what's going on, or if he came here to cause trouble for the training and got in someone's way?"

"Check his pockets. Maybe he's carrying something that will give us a clue."

His pockets were empty. No cell phone, no keys, no hint as to what he was doing here or who had taken an axe to his throat.

Task complete, they retreated into an alcove created by a

shed that abutted the yurt. "I need to get inside," Xavier said. "Cohen was in there."

Audrey's stomach churned. "It could be an ambush," she said, naming her biggest fear of the moment.

"I know."

She would go with him. No way was she staying out here alone.

The storm had worsened while she examined Jeb's body. Rain pelted the yurt's metal roof, drowning out all other sound. "We need to do it now, while the storm is heavy. If someone's inside, they won't be able to hear us over the rain."

He nodded. "I'll go in first. I want you right behind me. I'll give you my training gun. Simunition stings like a bitch. I wish it were more, but it's better than nothing."

She took a deep breath to steel her nerves. She'd faced a knife-wielding man on a cliff and searched the nearly decapitated body of Jeb McCutcheon. Might as well add walking blind into a yurt that could house an axe murderer to the list of horrific things she'd done that day.

She met Xavier's gaze in the dim red glow of his flashlight. His handsome face held fear and concern. Hours ago, the most traumatic thing she'd thought she'd face with him was telling him about their baby.

She straightened her spine. "Let's go."

*

With SEALs in the water, armed tangos in the woods, and a dead body outside the command center, there was no time to waste. Xavier needed to get inside and find out what had happened to the other trainers, turn off the signal jammer, and tell Naval Special Warfare Command to flood these woods with armed special forces operators. Naval Air Station Whidbey could have a team here in an hour. Two tops.

Plus there were Green Berets and Army Rangers stationed at Joint Base Lewis-McChord near Tacoma. They could end this before it took more lives.

But the dead-eyed stare of Jeb McCutcheon warned him it might already be too late to save his team of trainers.

Xavier gave Audrey his gun—a Glock, like hers, making him glad he didn't have to waste time with instructions. "It's chambered."

She pointed it away from him and looked down the sights. He noted her grip, thumbs aligned on one side, index finger along the trigger guard. She didn't look comfortable, but she had the basics down. Good.

She lowered the gun and met his gaze. "Ready."

From the determined set of her chin, he believed her. But from the shaking of her hands, he knew she was terrified.

"You got this," he said, touching her cheek. Her skin was cold and wet, but that wasn't the cause of her trembling.

She gave a sharp nod, and he dropped his hand. Precious seconds were ticking by.

"Have you been inside the yurt before?" he asked.

"No."

"The basement is divided into two semicircular rooms. We'll search both, then take the curved stairway along the wall to the main floor, where the command center is."

He turned, crouched low, and headed for the basement door. She followed on his heels. They reached the door, and he took a position on the opposite side. "I'll go in first. You come in behind me, covering the part of the room I'm facing away from."

"Got it."

Xavier couldn't believe he was about to enter and clear a building with an archaeologist armed only with a paintball

gun as his backup. This after finding a man who'd been
nearly decapitated with an axe, and before that, grappling
with a man wielding a knife and sporting an AK-47 on his
back.

This shit was real, and she had zero training on how to
handle it, but he had to give her credit for facing it head-on.
That was more than he had any right to hope for.

He slipped his key in the lock he'd oiled just yesterday. It
turned smooth and silent. He pocketed the key before giving
Audrey a nod. Go time.

He used his flashlight to scan the room, hoping to
temporarily blind anyone in the dark or wearing NVGs.
Audrey slipped in behind him, moving too quickly and
nearly tripping on his heel, but he was damn lucky to have
any backup at all.

The room was empty, and they repeated the flanking
maneuver and entered the basement utility room. A fast
search showed it was also empty.

He led the way up the stairs, footsteps muted by seventies-era shag carpet and rain pounding on the metal roof.
The yurt had the musty smell of wet dog and furnishings
made ten years before he was born. Add the scent of spicy
Mexican food to the smell and it could be his grandmother's
house. He'd been living in the yurt for the last week, and the
reminder of his long-passed abuela had been comforting
until now.

The lake-facing part of the main floor was a circular
living room with a magnificent view in daylight. A gas fireplace filled the center, the chimney running up the rooftop
spire, the ceiling high and cone shaped. The low fire offered
some light, but it didn't reach the tables his team had set up
beneath the windows that provided a two-hundred-and-
forty-degree view of the lake.

On those tables, they'd arranged a bank of monitors to

receive feed from closed-circuit lodge cameras, computers, phones, and a military-grade modem with direct feed to SPECWAR—NSWC's computer system. The signal jammer didn't affect the equipment they'd installed here. It was all hardwired.

The room felt vacant to Xavier even before he left the staircase, but he knew better than to go on instinct alone. He'd changed the flashlight beam from white to red and shined it low, below the window line. The windows reflected a flat, black void.

Rain on the metal roof reverberated through the room, masking all other sounds. He crouched low as he crossed to the worktables. The red light landed on one table, then another, and a chill ran through him as deep as any he'd felt on a combat mission. Every piece of electronic equipment on the tables had been destroyed. Smashed. Cleaved in two as if with an axe.

The table was splattered with a liquid that could be blood, but he couldn't be sure with the red light. Finally, the light hit an object that turned him hot and cold at the same time, and it answered the question about the splatter marks on the table.

Lying next to a shattered monitor was a tattooed, severed human finger that belonged to his partner in running this exercise, Master Chief Petty Officer Paul Cohen.

Chapter Six

It was dark by the time Jae made it to the Lake Olympus Road gate. Audrey's vehicle wasn't parked in or outside the gate as he'd instructed. His headlights shined on the heavy-duty lock designed to defy bolt cutters. Locked tight as it should be. But then, Audrey had a key. As did Jae.

The lock on the inholding entrance had been changed two days ago, but the park gate had the same master lock used for all gates. The Navy had requested the lock be changed, but ONP had remained firm—they were not to be locked out of their own facilities. Emergencies happened, and hikers could need rescue outside the training zone in other areas along the eighteen-mile road.

Had Audrey used her key? Surely she knew a training was set to begin tonight, making the area off-limits?

The splatter of rain on Jae's white and green law enforcement park ranger SUV increased in tempo. The front edge of the promised storm had arrived.

He'd wasted hours with a group of unruly Russian tourists at Mora Campground. They'd harassed the camp host to the point of Jae being called in, but when it was time to evict, their RV had mysteriously broken down. It had taken two hours for a flatbed tow to arrive to haul the vehicle away. Jae hadn't dared to leave the poor host alone with the campers.

There was something off about the whole ordeal, but not enough for Jae to make an arrest when expulsion from the park would do the trick. Getting them off park land with a heads-up to the chief of police in Forks—the nearest town that offered a repair shop and motel—had been the best he could do.

But it meant he was very late to his meeting with Audrey.

He'd checked with dispatch, and there was no word from her as to whether she'd entered the park or not. He called the security team that monitored all park cameras. "Has Audrey Kendrick reported in?"

The person he reached had just started their shift and checked the log before answering. "The last communication with Dr. Kendrick was at three thirty-seven p.m. She was en route to the Lake Olympus access road."

"Thank you. Please call me if she gives you an update on the cameras."

"Will do, Ranger Son."

He tried Audrey's cell again. Was it possible she didn't know about the training? After what happened, she might have been taken off the contact list. Jae certainly hadn't asked if she'd been kept in the loop. He'd avoided the subject altogether.

He still didn't understand what had happened between her and Xavier. He couldn't imagine his old friend would lie about something so important, but also didn't believe Audrey would behave unprofessionally.

All he knew was she *had* tried to use Jae to contact Xavier right before the SEAL dropped his bombshell about her. Was that because Xavier had blocked her number when things soured between them?

Jae had never asked what happened when he left after introducing them. He'd seen the sparks flaring and had figured they'd spent the night together, but it was none of his business.

His role in Xavier and Audrey's meeting was made even trickier because he'd known the SEAL couldn't reveal the truth about his job—which also happened to be the reason he'd been at the lodge that night. Jae had vouched for Xavier when the man had essentially lied about his work.

At the time, it didn't seem like a big deal. After all, he'd trust Xavier with his life. He was a good man and a very old friend. He'd warned Audrey that Xavier wasn't the relationship sort because he knew she was still hurting from a bad breakup and didn't want to see her hurt again, not because he had any misgivings about the two of them hooking up if that was what they both wanted.

He'd never dreamed Xavier would hurt her more than even Audrey's ex ever had.

None of it made sense. For Audrey to have denied the permit because she'd been rejected after a one-night stand, she'd have had to have known why Xavier was at the lodge. Which meant Xavier must have spilled the beans after all. But Audrey claimed she didn't know anything about his role in the compliance process.

None of it sounded like something Xavier would do.

The end result was an ugly tangle Jae had managed to avoid for the last month. Now he feared his neutral stance between two close friends was about to be tested.

If Audrey had entered the park and interrupted the training, she could be in serious trouble. Sure, the cameras gave her a legitimate reason for concern, but if Xavier or the other trainers believed she'd spoiled the training for revenge, she could end up in jail.

How badly did I fail her as a friend?

His call went straight to voicemail. Again.

He drummed his fingers on the steering wheel. It was possible she'd made it to the site, taken photos, and was back on the road and out of cellular range again. But wouldn't she have called him? Cell coverage was decent in the meadow.

Jae tried Xavier's number, knowing it was unlikely he would answer given that the training had probably started.

He looked out at the pounding rain, feeling sorry for the team that had to work in this. Xavier had said he hoped for a storm to kick off the training, but Jae figured he'd gotten more than he wished for. This rain would be brutal—not cold enough for snow, just heavy and miserable.

If Audrey had entered the park, she could be in trouble. If the training had been interrupted, the hundreds of thousands of dollars that had been poured into the setup and running of it could be wasted. Not to mention the national security implications. Jae had no idea what this training was about, but he figured it wasn't generic as the Navy had claimed. There was a specific op they were preparing for, and it was *big*.

He wished he'd never introduced the archaeologist to the SEAL, because if Xavier had lied about Audrey...that was unforgivable. No way could he defend his friend. And if Audrey really had denied the permit simply because she'd been rejected, well, he couldn't hold a grudge against Xavier for sidestepping her authority in this.

There'd been nothing he could do to ease the situation between them.

Until now.

He could enter the park and get Audrey out of there

before she landed in jail. He could vouch for the issue with the cameras and explain why the site was important—to Audrey, to the tribes, to the park.

He had legal right of entry and a role to play. As a law enforcement ranger, his job was to document the crime and search for the looters.

Plus, Jae hoped to move up into the investigative unit for the National Park Service. If he failed to do his job to protect this cultural heritage site, it wouldn't look good on his application when a position opened up in the unit.

He might get in as much trouble as Audrey for interrupting the training, but he could justify his actions and maybe save Audrey or Xavier from theirs. He donned his wide-brimmed ranger hat and climbed from the vehicle. Rain pummeled him, having picked up in the minutes he'd sat in the car making calls and debating his course of action.

He crossed in front of his headlights and pulled out the key to the heavy-duty lock. He would drive to the lodge, find Audrey, and extract her from the training.

It was the right thing to do and a good plan.

A great one, even. Except he hit a major snag: his key didn't work.

He studied the key and the lock. Had the Navy gotten a concession from the park on the gate lock after all? Or had the Navy changed the lock without permission?

But if they changed the lock, then Audrey didn't have a key either and couldn't have entered the park. At least, not on this road. And there was no other road to the lake or lodge. It was a dead end with only jeep trail spurs in a few places along the winding eighteen-mile stretch.

One way in, one way out.

Well, except for the SEALs, who were probably parachuting or being helicoptered in. Jae presumed they'd be airlifted out as well.

He returned to the vehicle, taking shelter from the rain as he considered his options. He couldn't ask about the gate lock over the radio because the exact timing of the training was secret—no details were to be broadcast over the radio. He would check in with park management about the gate at the end of his shift tonight.

His radio chirped, and the dispatcher spoke. "Ranger Son, we just received a request from George Shaw's family for a law enforcement ranger to check on the tribal elder in his cabin near Lake Olympus."

Jae frowned. George should have vacated his cabin with the other inholding landowners. But his cabin wasn't on the lake, so maybe he'd been excluded from that order? Jae had no role in the process, and so he didn't really know. It wasn't like he could have asked Audrey for the finer details.

"I'm unable to do a check tonight," he replied, "but I'll head to the lodge tomorrow." If the Navy had changed the locks without permission, he'd make sure they coughed up a key.

"Isn't tomorrow your day off, Ranger Son?"

He smiled, thinking of the attractive young woman who was on the other end of the conversation. She'd completed her law enforcement ranger training at the same school Jae had up in the Skagit Valley and was working as a dispatcher during the off-season as she applied for seasonal ranger jobs at all the major parks. She was kind and smart, and now it appeared she was aware of his work schedule. He wanted to ask her about that, but that conversation would be better if it happened over beers after work and not over the park radio.

"It is, but George is a friend, and I need to follow up on the cameras and potential looting anyway."

He pulled out onto the highway that skirted the north and western margins of the mountain range that defined the peninsula, heading north toward Forks. He'd check in with

Audrey later, after his shift. She lived only a few miles from him in Port Angeles. If she didn't call him back, he'd stop by her house.

Thick sheets of rain swamped his vehicle, and he imagined being a SEAL, out in the rainforest right now, role-playing combat in this miserable, drenching storm.

No, thank you.

Jae participated in plenty of search and rescue operations and could do the work that was necessary. But to be faking it? In this? He was more than thankful for the shelter of his SUV.

The thankful feeling proved to be short-lived when less than a mile from the intersection to 101 that would take him to Forks, he came across a mudslide that partially blocked the road.

He'd driven this road just twenty minutes before.

Still, he should have seen this coming with the heavy rain. Washington was among the most mudslide-prone states, suffering hundreds—sometimes even thousands—each year, and this stretch of the Olympic Peninsula had more than its share with the storms that roared in from the Pacific.

Thankfully, there was no sign of other vehicles on the road, and there were no homes or businesses in the area.

He alerted dispatch to the slide, then backed up well past the slide zone and set up barriers, alerting drivers to turn around. Anyone passing through would have to take the road all the way back to Queets to catch the main highway.

A long-ass detour, but better than getting swept away by a mudslide. He was informed that first responders in Queets were posting detour signs already. Good.

Jae left his warm, dry vehicle and inspected the slide area. It was risky, but he could drive forward. The pool of mud at the base of the collapsed hillside hadn't reached the road. The debris in the road was mostly rocks and splintered trees, with a thin layer of mud soup that just crossed the center line.

He could skirt it and close the other end of the road, which was too far from Forks to have a quick response. But he'd better do it fast because there was no way of knowing if more of the hillside would come down and take out the entire width of the road.

He made it past the slide area and kept driving until he reached the main road, glad there were no oncoming vehicles that required a stop until he was well past the slide area.

At the highway, he set up more barriers, closing the road. He then waited for an officer from Forks to show up with something more substantial than the portable "road closed" signs he carried in his vehicle.

Thoughts of Audrey, Xavier, and miserable SEALs faded as he redirected traffic in the pouring rain. He was going to have his own long, cold, uncomfortable night.

*A*udrey stared at Xavier's stiff back, wondering what was wrong. There was just enough light from the gas fire to see the shapes of things, but not enough to identify anything. That blob on the table under the window could be a throw pillow, roast turkey, or a decapitated head.

Given Jeb's condition outside, the third option might be the most likely, and once again, she felt bile rise.

"What's wrong?" she whispered. Xavier had frozen in place, and she needed the strong SEAL back.

"A finger," he said.

"What?" She stepped up behind him and focused on the table that held Xavier's attention.

He pressed the button on his red-beamed light, and she saw what he was talking about. It looked like a Halloween decoration. A prop. Except for the pool of blood, and the line below the knuckle at the base of the finger. A zigzag pattern. Like Charlie Brown's shirt.

"Is that…is it a tattoo?" she asked.

The red glow gave just enough light so the shapes she'd seen now made sense. The roast turkey was a small backpack, mounded on the table next to a smashed monitor.

Next to her, Xavier's head moved in a slight nod. "Cohen's wife would tease him about not wearing his wedding ring. Rings can get caught on things and are dangerous on ops, so most SEALs don't wear them, or they wear silicone bands. But Cohen had a better idea and got a tattoo. He told Carly he now had a ring he couldn't take off." Xavier's voice was hollow. Haunted.

It was easy to understand why. His buddy wasn't wearing his permanent wedding band anymore.

She'd managed to keep her lunch down when seeing Jeb's open throat, but the severed finger pushed her over the edge. She turned her head, spotted a trash bin, and dove for it.

She emptied her stomach, then wanted to stagger to the couch and sit down, but for all she knew, there was an axe murderer in one of the upstairs bedrooms. She needed to hold herself together.

She wiped her mouth on the wet sleeve of her raincoat and spoke to Xavier as if she hadn't just puked in the middle of the room like a child. "I'm sorry." She paused and searched for more words. "This doesn't mean he's dead." Although the amount of blood could argue otherwise.

"I know."

"If he's dead, they'd have left his body. Like they did with Jeb."

"Maybe Jeb caught them by surprise, but they knew

Cohen was here. And by leaving his finger, they're sending me a message."

"But what does it mean?" she asked.

"Fuck if I know." His voice had flattened. So unlike the Xavier she'd been with in the forest.

But then, this wasn't the sort of thing a SEAL trained for. This wasn't combat. This was a damn house of horrors. "Should we finish searching?"

"Yes, but this place is empty. They won't have stuck around after leaving a message like that." He stepped closer to the table and shined the red light on the thick male finger. "They probably chose to cut off his finger *because* of the tattoo. That's going to gut Carly." His voice held more emotion now, hinting at how much he was holding back. Every movement, every gesture, and every word seemed to be leashed, a restrained version of Xavier, showing her he was too well trained to break down right now, no matter how much he wanted to.

She reached into her pack and pulled out a small zipper-top bag and offered it to him. "Photograph it, then we'll bag it." One way or another, Cohen would get his finger back.

He snapped a photo, shielding the flash with a hand, but still, the room brightened for an instant and it was likely anyone watching the yurt saw the flare of light. He plucked the finger from the table and dropped it in the bag, then tucked it in one of his vest pockets.

Audrey pulled her water bottle from the side pouch of her pack and filled her mouth, then swished. She spit the water into the garbage before taking a long drink. Her hands shook, and the lip of the aluminum bottle tapped her teeth.

She'd been holding herself together by reminding herself she was with a SEAL. Navy SEALs were the closest a person could get to being a superhero, right? But he wasn't a super-hero. He was just as human as she was. Just as mortal.

His coworkers were also SEALs, and one of them had lost a finger.

"Cohen was in here alone?" she asked.

He nodded. "Besides me, there are five others. Cohen in HQ, and four playing tangos. Two in the woods, two in the lodge. I'd just finished my final inspection and was headed back here when Cohen saw you on camera pulling up in front of the lodge. He radioed me to intercept you."

She heard what he didn't say—if it weren't for her, he'd have been here. Watching Cohen's back. If she hadn't shown up, he might've been able to stop this from happening. Jeb would still be alive. Cohen would still have ten fingers.

"I'm sorry," she whispered. Her throat had turned dry again. She took another shaking sip of water.

"This isn't your fault, Audrey."

"I pulled you away. Maybe—"

"Don't go there. We don't know what would have happened. Hell, for all we know, it could be my finger on the table and Cohen with the butchered neck. Or vice versa."

"What do we do now?" she asked.

He picked up the phone handset on the desk. An old-fashioned corded phone in keeping with the seventies architecture. It was one of the few items on the tables that hadn't been smashed. "No dial tone," he said. He pointed to the kitchen to the right of the main room. "None of the digital clocks are lit. I tried a switch in the utility room because it doesn't have windows, and the light didn't go on. I'm guessing they cut cable, phone, and power lines at the road. No electricity and no communications for the entire complex."

"Several buildings, including the main lodge, have generators."

He nodded. "Phone is what we need more than anything, though, and a generator won't help there." He cleared his throat. "We're going to finish searching this house, we'll grab any functional supplies we can get our hands on, then we're heading to your SUV and getting you out of here."

She nodded. She was terrified at the idea of leaving him, but she could call for help once she was out of range of the signal blocker and in range of a cell tower—which, unfortunately, was at the other end of the eighteen-mile road.

"Do you have a vehicle?" Audrey asked. "That might be easier than backtracking through the woods to mine."

He shook his head. "They're in the garage of an inholding cabin on the far side of the lake."

"Which one?" She couldn't think of anyone who would give the Navy access to their cabin.

"The one owned by the Kalahwamish tribe. A tribal member is Army Special Forces. He's worked with a SEAL lieutenant I know. We went through channels and cut a deal."

"You're talking about Bastian Ford."

"You know him?"

"We've met—through George. George is part Kalahwamish, and he was in the Army once upon a time. Served in Vietnam. Bastian and George have hung out in the lodge a few times."

"I wish we could pack you off in one of our vehicles," Xavier said, "but yours is much closer."

She looked toward the windows. The pounding rain would make the trek to her car difficult, but at least the noise would cover their passage through the woods. And maybe they'd encounter some friendly SEALs on the way.

A girl could hope.

They searched the main and upper floor of the yurt quickly, finding no other trace of Cohen and no useful weapons. They were limited to what he had in his tactical vest and she carried in her pack.

There was a magnetic waistband gun holster that was salvageable, and Xavier showed Audrey how to hook it over her pants or the lip of a pocket to secure the Simunition Glock within easy reach.

"I think it's a good idea to keep the round chambered," he said. "You comfortable with that?"

She nodded as she tried to decide where to wear it. Finally, she tucked it in front of her left hipbone for easy reach with her right hand, if her raincoat had two buttons open. "I'll be careful."

"If someone comes at you, aim for the face if they aren't wearing eye protection. It's your best shot at doing real damage, and we know they won't hesitate to hurt *you*."

Her stomach churned at the idea of deliberately shooting someone in the face. She thought of poor Jeb and steeled her resolve. She pressed a hand to her belly.

She'd do whatever it took to get out of here alive.

※

The hike back through the woods to Audrey's car took far too long in the frigid rain and darkness. First, they had to head in the opposite direction to a culvert so they could cross the road without exposing themselves. After that, they trekked through the woods paralleling the road until it became the gravel track that ran behind the lodge complex.

Without his NVGs, Xavier was forced to resort to his red-tipped flashlight to illuminate the ground directly beneath their feet. She followed close at his heels, stepping where he stepped as they moved slowly and silently, always on the alert for tangos and SEALs as they traversed the slippery rainforest.

The team knew better than to signal trainers if they spotted them in the woods. After all, they were being judged on their ability to move through the forest unseen. If they spotted him, they'd tuck down and hide, presuming Xavier was a fake tango on patrol.

There was nothing he could do to change that, not without exposing Audrey to the men who'd killed Jeb. One of those men had already come after her with a knife, while another had left Cohen's finger on a worktable as a message.

He couldn't let her become collateral damage in...whatever this war was they were fighting.

At last, they reached the woods behind the blacksmith shop. Xavier studied the silhouette of her SUV. It was only ten feet away, and he was barely able to see it in the inky darkness and shroud of incessant rain. With no other choice, he shined a light on the vehicle.

Motherfucker. The front tire was flat.

He shined the beam on the rear tire. Also flat.

Audrey's audible curses were an echo of his mental ones. "Are those bullet holes in the gas tank?"

He focused the light on the rear panel and could just make out dark dots around the tank. He snapped the beam off. "Yes."

Audrey's SUV wasn't going anywhere.

He pulled her into the darker shadows of the woods. He felt her shiver as this new reality sank in. "I'm sorry, Audrey," he whispered.

She leaned her forehead against his chest. Rain hit her coat, splashing him in the face. "I knew it was too much to hope for, that there was a way out. That I could call for help." She raised her face, and he could just see the shape of her nose and chin in the inky darkness. Her voice shook.

"This is not my skill set. I'm a liability. I'm scared I could get us both killed."

He cradled her face. "I'm safer with you than I am alone." He ran his thumbs across her cheeks, wet from the rain. "And I will do everything I can to get you out of here."

She pulled her head back, twisting slightly to remove his hands.

He'd overstepped. "I'm sorry. I—I—I'm just sorry. Sorry I got you into this. Sorry I touched you."

"I started it. But…I'm just scared and not thinking straight."

He reminded himself she had pretty much zero reason to trust him now or ever again. That she'd hung with him for the past hour without complaint was a testament to their predicament.

"We'll head to the lodge, try to find the SEALs." In the pounding rain, it would be difficult to hear birdcalls that would signal the SEALs, so odds were they'd stay firmly hidden, but they were out of options. "We've got sixteen allies in these woods, and they're among the best-trained men on the planet. We'll find them and coordinate our efforts to get you out of here and find the other trainers."

They stayed in the trees, going back in the direction they'd just traversed, creeping along like fugitives.

Or prey.

As a SEAL, he was used to being the predator. This feeling of being at a disadvantage was foreign. Trainings like this one—no communication, unfamiliar woods and building, unidentified targets—were meant to address this, but still, on an op, they were doing the attacking. When SEALs were sent in to stop pirates, rescue a hostage, or liberate a seized facility, they were proactive. Swooping in to save the day.

They weren't targets; they were the response team.

But the objective here had flipped on its axis—on a training he, personally, had planned right down to the last detail.

This was all on him. He'd set these guys up for this. The platoon was based out of Coronado, and he knew all sixteen men by name. He and Flyte had been on the same team once upon a time. The lieutenant was the only reason Xavier was alive today.

He'd been the leader of the rescue mission that had landed Xavier in the hospital. The other two on their four-man team had died. Only Flyte had walked away from that mission on his own two feet, carrying an unconscious Xavier over his shoulder. He now was second-in-command of a new platoon, some shuffled from other teams, some new to the ranks.

He and Flyte were first-name kind of friends. On an op, it was always rank or last names, but out of uniform, Lieutenant Flyte was Chris. And Chris's wife, Pam, had attempted to fix Xavier up with half the women in San Diego before she finally introduced him to Lynn.

Shit. Carly. Pam. Those were only two of the wives he'd let down today.

And then there were the children. Xavier had Thanksgiving dinner at Paul Cohen's house. That night, he'd read bedtime stories to Olivia, Paul's six-year-old daughter. She'd chattered excitedly about how now that Thanksgiving was done, Hanukkah was just a few days away and her daddy would be home for the entire Festival of Lights because he was teaching now and no longer going on missions, which meant this would be the best Hanukkah ever.

His heart ached thinking of Olivia and Carly and the severed finger that was now in his pocket. The zigzag pattern of the tattooed wedding band was a nod to Carly's name: Carly Brown. She'd added Cohen to the end when she married Paul. When she realized Paul's finger had been cut off because of his tattoo, she would lose it. Xavier wouldn't tell her, but she was smart. She'd figure it out.

Where was Paul now? Was he bleeding out from that and other wounds? Was he a hostage?

Xavier had set up this training from beginning to end, selecting the lodge, planning the obstacles, even going so far as to undermine Audrey's job to make it happen. Everything that went down in these woods was his fault.

A noise caught his attention. Barely discernible above the pounding rain, he'd heard a click—a mechanical sound unnatural in these woods. He grabbed Audrey's hand and dropped, pulling her down with him. In the same moment, he pulled his flashlight—he didn't dare use the gun in case it was a friendly—and directed the full white beam in the direction of the noise, uphill from them.

He caught a man wearing night vision goggles. The light would trigger the NVGs to bloom out—blanking the screen, giving Xavier a temporary advantage.

Xavier's uniform had matte black infrared markers that glowed brightly through NVGs. Meant to signal friendlies with the SEALs, but in this situation, they would also identify him to the enemy. Lacking his own goggles, he didn't know if this man was a SEAL or one of the unknown enemies.

The bullet that whizzed by answered that question. The rifle—probably another AK-47—had a suppressor, but Xavier caught the supersonic crack as it passed his head. Without a suppressor, it would have carried through the forest, alerting everyone with the distinctive sound of an AK.

No SEAL would take that shot before his night vision returned. And no SEAL would shoot upon seeing the friendly IR markers. Not to mention that the team didn't have AKs with suppressors.

They'd walked right into the path of a tango.

"Stay flat on the ground," he told Audrey as he flashed the light again, this time on strobe to disorient the sonofabitch. Then he took his own shot, wasting a precious bullet.

The loud bang echoed in the woods, audible above the rain.

He took her hand and pulled her downslope, crawling across the muddy ground. After they moved several feet, he fired another shot. Two bullets down. He couldn't afford to shoot again unless a tango was directly in his sights.

Again, he pulled her downslope, away from the tango and now there was a thick patch of woods with several large trees between them. The shots hadn't been wasted; they'd served the purpose of providing cover so they could put distance between themselves and the tango.

With his mouth next to Audrey's ear, he whispered, "We need to get out of here. Without NVGs, we're screwed. They've got night vision and assault rifles. We need to find a safe place to hole up."

"The blacksmith shop?"

"Too close. We need to leave the lodge complex. Maybe go to a campground or, better yet, a cabin."

They crawled along, the rain covering the sound of their progress as they burrowed through the woods.

"The Jamison place," Audrey said. "It's on the lake, a few cabins over from the yurt. We'll have to go back to the trail that runs behind the command center."

He knew the cabin she was talking about. It was a good choice, with thick log walls. Bulletproof. They could break into the cabin, and he could tuck her safely away while he figured out what to do next.

Chapter Seven

$\mathcal{I}$t was slow going at first, but finally, they'd put enough distance between themselves and the encounter with the tango for Xavier to use his red light to find their way through the woods. Without his NVGs, it was just too damn dark.

Rain filtered through the evergreens, but they were more protected than not by the dense growth in this section of forest. Branches dumped water on his head and back as he brushed against them, but he didn't pay attention to the chill that penetrated his camouflage rain gear. He was more concerned about Audrey. She was an avid hiker and knew this forest, but hadn't been prepared to be in the woods in the dark during a winter storm. Her boots were light hikers, and her raincoat was more fashionable than rugged.

"You okay, Aud?" he asked softly as they reached a small but rapidly flowing stream they'd have to wade across. There was a footbridge on the main trail, but they couldn't risk the easy route, and there were no culverts away from the road.

"I'm better than Jeb. That's all that matters."

He nodded and stepped into the stream. They didn't

have time for sentimentality here. Just knowing she had the strength to keep going was enough. He was impressed by how well she'd held it together so far.

He didn't need to close his eyes to remember the shock of horror on her face when the guy came at her on the cliff or when she'd spotted Jeb slumped over the power meter. He guessed she was taking a *survive now, panic later* approach. He appreciated her ability to compartmentalize. Hell, he'd spent weeks of BUD/S training trying to achieve what she'd managed in just a few hours.

But then, she'd had a crash course in the real world, while his training had been a facsimile of the real thing. Grueling and brutal, absolutely. But still, deep down, he'd known it was fake.

He'd thought she was pretty damn amazing the night they met. Now he upgraded that assessment to include remarkable.

It was a short distance from the stream to the first inholding after the yurt, a small cabin that was cinched tight against winter storms. Xavier would have peeked in the windows to see if any electronics glowed with power, but the windows were all shuttered and the detached garage locked.

Three cabins later, they slipped through a barrier of blackberry vines and reached the outer perimeter of the Jamison cabin. Audrey's suggestion had been a good one. It was a fair distance from the lodge, and the lake curved in a way that it couldn't be seen from the yurt or lodge.

The cabin was one of the older structures in the area and constructed with thick logs, making it more bulletproof than newer cabins made with drywall, insulation, and siding. As with the other older structures, the windows were shuttered tight for the winter.

"What are you doing?" Xavier asked as Audrey ran her

hand down a corner where the cut ends of logs were notched and joined at the rear of the home.

"Getting the key to the back door." She stood and held up something small. He saw her smile in the glow of his red light.

He couldn't help but smile back, a strange pride blooming in his chest. He'd worried about breaking a window—it would be both a signal and entry point for the enemy, but of course, Audrey had access to the key. "What, it's not a color-coded one on your magical key chain?"

She laughed softly. "No. I don't know the Jamisons *that* well, and this cabin doesn't belong to ONP."

But clearly, she knew them. Like she knew Jeb. Like she knew this park.

And his lie could have taken it all away from her.

When they got out of here, he would call her boss and the ACHP. He would tell everyone he'd lied. The blowback on the Navy would be bad—no doubt it would end his career as a trainer—but it was fitting and the only way to make things right. He couldn't hold his career as more valuable than hers.

Which, of course, was exactly what he'd done a month ago. He'd had very good reason, but she would never know that part.

He took the precious piece of metal from her hand and moved to flank the back door, nodding to her to take the other side, just like they'd done at the yurt. "We'll go in fast and search the place."

The cabin was one story, but larger than many of the old lakeside cottages. It had a big kitchen with a walk-in pantry, dining area, living room, one bathroom, and three bedrooms of roughly equal size.

He relocked the rear door once they were inside. After the initial search, he did a second check of both doors and every window, making sure the cabin was secure. All the windows had exterior shutters and interior curtains. From the outside, no one would know they were here.

He looked at Audrey in the dark room, wishing he could turn on a brighter light than the red one. Even with the closed curtains and shutters, he wouldn't take the chance that light could slip through.

But the red light was enough to see she shivered in her soaking wet, mud-coated jeans and drenched raincoat. "If there are clothes in one of the bedrooms that fit you, you should change into something dry."

He circled the old woodstove in the corner of the room by the picture windows that overlooked the lake. Fully enclosed in black iron, the woodstove would pump out heat, but wouldn't emit light. Rain and darkness would hide smoke from the chimney. It was tempting to build a fire to cut the chill in the room and give Audrey's coat a chance to dry, but a heat camera could pick it up.

Too risky.

"I'll grab blankets from one of the beds. You can bundle up and get warm."

"What about you?" she asked.

He'd been thinking about this the entire long journey to the cabin and knew she wouldn't like it. "I need to head back out. I'm going to hike up to the van with the signal jammer. Disable the system so I can call NSWC and radio the SEALs."

"But you said it's too dangerous without NVGs."

"Too dangerous for you." It was the simple truth, and she knew it.

She swallowed. "I understand. There's a lot at stake here."

He nodded, thinking of Jeb's throat, Cohen's finger, the guy who took a shot at them in the woods, and the man on the ledge. "Getting communication back online is our top priority." He stepped toward her. "I'll leave you with the gun."

"No way. Out there, you'll need it more than I do."

"Fine." She was right, and between the SEALs, trainers, and the two of them, he was trying to save almost two dozen lives. "Let's get you settled and warm, then I'll go."

He paced, assessing the safety of the cabin as she changed. The idea of leaving her had him on edge, but he had a job to do.

She entered the living room in clean, dry purple sweat-pants that were too short and a University of Washington sweatshirt that was too tight across her chest. She carried a blanket in her arms. "These must be Harriet Jamison's great-granddaughter's clothes. Too small, but it'll have to do. At least the boots fit—cloth, but at least they're dry."

"Good. Keep the boots on. You want to be ready to leave in a hurry if necessary."

She nodded.

"How did you know where the Jamisons hide their key?"

"This cabin was part of an historic property inventory I did for the park. I interviewed the Jamisons for the report. Harriet—who's in her late eighties—inherited it from her grandfather. Daniel, her husband, is ninety. Given their advanced ages, they don't visit here in winter or spring. Their kids and grandkids have scattered; the closest one lives in San Francisco and doesn't get up here that often. Knowing I come this way frequently, Harriet asked me if I could check in on the place now and then during the off-season."

He raised a hand to touch her cheek, but stopped himself, hand hovering an inch from her face before he let it fall. "I'm lucky to have you with me in this."

She gave him a twisted smile. "Damn straight." Then she

grimaced. "And I'm lucky to have you. I close my eyes, and I see that guy coming at me with the knife. I see Jeb."

He took the thick comforter from her hands and draped it around her shoulders, wrapping her in the warmth while being careful not to actually touch her. "There's cereal and canned goods in the cupboards. Eat something. Rest. But don't sleep. You need to stay alert. You hear anything out of place, any strange knocks or noises that are unnatural, get your coat on, grab the pack, and be ready to flee."

"Will do." She paused, and her eyes showed uncertainty. "Xavier, I—" She shook her head. "Never mind. It can wait."

"If it's about what I did last month—"

She cut him off. "No. Now isn't the time for that."

"I—I want you to know, I *am* sorry. But I can't say I regret it." It was as honest as he could be.

She flinched. Her free hand formed a fist and pressed to her belly as if his words were a blow to the gut.

He shouldn't have said the part about not regretting, not when he couldn't explain. Stupid, stupid, stupid not to leave it at sorry. He cleared his throat. "After I turn off the signal jammer and call NSWC, I'm coming back for you."

"How will I know it's you?"

"If I can't get the phone to work, I'll knock in a pattern. One, two, one." He knocked on the counter as he said it, then repeated the knocking without the words. "If it's safe for you to respond, you'll knock back with a different pattern. One, one, two." Again, he demonstrated. "Got it?"

She responded by knocking on the counter, once, again, then twice in a row.

He smiled. Her strength never failed to impress him. And he was a monumental asshole for using her as he had.

He cleared his throat. "On the plus side, if I'm successful, I'll call you." He pulled out his cell phone. "What's your number?"

She gave him the number, and he typed it into his phone. How weird to be getting her cell number now, and not after their night together. He'd ruined something that could have been amazing. What he'd done was unforgivable, even if he could make it right with her boss. It was too much to hope she'd ever be willing to give him a second chance, but with each minute they spent together, that was what he wanted.

Giving in to impulse, he tucked away his phone and gathered the edges of the thick comforter in his fist and took a step toward her. "Stay safe. I'm coming back for you as soon as I can."

He still wasn't touching her, just the blanket, but their mouths were mere inches apart. He saw uncertainty flash in her gaze, then she did the impossible and rose on her toes and brushed her lips over his. But her kiss wasn't soft or fleeting. No. She opened her mouth and stroked his tongue with her own. In a flash of memory, he was back in the lodge as their mouths met for the first time.

Their first kiss had been sexy and sweet and a promise that delivered. Now, here they were again, mouth to mouth and he could lose himself in the heat of her. He remembered vividly the feel of being cradled between her thighs, skin to skin.

He wrapped a hand behind her head, taking the kiss deeper, just like the night when she'd been his. He wanted her again. And not just for one night.

All at once she pushed at his chest and jumped back a step. In her gaze, he saw confusion and a half dozen other emotions, including, miraculously, desire. "How do I know you aren't going to use that against me too?"

He ran a hand over his face. He sure as hell had that coming. She might still be attracted to him, but she had no reason to trust him. "I won't. I will never lie to you or about you again."

"And I'm just supposed to believe that?"

He was at a loss for how to answer. Why would she ever believe a word he said? He cleared his throat. "No. I guess not. But it's true."

"When you come back, we're going to talk."

"I wish we could, but there are things I can't tell you. I *can't* explain."

She grabbed the edges of the comforter and pulled the blanket tight around her shoulders, then she surprised him by smiling. Instead of hurt and anger, he saw something else in her eyes. Something mysterious. Knowing. "Well, in that case, maybe you'll be able to listen."

He nodded and slipped out the back door, waiting to hear the clank of the dead bolt behind him before setting off into the cold, dark, wet forest.

With Audrey safely tucked away, he could finally head into the storm.

Chapter Eight

$\mathcal{A}$udrey leaned against the thick wooden door and pressed a hand to her belly. "He's coming back for us," she whispered, as if she were talking to the baby.

She'd never spoken to the baby before, but it made sense that this would be the time she'd start, when his or her—or rather, their—father had just stepped into the dark, cold rain, facing an untold number of commandos while armed only with a pistol and thirteen rounds.

The kiss had sent her brain spinning back to their first kiss on the private balcony of the best suite in the lodge. Since mid-December, she'd been unable to think of that night with the pleasure it merited, but now, this crazy, scary night had restored the good part of that memory, and she'd slipped into the moment, reliving every fluttery feeling and remembering exactly why she'd tumbled into bed with him in the first place.

Xavier Rivera had been a masculine force then and now, and after everything that had happened tonight, she'd suddenly wanted to retreat into the comfort of his body. To be held tight and feel protected.

And then it hit her that he could be playing her again. She didn't know how or why, but all at once the anger and hurt came rushing back. She was a fool to have kissed him. He'd used her desire as a weapon once. He'd probably do it again.

In December, she'd realized that Jae had known Xavier was at the lodge to scout it as a location for this very training, which had made her wonder if he'd seduced her because Jae had said she'd be the ultimate authority for approval of the training.

But if he'd seduced her hoping she'd rubber-stamp his proposal, wouldn't he have submitted the proposal with his name on it? But his name had been absent from the EA and proposed action description. If she'd known his involvement, she might have called him and asked for an explanation before she denied the permit.

He'd nearly gotten her fired from the dream job she'd pursued since she was a kid—and he'd known exactly how important it was to her. They'd talked about it when she first joined him and Jae for drinks that night. The only thing he hadn't known when he complained to her boss was that she was pregnant with his child.

And he still didn't know that little detail.

What a mess.

She'd been so tempted to tell him before he left, but he needed a clear head as he set off in the rainy night. She pushed off the door and returned to the living room, settling on the couch and wrapping herself in several blankets. There was no danger she'd be falling asleep anytime soon. She was tired, but wired. And terrified.

When she closed her eyes she saw the specter with the knife. She saw Jeb. She saw a disembodied finger.

She kept her eyes wide open. She pulled the musty blankets tight around her, and warmth finally began to seep in beyond the surface. Her lips still held the memory of kissing him.

When she'd been unable to tell Xavier about the baby, she'd made the choice not to tell anyone. Not yet. It didn't seem right to share the news with someone other than the baby's father first. Only her OB/GYN, the physician's assistant, and the ultrasound technician knew. She'd heard the baby's heartbeat two weeks ago, but hadn't been able to share her excitement with anyone.

Her parents had divorced when she was fourteen, and her mom had gleefully left the Olympic Peninsula as soon as Audrey turned eighteen. The family had moved to Forks for her father's work, and her mother said living on the peninsula had felt like punishment for bad decisions.

Her mom now lived in Tacoma and refused to visit Audrey in Port Angeles. Needless to say, they weren't close. Not telling her mother about the baby hadn't been a hardship.

Her father was a different story. He'd left Forks as well, but for a different reason. His arthritis couldn't take the heavy coastal rain anymore. He'd retired to Arizona eight years ago. They exchanged regular emails, but distance had eroded their relationship. He would be excited to learn he was going to be a grandpa at long last, but he wouldn't have a big role in the baby's life.

What if she died out here without ever having told anyone about the baby? What if Xavier survived and learned the truth only then? He would realize from the timing, from her medical records, that not only had she known, but that the child was his.

She got up from the couch and went to the drawer where she'd seen pens and other supplies. She found a blank notepad in the drawer and returned to the couch. She'd write Xavier a note in case something happened to her before she could tell him. He needed to hear it from her, one way or another.

✦

*T*he wind was far worse than the rain, and the rain was a damn nightmare. Xavier tucked down in the thick shrubs, not to escape the wind, but to listen. The howl of the storm cut through his clothes and covered other sounds. A moment ago, he'd heard a grunt—the sound of someone who'd tripped and couldn't suppress making a noise.

One thing SEAL training had taught him over the years was patience. He could outwait any non-SEAL in these woods. Minutes passed. He waited and listened. A tango had made a noise. It was only a matter of time before they gave themselves away again.

It had been thirty-six minutes since he left Audrey in the cabin. In that time, he'd covered a scant quarter mile. The price of stealth without night vision goggles was a slow pace. He wouldn't let fear for Audrey's safety rush his actions.

Damn. Dr. Audrey Kendrick. Thirty-six minutes later, in the middle of a raging storm, while listening for what he assumed was a mercenary in the woods, and he could still taste her on his lips.

He hadn't planned or intended to seduce her the night they met. He'd found her simply irresistible.

Wicked smart. An outdoor enthusiast. Fascinating. So very enticing. But they were so different. He'd graduated high school and joined the Navy a week later. He'd passed BUD/S at the age of twenty-one and developed the ego of an elite special operator, but that same ego faltered when it came to higher education.

Even when he'd been at the top of his game, he would

have figured a woman with a PhD was out of his league. And when they'd met, he was far from the top of his game. That had been made clear when his girlfriend of two years had dumped him while he was in the hospital. She hadn't even waited until he was awake. She'd shown up after he finally was flown back from Germany, where he'd had his first surgery. She'd taken one look at his sleeping, bandaged self and turned around and left.

Apparently, the only thing he'd had going for him was his active-duty SEAL status. Without that, there was no point in sticking around. Not when continuing the relationship meant taking care of him after each round of surgery.

He'd met Audrey in a situation where he couldn't use his status as a SEAL to impress her. He'd just…been himself. Well, except for the part where he couldn't talk about himself, because any word out of his mouth, about his life, would tip her off that he was military, so he'd kept the focus on her and liked everything he learned. Given his evasions to her questions, there'd been no way she would have responded to him if Jae hadn't been there to vouch for him.

But Jae had been there, and she'd responded. She'd wanted him even when he had no special forces or even military credentials. She'd wanted the low-calorie, no frosting version of Xavier, and it had been a heady feeling, this idea that he didn't need to be an active-duty SEAL to appeal to a woman who had a PhD from Cal.

And then she'd shot down his permit, and his world imploded.

Getting the training approved was a national security imperative, but that could hardly be revealed in the application. Even though it fit the technical parameters, they couldn't slip it through operations—which weren't subject to environmental review—without putting the eventual mission at serious risk.

When the rejection came, in desperation he'd floated to his superiors the idea of going around the park archaeologist, suggesting that they could lean on her boss to sign the FONSI and override her objections if he presented evidence the park archaeologist was biased against the applicant.

He hadn't really expected them to bite, but his supervisors had jumped on the idea, not even flinching when he offered the argument he eventually presented to the park superintendent and Advisory Council on Historic Preservation.

The Navy didn't know or care if he'd really banged the archaeologist. They just wanted the permit. All was fair in war. Love had nothing to do with it.

But still, he'd hesitated. How could he do that to her? Then there'd been the chemical weapon attack in Prague. A dozen people hospitalized, two dead. According to intel, they had precious little time.

February was approaching fast, and it looked increasingly likely the attack would happen.

The team needed to prepare. Run every scenario possible to determine the best strategy. If the mission failed, many, many deaths would follow.

Still, he'd hated himself for using their night together against her.

Now, here he was, in the frigid rainy forest, and his actions in December could well make Audrey the next victim in an invisible war.

He'd created this mess, and in so doing, he'd endangered a woman he maybe could have fallen in love with. A woman he certainly had feelings for.

Seeing that man come at her with a knife had triggered something feral inside him. It rose again now.

Focus.

Rain pattered on the branches of the tall cedar at his

back. The wind rustled the same branches, dumping water on his head. Normal sounds. It was nearing twenty-one hundred hours. Still early, but the deep dark of the woods with wind and pummeling rain made it feel much later.

Had the SEALs managed to breach the lodge, or were they hiding in these same woods, still unaware this was no longer a training exercise?

A branch snapped behind him to the right. A soft noise, but he'd been waiting for it. Counting on it. Another step, another snapped branch, followed by a muffled curse.

Definitely *not* a SEAL. Even if the team still believed this was an exercise, they wouldn't make casual noises. Part of this training was practicing silence in the woods. It was sort of the whole point.

And then there was the fact that the guy cursed in Russian. Xavier would bet anything these tangos were mercenaries, and now he had a clue to where they were from.

Was this guy a sentry guarding a perimeter, or a scout looking for Audrey and him?

Had the guy on the ledge somehow survived?

Three minutes passed. Another sound. The guy was uncomfortable, shifting positions. Impatient.

Finally, he took several steps. Quiet, but Xavier could see his dark shape. He passed in front of Xavier, and he lunged, tackling the man and shoving his face into the moss-covered ground. The guy turned his head to keep from being suffocated in the saturated soil, and Xavier shined his light to get a glimpse of the man's profile.

He'd never seen the guy before. The tango bucked upward, trying to dislodge Xavier. He freed a hand that held a pistol. Xavier knocked the weapon aside as it fired. No silencer this time. The crack of the bullet was deafening even in the pounding rain.

If there were SEALs or tangos in the vicinity, they would hear it and know what it meant.

Xavier caught the man's wrist before he could take aim again and slammed it into a rock. The handgun dropped from his fingers. It was a wrestling match from there as they rolled downslope in the muck.

The mercenary was heavier, but not stronger. Until he punched Xavier in the shoulder.

Pain exploded.

Fuck.

The blow had dislocated his left arm, rendering the limb useless.

He punched with his right. Even as his mind wanted to blank out with the pain, he held on. If he died, Audrey would surely be taken. Tortured. Raped. Killed.

He didn't want to imagine what she would face.

He punched again and kicked with his two very good legs. He managed to roll until he had the man pinned, then used his good arm to position the bad one around the guy's neck. With a quick jerk of his right arm, his left twisted the man's neck, and it was all over with a snap of vertebrae.

He paused for just a moment, breathing heavily as his shoulder throbbed with a shock of agony. He needed to pop the ball back in the socket, but the pain was too much to attempt the maneuver right then.

Focus on the dead guy.

He searched the merc's pockets, finding a spare magazine for the handgun. Over one shoulder, he wore a short-barreled assault rifle with folding stock, and over the other, he wore a bandolier with a half dozen magazines tucked into the strap. The rifle—an AKS-74U—was fitted with a suppressor.

He claimed the assault rifle, slinging it and the bandolier

over his bad shoulder, then took the helmet with attached NVGs from the man's head and swapped it for his own. He clipped his old helmet to his pack. Audrey could wear it.

With the NVGs, he searched upslope where the fight began and spotted the Glock in the mud. He added it to his growing arsenal, then adjusted the goggles to the proper fit. They weren't as good as the US military-grade ones he'd lost earlier, but they were high quality. These guys were well funded, that was for sure.

Who did they work for?

They could be terrorists, but everything about this had the feel of a paid operation. Right down to the staging of their supplies months in advance. Terrorists couldn't afford to take chances that far ahead of an attack.

The rifle was troubling. Rare and Russian, it could be an important clue as to who these guys worked for. But after Osama bin Laden had been photographed with the same model, they'd been in high demand by several terrorist groups, so it could also be a red herring to make them think they were dealing with extremists and not mercenaries.

Done searching, he kicked the body, shoving it farther downslope, toward a rare spot of open ground. Maybe one of the SEALs would find it. The dead man would tell them this was no pretend war game.

Ready to go, he took a deep breath and attempted to pop his shoulder back into the socket. Pain exploded, and he wobbled on his feet. He couldn't black out now. Not here. The guy might not have been alone in this section of woods, and the gunshot would be a beacon for his comrades.

He set out, not going back the way he'd come nor heading in the direction he wanted to go. Misdirection was key here. Protecting Audrey's location was his first priority.

His shoulder throbbed, making him dizzy with the pain.

He couldn't head to the signal jammer. He'd return to Audrey and give her a real gun to protect herself. And hopefully, she could pop his joint back into place while he passed out.

Chapter Nine

audrey paced the cabin. She'd managed to choke down a can of cold pork and beans with canned pears for dessert. Adrenaline had faded, and now the chill air sapped her energy. Add to that pregnancy-exhaustion hormones and she was yawning in a perpetual loop. Forty-five minutes ago, she couldn't imagine sleeping, but now, she had no idea how she would manage to stay awake until Xavier returned.

So she paced, talking to the baby, or maybe she was muttering because she was falling apart. She wasn't quite sure. But really, after the night she'd had so far, a mental breakdown was fully justified.

She reached the front window and pivoted on her heel, turning too fast. Dizziness swamped her. She swayed on her feet.

It was unlike her to lose her balance so easily, but nothing was normal tonight. She fixed her gaze on a thick log beam. She took a deep breath to steady herself.

Rain pounded on the roof and wind rattled the shutters. She pulled the blanket tighter around herself. She'd keep walking to generate heat and stay awake. But no more fast turns. She placed her hand on her belly. "Your daddy is coming back for us," she whispered. "He's going to turn off the signal jammer and call for help. An hour, maybe two, and helicopters will swoop in. We'll be rescued."

But could helicopters fly in this storm?

Probably not.

When hikers were trapped in the mountains due to weather, search and rescue was often grounded until the storm abated. Black Hawks might be better equipped to fly at night and in a storm, but the basic physics of flight in bad weather remained the same. And this storm was a nasty one. The lake and lodge were nestled in the western foothills of Mt. Olympus. There were no taller peaks between the lodge and the Pacific Ocean to redirect or disperse the storm.

This was Mother Nature in all her Pacific Northwest January wrath.

The back door rattled, and she jolted, then twirled to face the door, again moving too fast, but this time keeping her feet. Was Xavier back already?

She took a few silent steps toward the door.

It rattled again. The knob turned, but the dead bolt prevented it from opening.

She froze, fear pulling the blood from her head and sending it straight to her belly. Someone was out there, and it wasn't Xavier. He would have knocked, using the pattern he'd chosen.

Could it be one of the SEALs checking out the cabin or seeking shelter? Would a SEAL have hiked this far, or was this out of bounds for the training? Of course, if they knew it wasn't a training anymore, nothing was out of bounds.

Her gut said this wasn't an ally, this was someone searching for her and Xavier. The SEALs in these woods didn't even know she was here, and weren't they supposed to be trying to breach the lodge?

She was going to vomit. Or faint. Maybe both.

She couldn't make a noise. If whoever was outside that door knew she was in here alone, armed only with a paint gun, they'd hack through the shutters and break a window. Entering the cabin would be easy.

They'd opened Jeb's throat with an axe.

She took a silent step backward and grabbed her coat from where she'd draped it over the cold woodstove and donned it, then she snatched her backpack from the floor. She'd exit through the door to the deck that overlooked the lake.

A thunk sounded from the deck, then that door's knob rattled at the same time the back door shook.

Icy terror slid down her spine.

There were two men, blocking both exits.

Tears spilled down her cheeks as she faced fear unlike anything she'd ever experienced. She could—probably would—die here. Tonight. By axe, knife, or gun.

Axe…

She turned to the woodbox next to the woodstove. The box was built into the wall of the log structure, so one could split wood outside, toss it in the box, and then from inside the cabin, grab logs to fill the woodstove.

There could be a hatchet in the box along with other tools, another weapon to add to her arsenal. But even more important, inside the cabin, the box looked small—not large enough for a person, but she might fit, and, even better, she might be able to slip out of the cabin via the box.

She gingerly lifted the lid, wincing when the hinges squeaked, but the storm had probably covered the sound. The front of the box was a third-full of wood, leaving a tight space for her to slip through.

A soft pop came from the direction of the back door. Were they shooting the dead bolt? Xavier had said their guns might have suppressors.

She scrambled into the box, wiggling backward into the narrow space, having no idea if she'd fit or if wood filled the back of the box and she was trapping herself. She'd just managed to fold herself into a ball and close the lid when she heard a door slam against the wall. If the outside hatch was locked, she was cornered, but her only choice was to hide or flee, and this box had the potential for both.

There was an unintelligible shout, followed by words in a foreign language. Her heart was beating so rapidly, she found it hard to concentrate, hard to breathe. It was a moment before the sounds registered: two men, speaking Russian.

She probed backward with her foot, feeling logs to her side, but nothing behind her. She scooted deeper into her hiding place, but she bumped into a log and it shifted, making a slight noise. The log landed on her leg, balanced, but ready to topple. She couldn't move without making another, even bigger sound.

One of the men said something sharply. She guessed he was near the kitchen table. Probably ten feet from the box.

The second man replied, and then the first spoke again, this time in heavily accented English, "Dear Xavier, if something happens to me, I want you to know…"

No! He was reading her letter. She'd forgotten it was on the table.

She would bang her head against the box wall if it wouldn't make a sound that would get her killed. But maybe it didn't matter. From the blankets strewn about and her damp clothes in the bedroom, they'd have figured out that she'd been there anyway.

While the men were distracted with the note, she reached back and silently shifted the log from her calf and set it in the space between her knees. She scooted farther back and discovered the exterior part of the box was empty, the wood having been piled at the front. She sat up in the larger area and probed the exterior lid, hoping, praying for an escape.

It lifted. Hope surged. Then the latch caught.

One centimeter. That was as wide as it would open. Just enough to slip a finger through the gap.

She was trapped.

Chapter Ten

*C*hris zoomed in the magnification on his NVGs. The tires on the SUV were flat, and those were definitely bullet holes piercing the gas tank. Rivera and Cohen had gone all out to make this exercise look and feel real. This didn't look like a beater SUV given to the Navy to use as a prop. It looked like it was maybe two or three years old. No big dents indicating it had been in any sort of wreck.

Must be a lemon. Or seized by the feds. However it ended up here, it looked strangely authentic. Like this was some horror flick where a group of teens find themselves trapped in the woods with a chainsaw-wielding psychopath.

"You think Rivera planned this to be like one of those murder-mystery dinner-party things?" Jonas asked. "Like, we're given clues and we have to solve some sort of puzzle?"

"If this was meant to be some sort of mental challenge, they could have saved a lot of money and just sent us to an escape room," Phelps said. "No need for the fricking HALO jump and cold swim. Or being out in icy rain at all."

It had taken them hours to traverse the forest, making their way slowly up and around the north end of the lake, skirting Kaxo Falls and crossing the creek upstream where the valley was narrow and the water ran fast and deep. Rain had pummeled them along the entire journey in an unrelenting downpour. Why couldn't this rainforest be the sultry tropical kind?

Just his luck that when the Navy sent him to a rainforest, it was in the Pacific Northwest. In January.

This was rapidly becoming one of his least favorite places.

"I dunno, man. This shot-up vehicle... It doesn't feel right," Jonas said. "It doesn't fit the scenario we were given on Whidbey."

Jonas had a point. Their orders were to infiltrate the lodge and extract two hostages, one female, one male, no further description. It didn't matter if they killed guards in the process. The only thing that mattered was getting in and out with the unharmed hostages without anyone sounding an alarm.

This wouldn't be easy, as they would need extraction via Sea Hawk—which required time. They had to radio for the helicopter and wait for it to fly in from a ship off the coast. No word on whether or not they could expect a real Sea Hawk in this exercise, but Chris doubted it. It would be damned expensive to have a ship and helicopter staged off the Pacific coast for the entire five-day training.

The fact that this was a hostage rescue mission had Chris wondering at Rivera's planning here. Few people knew what had really happened in Belarus on that horrible day twenty months ago.

But Chris knew, and he'd filled in the gaps in Rivera's memory for the hours after he was shot.

Was this crazy training Rivera's reaction to that nightmare? Was he running a simulation looking for a better outcome?

That really wasn't possible. And Rivera wouldn't waste Navy resources. Naval Special Warfare Command would never sign off on such a thing.

But still, one of the hostages was a woman.

What did this shot-up SUV have to do with the hostage scenario? They couldn't take the hostage out by road, rendering the vehicle useless to them anyway. The mission commander had been specific on that point—exfiltration had to happen by air.

Chris snapped a photo of the license plate of the SUV. Could be important for the test. A clue for the murder-party game.

A gunshot sounded. Distant, but close enough to be heard over the pounding rain.

What the hell? The shot had sounded real.

His gaze returned to the bullet holes in the gas tank. No one—not even the trainers—had real guns with real bullets on this exercise. That was the National Park Service's first stipulation, and the Navy had agreed. It was standard practice for all trainings in Washington state parks as well.

And it couldn't have been a hunter's rifle. Hunting wasn't allowed in Olympic National Park, and they were miles from state forest or Department of Natural Resources lands.

"That wasn't Simunition," Huang confirmed in a whisper. "Who the hell is firing real bullets out here?"

They retreated deeper into the woods. They needed better cover if they were going to figure out what Rivera and Cohen had cooked up to FUBAR this operation.

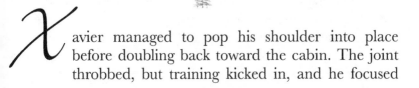

Xavier managed to pop his shoulder into place before doubling back toward the cabin. The joint throbbed, but training kicked in, and he focused on his next step and every sound in the stormy forest. Nothing would stop him from getting back to Audrey.

Even though he'd taken a circuitous route, it went a lot faster with night vision. He'd almost reached his goal when he saw the first sign that someone else had cut through these woods. Footprints in the soft mud—fresh given the amount of rain filling the treads. In another two minutes, the prints would dissolve altogether.

SEALs knew better than to leave prints, even ephemeral ones. These prints made an unmistakable statement: two mercs were headed straight for the Jamison cabin.

The urge to run and storm the place was difficult to fight, but exposing himself before he knew the situation would only put her in more danger.

He moved through the woods like a wraith until he met the blackberries they'd cut through earlier. He parted the thick, thorny vines with gloved hands and worked his way forward until he could just see through the last layer of vegetation. The west wall of the cabin was ten feet away. This was the wood-chopping area, with a sturdy lean-to that covered a cord of wood stacked high. A bolt rested like a table in the middle of the three-walled shelter, ready for the next round of splitting.

A few feet from the lean-to was a woodbox at the side of the cabin. With plenty of wood stored in the sloped-roof shelter, why did they need a woodbox?

All at once, he remembered the box inside the cabin next to the woodstove, and glanced up to see the chimney protruding from the corner closest to the outer storage box. He'd bet the outer box lined up with the inner one, and there was a gap in the thick log wall.

Movement caught his eye, and he adjusted the zoom on the night vision. Holy shit. The lid of the woodbox had lifted, and a finger poked through the narrow gap.

Audrey was in the woodbox?

He plunged though the last of the vines, exposing himself, but there was no other option. He had the Russian rifle at the ready.

He reached the box and was relieved to see carabiner clips hooked through two padlock hasps, securing the lid to the box, but not locking it.

He very quietly tapped once, twice, then once again. If Audrey was in there, she wouldn't freak out when he opened the lid, but no one in the cabin would hear the soft knocks over the wind and rain.

The lid rose as far as the carabiners would allow, and again, a finger poked through. Once, twice, then two times in quick succession. Her reply.

The lid closed, and he suppressed an audible whoosh of relief as he unclipped the carabiners and raised it again, opening it completely.

Audrey popped up like a jack-in-the-box and scrambled out of the thigh-high box as quietly as possible. That she uttered not a word told him how close the tangos were.

She pulled on her backpack as he relatched the box. If they were lucky, no one would guess they were ever in the cabin. Footprints around the box and broken vines would give them away, but he didn't have time to erase their prints. He would just hope no one would look in this area before the rain washed them away.

He took her hand and led her silently back into the woods. She followed without a word. But then, none were necessary at this point. They needed distance before they could debrief.

He was out of plans at this point. All he knew was no matter what, he wouldn't leave her side again.

*X*avier was sure-footed and fast as he pulled Audrey into the woods. She'd caught a glimpse of the NVGs and rifle before they left the faint light of the open yard and entered the forest. He must've had a run-in with a tango and won. He could see, at least. That was all she needed to know for now. She would hold on to his vest and follow him into the dark.

Lake Olympus was shaped like an irregular and blobby knee-high thick-heeled boot, with the lodge situated on the front of the calf and the cliff and waterfall on a swollen knee. The Jamison cabin was on a finger of the lake—or rather, the toe of the boot—that jutted to the east. A stream ran along the north side of the cabin, meeting the lake at the vamp of the boot. They crossed under the road on hands and knees, the stream soaking the sweatpants Audrey had borrowed from Harriet's granddaughter.

She didn't think of the frigid water as her hands found purchase on slippery rocks. Cold was nothing but a minor discomfort when compared to the terror she'd felt in the woodbox. She was alive. She would do anything she had to do to stay that way.

They reached the far side of the road and got to their feet. Xavier took her hand and led her deeper into the dark, saturated forest. He was taking her east, upslope, into the untamed wilderness. They were beyond trails here. No facilities. Just trees and moss and ferns. Fine with her. She only cared that they got as far from the Jamison cabin as possible.

She followed him, seeing only dark shades of gray to define contours under her feet, holding his hand and trusting he would keep her from stepping into a void as they wove between trees large and small, scrambling over downed trunks and crawling across rocks covered by a thick mossy carpet.

It felt like an hour must have passed by the time he drew her into the hollowed trunk of a giant cedar. "Let's rest out of the rain for a bit. We need a plan."

"Wait. Before you sit, I have a waterproof sheet in my pack. The only part of me that's still dry is my butt because my raincoat has kept it covered. No point in sitting down and soaking my ass now."

He let out a grim laugh. "Don't suppose you've got a sleeping bag in there."

"I wish." She plucked out the meter-square panel that was camouflage on one side and neon orange on the other and spread it out in the arched hollow beneath the large trunk.

"I feel I should say again I regret ever hassling you over grabbing your pack."

She smiled as she settled on the plastic. "I know. But it doesn't mean I don't like hearing the grovel." The sheet couldn't stop the cold from seeping through, but her butt remained dry.

Still, she shivered. They couldn't stop here for long. The cold ground would suck all the warmth from their bodies. He removed his tactical vest and slipped off the coat he wore beneath it. She did the same. He pulled her tight to his side and draped his thick jacket behind them, while she placed hers across their front.

His right arm circled her shoulders, holding her snug to his side. "I owe you so much groveling. And I promise, you'll get it all as soon as this is over."

Warmth bloomed from her center, and she realized it was because she was starting to believe him and his apologies. "I'll enjoy that when the time comes."

"You'll get it. I promise," he repeated. "But right now, we need a plan."

"Hiking out of here is impossible in these conditions—"

"I know. It's too far, and we don't have proper equipment. In these conditions, hypothermia would turn deadly fast, and it's not a hike anyone can do alone, and I refuse to leave my team."

"Good, I was afraid you were going to suggest I set out by myself."

"No. I won't leave your side again. So we need to find shelter to dry out and sleep when daylight comes. It'll be too dangerous to be out and about during the day. We need shelter with thermal pads. Sleeping bags. A heat source would be good too, but that's risky. The mercs might have thermal cameras."

"Mercs. You think these guys are mercenaries?"

"I do. They for sure aren't a formal military, but they're well equipped. Some are trained better than others. I don't think they're terrorists and here for a cause. They're moving through the woods like it's a job. Guns for hire."

"How many do you think are out here?"

"No idea, really, but my gut says more than eight, fewer than sixteen."

"Why?"

"The size of the storage pit, for one. But also, except for the two men who went after you in the Jamison cabin, the other ones we've encountered are alone. They should be working in teams. The SEALs are in four-man Fire Teams. These guys are working alone. Either they don't know how to work together, or they need to spread out to cover more ground because there's only about a dozen of them."

"So your guess is a dozen, then?"

"Ten or eleven now."

"You killed one of them." She'd known it when she realized he had a rifle and NVGs.

"I did. I hope the team finds his body so they'll know this is no longer a training exercise."

"What will they do if that happens?"

"The Fire Teams will have a rendezvous point they selected ahead of time. They'll gather. Share intel. Storm the lodge. Save my team of trainers."

"We need to get to the rendezvous point, then."

"I don't know where or when it is."

"Damn."

"So, got any ideas of where we can hole up when daylight comes?"

She racked her brain for a safe refuge. Obviously, all the lakeside cabins were out. "George's cabin? It's not on the lake."

"Too close to the storage pit. They could be all over that part of the forest."

"Right." She considered their options. Finally, she said, "I get why cornering ourselves in another cabin is a bad idea, but we can break into one and get supplies. Jeb repeatedly complained that one family—the Baldwins—rented out their place as an Airbnb. His evidence of this was always seeing tents pitched in the yard to accommodate extra guests. Park administrators looked into his complaints, and the cabin wasn't listed on any public site they could find, but that doesn't mean they didn't have an arrangement with a property manager to direct clients their way for a nonpublic rental. But what matters to us is, if Jeb's complaints were accurate, the cabin probably has a stockpile of supplies we could borrow—tents and sleeping bags at the minimum."

"Which one is the Baldwin cabin?"

"Southeast side of the lake—along the sole of the boot, a quarter mile from where the main road comes to a T at the lake." Lake Olympus Road didn't circumnavigate the lake—the cliff and falls being the one section that lacked road access—but the main road intersected with the lake at the south end, right at the boot heel, and a short gravel stretch ran up the ankle and back of the calf before dead-ending at a park service campground with an historic shelter built by the Civilian Conservation Corps in the 1930s, before the park had been established.

The main paved road was in the other direction from the T, winding around the foot, along the shin with all its knobs, ending at the lodge below the knee, with another gravel road that continued north—the one Xavier had driven like a madman hours ago to get them to the blacksmith shop in record time.

"That's not far from the Kalahwamish cabin where our vehicles are parked. We'll need to be careful, in case there's someone planted there, waiting for us to show up."

She nodded. "Makes sense. I have a feeling they'll have slashed your tires too anyway."

"Yeah. And there was a tree down on the road near the culvert we crossed under when we left the Jamisons. I wouldn't be surprised if they've cut off the main road at the fork too."

She hadn't seen the tree down, but she didn't have NVGs. It made her wonder what else she'd missed.

"These guys are really organized," she whispered.

He nodded. "They've been planning this since before they buried their equipment in the site."

Mid-November.

She shivered.

Xavier's arm tightened around her, and she leaned into him, taking the feeble comfort he offered and telling herself it was just because she needed his body heat. "So we break into the Baldwins for supplies, then retreat into the forest to sleep?"

"Not yet. I want to check out Jeb's cabin while it's still dark. Maybe there's a clue there as to why he went to the yurt tonight. After that, we can head deep into the forest, holding off on stopping to sleep until about an hour before dawn, so we know we're well out of range for any searching mercs. Then we'll pitch our tent and hide out until it's twilight again."

"We're going to hide that long? Lose a whole day?"

"The SEALs will be hidden during daylight too. No point in trying to find them when it's so risky with little chance of success."

"So we'll try to find them when it's dark again."

He nodded. "The rain should stop by then, so it will be easier to move. Easier to hear birdcall signals and we won't be exposed every step of the way."

She crossed her arms over her chest and rubbed up and down her own shoulders. She hadn't quite wrapped her brain around how long this would take. She could be trapped here for days as they played cat-and-mouse in the forest.

The problem was, she was pretty sure she was the mouse.

"What do you think the team is doing now?"

"If they found Jeb or the merc's body, then they're alert to the danger they're in. Probably looking at improvising weapons and figuring out a plan to assault the lodge."

"I hope they're giving the mercs hell."

He tilted his back against the inner wall of the trunk. His voice turned soft and wistful. "Me too, Aud. Me too."

Chapter Eleven

*S*omething was very, very off about this training. The disabled SUV was too random and not at all in keeping with the parameters of the mission, and the gunshot that had echoed through the woods had been a discordant note in an explosive- and bullet-free exercise.

Plus, Chris was certain there were more tangos in the woods than there should be. The forest was fricking *full* of people. They'd been told to expect a few guards patrolling the lodge, but that was all. Their objective was to breach the lodge and rescue the hostage. Intel had said there were only four men in the forest.

Sure, they might give them bad intel on purpose—that had happened on a mission more than once, including the last one he'd been on with Rivera—but this didn't feel like Rivera's touch. Nothing that was happening here even remotely resembled the last op he'd been on with Rivera, making him certain this wasn't a therapeutic mind fuck from his former team member.

He couldn't help but wonder who the hostage was supposed to be.

These thoughts swirled through his mind as he followed the tracks of a tango through the miserable cold, dark rain. At least the trail was easy to follow. These guys didn't care about covering tracks or snapping branches. Whoever Rivera had lined up to play the role of baddies was making it easy.

Either they were SEALs who were pretending to be less trained, or they were Army.

He smiled grimly at his mental joke. He'd have to rib one of his Ranger buddies with that one next time they went out for beers.

He paused and studied the ground where a bunch of leaves were smashed and branches broken.

"Shit," Phelps said, obviously noting the same thing.

"A fight," Chris said softly, thankful for the cover of the rain.

"One of our guys tangled here? With who? One of the trainers?"

That didn't make sense either. They were working in four-man Fire Teams. This looked like a two-man fight and not a group brawl.

His night vision goggles allowed him to follow a short trail of smashed leaves and gouged moss to where a swath of flattened branches suggested one of the combatants had slid downhill.

And there was the proof, in the middle of cleared ground, in glowing shades of green.

"Is that...a dummy?" Huang whispered in disbelief.

Chris had wanted to think the same thing, because the truth was too horrible to fathom.

This was an *exercise*. Fake. Training. Not *real*.

And yet, just a few feet away was a very real dead body with a snapped neck.

*T*he Baldwin cabin was a treasure trove of camping supplies. Not for backpacking—the tents were bigger and heavier, and the sleeping bags were base-camp style and not compact mummy bags—but Xavier wasn't about to complain about the bulky items and extra weight. They would need a good shelter when they rested come daylight.

He wished they could pitch the tent now. Audrey was exhausted. Soaking wet. At the end of the trek to get to the Baldwins', she'd been shivering with every step she took, teeth chattering and all.

But they couldn't stop now. Jeb's cabin wasn't far, and it might have answers.

So they'd gather supplies here, then continue on to Jeb's, which was the last one before the road dead-ended at the CCC shelter and campground.

At least here, in the Baldwin cabin, Audrey was no longer shivering. First thing they'd done was doff her rain gear and wrap her in a wool blanket that had been draped over the back of a sofa.

Once she was no longer shivering, they'd returned to the utility room at the back of the attached garage and raided it for gear: a green two-person half-dome tent, two all-season sleeping bags, two inflatable sleeping pads, a large-frame backpack for Xavier and another one for Audrey that she could clip her day pack to. They had a Sierra stove, fire bricks, and a small pot for boiling water. Now they just needed food.

Xavier led her into the kitchen, where they started with the pantry. They hit the jackpot when he found a stash of packaged Styrofoam noodle cups and mashed potato packets that only required hot water. He grabbed cans of tuna and chicken and threw those in his borrowed frame pack.

"Jeb was right about this being a vacation rental," Audrey said.

"Yeah, the notes everywhere give it away." There were little cards next to light switches and instruction sheets for how to use the compost bin and where to place the trash at the end of the stay.

"That and the locked closets and cabinets." She pointed to the lock on the cupboard above the fridge. "I'm guessing that's the liquor cabinet. It probably also holds the good knives and Le Creuset."

"Think there's anything we can use in there?" he asked.

"Doubt it, unless you want scotch or vodka."

"Gin is really my preferred liquor."

"Maybe you'll get lucky."

"Tempting but risky." He paused, then reconsidered. "Although alcohol is flammable. Wouldn't hurt to have the makings for a Molotov cocktail." He reached for a step stool and grabbed one of the cheap knives from the butcher block.

"*Suuuurrre,*" she said with a laugh in an unmistakably sarcastic tone. "It's for a *Molotov* cocktail."

He chuckled. "Tell you what, when this is all over, I'll introduce you to my favorite gin. It's made in small batches at a distillery in Portland." He slipped the knife blade between door and frame of the cupboard and popped it free of the cheap lock.

Behind him, Audrey said, "I'm not much for hard alcohol these days."

He scanned the contents of the cupboard, which, as Audrey had guessed, contained booze and quality cookware —but not Le Creuset. He was a little relieved by that deviation or he'd have to wonder if the woman was psychic. He grabbed vodka and a fifth of whiskey and passed them to her to drop in his pack.

After climbing down, he checked the cupboard above the countertop coffeemaker. "Coffee, filters, and a cone. Score!"

"Is there any decaf?"

"Nope. Why?" They'd had regular coffee the morning after their night together and she hadn't said anything then. If there was ever a time she might need caffeine, it was now.

"No big deal. I've just been off caffeine for the last few weeks." She shrugged. "I'll take some of that herbal tea instead."

He tossed packets of tea into the pack and grabbed two stainless steel travel mugs. "Any other food you want?"

From the pantry, she grabbed a sealed salami log, a box of saltines, a pack of bite-sized rice cakes, and a bar of dark chocolate. After placing those in the pack, she turned to the fridge and let out a squeal of delight as she grabbed a brick of unopened cheddar cheese. "Even better score."

She returned to the fridge. The remaining contents were mostly condiments along with jars of olives and pickles and other items with a long refrigerated shelf life. She opened a container of cottage cheese and took a sniff. All at once, she slammed the container on the counter next to the sink and retched into the basin.

He'd never seen anyone go from fine to sick like that in such a flash. Earlier, when she'd vomited in the yurt, she hadn't been anything close to fine. "You have a mold allergy?" he asked after shining the red light into the open container.

"It was the sour smell that got me. I've got a sensitive stomach right now, I guess."

"Understandable given the situation."

She turned on the water and dunked her face in the stream. She took a long gulp and spit the water out, then dunked her head under again, this time letting the water run over the back of her neck. After raising her head again, she shut off the spray and placed both hands on the lip of the sink, hanging her head over the stainless steel basin. "You don't know the half of it." The words were a soft mumble.

He wanted to ask what she meant, but every minute they were inside the house, the danger of being cornered again increased. He'd have to wait to continue this conversation when they were alone in the tent later. "You okay now?"

She nodded.

"'Kay. Let's go upstairs and see if we can find you better clothes."

She took a hand towel from the hook next to the sink and patted her face and neck. "I've been crossing my fingers for that ever since we decided to rob this place. Danielle Baldwin is about my size."

Before going up, Xavier grabbed a small crowbar from the garage. A knife probably wouldn't cut it—no pun intended—if the bedroom closets had solid interior doors.

His assumption proved correct, and he quickly pried open the locked closet in the master bedroom. It was a small walk-in, and they entered and closed the door, allowing Xavier to use the bright white lens on his flashlight to illuminate the fully enclosed space that included built-in shelves loaded with clothing. A tower of drawers filled one short wall.

"I joke about stealing, but I really feel terrible we're doing this." She ran her hand over a set of quality long underwear. "I'm going to reimburse the Baldwins for everything we pilfer."

"*Borrow.* And I will pay back every dime personally. I'll fix the doors and locks myself."

Audrey pulled open a drawer, then slammed it shut. "I can't take Danielle's underwear."

"Audrey, are your bra and underwear soaked?"

"Damp. Not soaked."

"If she has a sports bra that will fit you, you need to change. And you need to take a spare. You won't be comfortable hiking without a bra, and pulling on dry long underwear over a damp bra makes no sense. We can't have you succumbing to hypothermia out there."

She let out a heavy sigh and said, "Fine."

She found hiking pants and thick wool socks and took two of everything. "I'll change into one set now and keep the other in case these get soaked too."

He nodded and reached for the doorknob. "Hurry. We need to get out of here."

After making sure she had a flashlight, he left her in the closet and went downstairs to their pile of supplies that had yet to go into a bag. In the garage, he found a large box of heavy-duty garbage bags and set to work wrapping the tent, ground pads, and sleeping bags. He then strapped the wrapped items to the outside of their packs, making sure Audrey's would be lighter than his by quite a bit. She was strong and a hiker, but he was trained to carry extremely heavy packs on ten-mile hikes while wearing body armor.

He was in the middle of this process when he heard Audrey's footsteps behind him. He turned to see her arms loaded with clothing, including a heavy-duty raincoat made for winter hiking. "Danielle Baldwin might be my favorite person in the world right now."

"I'd suggest we leave her a thank-you note, but if someone else found it, they'd know what supplies we took. They'll guess we were here from the broken locks, but no need to advertise we've got camping supplies and food."

She frowned. "I—" She paused and shook her head. "Never mind. Later."

He cocked his head, but didn't probe. They'd lingered here too long already. "Let's roll."

"You don't want to see if any of Frank's clothes will fit you?"

"No. I need my IR patches visible for the SEALs."

"But aren't they visible to the bad guys too?"

He smiled at her use of the term *bad guys*. "They already know I'm the enemy. Doesn't matter. The team needs to know we're both friendlies. The patch protects us both." After a pause, he added, "If anything happens to me, you need to put on my coat. The tactical vest too."

She held his gaze. He guessed her face had just blanched, but it was hard to see in the red glow. After a beat, she nodded agreement.

He turned back to packing, making sure she had the stove and pot and half the food. If they had to separate, she'd have what she needed to survive.

When they were ready, she pulled on the heavy raincoat. Before she donned the bulky, loaded-down pack, he grabbed the lapel of her open coat and pulled her to him. "Can I kiss you?"

Her nostrils flared, then she gave a quick, slight nod.

He lowered his head and brushed his lips over hers. When he would have raised his head, she opened her mouth, inviting a deeper kiss.

He wasn't one to question her offering, short on time or not. He slipped his tongue inside, and they shared a brief but deep kiss. Without a word, he released her and stepped back, then slipped the straps of his loaded pack over his shoulders. The injured joint throbbed, but there was no avoiding the pain.

He would suffer any amount of agony to keep Audrey safe.

Chapter Twelve

$\mathscr{P}$aul tried not to think about the pain in his left hand, but the wound throbbed, shattering his ability to compartmentalize. It would be different if he were still in the fight, but he was trussed up in the cold ballroom, immobilized with nothing for his brain to focus on but worry for his team of trainers, who were all unconscious—or dead.

Only Reichmann's chest visibly rose and fell with the cadence of sleep. The others could be breathing, but Paul hadn't been able to detect movement. It could be the dim lighting and the fact they were half the distance of the ballroom away.

He studied Palmer, waiting for the man to inhale. No movement he could discern. Fear coursed through his pain-riddled body. As if it wasn't bad enough that they'd cut off his finger, they'd had to go and break his ribs and punch him in the kidneys too. He was in bad shape, but for now, he was alive.

He would focus on that. Try to forget he was missing a ring finger.

Impossible, but once upon a time, he'd been a special operator. The best of the motherfucking best.

His gaze dropped to his bandaged hand. He wouldn't look away. He tightened his fingers and felt a surge of pain.

All that mattered was he was still breathing, and as long as he was breathing, he would look for ways to help the team in the forest, who were surely working on a plan to rescue him and the other hostages.

If they knew there were real hostages, that is.

He went over what had happened, step by agonizing step, in his mind. This exercise would trigger a detail that would help. Something he could use against his Russian captors.

They'd dragged him to the lodge shortly after they'd destroyed the electronics and cut off his finger. He'd been taken into the public restroom near the check-in desk, where one of the mercs bandaged his hand, staunching the flow of blood that had left him light-headed.

It was around that point that Paul realized they wanted him alive. If this was because they thought he was going to spill the beans on future SEAL training exercises, then they were fools.

But that possibility meant he and his team had been beaten by fools. An added humiliation he hadn't anticipated.

Who are these finger-stealing assholes?

The humiliation had deepened when he'd been dragged into the ballroom and spotted the other four trainers, their team of fake tangos. The only person missing from their six-man band was Rivera.

He'd gone off on what Paul had figured was a boon-doggle with the archaeologist. He hadn't been in position when disaster struck. Hadn't been taken.

At least, that's what Paul hoped.

If the woman was in on this somehow, if it had been her

job to divert Rivera and the team, then they were all fucked. He figured Rivera had been distracted by the woman he'd screwed and then screwed over.

Paul's confusion about the situation only grew when he was dragged before the man who must be the leader of the merc team. He wore a balaclava hood with night vision goggles, making it impossible for Paul to make out his features in the dim light of the ballroom.

Why bother to hide his face? Was this man known to the US military?

That question became secondary when the masked man took one look at Paul, then decked one of his minions and yelled at him in Russian.

Luckily, Paul spoke Russian. Unlucky for the merc, he didn't know Paul was fluent in his language.

"This is not Rivera! I need the sonofabitch alive, and you bring me this piece of shit?" He'd kicked Paul in the ribs then, and the blow managed to eclipse the pain in his hand for a few moments.

What was this guy's beef with Rivera?

But that had been hours ago.

Now Paul was tied to a chair, halfway across the room from his team, wondering if they were sleeping or dead.

Two mercs entered the ballroom.

"Did you get him?" the masked leader asked in Russian.

"No," the taller of the two henchmen said, as the shorter man waved a piece of paper in the air.

"But we do have a letter. From a woman to a man named Xavier."

"Give it to me."

The short man hesitated, as if realizing the piece of paper was of great value, but handed it over after only a moment, likely realizing that holding the letter hostage would mean losing his own finger. Maybe even death.

Not the brightest bulbs, but not the dimmest either.

Paul studied the leader. He'd removed the NVGs to read the letter in the glow of a red flashlight, but he was too far away and the light too dim for Paul to notice anything distinguishable about his features.

It had been too much to hope the man couldn't read English, but he let out a nasty cackle as he set the letter on the table. "She's pregnant. With his bastard."

Paul had to work to keep his expression blank. Listless.

The archaeologist was pregnant with Rivera's child? And she'd written him a letter about it? Had she shown up tonight not because of her cameras—it had seemed like a far-fetched excuse—but because she wanted to slip Rivera the letter? Had she interrupted a military op so she could pass him a note like she was in middle school?

And why was their captor so damn happy about this turn of events?

The man spoke again. "This changes things. I need them *both* alive. Bring me the woman, and I'll pay double what I promised for Rivera." He lowered his voice, but still, it carried in the quiet room. "I will cut her while her lover listens to her screams."

Chapter Thirteen

*C*hris let out a birdcall, even knowing it wouldn't carry far over the tapping of the rain. The never-ending downpour cloaked them from the tangos in the forest, but it also made it difficult to find the other Fire Teams.

Four hundred hours and they were in the rendezvous area. All four teams should be here. He was certain the others had come across signs of trouble as his team had. They hadn't taken the lodge. They hadn't reached a single objective as it had been laid out for them on Whidbey Island.

Where was Rivera? Where were Cohen and the other trainers? Were they all in the lodge—real hostages and not the fake ones they'd been promised yesterday?

Surely someone was free if the guy with the snapped neck was any indication. The body had no weapons, which meant the trainer who'd taken the guy down had a gun that fired real bullets.

Good for him. It meant the platoon had an armed ally. Now they all just needed to find each other.

Chris made the call again. He waited several minutes, then tried again. When that failed, they changed positions and repeated the process. Finally, after thirty minutes, an answering call came.

Ten minutes after that, a third team checked in.

Three Fire Teams gathered deep in the woods. With no small amount of relief, Chris counted twelve uninjured men, including himself.

They just needed the fourth Fire Team to show up.

As the minutes ticked by, they shared the intel they'd gathered. Chris and his men learned of downed trees blocking the road—something that was strictly forbidden as part of this training. The trees here were old growth, the forest protected by state and federal law.

More disturbing was the news of another body, this one an older man with a Vietnam vet tattoo on his forearm. He'd been found by the back door of a yurt. The man had his throat cut wide—leaving his head barely attached.

"Sounds like a local," Chief Petty Officer Williams said. "NSWC said they hadn't employed any actors to play hostages in this exercise. We were assured there wouldn't be any civilians in the vicinity."

"That's our assumption too," Mock, the leader of the Fire Team that found the body, said. "Given the situation, we entered the yurt. The smashed electronics inside indicated it was the command center for the trainers. There was a lot of blood on one table, but otherwise, no evidence of the training team."

Blood in the command center.

Rivera? Cohen? Both?

Chris knew Cohen, but not as well as he knew Rivera. But then, he and Rivera had been longtime teammates and good friends before they shared the worst day of their lives.

Rivera was the only other person on their four-man Fire Team who'd lived to share the memory. Was he gone now too?

No. No. Dammit all to hell. *Fuck no.*

After an hour passed with no sign of the last Fire Team, led by Commander Odent, another terrifying truth sank in: they were missing an entire Fire Team.

Six missing trainers. Four missing SEALs.

With resignation, Chris took control. Without Odent, he was the ranking officer and in command of the mission. "Mock, I want your team on reconnaissance. We have more than two hours left before daylight, and we need to know if everyone is being held in the lodge, or if the prisoners have been divided amongst the buildings in the lodge complex. We need a count of how many tangos we're dealing with." He turned to Williams. "I want your team to check out the inholding cabins closest to the yurt. Power and phones are down but the inholdings will have generators and fuel. We can use the fuel for improvised weapons. The cabins could have guns and ammo. We've got two dead bodies—one of whom is probably a resident of the area—and we're missing six trainers and four SEALs. We'll do whatever it takes to rescue our team, even if it means breaking and entering areas that were restricted from the training."

Everyone nodded.

"It's possible there could be more locals hiding in their cabins," he added. "Be on the lookout for civilians and mercs."

"Maybe the blood inside the yurt was another local, like the one outside," someone suggested.

Was it wrong for Chris to hope that was the case?

Rivera lying in that hospital bed was far too fresh in his mind. Could the blood in the yurt be his?

He remembered Rivera's steely calm when he woke in the hospital—he'd finally returned stateside after surgery in the US military's hospital in Landstuhl, Germany. In Germany, he'd been delirious and asking for Lynn. But when he woke up in San Diego at last, Chris had been the one to tell him Lynn had been and gone while he was sleeping.

She'd dumped him without so much as a goodbye.

He'd lain in agony, pretending the woman hadn't just cut his heart out. This after the organ had thankfully remained intact when the bullet aiming for it landed just above and to the left.

Lynn hadn't wanted to stick around for the aftermath, and not just the playing nursemaid part as Xavier recovered from surgery. She was worried about PTSD.

Much as he wanted to believe otherwise, it was a looming specter in Chris's mind as well. Not just for Xavier, but for himself. He'd have been happy to never reveal to another soul what had transpired on that op. What he'd done to save Xavier after he'd failed to protect the others.

Pam had expressed the same fears to Chris. He'd promised to do the work.

But had he? Or had he pushed her away?

And, as far as he could tell, she'd moved on emotionally the same time Lynn did. Except Lynn made it a clean break, while Pam supposedly stayed by his side even as she took one of his closest friends as a lover.

But now he wondered, had he been the one to shut her out as he did the bare minimum needed to skate by and return to active duty? Not that anything could excuse her actions, but the thought still crossed his mind.

He shook his head. This was an *op*. He shouldn't be thinking about Pam. But then, it was a messed-up op, designed to shatter everyone's focus.

Xavier could be dead. A Fire Team was missing.

They'd been attacked on American soil, in a location that should have been absolutely secure.

He faced the men he was now leading. No more thoughts

of Pam. He couldn't even think of Xavier. No. He was Rivera. A stone-cold operator like the rest of them.

First, they needed to figure out who had killed the tango his team had found. That person had claimed weapons and was an ally.

"We need intel on the SUV you found. The one with the bullet holes and flat tires," Williams said.

Chris gave a sharp nod. "I was thinking the same thing. Huang and I will go check it out. Phelps and Jonas, your job is to hold this position. Update the fourth team when they show up."

Tasks set, the teams divided and set out into the pouring rain once again.

*R*ain continued to fall in torrents, making Audrey question her love of the Pacific Northwest and this park and the rainforest around the lodge in particular. Thank goodness she'd gotten wool socks and high-quality leather hiking boots from Danielle Baldwin, or her feet would be soaked and numb with cold as she trudged through the woods to Jeb McCutcheon's cabin.

She was weary in the extreme, but still wired with adrenaline. She'd had no idea her body could perform at this pace, especially at eleven and a half weeks pregnant, but survival instincts overrode hormones, apparently.

Jeb's cabin, at the farthest end of the road from the lodge, was closer than any other to George's forest hideaway on the opposite side of the falls. Kaxo Falls sat at the top of the lumpy boot, while Jeb's was on the back of the calf.

Between Jeb's place and the falls was a campground that had an historic CCC picnic shelter that was due for refurbishment this summer. Jeb often complained about campers on his property. A thinning of the clouds to the northwest allowed the moon's glow to penetrate and cast faint illumination across the lake, allowing her to read the half dozen "NO TRESSPASSING" signs Jeb had posted around his property.

They stuck to the shadows of the trees as much as possible as they watched the old cabin and carriage house, which now served as a garage.

"We'll wait for the clouds in front of the moon to thicken again, then make a move on the house," Xavier whispered, his lips brushing her ear so he could be heard over the steady beat of raindrops on her hood.

She nodded. After hours of wishing for the slightest bit of illumination so she could see her feet, it was bit odd to be wishing the light away. But the moon would be lost behind the hills and trees to the northwest in another hour or so anyway. It would set a little more than an hour before sunrise. According to Xavier, at that point, they would be setting up their tent deep in the woods, and her body ached for that moment when she could collapse in a warm sleeping bag.

She studied the cabin, which was one of the oldest structures on the lake—predating the lodge by at least ten years. She hadn't always gotten along with Jeb—the confrontation she'd had with him in mid-November when the looting was discovered was a case in point—but she grieved his loss. He'd loved this land even more than she did, and he'd devoted his life to protecting it, even if she disagreed with his methods and sometimes his views.

He'd been a gruff Vietnam vet with an understandable deep distrust of the government. He'd viewed every action by the park with suspicion. And of course, in many instances, he wasn't wrong. After all, ONP's early days had been rife with colonialism. It hadn't been a golden age for the tribal members who'd been locked out of their usual and accustomed fishing and hunting areas—theirs by right of treaties signed over a hundred and sixty years ago. But even Jeb recognized the progress of the last few decades. George's tribe had reclaimed their ancestral cabin, and George was granted unrestricted use of the woodshop and official title as master carver for the park.

The park didn't do *everything* wrong. But Audrey knew the park didn't do everything right either.

ONP could never make up for all the losses the tribes had suffered over the centuries, but at least they were making an inclusive effort and offered reparations in ways the park could give.

Now Jeb was dead and George… Where was he?

He'd been close to Jeb. They both had been sent to Vietnam at the tender age of nineteen, serving a few years apart. Audrey figured a bond had formed when they both returned, utterly changed from who they'd been previously and needing the touch point of someone who understood the experience.

Had George known Jeb planned to stay in his cabin during the training? What had been Jeb's plan?

She dearly hoped they'd find answers in his cabin. Plus, she harbored a hope that maybe his phone line—and all the phones on this side of the split in the road—still worked. Then Xavier could call the Navy, who would swoop in and rescue everyone.

Hope was dangerous, but it had enabled her to place one foot in front of the other for the last miserable hour. Hope was the only thing that kept incapacitating fear at bay.

*P*almer moved. Relief flooded Paul's system at catching the sudden twitch of the man's shoulders, just visible across the dark room. Palmer was alive. Waking up.

This was a good sign. Maybe Krieger was also asleep.

It made sense that the four men would have been drugged. Easiest way to take them down quietly before the training started. At the time, two had been in the forest and two inside the lodge. A tranq gun would do the job.

Paul had been inside the yurt. He'd heard the intruders and had put up a fight, but four on one had made for a lopsided battle.

It had to be a powerful tranquilizer for all four men to be out cold for so long.

Palmer moved again. Another twitch, then his body settled, and Paul wondered if he was awake enough to realize he needed to feign sleep.

The merc commander didn't notice the movement. He sat with his back to Paul, mask still on, but NVGs set aside, engrossed with something on his laptop screen. Paul wondered when the machine would run out of battery life, hoping they'd turn on a generator, which would signal to the SEALs they were in the lodge.

Not that the team wouldn't guess, but nothing quite like having X mark the spot when there were a dozen outbuildings they could have been taken to. They'd planned to run scenarios tomorrow with the hostages held in the boathouse, and another with mother and son in the maintenance shed.

He suspected the only reason he, as the lone awake prisoner, hadn't been moved to a separate room or building was because they didn't have enough men to guard him separately.

Paul had counted eight mercs so far. There could be

more in the forest, but how many? In most instances, a full platoon would be difficult to take down with just a handful of men, but no one had expected an ambush here, and the SEALs didn't have real guns or explosives.

But the mercs hadn't counted on Rivera eluding their net, and they were spending energy on tracking him and the Kendrick woman. The merc leader would be told the minute Rivera was caught, making no news good news for Paul and the other hostages.

The door burst open and a minion barged in, dragging a body behind him. Not Rivera or any of the SEALs, thank god.

The merc leader jumped to his feet and swore in Russian as he approached the dead man.

"We've got a problem," the minion said.

"So it appears."

The leader lifted the man's head. Paul could just make out streaks of blood covering the face, while something large protruded from the dead man's eye socket.

The masked man made a sound of disgust as he released the head. "What is this?"

The minion released the collar of the dead man's jacket, and the body landed in a pile on the floor. Discarded refuse, not a fallen brother.

These men had no loyalty, not even to each other.

"We just finished unloading the supplies from the boat onto the dock. I heard a pop and turned to see him scream and collapse. Shot in the eye with a nail."

Had the SEALs armed themselves by putting nails in front of the Simunition rounds in their rifles? That might work in a pinch, but a shot in the eye from any kind of distance was too accurate for that. A nail wouldn't fly far or straight with a Simunition round as the propellant.

No. This was something else. *Someone* else?

Rivera? His Glock only fired Simunition too. But Kendrick might know where Rivera could find weapons or where he could make them.

Paul averted his gaze and kept his body loose. He couldn't give off signs he understood their words, or they'd move their conversations to a different room.

"Put his body with the others."

Others?

He held back the smile that wanted to spread at hearing the plural word.

Rivera had been busy. Unless there was someone else in these woods.

Was it possible they had an unknown ally?

Chapter Fourteen

"*H*ave you ever been inside Jeb's cabin?" Xavier asked as he shined a red beam of light through the kitchen window.

"No. Jeb didn't want it included in my historical inventory. It's in the historic district nomination because it's a contributing element—Jeb's feelings don't change that—but the information is scant and the photos were taken from the lake without trespassing on his property. Jeb was pro-historic-preservation protections, but adamantly antigovernment."

"How did he justify both positions?"

She shrugged. "I'm sure it worked in his mind."

Xavier circled the cabin with Audrey at his heels. He found an unlocked window on the north side, glad he wouldn't need to break in this time. He hoisted the pane and found it moved smoothly in the old frame. From what he'd seen in daylight when they inspected all inholding properties two days ago, the hundred-plus-year-old cabin had been meticulously maintained. The thought triggered yet another pang at the death of the owner who'd cared so much for his lakeside cabin.

Xavier remembered seeing Jeb in the lodge the night he met Audrey. Jeb had been playing checkers with Audrey's friend, George. Both men were of a similar age, and for a brief moment, Xavier had imagined himself and Jae, friends since elementary school, facing off over checkers in the lodge when they were in their seventies.

On the other side of the room, he'd seen Harriet and Daniel Jamison enjoying a cocktail, and Jae had pointed out the couple had been married for nearly seventy years. At the time, Xavier had wondered what it would be like to have that kind of life partner, and he'd envied both their longevity and their relationship.

Hours ago, he'd invaded the Jamison cabin, and now he would trespass in Jeb's. Little had he known that night in the lodge that dominos were already falling. The thin rectangular bricks had twisted and turned as they fell, following switchbacks on a hillside, bringing him to this moment.

Somehow, someone had learned his reason for being in the lodge that night. They'd staged their weapons in the forest above the lodge complex two weeks later—a mere week after public notice had been sent to inholding landowners, a group that included antigovernment activist Jeb McCutcheon.

Jeb, who had stayed in the park after signing a contract to leave. Jeb, who had died hours ago outside the yurt before the training even began. Who had Jeb told in those first precious days after receiving the public notice?

Xavier hoped to find answers inside this cabin.

He paused just inside the window, listening for movement in the house. He didn't want to leave Audrey outside, but having her enter before he searched the place went against his nature. She followed her own nature, however, and was shoving both their packs through the opening and then climbing through herself before he could object.

They searched the small two-bedroom log cabin together, finding no one, and no obvious clue as to why Jeb had been at the yurt last evening.

Initial sweep done, Audrey made a beeline for the phone. Xavier spotted an old rotary-dial, wall-mounted phone next to the kitchen, but on the counter next to it sat a modern cordless phone.

"That won't work without electricity."

"Thank goodness for antiques," Audrey said as she pulled the plug from the cordless phone base. She then inserted the male plug into the bottom of the wall-mounted relic that dated to around the time the yurt had been built.

She placed a palm on the handset, then closed her eyes and took a deep, slow breath. If a wish could give a phone life, then certainly the intensity of her silent plea would open the line.

She lifted the handset from the hook and placed it next to her ear. She closed her eyes and gave a sharp shake of her head.

Damn.

He hadn't dared to hope. At least he thought he hadn't. Not until he'd watched her failed ritual and found himself hoping for her sake.

He didn't want to see the devastation she was feeling. Didn't want her to feel it.

She returned the handset to the hook and pressed her forehead to the wall. He suspected she was holding back tears. "I knew I shouldn't get my hopes up. But I couldn't help it."

He stepped up behind her and hesitated a moment, then wrapped his arms around her. She leaned into him, accepting his embrace. He had no clue what to say, so he just held her.

"I'm scared, Xavier. I've never been so scared."

"It's okay to be scared. Fear will keep you alive."

"But what if it paralyzes me? Like it did on the cliff ledge. I saw that guy coming for me and I froze. Deer in the headlights."

"You also screamed and got my attention. And then you threw a rock that saved my life—and yours. Fear didn't stop you."

She turned in his arms. They both wore thick, wool-lined rain gear, and he had his tactical vest loaded with tools between them, but still, she burrowed against him, undeterred by the stiff layers that separated them.

His heart did something strange when her face pressed against the bare skin at his neck.

"I'm in awe of you, Audrey. I hate myself for what I did to you. For the situation that has put you in. And even after all that, you're here, working with me. You know this park, and you know these people and their cabins. I'd be lost without you."

She lifted her head, letting him see the tears that spilled down her cheeks. She'd entranced him from his first glimpse of her face—those same broad cheeks had been smudged with dirt, and her dark hair had been pulled back in a scraggly braid. She'd looked earthy. Rugged. Utterly enchanting.

When he looked at her, he couldn't begin to understand the choices he'd made that had deliberately hurt her. He had to force himself to remember the chemical attack in Prague. And even then, his cruelty took his own breath away.

"I am *so* desperately sorry."

More tears spilled as she gazed into his eyes, reminding

him of the stare down they'd shared before their first intense kiss.

She smiled then, and he guessed she was thinking the same thing. "Blink five times if you want to kiss me." Her words were an echo of the exchange that had preceded that first kiss.

He chuckled and blinked the required number. "I always want to kiss you, Dr. Kendrick. You never need to ask." He brushed away the tears from her cheeks with his thumbs, cradling her head as he did so.

"I think I'm starting to believe you."

"About me wanting to kiss you?"

"That, yes. And also that you are genuinely sorry."

Now his eyes teared, which astonished him. It shouldn't, though. She'd given him no small thing, and it was far more than he had any right to hope for. "When this is all over, I want to take you to your favorite restaurant. Wine and dine you. I know it's more than I deserve, but please, give me something to look forward to and tell me you'll go out with me. Even if it's only once and only so you can tell me off."

She gave him a weak laugh even as more tears spilled. "Fine. I'll let you buy me dinner at my favorite restaurant."

He dropped a kiss on her cheek, brushing away her salty tears with his lips and feeling strangely light at her promise, even knowing she was probably only saying it to appease him. "Excellent. Where are we going?"

"It's an amazing seafood restaurant. Asian fusion. Everything on the menu is divine." She lifted her chin and gave him a crafty grin. "It's on Oahu."

He grinned back, imagining Audrey on a sandy beach under a bright blue sky. Bellows Air Force Station had oceanfront cabins on one of the best beaches on the island, available for rent by DoD civilians and active-duty military. The sound of ocean waves would lull them to sleep every night after he made love to her.

He would mentally explore this fantasy further when their situation wasn't so…completely and utterly dire.

"As soon as I have a working phone, I'll make us a reservation." He brushed his lips over hers, then stepped back. "Now, let's search Jeb's papers and see if his laptop will boot. I want to see who he's been corresponding with."

The damaged SUV looked exactly as it had when they'd found it hours ago. It rested low on the ground with four flat tires, six bullet holes in the rear driver's-side panel circling the fuel tank.

The holes were big. Whoever had shot up the vehicle had used high-caliber bullets—probably a .45. This was as much a warning as disabling.

Together, Chris and Huang approached the vehicle, standing back-to-back, rotating in a circle, taking no chances while they crossed open ground. At least the moon saw fit to hide behind clouds again, and the rain continued to provide endless cover.

When he reached the driver's door, he tried the handle. Locked, making him glad he'd remembered to get the tools he needed from Mock, who was the team's best car thief—or rather, commandeer-er—when a mission called for it. He quickly slipped a wedge between the window and the weather stripping and worked it in until the gap was wide enough for him to slip a thin bent rod through. It took less than twenty seconds to unlock the door.

He reached over the center console for the glove box and pulled out a faux-leather zippered case that probably held the owner's manual and would have pockets for registration and insurance cards. A quick glance inside and he had what they needed. Audrey Kendrick had renewed her insurance in October.

He snapped a picture of the vehicle registration and insurance card. Ms. Kendrick lived in Port Angeles.

A few years ago, Port Angeles had been at the center of a Ukrainian neo-Nazi group's terrorist plot to drop a nuke in the Strait of Juan de Fuca and cause tsunamis that would have wiped Seattle, Vancouver, and everything in between off the map.

Was there a chance the tangos here were part of that cell? Could this be related?

It was a razor-thin connection, but Chris wouldn't rule anything out without more information.

A quick scan of the vehicle interior offered another clue to the woman's identity. A medium-weight brown jacket with the Olympic National Park logo and an official-looking embroidered patch that said "Park Archaeologist" on the left breast was on the floor of the back seat.

Assuming the jacket belonged to Kendrick, he could conclude she was a park employee. What the hell had she been doing here during the training? He was certain now the SUV wasn't a prop, as they'd all assumed when they thought it was part of the exercise.

There was nothing else of interest in the front or back seats, so he and Huang moved in unison to the rear hatch. There he found a sleeping bag, muddy boots, a flannel shirt that had seen heavy use, a wool blanket, a professional-grade first aid kit, a box of flares, a portable car battery jump-start kit, and an emergency tire-inflator kit.

Kendrick clearly believed in being prepared. He wondered how many times she'd gotten stuck before those items earned permanent residence in the storage bay.

The portable battery kit and flares could come in handy. He dropped both items in his pack.

Done searching, he closed the rear hatch and returned to the front to lock the vehicle and reclaim the wedge tool.

There were dozens of structures on the lodge property, and he and Huang intended to check out the ones closest to the abandoned SUV if it appeared safe to do so. This was a good opportunity to obtain supplies.

A weatherproof waist-high interpretive sign by the building on the end informed him that he was looking at the oldest building in the lodge complex, the blacksmith shop. An adjacent sign indicated that the next building over was a replica of the carpenter's shop that had burned down in the 1980s. From late spring to early fall, the shop was open for wood-carving demonstrations by master carvers. A small, less official sign indicated carvings were available for purchase in the lodge gift shop.

He and Huang circled the blacksmith shop first, but there was nothing to see. There were no windows on the back, and the side windows were small and shuttered tight. The front was two barn-style doors that would be opened wide when the shop was open for tourists.

"There could be tools in there that we could use," Huang said.

Chris gave a sharp nod. "Let's check out the woodshop. It could have tools too, and there are windows."

He shined a light through the double-pane fake mullioned window and spotted a wealth of tools for wood-working—chisels, clamps, saws, and dozens of items he couldn't begin to name.

He also spotted a generator and several red jerry cans. If they contained gasoline, they were in business.

Every man on the team knew advanced-level improvised

weapon making. With gas and some of the tools he spotted, they could level the playing field with their unknown enemy.

Which raised the question, why hadn't the tangos secured this supply yet?

Maybe they were dealing with only a handful of men who were so busy chasing down the rogue trainer who'd snapped one tango's neck that they hadn't had time to search the outbuildings.

"If those cans are full, we'll take what we can carry and move the rest out of view of the windows."

Huang nodded.

The doorknob lock was basic and only took a minute for Huang to pick while Chris watched his six. In moments, they were inside, gazing at the wealth of tools through NVGs that lit everything in shades of green.

Chris's father would love this shop. Hell, he was half in love himself and he wasn't even a woodworker. One whole section was devoted to clamps of all shapes and sizes, meticulously organized and waiting for the next project. He'd salivate another time. They needed weapons.

He made a beeline for the row of jerry cans and picked up a metal jug. Heavy.

A good sign.

He unscrewed the top and took a whiff as Huang did the same with another can. "Yep. Gasoline."

"Diesel would be better, but I'm not gonna be picky," Huang said.

Yeah. Diesel would be too much to hope for. There was probably some in the lodge maintenance room, but that was near the heart of the complex and likely under surveillance.

Chris studied the row of fuel cans, noting the two smaller containers labeled "Two-Stroke" in black marker. It was probably fuel for the different-sized chainsaws that hung on the wall. Looked like someone did chainsaw art.

"I wish we could fill up a wheelbarrow and haul everything back to the team."

Chris wished the same thing. Instead, he pointed to a door in the back corner and said, "Let's see if we can hide the gas cans in there."

Behind the door was a large storage room full of cleaning supplies, broken tools, and other junk. Not nearly so organized as the main woodshop, which was more like a showroom. After moving the containers, Chris switched his focus to the cabinets and shelves. What gifts did they have to offer?

He popped the lock on a tall metal cabinet, and the door swung wide to reveal an assortment of power tools...and an old rifle with bayonet attached.

He studied the gun. Vietnam era.

Mock had said the body they found by the yurt had a tattoo on his forearm that indicated the dead guy had served in Nam.

Was this the victim's shop? His rifle?

And, even more important, would he find ammunition in one of these cupboards or drawers?

He looked in the adjacent cabinets and drawers, turning up nothing. Unfortunately, they didn't have time to search every tool and storage box. There were dozens, probably hundreds of small drawers holding nails, screws, washers, and every other metal thingamajig imaginable. It would be a waste of time to search each one for cartridges to a gun that probably hadn't been fired in more than a decade.

But damn. A gun would be pretty handy about now.

"Flyte, there's movement on the lake."

Chris turned to the window. Huang was crouched low, looking out toward the water. The rain had slowed in the few minutes they'd been inside. The patter on the roof was less frantic. But visibility remained poor.

Still, night vision caught things the naked eye would miss, and he saw it too.

"A boat."

Huang nodded. "It came from the dock in front of the lodge, I think."

The boat went farther out, toward the center of the lake, and Chris adjusted his NVGs to zoom in.

The boat stopped as the clouds thinned, offering a slight green glow to illuminate what had been dark shadows. He could just make out the outline of two men as they gathered at the stern of the small fishing vessel.

It wasn't a big boat, but it was a nice one. A fishing boat designed for comfort, with a trolling motor. It probably belonged to one of the inholding families. Trolling motors weren't zippy, but they could be powerful enough to move gear and people when roads were closed—as the lodge road was due to several downed trees.

This could be how the tangos were getting past the blockade they'd created. It didn't hurt that trolling motors were quiet, and in this storm, they would be invisible if not for the NVGs.

He watched as the two people—large men, from the looks of them—hoisted something. They rested the heavy item on the gunwale for a moment before pushing it over the side and into the lake.

In that frozen moment of rest, the dark green shape took form.

All Chris could do was hope the body they'd dumped in the frigid lake didn't belong to one of the missing trainers or the missing Fire Team.

Chapter Fifteen

*J*eb's computer was password protected and his papers were nonexistent, so Xavier and Audrey moved on to the carriage house that had been converted to a garage and shop.

Jeb had left a key chain hanging on a pegboard in the kitchen, and Audrey was relieved when the fourth key Xavier tried unlocked the dead bolt to the garage. It was so much better than smashing their way in. She had zero doubt that Jeb had the kind of soul that would haunt people if he could, and he'd hate any damage to his beloved property, even if it was done in service of finding out who had killed him and why.

Xavier ran his red flashlight around the room. On first glance, the shop looked disorganized. That didn't seem very Jeb.

In the center of the bay was an old beast of a pickup truck—from the 1960s or '70s—up on supports. It lacked tires and a front hood. It was a work in progress, or a parts vehicle. Something Jeb was restoring, she guessed, but it looked like the project had stalled long ago.

A long, L-shaped workbench spanned two walls. The surface was littered with tools and random items, bits of wire, baby food jars filled with nuts and bolts. Interspersed among the detritus of ongoing projects were open produce boxes—the cardboard kind cashiers at Costco used to pack groceries in lieu of using bags—some empty, some full with dirty shop towels, yet more tools, quarts of oil.

She puzzled over the incongruity of the messy shop and what she knew of Jeb, but then, this could be the place where he relaxed most and tinkered on multiple projects at a time.

Xavier's light landed on the corner of the L, revealing a jumble of items. Metal pipes, clamps, nails, and screws, all haphazard on the surface. Several incandescent lightbulbs—whole and broken—lay next to an old car battery and jumper cables.

The light went to the shelf above, revealing a stockpile of one-hundred-watt lightbulbs. "Jeb must've bought out Port Angeles before they stopped selling those," she said.

Xavier's light ran across all the upper shelves. Next to the lightbulbs were stacks of boxes of wooden matches, several dozen small black plastic bottles, a lifetime supply of toilet paper, boxes of borax, bottles of ammonia, bleach, and other household cleaners. "It doesn't surprise me that Jeb was something of a hoarder," she added.

"Usually antigovernment hoarders have a weapon stockpile."

"That also wouldn't surprise me. He served in Vietnam and knew his way around guns. He and George talked about—"

Xavier jolted, held up a hand, then the red flashlight went out, plunging the room into inky darkness. He made a soft sound she presumed meant for her to stay quiet.

She couldn't see a thing. Not even her hand in front of her face. Her heart pounded as she stood frozen. What was going on? Had Xavier heard something? Had they been found?

She took a slow, deep breath, trying to calm her racing heart. Her blood pressure was surely skyrocketing, which was not good for the baby.

But then, absolutely none of this was good for the baby.

With the deep breath came a scent that tickled at her memory. Her sense of smell, she'd noticed, had heightened in the last few weeks, which was one reason she'd vomited after smelling the moldy cottage cheese.

This scent was subtle. Lingering.

Recent.

She searched her memory, and then it hit her. At the quarry with Jae, when he'd taught her how to shoot her new Glock. Burnt gunpowder.

Had someone fired a weapon in this room recently?

She wanted to voice the question, but made no sound as instructed.

Instead, she took another breath and searched for other scents that would offer information. A faint whiff of singed electronics. A metallic smell that she didn't think was blood. Plus something acrid, like epoxy or another adhesive.

All this led her to one conclusion: someone had made something here. Recently. In the hours *after* Jeb was murdered.

Were they still here? Was that what Xavier had sensed?

He had night vision goggles. He could see, while she was limited to using her sense of smell.

After a long stretch of the only sound being rain tapping on the metal roof, he cursed softly. His voice came from across the room. How had he moved without her hearing a scrape of footstep or rustle of cloth?

She turned toward the sound, bumping into a high stool as she did so. It didn't make a racket, but it was loud enough.

Fear jolted up her spine as her stomach roiled. Had she just endangered them?

"It's okay," he said softly. "Someone's been here recently. I wanted to check out the truck, make sure they weren't hiding in the cab. I should have searched there before doing anything else."

She heard more movement and guessed he was searching the one cupboard that was big enough to hide a person. From what she'd seen before he doused the light, the room mostly had open shelves. No doors. No closets. Just one large bay.

Finally, he said, "We're clear. No one is here. But I'm leaving the light off. If someone is in the vicinity, I don't want them to see the red glow."

"I smell gunpowder," she said. "And something metallic, and epoxy or something equally stinky."

"You've got a good nose. There are several containers of black powder on the workbench. Looks like they were tossed aside after they were emptied. There are metallic shavings farther down on the bench—my guess is detritus from drilling a hole for a fuse."

"For a fuse?"

"Probably a pipe bomb. Jeb has a large supply of pipes and caps along with his stockpile of black powder."

"Is it legal? Black powder, I mean?"

"Sure. It's perfectly legal to own a black powder pistol. It's harder to buy black powder in quantity, but if he's been stockpiling for years, he could have acquired quite a lot. It's shelf stable, highly explosive, and versatile compared to just stockpiling ammunition."

"Jeb had a bomb-making factory here? Do you think he…was a terrorist?"

"I think he was a hoarder who wanted to defend his property. You said he served in 'Nam. He would know all about improvised munitions. It would be comfortable for him, but also not dangerous to own the pieces when they aren't assembled. He had supplies at the ready. The light-bulbs are part of the stockpile. File off the top and fill the bulb with black powder. Screw it in a socket, and when someone flips the switch, boom."

This was a bizarre conversation to be having in the dark, but it also crushed any desire she might have had to try a light switch anytime soon. "Thank goodness the power is out, then."

She could hear his approach as he moved across the room, finally stopping before her. His touch on her arm was a comfort as she remained sightless. He would guide her through this darkness, as he'd been doing all night.

"The lightbulbs—on the bench—you think someone was making bombs with those tonight?"

"Yes. I think the filament broke a few times—either while the top was being filed off or when soldering wires to the base."

"Soldering iron. I missed that smell. Or maybe I thought it was singed electronics."

"Could be both. A motor could have burned out."

"Why is soldering necessary? And how could he do it without electricity?"

"He made a soldering iron with the car battery, jumper cables, and the carbon rod from a regular household battery. As far as why he needed to solder, the power has been cut from this entire area, so screwing a hundred-watt-bulb bomb into a socket is useless. But if you solder wires to the base, and those wires are connected to a power source, it will ignite the filament and blow the black powder just the same. Making it a portable bomb. Like I said, black powder is versatile."

She leaned her forehead against his chest, coming into

contact with his stiff tactical vest and something hard and metal. The handcuffs? "It wasn't Jeb who made bombs here tonight."

"No. It wasn't. All we can do is hope whoever it was is an ally."

She raised her head, searching the dark for his features and seeing nothing at all, but she knew he could see hers through the NVGs. "George Shaw. He also served in Vietnam. He did his year, and my understanding is it was a rough one. He'd know how to make improvised weapons just like Jeb. And given their friendship, George knew exactly what Jeb had stored in his carriage house. He probably even had his own key."

Chapter Sixteen

From Jeb's property, they hiked more than a mile into the forest south of the lake. This area had no roads. No trails. Nothing but rocks, trees, and endless rain. The tent they'd borrowed was a pale moss green, meaning it would be well camouflaged in daylight, and Xavier would cover it with moss and ferns so it would be indistinguishable from the surrounding area.

They needed a place that was remote and untraceable, so they could both sleep without fear. The hike was slow going because Xavier had to ensure they left no mark of their passage. It was clear exhaustion was overtaking Audrey, but she didn't utter a word of complaint. She put one foot in front of the other like the soldier she never was.

At last, he found the perfect spot—a narrow valley between two downed trees that were in the process of becoming nurse logs. The tent would just fit between them.

He quickly assembled the structure then turned to Audrey. "Get inside and set up the bed. I'm going to hike back a bit and make sure our trail is completely erased. When I get back, I'm going to cover the tent to camouflage it." He cleared his throat. "Take care of business before you go inside. I'm going to bury the front in ferns and moss. We need to limit trips outside as much as possible during daylight, just to be safe."

She nodded.

He set out to cover their trail. He hated leaving her even for this, but he had to be certain no one searching for them would stumble upon their tent. They'd been careful, and he was back ten minutes later. He piled ferns and sticks and moss on the shelter.

"Turn on the red light," he said as he adjusted the covering then stepped back to view it from a few feet away.

There was no discernible light. He used the NVGs. Nothing.

He stepped closer and asked, "Is the light on?"

"Yes."

He felt a rush of relief. This was going to work. "Good."

He took a break to empty his bladder, then returned and piled a wad of moss and ferns across the opening as he joined Audrey inside the narrow two-person tent.

He noticed she'd zipped the sleeping bags together. Good. They both needed the shared body heat.

Audrey sat on one side of the double sleeping bag, her boots hanging off the end. "So—how do we sleep? Do we need to keep our boots and everything but our coats on?"

He paused to consider the question. If she were trained for this sort of thing, the answer would be yes. But she wasn't, and she was shivering and had been off and on for hours. She needed to get warm, and she needed sleep. The best way for both was to strip down to their base layers so body heat and the warmth from the bag would cocoon them. And the stiff, wet leather boots would be uncomfortable enough to keep her awake, especially if her toes were already cold.

"We're well hidden, and you need to get warm. Remove everything but the long underwear. Keep your socks on too if they're dry."

She let out a sigh of relief. "Good. I'm grateful for these boots, but they're chafing and uncomfortable at this point." She set to work removing the boots, followed by her outer layers.

He unclipped his tactical vest and set it aside. He then unholstered the Glock and set it at the top of the sleeping pad before doffing his coat, rolling it up, and placing it over the weapon. He turned to her. "Use your coat as a pillow, but don't put your gun under it. Not a good idea for you to be taking shots in the dark."

She let out a whoosh of relief. "I'm so glad you said that. I wouldn't begin to know what to do."

He did know what to do, but his standard operating procedure was skewed in this situation. Never in his wildest nightmares did he imagine being on an op on US soil with an untrained civilian as his backup while Russian mercs hunted them.

She rolled up her coat as directed, then finished removing her outer layers.

The long underwear she'd borrowed fit her like a glove, and he was glad she'd worn them for the last few hours. He imagined she'd be blue as a Smurf by now without them.

She placed her outer layers in the sleeping bag and pushed them to the foot. She caught him watching her and said, "Fieldwork trick. They won't get wet if they touch the sides of the tent and they'll be warm when I pull them on when we dress again."

He nodded. "Plus they're easy to grab in a hurry."

She burrowed into the sleeping bag as he finished undressing. He copied her actions and rolled up his combat uniform. When he reached to put it in the bag, she took it from him and pushed it to the bottom with her clothes.

Stripped down to his Under Armour, he slid into the double sleeping bag beside her. They were side by side in the small tent, only a dim red light providing relief from unrelenting darkness as rain pattered on the moss and leaves that covered the rainfly.

Bodies at rest at last. He switched off the light.

"I—I need to eat," she said. "The crackers and cheese I grabbed from the Baldwins should do it."

Guilt stabbed him. He should have thought of that. They'd been hiking in the cold rain for hours. Not to mention that fear drained energy fast. She needed fuel.

He snapped the light back on and reached for his pack, then pulled out the requested items. He handed her a sleeve of crackers, then plucked his knife from its sheath and cut into the brick of cheese, splitting the plastic and slicing a one-inch chunk in one stroke. He handed her the slice before cutting a piece for himself.

She ate several saltines in a hurry before taking a bite of cheese, eating as if cheddar were an antidote to a poison she'd just ingested. Catching his gaze, she wiped cracker crumbs from her lips, then covered her mouth with a hand and spoke as she chewed. "I hope you aren't the kind of guy to kick a girl out of bed for eating crackers."

He gave a half-hearted laugh. "If I ever was that guy, then it's not who I am now."

"So I can have cookies too?"

"You can have all the crumbly things you want as long as you're in my bed." The words were out of his mouth before he thought about what he was saying.

"You sure about that, Frogman?"

He deserved the bitter tinge to her tone. He cut off

another slice of cheese and offered it to her. "Yes." Might as well go full honest. "I will always want you in my bed."

She ignored his response and ate the cheese along with more crackers, then reached into the food supplies and grabbed a salami log. She peeled back the plastic wrapping and bit into it instead of waiting for him to slice it. When she was done, she let out a soft sigh as if eating had been a relief. She offered him the salami. "Want some?"

He took it from her and took a bite from the end as she had. He'd needed a protein hit too.

She took a long drink from her water bottle, then said, "Did you ever...consider...what it would do to me? The pain your actions would trigger?"

He cleared his suddenly dry throat and wished he'd taken a sip of water when he had the chance. "Yes. Every step of the way."

"But you did it anyway."

Nothing but honesty. "I did it anyway."

She shifted, putting space between them. He wanted to put his arms around her, hold her close and keep her warm, but he had no right.

"I can't tell you why I did it. I wish I could. I don't know if you'd understand, but at least it might make sense. What I did was unforgivable, and for that reason, I'll never ask for your forgiveness, but I hope someday you'll understand that it was never about you. Never about us. Never about that night."

"But you made it about that night."

"I had to. But I want you to know the night we shared was nothing short of incredible. *You* are incredible. If my job hadn't been paramount, I never would have tainted the memory of our night by lying."

"So you admit you lied?"

"Yes. I said as much before, and when we get out of here,

I will tell your boss, ACHP, and everyone who matters to you that I lied. I will own what I did, even though I can't say why."

"And I'm just supposed to believe that you'll do that. You. The one with the history of lying."

He shrugged. "It doesn't matter if you believe me, but it's what I'm going to do."

"And if you did, what will that mean for you?"

"Not sure. I'll be out of the military. On the extreme end, potentially a dishonorable discharge. Although higher-ups supported the tactic and probably guessed I was lying, so I don't think it would go that far—unless you pushed for it."

She raised a brow. "That's some power you're putting in my hands. Dishonorable discharge would destroy your whole world."

"I deserve to be dishonored. I acted dishonorably. I'm horrified by what I did to you. And it shouldn't have taken this extreme situation for me to get to this point, to see the wrong of it. Even worse, I did it for this"—he waved to indicate the thin sheet of fabric that protected them from a relentless rainstorm—"complete nightmare of a training that has endangered you, my training team, and a platoon of SEALs."

"I don't know about the rest of it, but I don't think you can take the blame for what's happening here. There was no way to predict any of this. For all we know, Jeb was in cahoots with the Russians."

He started at her words. "Wait, I know why *I* suspect they're Russian, but what makes you think so?" He suddenly realized they hadn't debriefed about what happened when she was alone in the cabin so many hours ago. All he knew was there were two men, one blocking each door.

She cleared her throat. "The men who came after me in

the cabin spoke Russian. At least, I'm pretty sure it was Russian."

"Any chance you caught some words? Even if you don't know what they mean, do you remember what they said?" He spoke some Russian. Maybe she heard something that would crack this wide open.

She shook her head. "I have no idea what they said when they were speaking Russian, but I did understand what they said in English."

"They spoke directly to you?" If they knew she was in the woodbin, why didn't they grab her?

"No. But one of the men can read and speak English, and I think the other man understood him."

He jolted. "What? How do you know that?"

She met his gaze in the dim light. "One of them found a letter." She paused, then added, "He read it aloud."

"A letter? What letter?" What was she talking about?

"I wrote…*you*…a letter. In case something happened to me."

"You wrote me a letter." He shouldn't be surprised. Seeing him again and then having the world go topsy-turvy in a lethal way was bound to trigger a need to vent. He deserved every nasty word she'd put to paper. "I hope…I hope it helped you process things."

"What?"

"I deserve all your anger."

"I wasn't venting in the letter, if that's what you mean."

"Then what was it?"

Audrey's hand covered his, and she threaded their fingers together, then she lifted her thermal top and pressed his palm to her belly. She moved closer, twisting to hold his gaze as she pressed his hand against her firm stomach. "Before you came to my office last month…I tried to reach you. The day before. Did you get the message from Jae?"

"Yeah. Someone from the Navy's regulatory branch tipped you off. You knew what was about to happen."

"No. I was *happy* to see you. Remember?"

"That was a front for your boss—"

She pressed a finger to his lips, even as her other hand remained entwined with his. "Shh. I mentioned earlier that if you can't talk about what you did, then you need to listen. We've reached that point in this endless night—or rather, early morning."

They'd entered nautical twilight. Outside, the sky would have lightened ever so slightly since he'd first climbed into the tent. A new day would dawn in just over an hour.

He held her gaze as he considered her words. "You have something to tell me."

"Yes."

She moved his hand, running his palm over her warm belly.

His throat constricted, and his own stomach seized.

All at once, he remembered her sudden nausea in the Baldwin cabin. And the way she'd desperately gobbled crackers and cheese a moment ago. He recognized the symptoms. His sister-in-law had been like that.

He knew what Audrey was about to tell him a heartbeat before the words left her mouth. He would have said it with her, but he'd promised to listen.

"That day, at the office, I was excited to see you, because it meant I could tell you in person that if all goes well, in late July or early August, you'll be a father."

His breath thickened in his already constricted esophagus as he tried to take in air and expel it at the same time. Emotion flooded him—horror and joy in equal measure.

Horror at what he'd done to her. She'd reached out to him to tell him she was pregnant with his child, and he'd assumed she'd been tipped off to the coming storm.

But it was the joy that sent the sting of tears to his eyes. And now he remembered the joy he'd seen on her face that morning a month ago. He could see it even now in spite of this terrifying situation. In spite of what he'd done.

He removed his hand from her belly and pulled her to his chest, holding her tight as unstoppable tears spilled down his cheeks.

He was trained to keep his emotional reactions in check. He was a stone-cold operator. But this news robbed him of his training. This night destroyed all his barriers.

Audrey is pregnant.

The nightmare he'd put her through for the last month ran though his mind. All this time, she'd been carrying his child.

"Oh, Audrey. I'm so sorry. I was sorry before, but…" He buried his face in her neck. Words to convey his absolute regret and remorse didn't exist. He would have to create a new language just for sorrow.

"We'll sort that out later," she whispered. "We'll sort everything later. You don't need to decide right now if you want a role in this baby's life. I just wanted you to know. I've been trying to figure out how to tell you for the last month."

"I don't need time to decide anything." He leaned back and pressed his hand to her belly again. There was a slight bump, her body roughly the same shape as she'd had the night they'd slept together, but where she'd been soft before, now her abdomen was firm.

My baby. Our baby.

"I'm in a hundred percent." Now all he could do was hope she had it in her to let him share actively in the parenting, because if she didn't, he wouldn't fight her. After what he'd done, he'd understand if she drew the line at tolerating him in their baby's life, but that was all.

The fun occasional uncle figure. Not really a dad. And he couldn't blame her.

Did she hate him? He wouldn't blame her for that either.

Tears burned again, and again he pulled her close. He'd wondered many times if he'd thrown away something special when he'd torched her reputation and career.

Now he knew the awful truth: he'd destroyed his family, before he even had one.

Chapter Seventeen

𝒫aul jolted awake at the sound of stomping boots. There was a rumbling noise in the hall outside the ballroom. A moment later, the door burst open. He squinted in the darkness to see who was entering. He found it hard to focus and wanted to rub his eyes, bleary with sleep and pain, but his bound hands prevented it.

All he could do was wait to make sense of what he was seeing as the mercs pulled something into the room. A moment passed before it did.

Four-wheeled garden cart. But there weren't garden tools in the green-sided metal wagon.

No.

Motherfucker.

No.

A SEAL.

The cart came closer, and even in the dark room, Paul could see the blood. The wound on the left shoulder, at the edge of the SEAL's body armor.

The merc pulling the cart stopped in the middle of the

floor. He lifted one side of the cart and dumped the body unceremoniously to the floor.

The SEAL groaned.

He's alive.

Across the room, the other trainers stirred. All four were alive, and now, at last, awake and no longer willing to hide that fact.

Smith, a medically trained Special Operator—SO—let out a curse and turned to the mercenary commander who'd followed the man with the cart into the room. "I'm a medic. Let me treat him."

The commander was silent. Would he ignore the request?

Finally, the masked man said, "You make a move to try to escape, and we'll slit the throats of every one of your bound comrades."

"I just want to stop the bleeding. Give him a chance."

The commander gave a sharp nod. "You may bandage him."

"I need my first aid kit," Smith said, nodding to the packs that were piled by the ballroom's cold fireplace.

The merc looked to his commander, who nodded.

No one was doing anything without express permission from the boss. Paul figured they were afraid of the guy, given the looks they gave his back.

With permission, the minion grabbed the large first aid kit and set it by the SEAL, then he released SO3 Smith from his handcuffs. "I need an assistant."

"No. Just you," the masked merc said.

Smith set to work, talking to his patient, who he identified as Collins. If Paul remembered correctly, the guy was a PO3—Petty Officer Third Class—and relatively new to the teams.

Smith tried to ask the barely conscious man questions—

whispering as he removed the petty officer's body armor and combat uniform to reveal a gaping wound just above and to the left of his heart.

The sound of a fist slamming on a table drew everyone's attention to the merc commander. "You work in silence, or you do not get to bandage him at all."

There went any hope of getting information from the SEAL about what was happening in the forest. Not that the man was capable of answering questions, but it had been worth a try on Smith's part.

Smith prepared a shot under the watchful gaze of the minion holding a gun on him. "It's so he can sleep." He administered the shot, and the minion took the needle and vial.

Collins's moans stopped as he slipped into a painless sleep, and Smith cleaned the wound, probing for bullet fragments.

Paul wondered if Smith had managed to pocket a syringe and drugs when the merc's attention had been on his volatile boss.

X avier's words, combined with his body pressed to hers as he held Audrey tight, triggered a flood of emotions. Tears rolled down her cheeks as she sank into his warmth. This was the warmest she'd been since he'd handcuffed her outside the lodge a lifetime ago.

Joy, fear, heartache, and even love swamped her as she breathed in his scent and absorbed his body heat.

She told herself the love she felt was for the baby. And the tears were from relief that they got to have this moment after the long, awful night. She cried because he hadn't hesitated to claim their baby.

Her child would have a father.

That's all this feeling was.

She slipped her hand between their bodies and stroked her abdomen.

Your daddy wants you, baby. He's going to love you just as much as I do.

She leaned back to meet his gaze again and saw matching tears on his cheeks.

It helped to realize he was as overwhelmed as she was.

He pressed his lips to hers, a soft, warm kiss that asked nothing. "I will be there for you and the baby every step of the way, if you'll let me."

She cleared her throat. "I want you there for the baby, absolutely. For me…I don't know. We'll have to take that one step at a time."

He nodded. "That's fair. I fucked up. You don't trust me, with good reason." He cupped her face between his warm palms. "When we said goodbye in November, I didn't want to leave like I did. My plan was to keep my distance until after the training was approved. Once that was behind us, I'd planned to ask you on a proper date. I wanted to wine and dine you and see if what I thought was between us was real."

"You were awfully cold with your abrupt dismissal when we said goodbye."

It had been the first sign something wasn't perfect. It had stung. A lot. More than she'd cared to admit at the time, actually. Later, she'd told herself that was who Xavier Rivera really was, and the man she'd had sex with had been nothing more than a pickup artist looking for another conquest.

She pushed away. She needed distance while she processed his words. She needed to figure out what was real. Was she merely seeing what she desperately wanted to see because she wanted to like the father of her child? Or was he the sincerely apologetic and intensely appealing man who'd protected her since this nightmare began?

Who is Xavier Rivera?

"Please, can I hold you? You're still cold, and I...I need to give you comfort after giving you so much pain."

"You're hoping to hug your way into forgiveness."

"If I thought that was possible, sure, but no. What I did was unforgivable. I've said that already. I'll never seek your forgiveness because I don't deserve it. I just...you could have died tonight, and that—along with every other awful thing you've had to deal with—was my fault. Please, will you let me hold you as I absorb the fact that the woman who bowled me over the night we met is going to be the mother of my child?"

She relaxed against him. "Well, when you put it that way..."

He let out a small laugh. "It was hands down the best sex I've ever had."

"Same," she admitted. "And potent too, apparently."

He let out a bark of laughter. "How did that happen? As far as I know, none of the condoms broke, and I was careful when I wasn't wrapped."

"The condom box in my kit expired more than two years ago. Apparently, those expiration dates matter."

"Don't condoms have a shelf life of like...five years?"

"Yes. I didn't realize how long it had been since I switched them out. I was in a long-term/long-distance relationship that ended a year ago, and I was on the pill the entire time we were together. I'd bought the condoms and tucked them in my emergency overnight field kit before my ex and I were a couple. I don't cheat, so they went unused. After the breakup, I stopped taking the pill and bought a new box, but I forgot to swap them out with the ones in my overnight field kit I always keep in my car. It wasn't exactly at the forefront of my mind since I don't fool around with subordinates in the field and don't go out to meet people much."

She let out a heavy sigh. "I want you to know I…I didn't plan this. We tried to prevent it. You had no way of knowing the condoms were suspect. That was *my* mistake. You offered to go to the store in the lobby, but I was too eager and vetoed that option with bad condoms. We made this fig together—"

"Fig?"

"In week eleven, the fetus is about the size of a fig. Anyway, it takes two, of course, but I was the one with the expired condoms and I'm the one who wants this baby with my whole heart."

She tilted her head down and studied his camouflage shirt, unable to meet his gaze as she said the important part. "You didn't ask for this, and I don't want my baby to have an indifferent father. I'm not going to force this on you."

A finger under her chin gently nudged her gaze upward until she had no choice but to look into his handsome brown eyes in the dim red glow. "I already said I'm in, and I meant it. We made this baby together. I will love our little fig with all my heart."

And me, Xavier? Will you be able to love me, or will I just represent shame and regrets?

The thought surprised her, but then, she'd given up on the fantasy of falling in love with her baby's father when he tried to destroy her career. The idea that a relationship with him could be back on the table was…not something she'd ever expected to wrap her brain around.

But then…this wasn't a brain thing. It was a heart thing.

She had to remember that when it came to Chief Warrant Officer Xavier Rivera, she needed to let her brain take the reins and leave her heart out of it.

Fig was going to have a dad. That's what mattered. "I'm

just glad we're talking, and you know I'm pregnant. That we're both going to love our little fig means more than I can say. Yesterday, I didn't know if that would ever be possible."

"Thank you for giving me a chance."

She placed her hand over his again, which had returned to her belly. "Thank you for knocking me up."

He let out a sharp laugh. "I think it's appropriate to say it was *literally* my pleasure."

She smiled. "And mine."

X avier held Audrey, spooning against him for warmth, as she dropped into sleep. He guessed it was the exhaustion of hiking and cold and pregnancy that allowed her to slip into sleep at all, given the situation. For his part, he'd been trained to sleep when needed on an op, and only waited for her to drop off before he gave in.

He knew little about pregnancy, but his sister-in-law had said it was draining, especially in the first trimester as the body adjusted to the work of growing another human. Add to that the terrifying day and near hypothermia she'd faced multiple times, and he'd had a small internal panic that the combination could trigger a miscarriage. But she was fine now, sleeping softly in his arms, warm and perfect.

It didn't seem possible to feel this deep and intense need to get her out of here. He'd never guessed his feelings could be so...boundless. It was like trying to grasp the expanding universe. Just when he thought he'd reached the end of his ability to feel, his mind—or heart—expanded.

Was this love?

It certainly was nothing like what he'd thought he felt for Lynn. But then, she'd made it clear when she dumped him at his darkest hour that it had only been attraction and affection on her part, nothing so powerful as love.

If this was love, was it love for the child that would one day be his? Or the woman who carried it?

Both, probably.

And he didn't think his feelings for Audrey were only because she was pregnant. No. He'd been feeling feral about her safety from the moment she'd been attacked on the ledge.

It was his fault she was in danger.

His fault they were being hunted and she'd been forced to burn energy until she had to inhale crackers and cheese.

He wouldn't fail her again. Not in these woods and not when they were back in the real world with a child to raise.

But first, he had to protect her and get her to safety.

Or die trying.

Chapter Eighteen

$\mathcal{U}$ ndine pressed the doorbell button for the second time. Maybe Audrey didn't hear the first one. After another long interval, she pulled out her phone to check the time and see if Audrey had messaged her with a change in plans.

No message. They'd agreed Undine would pick her up at eight a.m. sharp. She should be here.

Maybe she forgot?

But that wasn't likely. Audrey had texted yesterday to ask if they could meet for breakfast instead of lunch because her work had been interrupted yesterday and she had to return to Forks today to finish. Undine suspected Audrey would work well into the night if needed. After nearly losing her job a month ago, she was putting in long hours to prove to park management her dedication to the park.

Every time Undine thought about what Chief Warrant Officer Xavier Rivera had done to Audrey, she wanted to hurt the man.

Audrey wouldn't talk about him, and it was obvious she was devastated—not just by the fallout from work, but because she'd really liked the guy. She'd confessed as much in early November.

Undine had hoped to get her friend to talk over omelets and hash browns. It wasn't good to bottle up the pain. Her husband, Luke, had suggested Undine take Audrey out for a meal to try to get her to open up. He knew from experience how gutting it was to have a lover's betrayal destroy a career. That the lover who betrayed him had been Undine didn't change how much it had hurt at the time.

So here she was for her friendtervention, but Audrey wasn't here.

It didn't make sense.

She texted Audrey again, letting her know she was on her doorstep.

No response. Not even a read receipt, which Audrey's phone always sent.

She hit the Call button as she spotted a US park ranger law enforcement vehicle turning onto Audrey's street. Relief fluttered through her, and she tucked the phone away. Audrey was probably getting a ride home from a coworker.

She smiled, thinking maybe Audrey had a date that had extended into the morning. Had she and Jae finally hooked up?

Good for Audrey. She needed some fun after that prick Xavier.

Sure enough, it was Jae in the driver's seat, but she frowned when she realized the passenger seat was empty.

Jae looked weary as he exited the vehicle. His uniform was rumpled. "Hey, Undine. Good to see you." He leaned down and kissed her cheek. "You going somewhere with Audrey? I'd like to chat with her before you take off. It'll only take a minute."

Her heart sank. "I was hoping she was with you."

"She's not here?"

"No. I was supposed to pick her up for a breakfast date"—she checked her watch again—"fifteen minutes ago, but she's not answering her door. This isn't like her."

Jae frowned. "Agreed."

"Why are you here this morning? You look like you're just coming off a long shift."

He nodded. "I am. It went several hours over—multiple mudslides on roads near Forks." He ran a hand over his tired face. "Before the slides, I was supposed to meet her by the Lake Olympus Road gate. There were issues with the cameras monitoring the village site." He paused then added "I presume you know about that?"

She nodded. She'd have helped Audrey bury the cable if she wasn't busy with her own job.

"I was held up by some campers at Mora, and by the time I got to the gate, she wasn't there. I couldn't get ahold of her. I left a message for her with the dispatcher to call me when she got home. I was going to check on her last night... but then the mudslides happened. I called her as soon as I remembered this morning, but went straight to voicemail. Thought I'd swing by."

Fear squeezed Undine's heart. "Do you think she was on the lodge road during the storm?" It was a lousy, narrow road to begin with. Add icy rain and...well, there was a reason the lodge was closed this time of year.

Jae shook his head. "She shouldn't have been. The storm didn't start until at least an hour after she would've entered the park. Plus, the gate was locked—even my key didn't work." He cleared his throat. "That part of the park is closed right now—for everyone, including park employees."

All at once, what Jae was *not* saying became clear. "Oh, shit. There's a SEAL training going on. Xavier Rivera is at the lodge."

Jae gave the most imperceptible of nods.

"You think…she went there to confront him? And now she's missing?"

"Oh, god, no. Not like that. No. I would trust Xavier with my life."

Undine snorted at that. Jae had a history with the man, but Undine didn't know him, and he'd screwed over Audrey in the worst way. There was no way she'd believe he wasn't the villain in this scenario.

"Yeah, well, I don't believe Audrey would be so foolish as to confront him during a training exercise."

"I don't believe that either. I checked with the office. The issue with the cameras is real. But also, all communication —*all* the security cameras in that part of the park—are now down. I assume that's part of the exercise. Can't have anyone watching a secret training. And maybe Audrey's camera fail was part of that too. It could be nothing. But I'm worried because as far as I know, the last anyone heard from Audrey was yesterday around four p.m., before she entered the park —*if* she was able to get past the gate. At first, I was worried she'd be fired for interrupting the training, but now…" His voice trailed off as he gazed at the front of Audrey's small house. "If she's not here, I think she's missing."

"Surely there's some way to get in touch with Rivera?"

"I've tried every number I have. Email. Texts. Nothing."

Undine pulled out her phone. "My husband still has contacts in the SEALs and Navy spec war." She punched the button for Luke. "Maybe he can find out how to get a message to Xavier."

When Luke answered, she said, "Sweetheart, I'm handing the phone to Ranger Jae Son. There's something going on with Audrey, and I'm hoping you can help us."

꙳

*E*xhaustion won and Audrey had fallen into a deep sleep almost instantly. The hard part was staying asleep after that first blissful hour of rest. It remained dark in the tent when she surfaced, but she knew it was daylight outside. Their tent was well and truly buried. With Xavier pressed to her back, she was enveloped in a warm, dark cocoon.

His breathing was deep and even, and she forced her body to remain calm and still. She didn't want to disturb his slumber. If they were going to survive this, he was the one who needed sleep.

His skills, his team—those two things were her only hope of walking out of this forest alive. He'd never said a word about his shoulder, but she knew he was in a great deal of pain. He'd been injured again after he left her, when he'd fought whoever he'd gotten the NVGs and rifle from, but after she told him about the baby, they hadn't spoken more about what had happened in the woods last night.

It was probably a mistake, but part of her was glad they'd gotten to share that moment without the nightmare intruding.

He wanted and would love their child. She would hold on to those thoughts in the coming desperate hours. And she had zero doubt this day would be as desperate as the last. But the father of her child had her back—he was literally pressed against that part now as he slept—and would protect them. She would do her part to help. No one knew this part of the park better than her. Well, except George.

She'd spent months in these woods over multiple years, but George had spent *years* over multiple decades.

George.

He'd been in Jeb's shop last night, making bombs. Which

meant he knew what happened to Jeb. Knew there were enemies in the forest.

He'd prepared to engage them, resurrecting the guerilla fighting skills he'd learned fifty years ago.

George was an ally, but if the SEALs found him before she and Xavier did, would they know he was friend, not foe?

Chapter Nineteen

$\mathscr{D}$uring daylight hours, the platoon took turns sleeping in shifts. Chris wished he could be searching the forest for the missing Fire Team, but they all knew that the four men would be hunkered down during daylight as well. A search would be risky and likely yield nothing.

Still, concern for the missing team members gnawed at him.

As he lay inside a thermal blanket covered with moss and ferns with rain pattering his makeshift shelter, he went over again in his mind the size and shape of the body he'd witnessed being dumped over the side of the fishing boat. The person had been thick, with broad shoulders. Broad enough to be MCPO Mueller? Mueller was stocky. Thickly muscled.

Chris didn't think it had been the master chief petty officer, but the boat had been too far away for him to be certain.

He and Huang had returned to the rendezvous point with tools and several gallons of gas. They were facing the prospect of attacking the lodge armed with Molotov cocktails and Simunition tipped with nails.

It was a ridiculous plan considering the lodge grounds were too wet for anything to burn and the tangos had guns that could fire .45 caliber rounds, but they couldn't let this standoff last another twenty-four hours. One local was dead. Six trainers and four SEALs were unaccounted for. Plus, the park archaeologist could also be missing. They were potentially dealing with eleven hostages and an unknown number of tangos.

They'd debated sending two men to hike out, but they were stretched thin as it was with the need to maintain a presence at the rendezvous point, search for the missing team, and scout the lodge grounds for intel. Not to mention that they'd never gone over the maps outside the lodge area to determine best possible escape routes because this was meant to be a fricking *training exercise* and not the real deal, and without satellite connectivity for their GPS units they didn't have maps of anything except the lodge basin, so they'd be sending two men on a twenty-mile hike—at minimum—in a storm-drenched wilderness with no clue how to navigate.

As an alternative, they'd spent hours this morning poring over the maps they did have, trying to guess where the signal blocker had been placed. They'd managed to narrow the options down to a half dozen based on terrain and road access—the signal blocker would almost certainly be a vehicle of some sort—and would send a team at dusk to check out the most promising locations.

If they could contact NSWC, they could end this nightmare and rescue the hostages before more people died.

Chris just had to hope it wasn't already too late.

*R*ain drizzled down in icy fits, prompting Undine and Jae to agree to go to her house to hear the results of Luke's phone calls to NSWC. It was a short drive up the hill on the western edge of town to the newly built four-bedroom house on acreage that had a sweeping view of the Strait of Juan de Fuca. On a clear day, she could see Vancouver Island from her living room window.

The house was hers and Luke's dream home, and she still had trouble believing she was living out her every fantasy with a man she loved more than she'd ever dreamed possible.

Her dog, a sweet black-and-white mutt of unknown heritage, came rushing out to greet her, while their orange tabby cat watched from the window.

"Neah, you remember Jae, don't you?" she asked as she petted the dog. Neah turned to Jae on cue. Such a smart girl.

The only thing missing from her idyllic fantasy was a baby, something she and Luke had both wanted from the moment they got engaged. And just this week, her obstetrician had confirmed what the home pregnancy test had told her two weeks ago—she was officially nine weeks pregnant. Their first child was due in August.

She'd planned to share this news with Audrey at breakfast, and now her belly clenched at the thought that her friend was missing.

Surely, if she'd gone to the lodge, she was safe. Maybe she'd just gotten caught up in the storm and the road had washed out? Or maybe a tree blocked the way? Audrey could right now be sheltering in the lodge, unable to make calls because the phone line had been wiped out by the storm.

After all, phone and electrical lines to that old park complex weren't buried. Every year, the cost of burying utility lines was slipped into the park budget, and every year, it was skipped over in favor of improving cellular service and satellite upgrades.

But satellites failed in the worst of weather, which Lake Olympus had in spades in the winter, and the same storm could take out a cell tower as easily as a telephone line. She and Luke had been stranded by such a storm a few years ago in Neah Bay. But in their case, the lack of contact with the outside world had been glorious.

If Chief Warrant Officer Xavier Rivera wasn't such a prick—and in the middle of a job—she'd wish that luck for her friend, but as it was, she hoped to hell Audrey hadn't come across the SEAL in her foray into the park.

She and Jae entered the house with Neah following them, her claws clicking on the hardwood floor. She led the park ranger into the study, where Luke was on the phone.

She met his gaze for a signal that they should give him privacy, but he waved them into the room. Gone was the special smile he'd had just for her ever since they learned she was pregnant. His eyes were now filled with concern.

"Thank you, Captain. I will." He hung up the phone, then his gaze flicked from her to Jae. "Captain Barrett is going to go up the line to get authorization to share more information with me if he can. Everything about this training is highest level Top Secret." His gaze met Jae's. "You might have better luck. I understand Rivera had permission to share details with you from the beginning."

Jae frowned. "Only the barest details, but yes, I knew about the planned exercise before anyone else affiliated with the park was notified, simply because I helped Xavier scout the location."

"Barrett confirmed the training is happening now—which, of course, you knew already."

Jae nodded.

"He also said everything was normal on NSWC's end. I

don't know if that means they're in communication with the trainers and SEALs or not, but it doesn't sound like they've received notice that anyone interrupted the exercise."

"Is there any chance Xavier would hold back that information from his superiors?" Undine asked.

Jae shrugged. "I don't know. He's a straight arrow—but we all know he behaved strangely when it came to Audrey a month ago. It's possible he could withhold the information to protect her, if it wasn't relevant to the success of the training."

"Do you think he would contact you in that situation?"

"I'd like to think so, but if all comms are down for the exercise, perhaps he wasn't able to."

The whole situation made Undine uneasy. It didn't feel right. She wrapped her arms around herself as if to ward off the chill. Luke stepped to her side and draped an arm around her shoulders, then pressed his lips to her temple.

He didn't offer false words of comfort, and she appreciated that. Right now, there was little they could do and they knew even less.

To Jae, he said, "We'll go through channels right now, but if we don't hear from Audrey by four p.m., I want to go with you into the park to search for her."

Jae gave a sharp nod. "I hate waiting that long, but I also don't want to overreact, and this could be nothing. There's also the issue that the gate lock was changed. My master key doesn't work."

Luke frowned. "Then how did Audrey get into the park?"

Jae shrugged. "My best guess is she entered before the lock was changed. Maybe both the park gate and the inholding gate weren't changed until the last minute. But the problem there is—the Navy wasn't authorized to change the park gate's lock."

"Have you asked the park superintendent about that?"

"I left a voicemail for Jim this morning. I didn't tell him about Audrey, though—he stood by her after Xavier's allegations, but if he thinks she went into the park to disrupt the training, she could be fired."

Luke swore. "Glad I didn't use her name in my conversation with Captain Barrett, but it's bound to come out—sooner rather than later—that we're looking for Audrey and not some other random park employee."

Jae nodded. "I'll talk to Jim face-to-face and give him the full context when I ask for the gate key. There's no way the Navy could change the lock without giving the superintendent a key."

"Is it possible, do you think, that Audrey got stuck on the wrong side of the gate after the lock was changed? Maybe she had to return to the lodge because she couldn't get out?"

"I've considered it," Jae said. "But in that situation, she would have called from the gate. Cell service works fine there, and she could have called Jim to ask to be let out."

"Not if she was afraid of being fired," Undine said.

"Yeah, but I'm pretty sure she would have called me. I have pull with Xavier and a good working relationship with Jim. And she had the excuse of the broken cameras. I want this to be simple, but the more I analyze it, the more worried I get."

"Right now, it sounds like our best hope is she's safe in the lodge with Xavier, and he's protecting her with silence," Undine said.

It was strange to hope Audrey was with Xavier, but Undine had to consider that maybe, just maybe, Xavier Rivera wasn't a complete prick. It was possible he'd gone silent because he was protecting Audrey from getting fired.

Chapter Twenty

𝑎 udrey slept until early afternoon. That she slept at all was a testament to how exhausted she'd been, and that she'd managed to sleep for so many hours had to be because the fig she carried had drained her batteries to the bottom.

She woke with a jolt, completely ravenous, the same fig demanding food. Dim gray light penetrated the moss and leaf covering, enough to see Xavier's handsome face as he lay with eyes open, staring at the netting that hung from the apex of the half-dome tent.

He shifted to face her, and his mouth curved in a soft smile.

"I can't believe I slept so hard." Her sleep had been fitful for the first hour or two, but at some point, her brain must've released the fear, knowing that Xavier was by her side and would protect her. Strangely, the hours she'd slept in the early afternoon had been the deepest sleep she'd gotten since she'd learned she was pregnant. "And now, if I don't eat something in the next thirty seconds, I think I might implode."

His smile deepened as he handed her the sleeve of crackers. "Get started on that while I slice cheese. Want some canned chicken too?"

"Yes, please," she said as she rammed a saltine in her mouth. "I want it all."

He handed her a fork and the canned chicken.

She pulled the ring on the top and dove in, placing chunks of chicken on a cracker and taking a bite. She added a cheese layer when he handed her a stack of slices. Her stomach didn't settle until she'd inhaled her fifth fully topped cracker.

"Better?" he asked.

She nodded. "I was dizzy with hunger. That's new for me. Pregnancy is full of delights."

"Your blood sugar was probably desperately low. Your eating and sleep schedules are off-kilter, and your body doesn't know what to do."

She took a bite of cheese, this time chewing slowly as she felt her equilibrium return. "Thank goodness we got food from the Baldwins'. I have a few protein bars, but those won't last long."

"We should have enough for another day, but we can search more cabins tonight for supplies if need be."

"How did you plan to feed the team this week? Is there food in the lodge?"

"In the yurt and the lodge, although each team member also carries enough for days."

Xavier opened a can of tuna and ate it straight from the container. She offered him the crackers and her remaining slices of cheese.

"No. Those are for you. You need it more than I do. I'm content with plain tuna."

She wanted to argue, but she had no way of knowing what her body was going to demand in the coming hours.

She ate just enough to settle her stomach, then tucked the remainder away where she could reach it in a hurry. Yesterday she'd had two full meals in her belly before the nightmare began, and adrenaline had carried her the rest of the way. Today would be a different story.

Xavier set up the Sierra stove under the flap at the front of the tent and boiled water, making tea for her and coffee for himself.

They sipped their warm beverages while sitting cocooned in the sleeping bag. The moment was surreal. She loved camping. It had been one of the things she and her ex had enjoyed doing together, and being all alone in the wilderness, snuggled up as raindrops pattered the tent, had been her favorite way to while away the time. They'd read, make love, talk about the future.

Those were some of her favorite relationship memories. Now, here she was with a new man—one who also enjoyed camping, she knew—and they were alone in the wilderness, living what would be an idyllic romantic moment, except they weren't here by choice and were hiding out because they were being hunted.

Still, the moment had an odd comfort. He knew her secret now, and his betrayal didn't cut as deep as it had yesterday.

It still cut, but she was starting to see a path through that pain. Not to forgiveness, but maybe she could put it behind them. For the baby. But also…for herself.

Her attraction to him had gone dormant in December. Maybe it had burrowed down, hiding deep in her heart, and his actions since yesterday afternoon had allowed it to rise to the surface again.

All she knew was the kiss they'd shared last night had proven the attraction had returned…and as much as she cautioned herself not to trust him, a large part of her wanted to explore the feelings he triggered now.

She sipped her tea as she studied his shoulder. His Under Armour shirt was so tight, she could see the top edge of the raised scars on his left shoulder. She'd seen him wince several times in the long night as he moved his arm or adjusted his pack. "What happened last night, when you were alone?"

"A merc crossed my path. We fought, and I killed him."

His words were stark, but not without emotion. "You did what you had to do."

"Yes."

"And your arm? It was worse after that."

"My shoulder dislocated in the fight. I couldn't pop it back right away. Hurts like a bitch even now."

"I have some ibuprofen in my pack."

He gave her a half smile. "Of course you do."

"Want some?"

"Sure. Doubt it will cut into the pain, but might as well give it a try."

"You're used to hurting."

His nod was almost imperceptible. "Comes with the job."

"But not like this. You haven't been on an op since you were…shot, I presume?"

He nodded.

"Can you…talk about it?"

"I'm sorry. It's classified. An op gone wrong."

She dug out her pills and offered him the small pack. He took four and downed them with a swig of water. "Thanks."

"Were you…the only injury? On the op?"

He gave a sharp shake of his head.

"The other trainers—the ones who are missing—were any of them on that op too?"

"No. All five were SEALs too, but on different teams.

The only guy here who was on my team is—" He cut himself off.

She guessed he'd said more than he should. Or could.

"You know what? Fuck it. There's so much I can't tell you about my job, but that op is old news, and family members have the right to know some details."

She felt a small flutter at his words. They weren't a family yet, but if the pregnancy went smoothly, they would be at some point. Even if they weren't lovers in the future, they would be parents together.

He pulled her close to his side so they were hip to hip. They were leaning against their packs, giving them a slight backrest as they faced the door of the tent.

He raised his coffee to his lips with his injured arm while his other arm cradled her. "If anything happens to me… Someday, Fig is going to have questions. I want you to have answers. I don't want my child to not know who I was."

That fast, a tear spilled. Damn pregnancy hormones.

"There are limits on what I can share, but these are the basics. I was on a four-man Fire Team sent in to extract a hostage—the daughter of someone important in another country—who was being held in Belarus. She only had two guards, so it should have been a piece of cake."

His body tensed as he spoke. Other than the initial debriefing, she didn't imagine he'd spoken of this much. "Should have been…?"

"Yeah. But my team was betrayed."

She placed a hand on his thigh. "They knew you were coming."

"It was worse, actually. But I can't say more than that."

"I understand. So you were shot…"

"And two on my Fire Team were killed. Flyte, the fourth man, got us out of there. He saved my life."

"And the hostage?"

"She died."

"I'm so sorry." She couldn't imagine how it would feel to lose two men on his team and be injured himself, all for nothing. No rescued hostage. A completely failed mission.

She didn't doubt that he blamed himself for that failure. "You were betrayed."

He nodded. "It was a variable we hadn't considered. Never again."

She guessed at his underlying meaning. This training session had been designed to throw unexpected curveballs at the team. But then a bunch of armed mercenaries showed up, lobbing the ultimate curveball at Xavier and the SEALs.

He cleared his throat. "Lieutenant Flyte, the guy who saved my life in Belarus, is second-in-command of the platoon that's here now."

And that was what he'd been about to say before. His former teammate was here, not as a trainer, but as a SEAL. "Do you get along?"

"Chris is… I don't really have words that don't sound hokey. He did the impossible. Kept his head when the op went FUBAR. He's a hell of an operator and one of the greatest men I know. He can be pigheaded when he thinks he's right—which is always—and a total pain in the ass when he really *is* right. I owe him my life, and he ranks with Jae as one of my closest friends."

Again, she heard what he didn't say. Lieutenant Chris Flyte was in danger now, and again, Xavier blamed himself.

She did the only thing she could think of. She set down her mug, rose to her knees, then turned and straddled him. She took his mug from his hand and set it to the side, then wrapped her arms around his neck and hugged him. His arms slid around her waist and pulled her tight. She tucked her head down so their necks were skin to skin as their bodies fit together like a puzzle.

With her eyes closed, she held him, breathing deeply. And he held her back as rain softly pattered on their shelter.

The embrace was pure warmth and comfort. She was afraid, while he was hurting—physically and mentally. They were on a small life raft for this brief moment in time, hiding from the danger while it was too light out to emerge from their safe shelter.

They needed this nurturing break. A salve for open wounds so they could return to battle, not whole, but at least a little better off.

Eventually, she raised her head and cupped his face in her hands, the stubble of his beard a gentle abrasion on her palms. His eyes were damp as he said, "Thank you."

"We'll find a way to save them," she said.

"We will," he confirmed. "You're amazing, Audrey." His voice was husky and deep as he added, "I can't wait to take you to Hawaii so I can wine and dine you and try to convince you to give me another chance."

Truth was, she was pretty sure he wouldn't need to wine and dine her to get his second chance.

He ran a hand over her belly, then slid it around to her lower back. They both wore thermal underwear that went from wrist to neck, not revealing, but still skintight. The covering over his muscled body resembled a comic book hero's costume.

"I desperately want to kiss you right now," he said, "but I also don't want to ruin the moment. I know this was an embrace, not a come-on."

She smiled and lowered her head, brushing her lips softly over his. She lingered there, warm lips meeting sweetly. Her heart bloomed with a gentle heat.

This felt right.

She probed his lips with the tip of her tongue, and his

mouth opened. From that moment, he took over the kiss, transforming it from sweet warmth to spicy heat.

His hand cupped the back of her head, holding her mouth to his as he devoured her with his deep, stroking tongue.

Between her legs, she felt his erection thicken, and she rocked against him, generating a delicious friction that penetrated their layers of long underwear.

They kissed like that—rocking their pelvises together as his tongue caressed hers—for a long interval. Neither of them made a move to remove clothing or initiate an intimate touch. It was a burning-hot kiss, a temporary respite, and nothing more.

She felt his hand relax at the back of her skull by slow degrees as the intensity of the kiss lessened and the rocking of their hips subsided. She raised her head and met his gaze. His eyes were hot with desire, bringing back memories of their one delicious night together.

"I suppose it would be a bad idea for us to take this any further right now."

He nodded. "We can't take the risk of losing ourselves in the moment." He gave her a slow, sexy smile. "But you've given me something to hope for."

She brushed one last kiss over his lips before climbing off his lap. As she settled at his side again and picked up her mug of tea, she said, "You've given me something to hope for too."

*C*hris sat high in a tree with his binoculars trained on the dock in front of the lodge. He'd been watching the beach for the last hour, waiting for the rain and fog to lift and for the mercs to reveal themselves as twilight set in.

There'd been no discernible movement on the dock or beach all day, but now they were nearing dusk, and with the rainstorm finally abating and the clouds expected to clear, the waxing gibbous moon—they were just days away from full—meant the night would be too bright for covert maneuvers on the water.

If the mercs wanted to use their fishing boat to move people or supplies, they'd need to do it before the clouds dissipated.

The fog thickened again, and Chris lost sight of the dock. He kept the binoculars fixed and waited for the fog to thin, knowing the mercs could take advantage of this cover.

Minutes passed and finally, so did the low cloud. Where the dock met shoreline, the dark shape of a shrub next to one of the waist-high park interpretive signs emerged, but unlike the previous times he'd watched the fog dissipate, now he saw the shrub *move*.

Once again, he wished their damn radios worked. Without it, he'd have to climb down to tell his team what he saw.

The figure moved slowly, crouched low. For a moment, Chris had to wonder if it could be an animal—this was bear country—and he never got a clear view of the figure as it jetted off into the woods.

But it didn't head toward the lodge. No, it stayed to the shadows just beyond Chris's clear line of sight, an uncanny ability to never quite show itself.

If it had been bigger, he'd wonder if it was a sasquatch. This was the Pacific Northwest, after all.

In moments, the figure was gone.

Chris scanned the boat and dock again. Nothing looked out of place. Darkness crept in slowly, the white fog mists taking on shades of gray, each one a pixel darker than the last.

He waited until his replacement climbed the tree to relieve him, then passed on the binoculars after explaining what he'd seen.

Someone had been on the boat, and he was certain the person hadn't been an enemy tango.

Chapter Twenty-One

"Would you consider...staying here while I search for the team tonight?"

The look Audrey gave Xavier let him know *exactly* how much she loved that idea. Her words made it even clearer. "You've got to be fucking kidding."

"Did I sound funny?"

"You promised you wouldn't leave me alone again."

"That was before we had a safe place for you to hide."

"You mean it was before you knew I was pregnant."

He held her gaze in the rapidly fading light. Dusk was descending, and while they'd spent the last two hours making plans, now that it was time for them both to leave this haven, he couldn't bear the idea of her being at risk.

He'd endangered the lives of too many people already. If Audrey and their baby died in these woods, he didn't know how he could go on. "You'll be safe here."

"But what if I'm not? What if those bastards are out there, just waiting for you to leave me alone?"

Fuck. That was the one argument he couldn't counter.

"I'm not staying behind. Do you have any idea how terrifying it would be for me to wait out here for you to return? Even if we had cell service, it wouldn't work out here. I'd be stuck, waiting for you to return or for someone to kill me."

"I'd give you my radio. Once we get the signal blocker turned off, my team could radio you."

"I'm not staying here alone, Xavier. The fact that I'm pregnant changes nothing. I was pregnant yesterday too, and you weren't questioning my ability to handle myself in these woods."

"I didn't—"

"I know these woods better than you do. I'm healthy and strong. We've got food, and I have the right clothing. Plus, I'll be a hell of a lot safer with you than stranded out here alone. I would have been taken hostage or killed last night if you hadn't returned when you did. Don't pretend it's better for me to hide when we both know you're just afraid something will happen to me."

"Of course I'm afraid! I've never been so scared in my fucking life, and I'm not afraid for me. I'm afraid for Paul. For Chris. And for you and Fig. I'm terrified I've killed you all."

"This isn't your fault, Xavier."

"Oh, but it is. I planned this training from beginning to end. It was my brilliant idea to make sure the SEAL team wouldn't have direct communication with NSWC."

"But surely NSWC will expect to receive updates from your training team?"

"Only in the event of an emergency. Which of course, this is, but no one counted on the fact that we would lose our landlines and computers."

"But wouldn't NSWC know your computers are offline?"

He shrugged. "They might. And they might think it was part of the exercise—it fits with the mission scenario we're running."

"So at what point will NSWC start to worry that they haven't heard from you?"

"Could be as long as two…maybe three days?"

Even in the gray light, Xavier could see her face blanch. "Two or three days before they even start wondering if something is up?"

He nodded.

She placed her hand on her belly. "I think I might puke again."

He handed her a helmet to use as a basin.

She held it before her, taking deep breaths as she stared down at the cheap helmet with the broken clip that had saved his life a little less than twenty-four hours ago. After a long silence, she set it aside and met his gaze. "What would the Navy do if I were reported missing? Would they send someone into the park?"

"Is that likely?"

"I don't know…maybe? I was supposed to meet a friend for breakfast today before I was going to return to the Forks Ranger Station. And my colleagues in Forks were expecting me to return."

"But it's not your regular work site. So they might assume you're at park headquarters in Port Angeles."

"True. But also, last night, I was supposed to meet Jae at the gate. He might follow up. I never miss work without calling in."

"ONP has their own search and rescue, right?"

"Yeah. With assistance from the Coast Guard. They're more active in the summer when hikers go missing, but winter storms bring new dangers."

"The Navy might balk at sending in a team." Now it was his turn to feel like he was going to puke, but he had to say it. "And the reason is…they might not be concerned because the missing person is *you*, and they know you were opposed to the training. They might think—like I did last night—that you entered the park to disrupt the training. For revenge."

🌲

*H*is words made Audrey feel sick again, but she knew he was right. Her motives for entering the park would be suspect. Jae could raise all the alarms, and the Navy could refuse to allow a search party.

"If they won't come looking for me, then we should hike out. The storm is lighter now—"

"I can't leave my team, Audrey, and you shouldn't take on a hike like that by yourself. For starters, we don't have the right camping equipment—not backpacking gear. What we have is too heavy for one person."

He was right. She was an avid hiker, but she knew better than to hike alone, especially in winter conditions. One bad step, and a sprained ankle could be her death.

But if she wasn't alone, it would be worth the risk. "We need to find George."

"You want to hike out of here with a seventy-two-year-old as your backup?"

"He's been hiking these woods for seventy of those seventy-two years, so yeah. I do."

"And how do we find him?"

An idea stirred. "We don't. We let George find *me*."

Xavier's brow furrowed. "What makes you think George even knows you're here?"

"I left him a half dozen messages and told him I was coming. Plus, my SUV is parked right in front of his wood-shop. He knows my vehicle."

"He might not have listened to your messages. He might not have seen your SUV."

"But what if he did and has? He made pipe bombs in Jeb's garage last night. He knows what's going on—probably better than you do, because he might've witnessed them digging up the weapons cache. And if he knows I'm here, I think I know where he'll expect to find me."

She reached for her clothes from the bottom of the sleeping bag and pulled them on. It was time to pack up and get out of here. They had a long way to go if they were going to have a chance to meet up with George before the moon rose and lit up the forest like a football stadium.

"Where are we going? His cabin? I told you, it's too close to the storage pit. And the tango we ran into on the cliffside trail could be a sign they were looking for him or his cabin."

"No. Not his cabin." She grabbed the zippers of their joined sleeping bags and made quick work of separating them. "Let me tell you a story about a summer afternoon ritual I called 'teatime with George…'"

*P*aul was dizzy from loss of blood and lack of sleep, and his legs wobbled as he was led to the restroom for the third time in the last twenty-four hours. Each time he passed through the great room, it was an opportunity to gather intel. Count mercs.

He and his fellow trainers might have been gagged to prevent them from communicating after Smith tended Collins's gunshot wound, but they'd all been SEALs once upon a time, and they knew how to communicate without words. Between them, they'd determined the minimum number of living mercenaries was eleven.

The current number of living hostages was six. Collins was hanging on. Unconscious thanks to the drugs he'd been given, but breathing.

Now Paul walked across the lodge great room as if he were drunk. The gag chafed, but he paid it no mind. This restroom break was a reconnaissance mission, a chance to see out the front window toward the dock. One of the mercs had just been ordered to pick up more supplies now that the sun had set and the sky remained cloudy. The storm had ended, and the clouds were thinning. The moon would be bright tonight and the boat easy to spot.

Paul wanted to see which direction the boat headed. Maybe they could get a fix on where the mercs had staged their supplies. He didn't think they were storing their weapons here—which made sense if they expected an assault from an entire platoon at some point. They wouldn't want to lose their stockpile all in one blow.

The darkness of the lodge allowed him to see through the large picture window toward the lake. There was just enough shine from the moon to see the outline of the boat bounce on the water as two mercs stepped aboard.

He paused, and the merc who'd been assigned to ferry him to the bathroom jabbed him in the back.

Paul took advantage of the motion to pitch forward as if the guy had shoved him hard enough to make him lose his footing. It wasn't that far off given how cramped he felt after being bound to a chair for hours and only catching minutes of sleep at a time.

The man cursed in Russian and kicked at Paul to get up. He rolled and stumbled, drawing out the process as he watched the boat. If he could just delay long enough…

All at once, a massive blast rent the air, and the boat disappeared in a blinding flash of white and orange.

Satisfaction filled Paul as he adjusted his calculations.

Now there was a minimum of nine living mercenaries.

Chapter Twenty-Two

*X*avier led Audrey through the forest, moving as fast as he dared. She kept pace with him without complaint in spite of being burdened with an unbalanced pack due to not having proper hiking gear. With each rapid step, he was reminded how incredibly lucky he was to have this knowledgeable woman and experienced hiker at his side.

Without warning, a massive boom split the air. Beneath their feet, the earth quaked. Raindrops fell from shaking tree limbs.

They stood on a steep hillside, and he could see glimpses of the lake through gaps in the trees. He turned his NVGs toward the water as the sound echoed across the basin.

The forest went silent once the earth settled, as if the wildlife all held their breath, waiting to see what was next. Then a cacophony of bird chatter broke out, filling the woods with discordant sound.

"Holy shit," Audrey whispered, her words nearly lost in the distressed bird noise. "A pipe bomb did *that*?"

Pipe bombs could have massive explosive power, amplified by the point of detonation, but given their distance from the lodge, he guessed this had been something bigger.

His mind ran over the other items he'd seen on the workbench, remembering the small Dutch oven with the cracked lid. Had the lid broken when George attempted to drill a hole for the fuse cord?

There'd been Dutch ovens in various sizes stacked along one wall. If George was successful in drilling a hole in the lid of one and filled it with black powder—which Jeb had in abundance given all the empty bottles they'd spotted on the counter—it would make a sizeable bomb.

He shared this theory with Audrey. "So you agree with me that George is our bomb maker?"

He nodded. "I believed you before. The blast just confirmed it."

"Why don't you think it was the Russians?"

"They're all about stealth and silence. Most of their guns have suppressors. That blast was a beacon. Meant for the SEALs."

She smiled. "Let's go find George."

He dialed in his focus, becoming the operator he'd once been. Gone were thoughts of pending fatherhood. There was no room for that now. Not when they were in the forest and he had a team in danger and, finally, a path to victory.

He discarded his planned argument that he should be the one to meet George because the meet point she'd described was too close to the mercenary stronghold. Audrey knew George. And his SEAL team needed the Native American soldier's intel and weapons.

*C*hris stopped in his tracks as a massive blast shook the ground under his feet. When the world stopped quaking, he and his Fire Team picked up their pace to return to camp. He guessed the explosion was good news to offset their disappointing find in the forest. They'd found the signal-blocker van, and it had been destroyed, probably yesterday.

Something else in the forest was blocking all signals, and the device—or devices, he now suspected—could be anywhere.

Given that disquieting find, the explosion could be the boon they needed. The SEAL on lookout duty might be able to tell them where the blast had occurred.

Chris had a strong suspicion that the ghost in the mist had left a little something in the boat for the mercs. If so, then they had a friend. A very good friend. With firepower.

But how would they find this friend? Whoever the person was, they moved through the forest with ease, managing to avoid both a platoon of SEALs and, he figured, about a dozen mercenaries.

Undoubtedly, he or she was one of the inholding landowners, but who? Which cabin held the arsenal? He would very much like to visit that place. All they had right now were Molotov cocktails, and in this wet forest, those would be ineffective as assault weapons.

His team reached their hidden HQ. Three men guarded the perimeter while another climbed the tree to relieve the seaman who, hopefully, had witnessed the blast.

The lookout descended, a wide grin on his face. "The blast took out the boat and dock. It even took out a few trees close to the shore."

Chris nodded. "Must've been set by the ghost I caught a glimpse of."

"Two tangos down," the lookout added. "They were on the boat, turned the key, then boom."

"Tangos? You're sure there wasn't anyone else?" Everyone knew the question Chris wasn't asking: *No bodies to be disposed of?*

"Just tangos. Pretty sure it was the same two we spotted entering the lodge before dawn."

That was a relief. Even better, the enemy was down two mercs.

Now they just needed to figure out how to make contact with the ghost.

⁂

Two hours after they set out, Audrey and Xavier reached the perimeter of the lodge complex. They'd traveled a long and twisted route high on the hillside along the backside of the boot until they reached Kaxo Creek. After crossing the stream, Audrey directed them on a route that skirted George's cabin along with the meadow and forested area that were home to the village site, but still brought them around to the rocky outcrop where she'd enjoyed tea with the elder two or three times a week for most of a summer.

Thousands of years before, glaciers had carved this land, including the falls and lake, and the five boulders that formed her favorite break hideout ranged in size from a Mini Cooper car to a basic minivan. They were jumbled together, with trees and ferns sprouting in the crevices and a thick layer of mossy padding that made the flat top of one boulder comfy to sit on.

She'd called that rock her *Flintstones* recliner.

There was a gap between her recliner rock and the next boulder in which she and George would leave their mugs, snacks, and whatever book or magazine George was reading at the time, sealed in a round bear canister that she restocked at the beginning of each week.

The crevasse was hidden by moss and ferns, a perfect hiding place, but also, nothing of real value was left behind so if hikers discovered her cache and absconded with the canister, it wouldn't be more than an inconvenience.

The canister had been packed up at the end of the summer along with the rest of the field school equipment. There would be no stale protein bars or tea bags to be found. But Audrey knew without a doubt if George wanted to find her, this was where he'd come.

They circled the rocks and logs, moving quietly as Xavier scanned the ground and trees, looking for evidence George —or a mercenary—had been here. Xavier gave her his NVGs so she could scan the rocks, and she was disappointed to see her recliner was empty. But that didn't mean George wasn't on his way, or he hadn't been and gone already.

At last, Xavier decided it was safe to approach. She followed him in the darkness, crouching low as she climbed over logs and rocks. Adrenaline surged as they moved in, her heart pounding so hard, she could feel her pulse in her fingertips.

She climbed up onto the rock and crawled across the soft surface as Xavier stood guard at her back with the rifle he'd acquired last night at the ready.

She flicked on her red-tipped flashlight and shined it in the gap between boulders, lifting the moss blanket as she did so.

Her light landed on a silver cylinder, sealed tight against the elements and bears.

Chapter Twenty-Three

*A*udrey tucked deep into the hollow in the roots of a large tree and waited for Xavier to settle in beside her before she twisted open the top of the bear canister. She'd peeked inside before they left her *Flintstones* recliner, and seeing a note along with some pipes and boxes of matches, they'd agreed to move to a less-exposed position to read the letter and figure out the gift George had left for her.

Xavier grabbed the camouflage and orange panel from her pack, but instead of sitting on it this time, he tacked the square to the opening with the mottled-green side facing out to ensure the light from her flashlight wouldn't be visible. Secure in the knowledge they wouldn't be easily spotted, she flicked on her headlamp, choosing the dimmest setting as she directed the beam at the piece of folded paper.

She unfolded it and studied what appeared to be a page from a bored high school student's notebook: quick sketches —line drawings that looked like petroglyphs and pictographs —numbers, letters, random words. And interspersed among it all, a few names.

Familiar names.

Inholding landowners: Harriet Jamison, Jason Caruthers, Bastian Ford.

But wait. Bastian Ford wasn't an official inholding landowner. He was from the Kalahwamish Tribe. Their reservation was on the shores of Discovery Bay, an inlet of the Strait of Juan de Fuca. Many Kalahwamish Tribal members—including George—had family ties to the coastal tribe that claimed Lake Olympus as part of their traditional territory. The Kalahwamish Tribe—which included Bastian —owned a lakeside cabin that had been transferred to the tribe two decades ago when Millie Thorpe Montgomery's last will and testament had been found nearly sixty years after her death. Millie's great-grandson, Jason Caruthers— another inholding landowner named on this page—hadn't waited for the courts to sort out the legalities of the bequest and handed over every property he'd inherited that had been owned by Thorpe Log & Lumber to the tribe, including the lakeside cabin that had been built by Jason's great-grandfather in the 1920s. The trainers' vehicles were stored in this cabin's garage.

Jason remained an inholding landowner, though, because he and his wife, Dr. Simone Atherton, purchased a lakeside cabin several years ago. Simone was a contract archaeologist who did lots of field projects on the peninsula, and Audrey had first met the woman when she was in her teens at a summer archaeology camp run by ONP archaeologist Roy Heller.

Why had George listed these people specifically?

Harriet Jamison. Jason Caruthers. Bastian Ford.

She'd assume he was indicating cabins, except she'd been in the Jamison cabin last night and it wouldn't be safe to return there. Plus, there was no mention of Jeb, whose cabin they knew George had plundered to build weapons.

Technically, Bastian Ford didn't even have his own cabin.

It was a tribal holding, not personal. Why name him and not someone else in the tribe?

Bastian and George were close, as she'd mentioned to Xavier, due to their tribal and Army ties. Bastian was Special Forces, and when he visited the elder, they would trade stories in the lodge, sometimes with Jeb joining them.

"What does it mean, Aud?" Xavier whispered.

"I'm not sure. There's a connection here. Meant for me to decipher. I know it."

Harriet Jamison. Jason Caruthers. Bastian Ford.

They each had long ties to the peninsula. Jason's and Harriet's families had owned cabins at the time the lodge was built, before the park even existed. Bastian was Kalah-wamish, like George. A soldier, like George.

Think, Audrey. Think. What do these people have in common?

All at once, it hit her.

The Jamison library. The Thorpe—not Caruthers—ballroom. And the Ford dining room. All public rooms in the lodge, named after a patriarch who'd donated money to the park when it was founded. Except, in Bastian's case, the donor with the last name Ford wasn't a relative; it was automobile manufacturer Henry Ford. The name was a coincidence, which George had used.

"These are rooms in the lodge," she whispered. She studied the numbers next to Jason's name. He represented the Thorpe ballroom. "I think this means there are five hostages in the ballroom."

"That fits the count for my team, but why do you think the number refers to hostages?"

She pointed to a crude drawing that looked like it was supposed to be a petroglyph. George was a tribal artist, a carver. He had excellent drawing skills. He'd intended to make this look amateur. "This human figure only has four fingers on one hand."

Xavier sucked in a sharp breath. "He saw what happened in the yurt."

"Or he watched them move your team to the lodge and saw Cohen's hand. But yeah, if he saw the men at the site digging up weapons, he might have followed them. Saw them kill Jeb. Watched what he could until he slipped away to make weapons."

She looked into the bear canister. "What are those, by the way?"

"It looks like he made match guns."

"What are those?"

"Improvised munitions. Standard in the handbook that was produced during the Vietnam War. You can use match heads as the propellant and shoot projectiles like nails thirty or forty yards with a fair amount of accuracy. That explains Jeb's stockpile of matchsticks. Could have been a hobby of his."

There were three homemade guns in the canister, along with a bunch of nails and several boxes of matches.

"It would take a while to reload."

Xavier nodded. "Forever. But better than nothing if you're sneaking up on an armed merc." He returned his attention to the paper. "What else does it say?"

She studied the drawings, words, and numbers, reminding herself George was an artist. None of the markings on the page was done in error.

"Those are lightbulbs." She pointed to the three balloon-shaped drawings by Harriet's name. "He's colored them in with black dots, like a comic book drawing. I presume that indicates black powder? And this one on the end…it's shattering, and inside is a shape that looks like a comic book *kapow!* bubble. He couldn't know we've seen Jeb's workbench, so I think he's telling us the lightbulbs are bombs."

"He'd probably guess that once I saw the match guns in

the canister, I'd recognize other improvised explosives." He touched Harriet's name on the page. "So…does this mean he's planted explosive lights in the second-floor Jamison Library?"

"How could he? He'd need to have gotten inside to do that, before he left this message for me."

"Or he has a plan for getting inside. And he left you this note to tell you what he's up to. We just need to figure out how he plans to do it."

"He has special access because he uses the woodshop year-round and has wintered here for the last three years. He has the full employee key chain. Hell, he probably has keys I don't even have."

"His keys wouldn't work because we substituted all the exterior doors."

"*All* the doors? Even the third-floor doors and windows?"

"The balcony doors don't have mechanical locks with keys. It's all pegs and bolts that can only be locked and unlocked from the inside. Same with the windows."

"Not the attic window on the end, and not the interior door that leads to it."

"What do you mean?"

"On the third floor, there's a half door at the end of the hall. It goes to the old fire escape."

"That door goes to the eave crawl space. No outside access."

"At the far end of the crawl space is an octagon-shaped window that opens onto a widow's walk. Once upon a time there was a wrought iron fire escape ladder that extended down, but it was removed as a hazard about fifteen years ago. The bolts for the old escape are still in the wall. An agile person could climb up using the bolts as handholds, open the window—which I doubt has a lock because it was an emergency escape—and slip inside the lodge. The hallway door is locked to keep guests from snooping and getting injured in the attic, but it's probably the same key as the other utilitarian exterior doors. I bet my basement key could open it." She pointed to an octagon that sat above Harriet's name. "This isn't a stop sign. It's the shape of the window."

*avier stared at the drawing, disbelief peppered with excitement coursing through him. Was it possible George Shaw was inside the lodge, setting a trap for the mercs? It was clear from what they'd found in Jeb McCutcheon's workshop that Shaw was exceedingly smart and capable. But damn, this note for Audrey was a level of cunning he'd never have dared to hope for.

Shaw had ensured that if anyone spotted him planting the message and intercepted it, it would be meaningless. And it said something about Audrey that George had trusted she'd zero in on their teatime spot.

Fucking brilliant.

Shaw must have slipped into soldier mode the moment he saw his friend murdered at the hands of mercenaries. His home territory was under attack, a friend and fellow vet killed. At some point, he saw Audrey's vehicle, knew she was in danger too, and George went to work.

What had been McCutcheon's role? Xavier was beginning to think that the man had shown up at the yurt to give warning. He might have stayed in the training zone so he could spy on the SEALs, but then he saw something that alarmed him enough to reach out to the people he distrusted most.

Xavier cleared his throat. They needed justice for

McCutcheon. And he needed to get Audrey out of danger. "We need to find the SEAL team. Tell them we have an ally who might be inside with bombs planted in the library."

"And the dining room," she said, pointing to the light-bulbs by the name Bastian Ford.

"That'll be risky. It's on the same floor as the mercs and hostages."

"But the other end of the lodge from the ballroom. As a point of surprise attack, it will leave the hostages out of it."

She pointed to a drawing that looked like a skeleton key and what he recognized from the gift shop as a Native American sasquatch drawing. "He's going to unlock the exterior door by the bigfoot display. That's how your team can get in. The display is by the public restrooms on the forest side of the lodge."

He knew exactly the door she was talking about. "It would help to know when he plans to do all this."

Audrey stared at the page another moment and let out a squeal, then pointed to a series of symbols that were next to both sets of lightbulbs. "It says right here twelve thirty a.m."

"What?" He stared at the lines of neatly printed stacked symbols. From top to bottom they read:

$$\bigcirc$$
$$\text{ⅿ}$$
$$\triangle$$
$$N$$

She turned the page on its side, and the stacked symbols transformed.

$$Z \triangleright \ni \bigcirc$$

"He went to some effort to make sure it wasn't obvious it says Z-D-3-0."

"Zero Dark Thirty doesn't always mean twelve thirty a.m.," he pointed out. "It's really any time after midnight."

"But what is the time most frequently suggested?"

"Good point. He's not aiming for obscure. So he's telling us when he's going to create a diversion from the inside—set off explosives on the second-floor library and in the dining room—and we can slip in through a side door while the mercs are scrambling and seize the lodge."

"Yes. That's exactly what I think he's telling us."

He glanced at his watch. It was after nine. They had three hours to find the SEALs and get into position to make this work. "We just need to know where the team is."

"Not to worry. George tells us right here where they are." She tapped another drawing, the last ones at the bottom of the page. He could hear the excitement in her voice. The elation. She was enjoying this moment. But then, so was he.

George was a damned miracle.

Or would be, as long as he was able to slip into the lodge as planned.

"Where are they?"

"See this drawing? It's a famous petroglyph on Vancouver Island. Well, the head of one. Not the whole body, or it would be obvious to anyone who looked it's a representation of a seal. George is being careful, and he knows I'll recognize it."

"Okay, a seal symbol makes sense, but why the donkey?" It wasn't even a petroglyph-style donkey like the other line drawings. No, this one looked like Eeyore, and it had the number "277" written on the animal's rear.

Even in dim light, her grin was radiant. "George is fucking brilliant." She tapped the number. "That's the archaeological site number of an ancient, rusting steam donkey that's about a mile from here. A left over from early twentieth-century logging. George is telling us the SEAL team is in the forest somewhere near the donkey."

Chapter Twenty-Four

*a*udrey described the route they would need to take as best she could without a map. They were heading into an area they'd ignored so far, as it was high on the hill above the lodge and cabins they'd explored last night, and on the opposite side of the lake from where they'd camped today.

As a remote meeting point for SEALs, she supposed it made sense. It was far from the complex of buildings and roads that provided infrastructure to the lodge, and upslope so they'd have a good vantage point to view the lodge and lake from the top of a tree. A hiking trail passed within a half mile of the area, making the area one that was usually only accessed by hard-core backcountry hikers.

Audrey figured George had provided just the general area. The odds that the SEAL team was sitting on the donkey sled were slim, but the basic direction was all they'd need, Xavier assured her. He knew how to connect with the team.

It was nearing ten p.m.—or twenty-two hundred in military parlance—when Xavier let out a birdcall that received an answer.

Even in the dark, Audrey could see the shift in his posture when the soft whistles carried on the night wind.

He raised a hand in signal to halt, and she froze in place, barely able to breathe.

A moment later, a second call came, this one different. Xavier answered, also using a new cadence.

Another response followed, and Xavier sagged back against a tree. "Thank fucking god. Flyte's here."

Seeing his reaction triggered the burn of tears, which she quickly swiped away. She would not be the emotional female in this reunion of hypermasculine special forces operators.

Still, she fought the burning sensation and her nose tingled as a Black man emerged from behind a tree and greeted Xavier with a handshake. "Shit, Rivera. I was braced for the worst."

Xavier's voice was a low whisper. "Same, Lieutenant. And I'm still afraid it might be for the others."

She cursed her overloaded pregnancy hormones and stifled the last of her reaction as Xavier introduced her. "Dr. Audrey Kendrick, this is Lieutenant Chris Flyte."

He'd flipped up his NVGs, so she could see his eyes, but the rest of him was decked out in full combat gear. She shook his gloved hand, then followed him into the SEAL team's lair, Xavier and another SEAL falling in line behind them.

They'd set up a headquarters of sorts in an alcove created by a large fallen tree that draped at an angle as it was propped up by a large, thriving Douglas fir. Sheets of moss provided cover that had been embellished with ferns and forest-patterned camouflage sheets.

"We've got two men patrolling. One in a tree on lookout. He caught you with his NVGs ten minutes ago." One corner of Flyte's mouth curled up. "If I were grading you, Mr. Rivera, that would be a fail."

She knew the official address for a warrant officer was "mister," but it sounded odd to her ears given the military hierarchy present. This was her first time seeing Xavier in this element. She could swear his posture was straighter. He'd let her see his pained shoulder, his unpolished edges. But none of that would be on display here.

She felt a surge of emotion at the realization Xavier had let her see beneath the surface to the wounded SEAL.

She shoved her feelings aside and paid attention to the report Flyte gave Xavier. As a commissioned officer, the lieutenant held the higher rank, but it was possible Xavier was in charge here because he'd been in command of the training exercise.

She settled on a log as she tried to make sense of the jargon. Flyte's team had found a dead body in the woods with a broken neck, and Xavier pointed to the weapons he'd acquired from that encounter. Her belly twisted when Flyte reported that one Fire Team never made it to the rendezvous and had yet to be located.

Xavier let out a low curse that was echoed by Flyte and others in the circle.

"On a positive note, we have a ghost who took out two tangos when he blew up a boat earlier."

Never in her life had she imagined she would smile at hearing a boat explosion on Lake Olympus had killed two men, but her life had changed a lot in the last thirty-plus hours. "Good job, George," she whispered.

Flyte did a double take. "You know the ghost?"

She nodded and met the man's gaze. "Even better, I know where he is now and what he's planning."

And with that, Xavier began his report. The team gathered to strategize their assault on the lodge armed with three match guns, an assortment of Molotov cocktails, two pistols, and one assault rifle, in addition to two dozen handguns and rifles loaded with paint pellets.

*J*ae wasn't a fan of going against his boss's wishes, but he'd been getting the runaround all day from both the park hierarchy and the Navy. Luke Sevick was equally fed up with Navy brass. When both the park and the Navy refused to offer up a key to the gate, they came up with their own plan.

It wasn't complex by any means. It was as basic as possible. An hour before the first light of dawn, Jae and Luke were going to drive to a trailhead for a loop that included Mount Olympus. One section of the trail came within five miles of Lake Olympus Lodge as the crow flies. It was a gruesome, nasty, backwoods five miles that went up and over a ridgeline before descending into the lake basin, but it was as close as they could get without road access.

With no real word on what had happened to Audrey and stonewalling from the Navy, it was the right thing to do. The superintendent admitted the lock shouldn't have been changed, but he wasn't doing enough to push back against the military powers that be.

Audrey's SUV could have slipped off the road in the storm, and no one was looking for her. He and Luke would change that. Something just wasn't right.

No way would Xavier fail to reach out if Audrey had been stranded at the lodge. He'd know Jae would worry.

The lack of contact meant something had gone terribly wrong. For Audrey, and maybe even for Xavier.

*T*here was a lengthy debate on what do to with Audrey while the team moved in on the lodge, and Xavier knew she was ticked that absolutely no one considered her opinion on the matter. Not even him. But in the end, she'd accepted their decision and agreed to the plan.

Much as he wanted to leave her safe in the deep woods, it was safer to stick as close together as possible. Leaving her by the donkey sled hideout would mean having to send someone back for her after the lodge was secured, and that only invited more risk.

So she made her way toward the lodge with the team and would take cover in the post office that was attached to the museum across the street from the lodge, where she'd wait out the battle alone.

They couldn't spare a man to protect her, not even injured Xavier. They were thirteen strong, moving in to rescue their fellow SEALs—five trainers and, they hoped, four SEALs.

They had to be ready to strike when George set off his lightbulbs.

Audrey insisted a SEAL take her Glock. They needed bullets more than she did. She had a paintball gun and a Molotov cocktail to defend herself should she be spotted by one of the mercs.

Xavier felt sick at the plan, but it was the only option. She couldn't storm the lodge with the team. That would be far riskier.

He accompanied her to the back door of the post office. With a SEAL watching his six, he quickly picked the lock and pushed the door open.

He followed her into the small back room and did a fast search of the mail bins and under the tables, ensuring the space was empty. He didn't have time for more.

"I'll come for you once we have the lodge."

"Watch out for George."

He nodded and turned to leave, then stopped. He faced her and placed a hand at the back of her neck. She was trembling.

It was a punch in the gut to feel the physical manifestation of her fear, but he understood it. This wasn't her world.

Hell, it shouldn't even be his anymore.

"When this is over…" He shook his head, unable to say the words.

If you'll let me, I'm going to love you like you deserve. I'm going to do everything I can to be a man worthy of you.

Instead, he pressed his mouth to hers. She opened her lips, and he slid his tongue inside for a deep, intimate kiss that ended far too soon.

He released her and headed for the heavy wood door. "Bar the door behind me. You know the knock."

If Xavier wasn't able to retrieve her, Flyte or one of his men would. They all knew the knock pattern.

Without looking back, he left her in the tiny, musty post office and slipped into the woods to take his position with the team. In twenty minutes, the most important op of his life would begin, with nothing less than his future family at stake.

Chapter Twenty-Five

The back room of the stamp-sized post office was what one would expect for an office that was only open for four hours twice a week during the off-season. Audrey figured they'd committed a federal crime by breaking in, but Xavier had wanted her inside the log structure because the thick log walls were as close to bulletproof as possible and there was only one small window at the front, which was inset in the door.

It was a tiny fortress.

But the thick walls and lack of windows also meant Audrey couldn't see what was happening outside, just a hundred yards away.

The next hour was destined to be the longest of her life as she would wait and wonder if the father of her unborn child would return.

And then there was George. He'd more than proven he was an adversary for the mercenaries who'd invaded his forest, but he didn't have body armor like the SEALs, and it had been more than fifty years since he'd fought in a war.

It was useless to pace such a small room, so she dropped

down in a corner and wrapped her arms around her knees. But it didn't take long for shivering to overtake her, and she was back on her feet.

She was nauseated and dizzy. She needed to eat, but knew without a doubt that she'd vomit up anything she put in her mouth.

How the hell did Xavier and the others *do* this sort of thing?

This was their job.

She'd always respected the men and women who served in the military, but this was the first time she'd ever faced the reality of their world.

She'd spent hours chatting with Undine's husband, Luke, and even knew a bit about what he'd done when an old Russian nuke—a Cold War leftover—had been found in the Strait of Juan de Fuca a few years ago. But even that threat —which could have resulted in a massive tsunami that would have wiped out the Pacific Northwest—hadn't held this level of tangible fear, because she'd heard about it more than a year after the danger had passed.

Now she understood in a way that she never could have grasped before. This was even worse than last night, when she'd paced and talked to the baby alone in the Jamison cabin.

Last night, she'd believed she was safe and Xavier would be back in a matter of hours. Tonight, she knew that improvised bombs would begin to go off in a matter of minutes.

What if she was wrong in her interpretation of George's note? What if he hadn't been able to enter the lodge and the bigfoot door was locked and guarded?

Sure, she'd been right about the donkey engine, but that had been easy. Lightbulbs in the library was a bigger leap.

This was the world's worst game of *Clue*.

Time moved with aching slowness as she committed

more federal crimes by looking at the stack of mail in the "undeliverable" bin.

Even though there were no windows for light to leak through, she used the red-tipped flashlight to read the envelopes.

This was a rotten invasion of privacy, but it was keeping her from losing her mind.

She paused on an envelope addressed to Jeb. "Addressee unknown" was written in his messy scrawl. She knew his handwriting from the numerous times he'd petitioned her office to step in and use the National Historic Preservation Act to prevent something from happening in the park.

Jeb would always be a mystery now, and her grief at never really having known him grew.

She left the stacks of mail and slipped into the front of the post office. She'd been in this vestibule many times. The entire building—including the attached museum—was a contributing element to the National Register Historic District. But never had the tiny space seemed so...ominous.

Across the street, a battle would be waged in a matter of minutes. And it wasn't just any battle, it was potentially the first salvo of a Russian invasion of American soil.

Take away everything personal about it, and it was *still* gut-wrenchingly terrifying.

This was a meticulously planned assault on a United States special operations team on US soil. It didn't get more dire than that.

Add in the personal aspects, and she could barely breathe.

She'd wanted her baby from the moment she'd realized she was pregnant, and now, after a month of heartache and turmoil, she had a new truth: she wanted Xavier with the same ferocity.

And she could lose him. Tonight. In a matter of minutes.

And there was nothing she could do about it. She'd played every card she had already.

Then there was George, who'd been something of a mentor to her along with Roy when she was young, and who'd become a friend in adulthood. If any of them survived this, it would be thanks to George. His cunning. His knowledge. His badass guerilla fighting skills that he'd acquired a lifetime ago in a foreign land, forced to serve in the military by a government that had betrayed his people for hundreds of years.

George was an artist. A carver of totem poles and other Native art—yet there was no monument great enough that could fully honor *him*.

She swiped at tears that fell without permission. She wanted to blame pregnancy again, but this was straight-up fear. She'd be crying now even if she weren't pregnant.

She returned to the back room and locked the door that separated the two areas. She stood behind the wall of post office boxes—a grid of cubbyholes, with each rectangle measuring five by four inches. There was a box for each cottage, plus extra for local businesses and renters who wanted a coveted Lake Olympus address. George's cabin had a box, as did tour operators who held park concession contracts, but were based in Port Angeles.

Audrey scanned the boxes. Jeb's box—identifiable because "McCutcheon" was printed on a label taped to the back end of the cubbyhole—contained a grocery store mailer, junk mail that couldn't be avoided even in the most remote of places, and a notice from the US Navy that access to Lake Olympus Road would be cut off as of Monday of this week—four days ago, given that they were now minutes into Friday morning.

The Navy had been required to send these notices in a timely manner to all inholding property owners, but now it occurred to her to wonder, did everyone with a PO Box receive a notice?

She checked the rental boxes for tour operators and felt a surge of adrenaline at seeing the same notice. These groups didn't have a gate key and wouldn't be able to access their box until the road opened, but they'd received the same notice as all box renters.

But…not everyone who owned a box collected their mail from here. There were forwarding services for PO Boxes to deliver to street addresses. What if someone had learned of the training and managed to get a box, then had the mail forwarded?

It could explain the leak of the timing for the training, without Jeb or someone else playing the role of traitor.

Deep down, Audrey didn't want Jeb to be a traitor. Even unwitting as he would have been. Partly because she hated the idea of him being killed by the very men he'd unintentionally abetted.

Not that it mattered. He was dead either way. But there was something a little extra horrific at the idea of being duped into sharing information and then being killed by the same people who'd manipulated him.

She continued with her lawbreaking, going through the mail of each box, not for any purpose, but to pass the seconds that ticked away to the moment she both anticipated and feared.

Still, the clock hands on the wall behind her moved achingly slow, yet somehow, she found herself lost in emotional spirals that made her lose track of time.

It was during one such lost brain spiral that she heard the first explosion.

Chapter Twenty-Six

$\mathcal{L}$ ight flared behind the second-floor library window as the first roar of explosives split the air.

Like fireworks, more booms followed, each lighting the night before the other had fully faded. Xavier didn't know how George did it, but he'd managed to rig his lightbulb igniters in a series so they went off in succession.

Beautiful and deadly.

From his position, he could see the flashes of light from the dining room explosions reflected on the water.

Nine SEALs had breached the lodge—entering from both the octagon window and unlocked bigfoot door. Because he lacked body armor, Xavier was among the SEALs tasked with watching for escaping mercs. The lodge had exits through the game room, deck, ballroom, dining room, plus in the service areas. Too many doors for only four men, but with minimal weaponry, they needed a full force in the lodge to secure the hostages.

Plan B went into action: the main generator went on and interior and exterior lights flared bright, lighting all the dark corners outside the lodge.

A mere fifteen feet away, a suddenly exposed balaclava-clad merc crept along the side of the building. The man stumbled, thrown off by the flare in his NVGs. Xavier took aim with his match gun, which he'd test-fired in the woods before they set out. The reload time meant he only had one shot at this man who wore body armor and carried an AK-47 that Xavier very much wanted to add to their limited arsenal.

The merc dove for cover, and Xavier fired. The makeshift gun was true, and the shot landed above the chest plate, embedding in the merc's shoulder, just above the right clavicle. Not a killing blow, but an exceedingly painful one.

A Molotov to the chest should incapacitate him to the point where Xavier could claim the AK. As he prepared to light the improvised explosive, a shrill scream split the night.

A woman's scream.

He didn't pause to come up with a plan. No time to grab the rifle from the masked merc. He just reacted, bolting for the post office and the woman who meant everything to him.

One minute, Audrey was huddled in a ball listening to the sound of explosions, and the next, she heard glass shattering on the other side of the vestibule wall.

The window inset in the door. It had to be.

She looked through the rows of post office boxes—each had a tiny glass pane at the front—to see into the front room. Light from the lodge—they must've gotten the generator going, as planned—lit the opening as a gloved hand reached through the shattered window and twisted the knob on the dead bolt.

Someone must've spotted her entering the post office, and now that they were under attack, they'd come for her.

She turned for the back door and threw up the old-fashioned wood beam that barred it. She didn't take time to grab her pack as she bolted into the forest that backed up to the post office.

The night was no longer pitch-dark. With the generators on, halogen lights mounted to high poles lit up the grounds like a stadium and bled into the forest, reducing her options for hiding.

That had been the plan—a weapon to be employed against mercenaries—but now she was caught in the same trap.

She sprinted through the lit woods, jumping over logs and roots like they were hurdles. This was the race of her life, and she wasn't a runner. Never had been.

A shot rang out. She mistimed a jump, and she landed hard, face forward onto hard ground littered with rocks and sharp sticks.

She pushed herself up, pressing her palm on something sharp, and was moving forward before the pain registered, before she was even fully on her feet.

Her pursuer was right behind her. He caught her foot, and she went down again, letting out a sharp scream.

He yanked her back. She screamed again. Wondered why she hadn't been screaming all along. But then, screaming took breath, and she'd been too focused on running to spare her lungs for anything else.

He dropped, the length of his body pressing her into the dirt. Her breath left in a rush, silencing the screams that were her only hope at this point.

He was large. Heavy. His weight immobilized her, no matter how much she bucked against him. She couldn't draw in a breath. She was utterly trapped.

He spoke in her ear, his accent heavy. "You're my ticket out of here. The boss wants you alive."

She tried to buck him off again, her journey to panic nearly complete.

When that failed, she managed to elbow him in the side. He grunted and shifted slightly. She used the opportunity to draw in a deep breath and scream for all she was worth, then head-butted him in the nose.

He grunted in pain. "Just because he wants you alive doesn't mean I can't hurt you first." An arm snaked around her neck, and fingers gripped her throat. "I can do whatever the fuck I want. No one is coming. They're all inside getting shot. Burned."

Explosive bangs interspersed with bursts of automatic weapon fire underscored his words.

"Your SEALs are all dying. They're no match for us."

"If that's true, then why are you here and not inside the lodge?" Her voice was a low rasp as he controlled her airflow.

"You. Our commander put a bounty on you. You are money."

She gathered breath for one more scream, drawing it in slowly through her compressed airway, but before she could release it, his fingers closed tight on her neck, preventing the release.

She bucked again, trying to dislodge him as she scratched at the hand on her throat.

She couldn't breathe. Couldn't make a sound. His weight crushed her, prevented her from fighting.

No one would save her. They were facing their own nightmare in the lodge.

She'd been left behind because she was a liability. The stakes they faced were far bigger than a single woman's life.

She felt hands at the waist of the hiking pants she'd stolen from Danielle Baldwin. She was near blacking out from lack of oxygen when she felt chill air on her bare butt. He was going to rape her as he strangled her.

Her vision tunneled to a pinpoint. Unconsciousness would be a relief of sorts.

All at once, she heard a roar, and the man at her back was lifted from her. She curled up in a ball, pulling her knees to her chest as she choked and cried, taking in painful, wheezing breaths.

"Run, Audrey!"

The sharp command from Xavier had her scrambling to her feet and yanking up her pants as she lunged forward, moving deeper into the woods before she could turn and see what was happening behind her.

Xavier and the merc rolled on the ground, exchanging blows. Her attacker was bleeding from a slash on his arm, and she spotted Xavier's knife on the ground several feet away.

He'd gotten one good cut before being disarmed. Now they fought barehanded, with Xavier's injured shoulder putting him at a disadvantage.

"I said, run!"

The merc landed a blow to Xavier's wounded shoulder. He let out a grunt and fell back. He reached for his lost knife, just as the merc pulled a pistol from his holster.

Audrey didn't hesitate and launched herself forward, throwing herself on the mercenary's back.

Caught off guard, he dropped the gun as he tried to dislodge her. She wrapped an arm around his throat and squeezed, using her other hand to cinch her arm tight as she clung to his back with her legs wrapped around his hips.

She didn't have the strength to bring him down, but as long as she was behind him and constricting his airflow, his ability to hurt her was limited.

Xavier claimed the dropped pistol, but with the merc's

body armor and Audrey on the merc's back, she knew he didn't have a shot.

An elbow to her side loosened her grip, and she let out a yelp. The merc tripped on a root or a rock and fell back, pinning her beneath him on the ground. She released his neck as she tried to scramble from beneath him.

He twisted to grab her, and Xavier struck. A swift stroke of a knife blade opened his throat. Blood spurted from the wound, hitting Audrey in the face.

Chapter Twenty-Seven

*I*n a daze, Audrey entered the lodge a half hour later. The building smelled of gunpowder and singed electronics. The power was out again, and there were dead bodies lined up against the wall in the great room.

One of them was the man who'd attacked her in the woods behind the post office.

In spite of the carnage and destruction, this was still her lodge. Or maybe it was her lodge once again, no longer held by mercenaries who'd seized it without firing a shot.

With George's groundwork, they'd reclaimed the building, rescued the hostages, and won the day.

Or rather, night.

It wasn't over. At least five mercenaries remained at large. Three SEALs remained missing. And they still didn't have communication with the outside world. Two SEALs had been injured in the battle for the lodge, and one of the hostages was critically injured. The injured hostage was a SEAL from the missing Fire Team.

The great room was in a shambles. Antique sofas and

wing chairs upended, blood marring the upholstery, lamps shattered.

From the smell, she guessed George had managed to exchange some of the lightbulbs with his ignitors. When the generator powered on, the lights exploded.

She spotted George sitting on the stone lip of the massive central hearth, a medic tending to a wound just above his knee. She crossed the room and planted herself beside him on the side that wasn't injured, throwing an arm around his shoulders and giving him a grateful squeeze.

She'd never hugged George Shaw in her life, but figured this was an appropriate occasion for it. "George, you beautiful, brilliant, badass—" She stopped. Her mind went blank as she took in everything he'd done, so she just spoke the truth. "I don't even have words…"

For the hundredth time since this ordeal began, her eyes teared. But the feeling behind it now was different.

He wrapped an arm around her waist, squeezing back. "With that list, I think the next word should be bastard."

Tears leaked from the sides of her eyes. "No way. I think saint is more appropriate."

He shook his head. "Hell no. I'm much more bastard than saint." He leaned back and studied her face. More tears spilled, as she took in his lined cheeks and long dark hair streaked with gray.

His gaze landed on her throat, which she imagined was red from her encounter with the tango in the forest. "You okay, Aud?"

She nodded. "I'm fine. That we're even here at all is thanks to you."

"Hear, hear," the medic tending George's leg chimed in.

Audrey turned her gaze to him and realized he wasn't one of the SEALs she'd met in the forest. He must be one of the men from Xavier's team who'd been taken hostage.

"It was your call when the cameras went out that alerted me," George said. "I got your message right away and grabbed my binoculars and went to see what the hell was going on. It was clear they weren't looters. They were dressed for combat, and when I saw them recover their cache of weapons from the site, their plan to attack the training was obvious."

"Why didn't you call or text me?"

"I think they had a shorter-range signal jammer on them. My phone worked one moment, and the next, it was toast. If your cameras had been wireless with a satellite feed, there would have been no need for them to cut the line."

She thought of those days in November of backbreaking work as she buried the conduit for the cables. It was common for satellite signals to be interrupted, and the security team monitoring the camera feeds might never have noticed—especially if the signal was restored once the weapons had been retrieved.

Without those cut cables, George never would have been warned. Audrey wouldn't have entered the park. Xavier would have been ambushed along with the rest of his team.

The events of the last day and a half would have played out very differently.

Several SEALs, including Xavier, gathered round as George gave his account. He'd witnessed Jeb's murder and watched as a man was forced at gunpoint into the lodge, his hand dripping with blood. He'd seen the other trainers all get dragged into the ballroom. He'd then gone to Jeb's and set to work making weapons, unsure how he could use them, but aware his ability to move unseen in a forest combined with his knowledge of the lodge complex and surrounding woods could be used against the intruders.

Others chimed in when his account intersected with their

experiences. A man she guessed was Paul Cohen due to his bandaged hand shared the story of a dead merc being shot with a nail to the eye in the wee hours of yesterday morning. Huang and Flyte had witnessed that body being dumped in the lake.

The mercenaries had no intention of taking their dead home, it seemed. How many more had been deposited in the lake? Cohen stated the mercenary leader's words indicated at least two others had died.

The one Xavier killed in the forest, and possibly the man who fell from the ledge before the SEALs had jumped into the lake?

When those accounts were complete, Cohen cleared his throat. "There was another exchange I witnessed, between the leader and two goons." His gaze shifted from Audrey to Xavier, then back to Audrey. "I believe these men were the ones who cornered you in one of the inholding cabins, Dr. Kendrick."

"Audrey, please," she murmured. She was fairly certain she knew what Cohen was about to reveal. Her hand went involuntarily to her belly. She'd gone from no one but her doctor knowing about the baby to telling Xavier, a group of mercenaries, and now a platoon of SEALs. Not the usual progression for sharing big news, but at least she was alive to do it herself. "They found my letter to Xavier."

Cohen nodded.

"They know I'm pregnant."

Again, Cohen nodded. He turned to Xavier. "But the part that interested the leader most was the fact that *you* are the father. It was the second time he'd made it clear he knows you."

Xavier jolted. "Knows me? By face?"

"Yes. The first time was when I was delivered to him. He

was angry when he saw me. Said I wasn't Rivera." He faced Audrey again. "He'd put a bounty on Rivera. He doubled it for you. He said…well, he said he wants to hurt you in front of Rivera."

Chapter Twenty-Eight

$\mathcal{G}$uilt threatened to swallow Xavier whole. This had been about him all along. It didn't make sense. He was nothing. No one. Not a SEAL anymore. Just a trainer.

How could it be about him? This was a trial run for a vital op. If not Xavier, some other trainer would have planned it.

He studied Audrey. She'd been strangled and nearly raped less than an hour ago. And the merc had been after her because of *him*. Because she was pregnant with his child.

But how was that even possible? And why? SEAL ops were top secret. No one knew which SEAL went on which mission. And usually no one outside NSWC and the highest branches of government ever learned about the mission at all.

No one would have known who shot Osama bin Laden if the SEAL hadn't broken his vow and publicly claimed the kill. And Xavier sure as hell had never done that. Not even to Lynn in the days when he thought he might marry her.

"What's going on, Xavier?" Audrey asked.

"I don't know. None of it makes sense. This is a training. One I was assigned to plan and execute."

"A training with very specific parameters," Flyte interjected. "It's been clear from the start this is a planning session for a specific op."

"Let's start there," Cohen said. "I think at this point, every person in this room has a need to know why we're here at all."

Xavier's gaze landed on Audrey and George. With the exception of the two civilians, he was authorized to reveal the details of the mission. The plan for the training was for the team to brainstorm various plans of attack to liberate the hostages, which this team would then use when they carried out the mission as soon as possible.

He'd be violating his security clearance in sharing the details with Audrey and George, but no way in hell was he asking either of them to leave the room. They'd used their knowledge of the lodge and forest and each other, and in so doing had saved all their asses, bringing everyone to this debriefing with the lodge firmly in SEAL control.

Hell, he didn't doubt that George could seize it back if he wanted to.

"I think everyone here can agree that Dr. Kendrick and Mr. Shaw have a right to know every classified detail."

There were nods from everyone present, including the four SEALs who guarded the corners of the room, each armed with a liberated assault rifle. They were listening, but on the alert, making sure the lodge remained safe.

He shook his head. "Where to begin?" This was unlike any debriefing he'd participated in before.

"How about explain why we found two prop dummies in one of the guest rooms," Mock said. "One was a woman. The other the size of a kid."

"Good place. Okay. I'll share what I know, which, of

course, is just a fraction of what NSWC has gathered from the intelligence community. Last fall—my guess is early October—intel was spiking with warnings that a chemical weapons attack on the US mainland was in the works. The attack would look like the work of terrorists from the Middle East, but it would really be a Russian operation.

"The threats were credible, and the timeline for the attack indicated it would happen in the first or second week of February. The magnitude of it is huge and requires months to set up. It would be an attack on a major city. Possibly subway, stadium, or large office building. Expected death toll anywhere from five hundred to over thirty thousand people."

"What kind of chemical can do that kind of damage?" Audrey asked. "Are they planning to attack the Super Bowl?"

He shook his head. "Unlikely, but nothing can be ruled out." He rose to his feet and began to pace, as he'd done so many times in the last months as his mind played over the variables he'd been handed when he was tasked with shaping this op.

"From what I've been told, the chemical compound is unlike anything we've dealt with before, hence the expected high death toll. I don't know the science behind it. I don't even know if the US has managed to obtain a sample or if it's all theoretical. Rumor has it the gas is odorless. Invisible. Like propane or natural gas, you wouldn't smell it without the additives. But it's a thousand times more toxic, rendering a person unconscious with a few breaths. Brain damage occurs if the person inhales it for just a few minutes. Death follows soon after."

"Damn," someone muttered.

He nodded. "It's believed that the gas explosion at the elementary school in Lithuania was a cover-up for the first field test of the compound."

Audrey's face blanched. "Last September? The one that killed nearly a hundred and fifty children?"

He nodded. "No way to prove it, of course, but the *accidental* explosion was a little too thorough in destroying the building." He'd stared at photos of the bombed school for hours, remembered every gruesome detail. He cleared his throat and continued. "As you may have figured, the chemical compound is the brainchild of a Russian scientist."

"So why are we in Washington and not in Russia, taking out their chemical weapons lab?" a SEAL asked.

"Because sometime after the school explosion in Lithuania, a team was sent to extract the chemist. She'd signaled through intelligence lines she would help the US if we got her and her son out of the country safely. She could even stop further attacks by uploading corrupted data. But as long as her son was a hostage, she couldn't make a move without her child facing retaliation.

"The first mission to extract her was a disaster—a CIA special operator died, while another was severely wounded. After that, she and the boy were moved to a location very much like this one—far east Russia, on the Sea of Japan. Complete with mountains and a temperate rainforest. She and her son are ensconced in a remote mountain mansion. It's the vacation home of an oligarch. She's being forced to complete her work to set up the upcoming attack from there."

"So we're here to do a practice run for the extraction of the chemist and her son," Mock said. "And the clock is ticking down to the attack."

Xavier nodded. "There's only one road to the mansion. It's in the mountains about thirty miles from the sea, and about a hundred and fifty miles northeast of Vladivostok in the heart of Primorsky Krai. Very isolated, as there are only small villages along the coast. There's absolutely no communication in or out. Signal blockers have dampened all communications from the mansion. There is no landline or cable. No internet. Nothing."

"So how does she do her work? How does the Kremlin keep track of her progress?"

"Twice a week, an armored SUV drives from Vladivostok or one of the villages on the coast to the lake. We believe the purpose is to deliver hard drives for data transfer. There's another vehicle that delivers food once a week. We initially hoped to be able to infiltrate the food delivery, but intelligence suggests we'd never get past the guard at the gate without the proper password, which changes daily."

"So shoot the guard," one of the SEALs said.

"It's believed there's a helicopter at the ready to remove the chemist if there's any indication the guard has been incapacitated. The chemist has been warned that if they were forced to do another emergency extraction, this time they would leave her son behind with a chemical bomb that would explode when SEALs breached the building."

"Okay. So we leave the guard alone."

"And here I thought you were just fucking with us with the no-comms shit," Flyte said.

"I wish."

"So we were going to run scenarios here to plan the op," Phelps said. "Figure out how to do the impossible."

Audrey rose from her seat next to George and stretched. They used small red lanterns to light the room, making it impossible to see the red marks on her neck, but he knew they were there. Her voice had a slight rasp as she said, "I don't understand. What you've described is part of military operations—not a training exercise. Why didn't you just submit your plan to the park under that regulation? Ops don't fall under environmental review. You could have left me out of it and the lodge would have been yours to use."

"Inholding property owners couldn't be here, so we had to have a public notice period. We couldn't go out with a public notice saying the Navy is going to run an op in Olympic National Park, so we called it a training exercise, which left it open for review."

It wasn't lost on him that every man in this room had learned tonight that she was pregnant with his child, but only Cohen and the other trainers knew what he'd done to her to get them here. He'd never expected to have the opportunity to justify his actions, but here it was. He'd be a fool to let it go by, even if this wasn't the most opportune moment. "When the training was denied, I would have walked away and come up with a different plan, except then there was the chemical attack in Prague at the beginning of December."

Audrey's gaze whipped to his. "That was a gas attack?"

He nodded. "Intelligence gathered indicates upwards of eighty-two people died. Of course, this is all highly classified, but at this point, you all have the right to know what brought us here." His gaze met Audrey's. "And why I did what I did to you."

He'd never expected to be able to tell her, but now that he had, a weight lifted from his chest. At least there was a chance she would understand. Would know that it truly had nothing to do with her and everything to do with hundreds, even thousands of lives hanging in the balance.

She gave him a small nod, and he moved on. They still had a lot of ground to cover. Like how the hell they were going to end this nightmare once and for all.

"So if everything hadn't gone to hell before we even splashed down," Williams said, "we would have taken the lodge the first night, and then what?"

"Then we would have run different scenarios for how to extract the hostages. As we've learned, it's one thing to get in, and another entirely to get out."

"As far as I can tell," Flyte said, "the only way out without being seen, without being able to call for a helicopter, is hiking overland."

Xavier nodded. "Yes. I believe that would have ended up being the only scenario that would work. That's why the dummies representing the hostages are the right height and weight of both hostages, although the boy will have grown in the months since he was last seen, so his dummy is based on averages."

"And that's what we need to do now," Smith said. "Hike beyond the signal blocker and make the call with a satellite phone."

"The best way to do that is to go deeper into the forest," Audrey said, "toward Mount Olympus. Get high, above the tree line, to have the best chance to get a signal."

"We could try to find the signal blockers the mercs set up," Cohen suggested.

"I've considered that," Flyte said. "But from the coverage, I'm guessing there are several. We could waste days searching. In the meantime, we've got a critically injured SEAL and three missing team members."

All at once, Audrey jolted. He knew her body language. She had an idea.

"What is it, Aud?"

"Remember the night we met?"

He couldn't help but smile, his gaze landing on her belly. "Uh. Yeah."

Cohen snickered.

She rolled her eyes. "I mean what *I* was doing. The project I was working on."

"You were doing a survey to determine if an archaeological site would be harmed if an emergency shelter was built near a trail."

She smiled. "You were paying attention." She crossed the

room to a table that was stacked with brochures for tourists, unharmed by the battle that had taken place here. She grabbed a stack from the tabletop and returned to the group, setting the trifold pamphlets on the coffee table in front of the hearth, between the facing couches where everyone had gathered.

"This is a park guide for trails in the vicinity of the lodge." She opened one and pointed to a dotted line a fair distance from the line drawing of the lodge.

Flyte grabbed a map, as did others. Audrey moved to stand by Xavier so he could look over her shoulder at the page.

"They weren't just building an emergency shelter for hikers caught in a storm. The plan was to put in cellular antennas, giving my project area a bigger footprint. It'll be one of the few lower elevations where a cell signal is possible—there isn't much point in putting up a tower in the middle of the trees where the signal won't carry far."

"But the terrain is better there?"

"Yes, there's a decent rise and clearing."

"How far is it from here?"

"Roughly seven miles. Four by road—backtracking toward the gate. There's a wide pull-off for parking where there's a mile long trail that gets you halfway to the ridge, then it's nearly two miles of backcountry hiking to reach Lost Goat Trail and the proposed emergency shelter location."

"But avoiding both road and trail, how far is that?" Xavier asked.

"All backcountry? Five, maybe six miles. You still can't go as the crow flies because it's steep and heavily forested. The ground will be really slippery, requiring a lot of switchbacks instead of hiking straight up."

Cohen frowned at the brochure. "Please tell me there's an antenna in place there now?"

She shook her head, "Sorry. No. But it's a hike no one would expect. They'll be watching for us to head west, toward the edge of the park and the towns along the coast, or to go north along Lake Olympus Road toward the gate. Like last night, when we sheltered far from the lake and lodge, it'll be safer. Unexpected because it's such a difficult hike that seemingly goes nowhere that would help us."

Chapter Twenty-Nine

"We won't leave without Odent, Mueller, and Hobbs," Flyte said. Audrey assumed he'd named the three missing SEALs.

Xavier nodded. "We'll send a Fire Team to make the call. NSWC will send reinforcements."

Flyte shook his head. "We need every man here—to protect the lodge and to search for the missing team members."

Audrey cleared her throat and made her terrifying offer. "I'll go."

"You can't do that," one of the SEALs said. "You're pregnant."

She turned to glare at the man. "I've been hiking these woods for over twenty-five years. And I was pregnant last night when Xavier and I hiked all over the damn forest in pouring rain."

The man looked a bit sheepish. "I just meant…you said it would be steep."

"I'll go. Alone," George said.

"You aren't hiking on that leg," the medic who'd just stitched him up said.

"I've survived worse."

"I know, George," she responded. "And if we were choosing teams and you weren't injured, you'd be my first choice for this. You know this forest better than anyone alive. But you haven't slept in two days, and that cut looks like it went deep."

The medic nodded. "It *is* deep. You lost a lot of blood, and your leg could give out in a tight spot. You've saved all our asses, and we're grateful. It's time for you to rest and let the team do what we're trained for."

"They invaded *my* land," George said. She could see the fire in his eyes. "Killed *my* friend. I can do this."

"So can I," Audrey said.

"You can barely stand," George said. "Don't think I didn't see your face turn white as you tried not to puke the minute you walked in here, and your hands have been trembling for the last twenty minutes."

She'd thought she'd hidden her stress pretty well, but nothing slipped by George. "The nausea is from stress, and I need to eat. Some protein and a few hours of sleep and I'll be fine. I can do this, George. And don't forget, after you, I know these woods better than anyone else here. Plus, I've learned a lot from Xavier about how to move quietly through the forest. I can do this."

"I'll go with her," Xavier said.

She didn't know if she was irked or not that his words weren't addressed to her, but then, this was a military operation and he was a SEAL and not exactly in command of the op.

Sure enough, his gaze wasn't on her or even George. He addressed Lieutenant Flyte, his former teammate and close friend. "I'm useless here with my shoulder, but my legs work, and I can protect Audrey and make the call to NSWC. They'll listen to me."

All at once, she remembered that there was a chance NSWC might try to disregard a call from her. They'd listen, surely, but it would take more convincing than if it was one of their own.

Finally, Xavier faced her. "I hate the idea of you leaving the safety of this lodge." His gaze flicked to her belly, and she knew he wanted to mention Fig, but he wouldn't do that now, not in front of his team. "But you're right about being the best choice for this, and I know you've got the grit and stamina for it. I will have your back every step of the way."

She nodded. "We should go now, then, while it's still dark. We could probably be halfway there before dawn."

"No way. As you said, you need to eat and sleep first. You're running on fumes. We'll head out an hour before dawn and get well away from the lodge complex before daylight."

She nodded. It was a reasonable plan.

She resumed her seat on the stone hearth next to George and listened as the men made a plan for searching for the missing SEALs and protecting the lodge while she and Xavier hiked up Mount Olympus.

Given the conditions, she figured the five- or six-mile hike would take at least six hours. Possibly longer as they would have to avoid areas that were too steep to traverse without ropes. This wasn't a good time to attempt rock climbing an unexplored cliff face. Audrey was already mentally preparing her route when George nodded toward one of the large topo maps hanging on the far wall. "You'll want to take a Thunderbird trail."

"Thunderbird?" Cohen said. "There aren't any trails by that name around here."

"They're traditional trails," Audrey said. "Used by tribes

since the beginning of time. Hidden routes through the Olympics that connected the coastal groups with the Puget Sound tribes."

"My people would meet in the mountains to conduct trade," George said. "The mountains were neutral ground, allowing for commerce. Bypassing the range and crossing the lowlands to the sound could be considered an act of aggression and war."

"There's a Thunderbird trail near here?"

"Not so much trail as a general course, but yes, we had a route that connected Lake Olympus with the top of Mount Olympus, which would intersect with the Lost Goat Trail not far from the area where you surveyed last November." He nodded again toward the topographic map that hung on the wall. "Come. I'll show you."

She and George left the SEALs to their strategizing session and crossed the dark room to the framed map he'd indicated.

George ran a finger across a section of closely drawn contour lines, indicating a steep slope. "This section is going to give you the most trouble without a trail. Over here"—his finger traced a small adjacent area—"might as well be a cliff, and the ground is too exposed. You'd be visible from a distance. This area to the north is your best bet. The ground is supersaturated. You'll have to watch out for areas where downed trees have caused water to collect. Some parts of the hillside could be more bog than ground, but you won't know until your foot sinks deep, because ferns will hide the water."

She closed her eyes and tried to envision the area he'd indicated, but she couldn't. She'd never explored that area. For the first time, she recognized her words about knowing the forest might be nothing more than bravado.

But still, even if it was bluster, she was the team's best

bet. They couldn't spare SEALs for this, and none of them had ever visited that part of the forest either.

"Okay. Thanks. This helps a lot."

Xavier approached from behind and offered George a thick black marker. "Draw our route, and I'll take a picture with my phone."

Lieutenant Flyte joined them, and George talked them through the route again as he marked the glass that covered the topo map. Audrey felt better with Xavier being part of the discussion of the route.

They could do this.

They *would* do this.

By tomorrow evening, she'd be safely in her Port Angeles home.

She'd call her parents and tell them she was pregnant and that she loved them and missed them. She'd tell her mother she wanted to see her more.

She'd even call her ex-boyfriend and…well, she didn't know, really, but try to find some peace with the way they broke up. He'd dumped her the day she got the park archaeologist job, because he knew the permanent position meant she would never leave the peninsula.

It had been a blow on the day she'd achieved a goal she'd held since she was eleven years old, robbing the moment of all the joy it deserved.

He'd meant the world to her once upon a time, but now she realized that no, she'd never loved him more than her park, and she could see how that must have hurt him to come in second place to a…place.

Much like it had gutted her that Xavier prioritized his job over hers, and they weren't even in love like she and Kevin had been.

But now she knew *why* Xavier had prioritized his job, and

he'd been right. She did understand. It had never been about his job or her job at all.

It had been about preventing a massacre of epic proportions.

He hadn't been able to tell her the truth, the reason it mattered so much. She didn't feel the need to judge him for his decisions now that they at least made sense. He'd done, if not the right thing, then the only possible thing.

She stared at the map, mentally planning each step she would take, climbing over logs and burrowing through branches draped with moss, wading through tall ferns.

In the flatter areas, the ferns had been tamped down by snowfall, but the steeper hillsides hadn't collected snow, and the green fronds remained perky. In the summer, they grew so high, one could take cover from the rain under the thick overlapping plants.

The edges of her vision darkened as she focused on the black line George had drawn on the map, and the men's conversation around her faded into meaningless chatter. Like birds.

A cold sweat broke out on the back of her neck. So odd. She'd been warm since she entered the lodge and had even removed her damp coat before she accosted George with a hug.

But now chills settled in and her vision continued to narrow. She wobbled on her feet and made an incoherent noise as she realized she was about to faint.

Strong arms gripped her, and the buzzing voices took shape again. Xavier. Asking if she was okay.

Supporting her.

She shook her head, causing her vision to swim. Like mixing paint, the dim light of the room transformed everything to swirling shades of gray.

She could not lose consciousness. She forced herself to

take a deep breath. She had to shake off the dizzy spell that had wrapped around her without warning.

"I'm…I'm fine. Just. I just. I…need to eat. I think."

"You aren't up to this hike," Xavier said. "We'll send someone else."

"No. I can do it. I haven't eaten in hours. Add to that an adrenaline crash. I was assaulted not too long ago. All the stress… I think my body's saying it's safe to take a break, so I should get to it."

Truly, this had been the first moment she wasn't on edge or needed to be vigilant since she woke in the tent with Xavier in the late afternoon. And even then, they'd had to be alert for an attack on their hideaway.

It was all catching up with her.

"Take her to one of the guest rooms." Flyte turned to face her—as if remembering she wasn't in his chain of command. "I want you to eat, take a shower if you think it would help, then sleep. We'll have a guard patrol the hall to make sure you're safe."

"You don't need to—"

"We're going to move the wounded to one of the rooms as well. Third floor, so pick one of those rooms. A few SEALs will take sleeping shifts too, so you aren't the only reason we'll have a guard posted." He turned to Xavier. "You're off too. Rest up so you're ready to leave with Dr. Kendrick before dawn."

"We need to go over—"

"You need to sleep, Rivera."

Audrey sensed the two men needed to talk, and Flyte wasn't wrong. She needed to eat and get off her feet. She crossed back to where the rest of the team was gathered and grabbed her pack, which contained protein bars, then headed for the stairs.

She didn't even think about which room to take. She was

drawn there like a magnet after her slow climb of two flights of stairs.

She reached for the knob, expecting it to be locked, but the door swung wide, and she stepped into the honeymoon suite and faced the four-poster log bed she'd shared with Xavier in early November.

🌲

"Go to sleep, Rivera," Chris said. The guy looked like death warmed over, his face ashen with pain that Chris could only guess meant his shoulder had been hurt during the assault on the lodge, or when he'd saved Audrey from being taken by one of the mercs. "But before you go, have Smith give you some painkillers."

"I'm fine."

"Bullshit." He placed a hand on Rivera's arm. They were alone in the corner of the room, having retreated from the others after Audrey made her exhausted ascent of the curved staircase to the left of the great room. "Listen, man. Go to her. She's not trained for this and won't be able to sleep unless you're by her side."

"I should be helping the team."

Chris knew guilt had to be eating the man from the inside. "You are helping the team by getting rested up for the mission." He smiled as he gazed at the banister where he'd last seen Dr. Kendrick. "I like her. She's strong. Brave. Smart as hell."

A shadow of a smile crossed Xavier's face. "Tough as hell too."

"Did you know about the baby? Before this?"

He shook his head. "No. That's why she wrote the letter. In case something happened to her. She wanted me to know how much she wants our baby, how elated she was to find out she was pregnant, even though it was an accident."

"Go to her, man." Chris thought about his soon-to-be ex-wife and the mistakes he'd made in the months following the op that shattered their team. His situation was nothing like Xavier's. Hell, his marriage had probably never been solid for reasons that could be laid at both their feet. But Xavier could have something real come out of this nightmare.

"Go to her," he repeated. "And don't forget, tomorrow isn't guaranteed, so if you love her, don't fuck around with euphemisms. Tell her how you feel. What you want."

"We're in the middle of an op——"

"That never should have been an op in the first place. Hell, you aren't active duty with the teams anymore. I will see you at six hundred hours and not a moment before."

Chapter Thirty

*X*avier went to the kitchen before heading upstairs. It was clear the mercs had raided the food supplies his training team had stored in the restaurant's large walk-in fridge and freezer, but they hadn't eaten everything. He grabbed a precooked baked potato stuffed with broccoli and chopped it up, then tossed it into a frying pan and heated it on the gas stove.

If the power were on, he'd microwave it, but this would do for now. They'd shut off the generators because they didn't want the noise to provide cover for the enemy.

He grabbed a cooked chicken breast and, after shredding it, added it to the pan. He knew Audrey could use the protein, and it would taste better than the canned stuff she'd been eating for the last twenty-four hours.

Once everything was heated through, he tossed on a handful of shredded cheese and a dollop of sour cream, remembering that was how Audrey had eaten her baked potato in November.

Sheesh. He'd remembered everything about her, right down to how she'd topped her side dish.

The plate was piled high with food—more than enough for two people—when he headed up the back stairs to find Audrey. He paused on the third-floor landing, for a moment wondering which door she'd be behind, then he smiled.

He knew exactly where she'd be.

He paused outside the room, then knocked in the pattern he'd taught her the first night, then pushed the door open.

The room was dark, lit only by a camping lantern on the nightstand that she'd covered with a towel to keep the light from reaching the windows. He spotted her in the gray light, fully clothed and sprawled on the bed, her backpack beside her.

She slowly rolled to her side, her eyes remaining closed. "Oh my god, that food smells so good. I need it in me now."

He laughed. "I have never been jealous of a baked potato before."

"There's a first for everything." She sat up and shoved her backpack unceremoniously to the floor. "I inhaled a protein bar. I thought it would be enough, but my reaction to the smell tells me it wasn't."

He settled beside her on the bed and held the plate between them, then handed her a fork and cloth napkin.

"My, haven't we moved up in the world. Utensils *and* a napkin." She then speared a piece of potato, making sure she loaded the bite with broccoli and chicken. It disappeared into her mouth, and she leaned back and chewed, eyes closed.

After she swallowed, she said, "I might cry, that's so good. I didn't know you could cook."

He leaned over and kissed her neck, then straightened and loaded his own fork. "You're going to be sorely disappointed in the future when you realize this is pretty basic and required no actual skill."

He took his bite and was surprised to realize he felt a

similar rush of emotion, but figured it was because not only was he enjoying his first hot meal in days, but also, he was sharing it with Audrey. She was safe, and they'd have a warm bed for the next few hours.

They ate in silence. He noticed she paced herself tonight —she didn't gobble it down like she had the crackers yesterday.

Finally, she set her fork aside. "Thank you. That was just what I needed." She placed a hand on her belly and said, "Fig is happy too."

"How can you tell?"

"Well, I'm no longer dizzy and I don't want to vomit."

He set the plate on the nightstand, then turned and placed a hand on her belly. "When will you be able to feel the baby move?"

"According to the pregnancy guide, maybe around sixteen or seventeen weeks? They say it takes longer to notice the sensation with first pregnancies. If this were my second child, then as early as fourteen weeks."

"And you're eleven weeks now?"

"As of tomorrow, I'll officially be twelve weeks. Last week of the first trimester."

"But…we had sex ten weeks ago. I'm not saying I question paternity or your counting, I'm just confused."

She let out a soft laugh. "You aren't the only one. The first two weeks of pregnancy are actually before conception. The number of weeks are counted from the first date of the last menstrual cycle—which is because women don't always know when they conceived but we're trained by medical professionals to always remember when we last had a period. I've gone to the doctor for a very obvious sprained ankle, and the first thing they ask is when I last bled."

He stroked her belly, enjoying the normalness of this

conversation. This was how it would have been last December if he hadn't fucked everything up.

"Anyway, given that I know exactly what day I conceived —you're the only man I've had sex with in the last sixteen months—there isn't a lot of guesswork as to due date, but the weeks are still counted like everyone else."

"Do you have a good doctor in Port Angeles? Do you plan to deliver there?"

"Yes. I like the doctor and hospital, and it's not like I can relocate to the Seattle area for the last trimester just because I want to be near a bigger hospital."

Without thinking, he said, "I'll move to Port Angeles, then. If I haven't been released from the Navy yet, it might mean commuting to the shipyard in Bremerton while we get things sorted, but I'll make it work."

"It's too soon to be making those kinds of decis—"

"No way. Not too soon. You don't want to leave your job or the peninsula, so I'll come to you. I'm not going to miss a minute of this, Audrey." He felt his eyes burn, but he pushed through, speaking with his whole chest. "If you don't want me in the delivery room, fine. I'll respect your wishes in all things, but I will hold my child on the first day of their life. I'll be there for you and the baby in every way you'll let me."

She made a sound, and he raised his gaze from her exposed belly that he'd been caressing to see her face.

He'd been afraid to look into her eyes as he spoke, terrified of the rejection they might hold, but instead, he saw something else entirely. A warmth he'd had no right to hope for, accompanied by tears that might just be the good kind.

"You can be in the delivery room. I think I'd like to hold your hand."

He scooped her up—ignoring the pain in his shoulder— and pulled her onto his lap. He held her against his chest. "Thank you."

He thought about Chris's advice. Did he love Audrey? It was hard to know. They barely knew each other. But damn, what he did know had him in awe.

"I want to be with you, Audrey. Not just as the father of your child, but your partner in everything. I want to share a home and a bed."

"I don't know if I'm ready to go there, Xavier."

"I know. I just wanted you to know that's how I feel, what my goal is."

"We have a lot we don't know about each other. I mean, I only just found out you're a SEAL."

He grimaced. "I'll tell you anything you want to know."

"Have you ever been in love?"

He paused. He'd thought he was in love with Lynn, but wasn't certain if the feelings had never been there or if the way she'd dumped him had killed his connection to the deeper emotions. "I don't know." He went on to explain the relationship and the breakup in brief terms. She needed to go to sleep, but he didn't want her to think he was avoiding this conversation.

"Have you ever been arrested?"

He laughed. "What? I thought you were going to ask favorite color or favorite movie. We're going straight to jail?"

"Yep. Favorite movies and colors can change over time, but a criminal record follows you."

"Well, not if you were a minor…"

She grinned. "You *were* arrested. What did you do?"

"I was arrested, but no charges were ever filed, and it was juvie, so no record of any of it."

"I'm waiting, Mr. *I'll-tell-you-anything*."

"I…shit. Jae's going to kill me."

"What? Jae was involved?"

"We were fifteen and full of ourselves. A senior who was our team's quarterback and even more full of himself comes driving up to the school in a flashy sports car on game night. He nearly hits Jae and me and two freshmen as we're crossing the lot. I called him a dickhead, and he puffed up, tossed a few racist slurs against me and Jae. During the game, we decide to get some revenge by stealing his pretty car. We just planned to move it a few blocks from the school. Jae was on the JV team, so no one paid any attention when he slipped into the locker room and took the asshole's keys."

Audrey put a hand over her eyes. "I don't like where this story is headed. Please tell me no one gets hurt. Did you even know how to drive yet?"

"Well, not a stick shift. They didn't cover that in driver's ed. So yeah, that was part of the problem. We get pulled over two blocks from the school by a cop on patrol. It's kind of obvious when someone who has no clue how to drive a stick shift is behind the wheel of a fifty-thousand-dollar car that the car *probably* doesn't belong to them. Especially when said driver doesn't even look like he's hit puberty yet."

Her eyes went wide. "You or Jae?"

"Me. I was a late bloomer."

She kissed his neck. "But you did bloom."

He smiled. This was a bizarre but wonderful moment to be having with her.

"So what happened?"

"Well, we were arrested for stealing—grand theft auto —but it turns out, the car was already stolen by super jock, whose dad worked for the dealership. The guy's finger-prints were everywhere inside the vehicle, and once the cops knew what to look for, they had video of Mr. Football swiping the keys from his dad's desk, who had them after a test drive. Jae was a fast thinker—he'd noticed the dealer key chain and of course, the car had dealer plates—so he told the cop we were just trying to return the car to its rightful owners. They didn't believe us, but also knew it wasn't like we were going far or on a joyride and it was obvious who had *really* stolen the car. Jock boy was eighteen, so it would have been a much bigger problem for him, plus what he'd done could get his dad fired. So basically, it all went away, but Jae and I spent a terrifying night in jail and were told very sternly to never do stupid shit like that again."

"Whew. And did you follow that advice?"

"For the most part. Never got arrested again, anyway."

"And now Jae is a cop."

"Yeah. He made me swear I'd never tell anyone that story."

"Oops."

He brushed his mouth over hers. When he would have raised his head, she opened her mouth and slipped her tongue between his lips.

What followed was a slow, languorous kiss as she tasted and explored him and he did the same.

He could get lost in this moment. Forget everything except her. Even the ache in his shoulder seemed to dim with the endorphins of having this woman in his arms.

Her fingers went to the buttons of his shirt, while his went to the hem of hers. They broke apart long enough for him to pull the sweatshirt over her head.

In the dim light, he could see the outline of her breasts in the sports bra she'd borrowed. The reality of the moment came back to him.

They might be on the same bed where they'd first made love, but this wasn't the time for this. They were in the middle of an op.

Chris, who was the de facto leader now that it had become an actual op and the lieutenant commander of the team was one of the missing SEALs, had made it clear he didn't give a damn if Xavier got it on with Audrey tonight, but that didn't mean his conscience could bear it. "You need sleep, Audrey."

"I'll sleep better after you've made love to me."

That was solid logic right there.

Still, he resisted. "We don't have—" He stopped short.

She snorted out a laugh. "Were you about to say condoms?"

He cleared his throat. "Maybe."

She cupped his face and kissed him softly. "You're adorable." She wiggled on his lap, causing his already heavy erection to thicken further. "You want me, that much is clear."

"Dr. Kendrick, I've wanted you from the moment I stopped being inside you last time. I'm pretty sure I'll never get enough of you."

"I've wanted you since then too. That night felt... momentous. Even then, I was sure it was more than just a one-night stand."

"I'm sorry I—"

She put her fingers to his lips. "Shh. Let's set that aside for tonight. This is you and me, coming together in the way we were meant to." She let out a soft chuckle. "And I didn't mean 'coming together' in *that* way, but it fits too. Let's try it and see."

And with that, he no longer had even weak resistance. He was enthralled by her. Had been from the start. They had a few hours and an uncertain future. He would show her with his body what she meant to him.

She climbed from his lap and pulled off the bra as she said, "Get naked."

As a Naval warrant officer, he knew how to respond to a direct order and rose from the bed to doff his clothing.

As he removed his shirt, he recognized his shoulder was

going to be a problem. He wouldn't be supporting his weight with his left arm any time soon.

But there were work-arounds they'd both find satisfying. Fully naked, he stretched out on his back, his erection pointing to the ceiling. She sat to the side with her legs tucked beneath her.

She was more shadow than light, her soft curves a dark silhouette. Beautiful, but he wanted more. "If we close the curtains around the bed, we can remove the towel from the lantern, and I can see you."

Without a word, she pulled the canvas curtains closed on one side while he closed the opposite. They each grabbed the curtain at the foot and met in the center.

The four-poster had log beams to form a canopy. Between the foot-diameter logs that made up the posts, the five-inch-thick beams, and the king-sized mattress, the bed appeared fit for Paul Bunyan.

Tonight, this bed where they'd first made love would be a haven. An escape from cold and danger. And maybe it would be the start of something real with Audrey.

He grabbed the lantern from the nightstand and placed it on the log headboard, then pulled off the towel, giving their tented bed a soft yellow glow.

The warm light caressed Audrey's skin. "I wish I'd washed my hair instead of just using a washcloth to scrub myself when I first stepped into this room."

"Sweetheart, this is an op. Doesn't matter. And you're beautiful and perfect just as you are."

"Is this what all ops are like?"

He snorted. "Hardly."

"I have to say, I don't care for it much. Well, except for being with you now. The rest is really scary and feels a bit…lethal."

"I'd say you get used to it, but the truth is, if you do get used to it, then it's a problem."

"I think that's what happened to George. His year in Vietnam. He got used to it, and it changed forever who he was."

"That's true for a lot of Vietnam vets. It's why they changed how they rotate in soldiers. In Vietnam, a guy was sent in on his own with a three-hundred-sixty-five-day clock. Now a deployment is an entire ship or garrison. And special forces teams serve together, with new members rotating in as others leave."

Or die.

He shook his head. "Why are we talking about this? I thought we were here to forget for a few minutes."

"I guess this is part of who we are now too. Like George and Vietnam, this experience is going to change who we are." She placed a hand on her belly. "You've already changed my life completely."

He smiled at that, the look of serenity on her face as she touched her abdomen. He'd done one thing right in the twenty months since his injury. It had been an accident, but it was right. "I've only known about Fig for less than twenty-four hours, and already I can't wait to hold our baby. Can't wait to see you holding them." He rose to his knees. "There's probably going to be a period of time in which your breasts are going to be off-limits to me, so, if you don't object, I'd like to lavish them with attention while I can."

He leaned down and licked a pert nipple and she let out a soft sigh. "No objection, Your Honor."

He started slow, but weeks of fantasy and two days of adrenaline combined with having her beautiful body in his arms again couldn't compete with his limited control. It didn't take long for him to find himself with his face between her spread thighs.

He took a deep breath, the smell of her arousal erasing everything bad from his mind.

He'd dreamed of pleasuring her like this again. Of hearing her shout his name, and now he was improbably here. In spite of everything, she wanted him. And he—he didn't just want her. He was desperate for her.

He gave in to that desperation and stroked her clit with his tongue. She bucked at the sensation and slid her fingers in his hair, her nails grazing his scalp and sending pleasure up his spine.

He explored her with his mouth, his tongue tracing the contours of her labia before sliding inside her wet heat as she moaned and panted. He lifted his gaze to see her face as he thrust his tongue inside her, then licked his way back to her clitoris. Her eyes were half closed as she peered down at him and made a soft sound of pleasure that swelled his erection to new heights.

The look on her face. The sounds she made. He'd never have believed it possible, but this was even better than November. She was his future. His family.

No matter what happened between them in the future, they would always be family.

Her thigh muscles tightened as he brought her closer to the edge. She panted his name and gave praise to a deity, all while continuing to stroke his scalp.

He abraded her sensitive sex with his tongue, then sucked on the bud until she thrashed against him, letting out a soft shriek that he knew she fought to hold in, lest a SEAL on patrol should hear.

She lay panting, wrecked in the best possible way. Breathtakingly beautiful. Her eyes remained closed as the fingers threaded in his hair shifted and tugged, urging him up. "Inside me. Now. Please."

"Yes, ma'am," he whispered as he licked his way up her body until his cock nudged at her opening.

She opened her eyes. The pleasure and heat he saw there brought him back to the stare down they'd shared before their first kiss. This woman was everything to him.

He kissed her, breaking the intense stare. Her tongue slid against his as he shifted his hips and thrust deep inside her, burying himself with one smooth stroke.

Holy hell. Sex without a condom with Audrey was fucking amazing. She made a soft, satisfied groan as he filled her. He took her slowly, loving watching her face as she was lost in the pleasure of what he was doing to her. With her.

It wasn't long before his shoulder complained, forcing him to give in and grip her waist so he could roll onto his back. Now she straddled him. "Sorry, sweetheart, but my shoulder was going to give out at an inopportune moment."

She leaned down and kissed him again, then ran her lips over his scar, before straightening her back to a full upright position as she straddled him with his cock buried deep. So damn beautiful. Majestic.

She looked down on him with a luminous grin. "You need to save your strength. Let me take care of you as you took care of me." Her dark hair was loose around her shoulders. She tilted her head back and used her thighs to control her slide up and down his shaft.

He'd had a thousand incredible fantasies of her since their night together, but the reality of this moment put them all to shame. No mere fantasy could hold a candle to the real woman.

He placed his hands on her hips, helping guide her as she rode him. He moved his thumb to her clit and stroked as he thrust upward with his hips.

She let out a screeching gasp and ever so slightly adjusted her hips, and he increased the pressure of his thumb to match her movements. From there, it was a long, sensual, and yet frantic slide to the finish as she clenched him tight while he thrust and stroked.

He might have been on the precipice forever—he would never be sure—but after a glorious never-ending agony, he came, spilling inside her. He felt her clench again as she pressed her clit to his thumb. He ground into her with both cock and digit until her body convulsed again with orgasm. She made a sound of pleasure that would live in his memory forever.

Spent, she collapsed on his chest. He adjusted her position to allow his cock to slide from the sheath of her body. His semen spilled from her, a sticky warmth that usually he'd jump up to wash away, but in this moment, he lacked the energy. Plus, it was kind of great to not have to get up and get rid of the condom when all he wanted to do was hold her and feel her racing heart beat next to his.

He'd never dared to hope for this, but here they were. He didn't even feel the pain in his shoulder, he was too busy marveling at the gift of having this moment with Audrey after the nightmare he'd put her through.

"I'm falling in love with you, Dr. Kendrick. I have been since that first moment we met." The words slipped out, too big to keep inside after all the pain he'd given her. A truth he'd denied out of necessity so he could do the unthinkable to maintain his status as the warrior he was no longer capable of being.

He loved her. With his whole being. In ways that terrified him. And his feelings weren't because of the baby. No. It was simply Audrey, who had a passion for nature and the world and her place in it and grit that left him in awe.

She rolled to her side, and he followed so they were chest to chest with his right shoulder bearing his weight. She met his gaze in the lantern light and smiled. "I'm thankful we have this moment," she said. She touched his lips with her fingers and added, "And I'm hopeful for our future."

He kissed her forehead, her cheek, her lips, and nuzzled her neck, then whispered, "We need to sleep."

She nodded and rose to use the bathroom before returning to slide beneath the covers. He held her and listened to the even cadence of her breathing, making certain she was asleep before letting go himself and sliding into slumber. As he drifted off, he knew her response to his declaration was the best he could have hoped for.

He also had reason to hope she might someday love him back.

Chapter Thirty-One

*a*udrey felt Xavier slide from the bed after a few short hours of sleep. She wanted to grab his hand, pull him back to bed, and make love to him again. Maybe even say the words back to him that he'd given her. But deep down, she knew their respite was over. He was back on duty and wouldn't permit any more deviation from his role as special forces operator.

She wasn't sure if she regretted not saying the words back to him when she'd had the chance. She'd been caught off guard and had yet to explore her emotions given the distance they'd traveled in the last two days.

Two days.

It had only been—she glanced at her watch—thirty-eight hours since she'd approached the basement door of the lodge. In that time, her entire world had changed. But not just hers. There was a platoon of SEALs who were missing team members. One was missing a finger, and another might yet die from a gunshot wound to the shoulder—so much like Xavier's wound.

She heard him pull on his clothes on the other side of the

bed-curtains, then pad quietly into the bathroom. A few moments later, the hall door closed behind her favorite SEAL, and she was alone again in the honeymoon suite.

Making love with Xavier had been exactly what she needed. It had bolstered her. Given her hope. Made her feel connected to him on a level she'd never experienced.

They'd been partners these last two days, and they would be again today as they set out on a hike that would be difficult under the best of circumstances.

The intimacy of the last few hours would sustain her in the coming journey.

Now she rose from the bed and used a washcloth to wash up in the bathroom. The water was icy cold and bracing, just what she needed after less than four hours' sleep.

It would be enough, though. It had to be. And she wouldn't trade the time she'd spent making love with Xavier for anything—certainly not sleep.

She donned clean clothing she'd borrowed from Danielle Baldwin, again vowing to make sure the woman knew that the items they'd taken from their home had been lifesaving.

All traces of Xavier's scent had been washed away by the time she descended the stairs to the great room, where yet another meeting between the operatives was taking place.

Four men had gathered around the coffee table where the framed map from the wall now lay.

Xavier turned, presenting his back to the others. Only she was able to see his face as he smiled at her in the dim light. She felt his gaze as the caress it was meant to be. His features shuttered, and he turned back to the team.

When she reached the table, he said, "You should still be sleeping. I wasn't going to wake you for another half hour."

"We should go soon. While it's still full dark. Put some distance between us and the lodge before the sun rises."

"You sure you're up for it?" His gaze probed her face,

and she knew he was worried about her pushing too hard. He was probably worried about the baby, but she was in good physical shape, so there was little risk as far as the pregnancy was concerned.

"I can do it."

He gave a sharp nod. He was in professional mode in front of the others. She was glad for it.

It took less than ten minutes to go over their plans once again and to receive a full debriefing on intel gathered during the hours they slept.

A thorough search of the boathouse, shop, and other buildings in the lodge complex had been conducted, turning up no trace of the missing SEALs or the mercenary team's refuge.

In her absence, they'd come up with an estimate of the number of mercenaries unaccounted for. They guessed that the leader—who, she now learned, had remained masked in front of the hostages—and five minions remained at large.

The general consensus was they were holed up in one of the inholding cabins, but that search would take an entire day and could be a moving target if the mercs had divided and were on the run.

No one believed they'd left the forest. They'd had an end goal that wasn't met. They'd taken hostages instead of killing them, and for some reason, they wanted Xavier and her.

The men were still in the forest somewhere, and they had three SEAL hostages with them.

The alternative—that the SEALs had been killed instead of taken hostage—was unfathomable and not discussed as an option.

They were alive until proven otherwise.

The trainer who was a medic—Smith—was now resting upstairs in the same room with the wounded SEAL. It was unlikely the injured man would wake and be coherent enough to share his story, but if he did, the medic would be there to find out what happened to the team.

The meeting adjourned, and they prepared for the hike. They needed enough supplies to see them through a few days in the forest, just in case. First, they headed to the lodge storage room in hopes of finding better outdoor gear. They traded out their bigger, car camping tent for a small, light-weight four-season backpacking tent.

"We should probably trade out our sleeping bags too. Get mummy bags that pack really small."

"No," Xavier said without hesitation. "I don't care that they're bigger and heavier. If we have to camp out another night or two, I'm holding you while you sleep."

She felt a little flutter at the intensity of his eyes.

"To be clear, I'm not talking about fooling around. Dropping my guard like that could be a monumental mistake, but I will hold you close, feel your heartbeat, and know you're safe."

Since there was no one around, she rose on her toes and kissed his cheek. "Okay, then."

He smiled and reached for ultrathin sleeping pads. "Unfortunately, we should trade out for these."

She nodded even as she grimaced. The larger, thicker pads they'd used yesterday were comfortable, but far too bulky. The pads he'd selected would do little more than provide a thermal barrier from the cold ground. She was a fan of comfort, but understood the need. The sleeping bags would be their only extravagance comfortwise.

But given that they could only afford one extravagance, she was glad that was the one he chose. She wanted to be held as much as he wanted to hold.

Being pressed close to his warm, muscled body as they made love, then slept had been glorious. His body was a masterpiece, and she'd loved exploring every inch of him. Of kissing his scars. Bringing him to pleasure.

Camping gear set, next they raided the food supplies and loaded up on protein bars and trail mix in addition to Meals Ready to Eat and more cooked chicken and cheese.

Between the cold and the exertion of the hike, they'd need a lot of fuel, so they packed far more than Audrey would normally eat. They weren't going to take chances, even though it meant more pounds on their backs. That part of the load would get lighter at least as they continued.

Packed and ready, the team members who weren't guarding the perimeter or searching for the missing men all gathered. Even George was present.

He surprised her by giving her a full hug. "Roy Heller would be damned impressed by all you've done here these last days. Jeb too. Not to mention, *I'm* impressed, Audrey, and damn proud to call you my friend."

She blinked back tears. It was incredible praise from a man who rarely gave it. "While I'm in awe of what *you* managed here. We wouldn't be in the lodge right now if it weren't for you."

He grinned and tweaked her braid. "Gotta look out for the brat who always asked way too many questions."

She swiped away another tear, remembering George's curmudgeonly complaints the first time they met when she was eleven and full of questions about the Ozette village— an archaeological site she'd visited on a field trip with Roy's "junior archaeologists" group. George had been one of the guides on the trip.

Finally, she and Xavier set out, leaving via one of the service doors, which spilled out into a side parking lot that was cloaked in darkness.

They moved silently as planned, heading straight for the

culvert so they could cross the road without being spotted. The SEALs on scout duty were patrolling the area, ensuring they wouldn't be ambushed when they were under the roadway.

They emerged and entered the forest. Audrey fell into her place behind Xavier. He had her gun, returned by the SEAL who'd used it in the battle for the lodge. Four bullets remained.

Audrey had the clip-on holster with a Glock that only fired Simunition, but she had more than a hundred rounds.

Xavier had traded the NVGs he'd gotten from the dead mercenary for the US military-grade ones the SEALs used. Most of their hiking would be in daylight, so Audrey, being unfamiliar with the equipment, had opted not to take a pair that would be better utilized by a SEAL.

If all went well, they'd need neither guns nor night vision. The most important items they carried were satellite phones—one in each of their packs.

If something happened to one of them, the instructions were clear: the other would continue on to the promontory, where they should be able to get a satellite signal once the clouds thinned.

Fingers crossed the new storm that had rolled in overnight would clear in the afternoon—around the time she estimated they'd make their destination.

Xavier alone would probably be faster, but this wasn't the kind of hike one should do solo in this weather.

As agreed, they went hard at the start, trying to get at much distance as they could while night still clung to the mountain. But all too soon, they passed through the varying stages of morning twilight and the morning mist rolled in, a flat white shroud enveloping spruce trees that had sprouted before the Ozette mudslide five hundred years ago, growing next to firs that predated the birth of Chief Sealth—commonly known as Chief Seattle—around 1786.

This time of morning, in this remote place, it could be any century. No planes flew overhead. And to their great distress, no radio signals transmitted through the air.

It was just her, Xavier, birds, deer, and the occasional mountain goat. There were cougars and bears too, but as Xavier had pointed out on the first day, the bears were probably hibernating, and it had been several months since she'd spotted a cougar.

They came to a steep slope, and Audrey stared at the slick hillside, looking for the best route. There was a band without trees, but she was uneasy about being exposed as they traversed the difficult section.

Why couldn't the fog be thicker right here?

There was no option but to move fast, spend as little time in the open as possible.

Easier said than done, as she slipped twice on the slick moss and ferns that still managed to cling to the hillside. But eventually, they made it back under the thick canopy, Audrey panting with the effort of the steep climb with heavy pack.

"Need a break?" he asked.

She did, but they needed to move deeper into the forest first after being out in the open for several minutes.

"Soon," she wheezed.

They continued upward until the canopy was thick enough to recreate the feeling of twilight and Audrey called a halt. She pressed a hand to a tree trunk and leaned, taking slow, deep breaths. Sweat coated the back of her neck and dripped between her shoulder blades. When her breathing evened out and exhaustion receded, she was going to be chilled.

Xavier—*the bastard*—was barely winded. She gave him a grumpy look. "Weren't you wounded for a while and laid up? Shouldn't you be out of shape?"

He grinned. "I was shot twenty months ago. I've been

back on my feet and working out for almost a year since then. Except for my bum shoulder, I'm in excellent shape."

Much as she appreciated his fit body when he was using it to please her, right now it seemed a bit showy. A vulgar display of perfection that made her feel inadequate.

"You know, you're adorable when you're exhausted and grumpy."

"It's a good thing you think that, because I have a feeling lack of sleep and taking care of a crying baby is going to render me just as cute."

He kissed her, his tongue sliding between her lips, stealing the little breath she'd managed to take in. "Bring it on."

Dammit. He was too freaking sexy. She was melting on a thirty-seven-degree day in the middle of a misting rain.

His kiss proved effective in erasing her grumpiness. She'd have to remember that. It was quite the mood enhancer.

He leaned his forehead against hers. And she noticed that *now* he was breathing heavily. She'd taken each moment as it came these last two days. Even making love with him had been an in-the-moment experience, separate from thoughts of a future, because except for him wanting to father their baby, his feelings for her as lover and partner might dissolve to nothing over time. This was a surreal situation, and she couldn't expect real emotions to be in play.

His words and promises were wonderful. She felt fluttery at the idea that he might really be in love with her. But she wouldn't hold him to those words when this was over. It wouldn't be fair to him when she couldn't even trust her own feelings.

But standing on this steep, wooded hillside, she wanted to believe in everything. She wanted to believe in love and marriage and happily ever afters that included him pushing a baby carriage while she held a toddler's hand. As an only child, she'd always wished for siblings. He'd mentioned a brother, so she knew he had at least one.

Good Lord. She didn't even know how many siblings he had.

Did he have religious beliefs? What were his political leanings?

It was okay. They had time and nothing else to do but talk as they climbed the lower slopes of a mountain.

"How many siblings do you have?" she asked when they set out again.

"One. A brother. He's older. Married with a one-year-old. I expect they'll be trying for another soon. Fig will have cousins."

She smiled at that. She'd also always wanted cousins, but she was the only child of only children.

"You get along with your brother?"

"I was the best man at his wedding, and it wasn't merely a nod to tradition. He's my best and oldest friend. He and Jae are good friends too."

"You have a lot of friends, don't you? Jae, your family, your SEAL team members."

"Yes. I'm a lucky guy. I have a lot of worlds I fit in."

She'd never had that—an abundance of friends. Mentors, yes. Friends had been harder to come by for a nerdy girl. She'd arrived in Forks more than a decade before the *Twilight* boom started and graduated a few years before the first book was published.

Forks had been a normal, financially unstable small logging town during her teen years, and she was the crazy girl who believed in protecting spotted owls, archaeological sites, and preserving the beauty of Olympic National Forest.

She was decidedly unpopular, and that didn't change even when Forks's economy shifted to tourism during the *Twilight* boom.

Now Forks was Forks again. She loved her small town and was glad they got to profit from the wildly popular books and movies while there was gold to mine. But she still didn't quite fit in her hometown. She was more comfortable in Port Angeles and most comfortable in her park.

But she did have Undine and Jae, and a few other friends in her adopted peninsula town.

She slipped on the wet ground and landed on her knees, her gloved hands sinking into the soft earth. "The ground is really saturated from the rain. We'll need to watch out. Mudslides could occur on the steeper slopes where water has pooled."

He nodded. "I was thinking the same thing. We'll need to avoid the steeper section George suggested. It might be unstable."

That route would save them a half mile, but she had to agree. Better to lengthen the hike than to have regrets.

They adjusted their trajectory up the slope to avoid the worst of the steep section.

The hike was more grueling than she'd expected, but then, she never hiked in these conditions and never before had so many lives depended on her success.

"What about your parents? Are they going to give me the side-eye for trapping you with a baby?" she asked when they were moving again.

"Are you kidding? My mom is going to be thrilled. She's been on me about grandkids ever since I stopped going on ops. I'm forty and my brother is forty-two. She's complained about the long wait."

She felt a flush of warmth. It hadn't even occurred to her that her baby could have doting grandparents—another thing Audrey's childhood had lacked.

"And your dad?" she probed.

"He'll be thrilled too. He retired last year and wants to

do the RV-living thing, which my mom has been resisting because she wants to be close to the grandkids, but once she has a grandbaby up here, she might be agreeable, knowing having an RV would mean being able to visit the Olympic Peninsula for longer periods of time."

Wow. Xavier had really thought about this, and he really had gone all in. Once again, the damn pregnancy hormones made her eyes well with tears. Her baby was going to have a real family.

And maybe, just maybe, Audrey would have a family too.

Chapter Thirty-Two

*H*er questions about his family lit a fire of hope in Xavier's chest. Hours ago, when they'd made love, when he'd held her, he'd known she didn't fully trust the commitment he offered, and now she was probing, asking about the people who were most important to him. The people who would lavish love on their child.

But they wouldn't just love the baby. They'd embrace Audrey too. And she needed to know that.

"If anything happens to me, if I don't walk out of this forest, I want you to know my family will love not just the baby, they'll love you too."

She stopped dead in her tracks at his words. "We're both walking out of here. Don't even *think* there's going to be any other outcome."

He touched her cheek. "I will move heaven and earth for us both to survive this, but at the same time, I need you to know my family will be there for you, just like you needed to write me that letter. Some things need to be said. Some things need to be heard."

She nodded. "Okay. But let's focus on getting out of here together."

"Of course."

He could tell the hike was more of a struggle than she wanted to admit, but then he couldn't judge. His shoulder ached like it was on fire. He'd taken ibuprofen this morning, which didn't really touch the pain, but anything stronger would slow his reflexes.

Two hours after they set out, the sky opened up once again. The downpour was so heavy, it penetrated the canopy with enough force to fall in sheets. They huddled under a cluster of branches and ate protein bars, hoping the cloudburst would pass quickly.

"I gotta say, I'm not a big fan of the weather here," he quipped.

"I'll admit, I'm not too fond of it right now either. Days like today, I'm usually in my office or, if it's a day off, I'm home, sitting by a fire and reading a good book."

From there, they traded book recommendations and talked about their favorite authors, and he looked forward to a time when they'd sit by a fire together, content with their own books while spending time together.

He'd never had that with Lynn. When they spent time together, she'd wanted to be the focus of his attention. Which was fine, but also exhausting. It had never occurred to him that he could have set a boundary and asked that they share downtime together too. Maybe it had been just as exhausting for her. He didn't even know if she liked to read and was fairly certain she never realized he liked to read a few chapters each night before sleeping. They'd never spent a night together that didn't follow sex, and he was damn certain she would have been miffed if he'd picked up a book after pleasuring her.

He realized now he'd never really been himself with Lynn. That had been unfair to them both.

"If we had sex, and then before going to sleep, I wanted to read a book or watch TV…would you have a problem with that?"

"Of course not. I usually read before I go to sleep. Why do you ask?"

"I just realized I never felt comfortable reading when my ex spent the night. I think it would have bothered her that my attention wasn't on her. But to be fair to her, I never asked."

"Sex is great and all, but there's got to be more to a relationship than that."

He took her hand in his and brought it to his lips. Neither of them wore gloves while they'd been eating, so it was bare skin to skin. Her hand was icy cold against his lips. "There's more between us than sex. I know this started as a one-night stand, but even then, I felt something with you that went deeper. These past two days have only confirmed it."

She gently extracted her hand. "It could just be the baby muddling things."

He shook his head. Her concern was reasonable, but he knew his mind—and his heart. "I meant what I said last night. And I get that you can't say it back. I know you might never be able to. But I want you to know for me, this—us—is real." He rose to his feet. The rain had lifted slightly. They needed to keep going. "Now, what else do you want to know about my family?"

"Did your family immigrate, or were they in California before statehood?"

"My grandparents on my father's side immigrated from Mexico just after World War II—before my dad was born. My mother's side was here a generation before that. I never knew her parents, but I was close to my paternal grand-parents."

"Do you speak Spanish?"

"Not as much as I'd like. My grandparents—on both sides—were eager for their children to be seen as Americans and so didn't speak Spanish much at home. Neither of my parents are fluent, my brother and I less so. But my brother's wife is from Costa Rica, and she's teaching their son Spanish along with my brother."

"Oh, I love that. I'd love to have a second language and would love it even more if our baby were multilingual."

"I've always wanted to take classes. This would be a good time. Maybe hire a tutor. I've studied Russian and Arabic for the job, and having a tutor for intensive training really helped. I'm not fluent like Cohen is in Russian, but I often get the gist."

Behind him, he heard the snap of a stick followed by the click of a gun being cocked, followed by a man's voice—speaking Russian. "Oh yeah? Then you should understand what I'm about to tell you. You both are coming with me, or I will shoot your pregnant girlfriend in the stomach."

Chapter Thirty-Three

*a*udrey heard the Russian words, but didn't need to know what they meant. The man stood upslope, and Xavier's body blocked him from her view.

"Get behind the tree to the left and keep it between you and him at all times," Xavier whispered.

He referred to a very large old-growth cedar. She dove for it without hesitating at the same time Xavier moved to the right, taking cover behind a much smaller tree.

How the hell had this man found them? If they were needles, then the haystack would be the size of Lake Olympus.

Xavier moved farther to the right, skipping from tree to tree. She couldn't see the merc, but could hear him as he shouted in Russian. He switched to English and said, "Mikhail has tripled the bounty on the woman, but he wants her alive."

Mikhail. That must be the mercenary leader's name.

"Why does your boss want her?" Xavier asked as he slowly drew the man away from her.

"Who the fuck knows?" the Russian said. "He's crazy. All he cares about is killing you."

"Me, specifically?"

"You are the one called Rivera, no? He wants you, the woman, and the Black one. Flyte."

Lieutenant Flyte? Xavier's friend?

She inched her way around the tree, so she could see both men. They were downslope from her now, moving south toward steeper ground. She had a full view of the Russian's back. If she had a gun with real bullets—and was anything close to a decent shot—she could shoot him. As it was, firing a paint pellet at him would only alert him to her position.

"Why me? Why Flyte?" His voice held a different note. He'd been trying to distract the man with his questions, but this…this was important.

The Russian's shoulders moved in a shrug as he shifted his pistol, trying to get a better line of sight on Xavier, who'd disappeared behind a tree. "Something about a woman and Belarus. I don't really care. He's fucking nuts, and I was leaving before he kills us all like he did Pyotr. But then I spotted you and realized I can have my payday after all."

Shit. This man hadn't tracked them. He'd been escaping. He'd probably looked at the maps and realized Lost Goat Trail was his best route out of the park too.

Dumb luck and bad timing.

"Mikhail wants the woman alive, but you…you're different. Showing him proof you're dead is all I need."

Xavier chose that moment to bolt to a different tree.

The Russian fired his gun. The single shot echoed through the forest.

She didn't think Xavier had been hit, but she held her breath, waiting for a sign.

She knew what he was doing as he widened the distance between them on the steep, rainy hillside.

He wanted the Russian to forget about her.

She had her instructions. They'd been repeated over and over. If something happened to one of them, the other had to continue. He was drawing the man away so she could do just that. Taking risks and moving from tree to tree, giving the man a target, pulling him downslope and farther south so Audrey could continue east.

"Help us get Mikhail, and my government will pay you. Better than he would have." Xavier's shout was strong. Not the words of a man who'd been shot. He was letting her know he was uninjured.

"But we must go now for the deal to work!" The words were directed at the Russian, but she knew they were intended for her.

She didn't want to leave him.

She remembered last night, when he'd shouted for her to run, but she hadn't. She'd turned and attacked.

This was different. This time, he wasn't just sacrificing himself for her. He was protecting the entire team.

Shame washed through her at her selfish hesitation. She moved silently upslope, tucking behind a tree before looking back. Below her, the scene played out again, Xavier moving left, another gunshot.

Another shout that indicated he was fine.

He was heading toward the hillside they'd avoided because it was too steep and likely to be unstable with the torrents of rain in the last two days.

She moved again, and this time when she peeked downslope, the mercenary had turned and was scanning the hillside for her.

He hadn't forgotten her, and he'd clued in to Xavier's ploy.

A pistol fired. This time, the shot was taken by Xavier, drawing the mercenary's attention back to him, using one precious bullet.

She ran uphill. She couldn't let that bullet be wasted. As she ran, she heard Xavier shout, this time the words aimed at her. "I love you. And Fig. Tell Fig."

She ran without looking back. Her lungs burned, and her heavy pack felt like it could tip her backward and she'd tumble down the steep hillside.

She scrambled and climbed. There was forest between her and the mercenary now. Logs and trees and moss and branches that prevented her from being easily spotted as she clambered over and under.

She didn't dare look back. She needed to disappear.

But her lungs burned, and she was getting dizzy.

She spotted a thick patch of ferns and branches and burrowed into it. She had to catch her breath, or she might pass out. A long interval passed before her heartbeat began to settle and her breathing was less ragged, vision less blurred.

She pulled out her binoculars and shifted in her fern hideaway, moving fronds to make a window to look downslope. It took a moment to spot the Russian, who was searching the lower slope where she'd been minutes ago.

Xavier's voice was a distant shout. "You won't find her. She's long gone. It's just you and me now."

The merc's gaze ran upslope, and she lowered the binocs lest he catch the shine of a lens—although that was unlikely given the gray weather and steady rain.

She looked again, and saw the man had turned. He must've accepted the truth of Xavier's words and decided the bird in the hand was worth more than her in the bush.

And now it appeared he'd lost track of Xavier, who, she finally spotted, was now upslope of the mercenary. Only a tree between the two men prevented her SEAL from taking a shot.

He was okay. He had the high ground even.

This was going to work. He'd find her after he dealt with the merc and they'd finish the hike together.

She rose slowly, turning her back to both men. She had to keep going. A platoon of SEALs was counting on her to not screw this up.

More shots echoed through the forest, and her eyes burned even as she continued upward, moving more on hands and knees now, pulling herself upward and staying out of sight.

When she reached a small shelf, she saw it was a good place to rest and it had a good vantage point. The perfect place to wait for Xavier after he disposed of the mercenary. Again, they were difficult to spot between the trees, but at last, movement caught her eye, and she raised the binoculars and adjusted the focus.

They were fighting hand to hand now. Xavier must've used all his bullets and had managed to divest the mercenary of his pistol.

All at once, the mercenary took a tumble, falling down the steep slope. She watched him grapple for purchase as the ground beneath him gave way.

Satisfaction roared through her. If he kept sliding, he'd hit the steep hillside they'd skirted to avoid.

Xavier was home free.

But then she saw the mercenary grab something attached to his vest and throw it at Xavier even as he dropped out of her line of sight.

Xavier batted at the object, and it flew to his left, out of her view.

A heartbeat later, a loud boom split the air.

The binoculars remained fixed on Xavier. He stood tall, unaffected by the blast. Relief swamped her.

He was okay.

She rose to her feet. She would call out to him, he'd hike to her, and they'd finish their quest.

But before she could draw breath to shout, she heard a crack. Not a bullet, but still loud, like a tree branch but bigger. Far bigger. Like the roots of a tree upending.

And that's exactly what it was. Only it was more than one tree.

She watched in horror as the line of trees below Xavier gave up their battle to cling to the saturated hillside. The soil turned to liquid. Moss, branches, plants all flowed downward, following the trees that cleared the way as they swept down the hillside.

The uppermost boundary of the slide was just below Xavier. She watched as the ground gave way beneath his feet, and he tumbled down the river of mud.

Chapter Thirty-Four

*J*ae and Luke had halted at the first sound of gunfire. They'd left the main trail an hour ago and were making their way downslope toward the lodge when the crack of a bullet pierced the air.

"What the fuck?" Luke scanned the hillside. "That wasn't Simunition."

"And hunting is illegal in the park."

Another shot sounded, and they both scanned the woods. It was hard to tell where the noise came from, but it couldn't be far.

Jae nodded to a spot downslope that jutted out a bit and was free of trees. "Might be able to get a view from there."

They scrambled down and planted themselves on their bellies, with binoculars pressed to their eyes, looking out over the treed hillside while keeping their exposure to a minimum.

Another crack of a bullet, and Jae zoomed in on the forest to the left and above, not far from a creek that flowed down the steepest part of the slope. Another degree or two and it would be called a waterfall, not a creek.

A person would have to be insane to climb that slope with the ground as saturated as it was. He and Luke had opted for a longer route to the north to avoid that very stretch of hillside.

"Can gunfire cause a mudslide?" Luke asked.

Jae shook his head, "Not a geologist, so not sure, but it's not a risk factor I've heard of, not like an avalanche."

After an interval, the gunshots stopped. Jae thought he caught movement on the hillside. He adjusted the distance and scanned the area. Before he could get a fix on anything, a massive boom echoed across the basin.

Jae caught the edge of the flash and scanned upward from there, seeing a man standing above and looking down. "That's Xavier, above the blast zone."

"I see him."

Then there was a loud crack, followed by another. Jae watched in horror as Xavier was dragged down into the slide.

*udrey wanted more than anything to run down to Xavier. To save him. But how could she save him? She'd probably get sucked into the mud river and die with him.

Die with him.

No. She couldn't believe he was dead. He was above the debris, not below it.

But still, she knew mudslides and exactly how deadly they could be.

NO. No. *No.*

She knew what Xavier would want her to do. What he *did* want her to do. She had to keep climbing. Head toward the destination they'd decided on last night and make the vital call.

She turned her back on the collapsed slope and let out a loud sob even as she took steps that would widen the distance between herself and the father of her unborn child.

She placed her hand on her belly and sobbed as she placed one foot in front of the other. Over the ridge and into the next drainage. Up another hill. Then, and only then, could she make the call that would end this nightmare.

But with Xavier gone, the nightmare would never be truly over.

Chapter Thirty-Five

"*H*oly shit. We have a mudslide on the east hillside," Palmer said to the team gathered in the lodge.

Chris bolted to his feet. "How far from the route Rivera and Kendrick were taking?"

"Close. Possibly *on* the route."

"Not a random act of nature, then."

Chris felt sick. Kendrick was pregnant. And shit. *Rivera...* He didn't want to think about the possibility of losing another close friend, let alone the fact that the entire team was fucked if help didn't arrive soon.

Collins wouldn't last much longer. He needed an IV. Blood. Surgery. And they still had three missing teammates.

"We need to send another team." He turned to face the others. "We can't wait for full dark. They found Rivera and Kendrick anyway. How the fuck did they do that?"

"No fucking clue."

"Jonas and Phelps, I want you to set out within thirty minutes for the area where we're likely to get a satellite signal. Check with Corporal Shaw"—they'd adopted George

Shaw's former rank out of respect—"to determine a route that avoids the mudslide area."

"Yes, sir," they said in unison.

Both men had just returned from searching the forest for missing SEALs and hiding mercenaries, and they'd been slated to head back out after eating and debriefing.

This would spread the search even thinner, but they couldn't count on either Rivera or Kendrick to have made it past the mudslide.

Collins was running out of time.

＊

*J*ae kept his binoculars on Xavier as the hillside threatened to swallow him. Twice, he lost him, but then a hand would wave or a leg flail. Hell, he hoped that was waving and flailing and not the wave action of liquified mud moving his limbs.

The mud river flowed out of Jae's view, and he bolted to his feet, trying to see beyond the lip of the hillside.

"I don't see him," Luke said.

"Me neither. Let's go. We need to move closer to get eyes on him."

They took the slippery hillside at a dangerous pace, but every second mattered if Xavier was to have any chance at survival.

What the hell had happened? Why had there been gunfire and an explosion that triggered a mudslide? Wasn't this a training exercise? "Are SEAL trainings always this fucked up?"

"Hell no. Never seen anything like this."

Back in the trees, he had no perspective to look upon the glacier-carved bowl that surrounded Lake Olympus.

Finally, they came to another rock projection that offered

a view and could see that the slide had stopped, forming a pool at the base of the slope just a hundred yards away.

A mere football field separated him from his childhood best friend. But he couldn't see him. It was all shades of brown with flecks of bright green moss that had somehow escaped being fully saturated in the liquid ooze.

He scanned with his binoculars, looking for a sign.

And then he saw it. Movement.

But no. It could just be debris settling.

Except it was a hand.

Holy crap. Xavier was trying to swim through mud to get to solid ground. The man had ridden the top of the slide like a damned deity surfing the apocalypse, and now he was *swimming* to shore.

"Holy fuck," Luke said with similar awe in his voice.

They ran together toward the clearing created by the slide, facing the massive mud pool.

They stopped as close as they dared to the unstable earth, and Jae dropped his pack and pulled out a rope. "I'm going in for him."

"You a good swimmer?" Luke asked.

"Good enough."

"Let me, then. I'm more than good enough, and I've swum in water almost this thick."

Jae wanted to argue, but he wasn't a dumbass. Their best shot at saving Xavier was the former SEAL and current NOAA lieutenant commander whose entire life revolved around swimming and scuba.

Luke quickly rigged a rope harness, which they wrapped around a tree, then hooked to Jae as anchor. He'd pull both men in once Luke reached Xavier and tied him on.

*a*udrey forced her sobs away as she continued upward. *Focus on the mission and forget everything else.*

The mission. As if she were one of the team. She didn't begin to know how to cope with all that had happened. On his last op, Xavier had been shot and lost two team members, but he hadn't given up. He'd instead focused on what he could do to prepare the teams for nightmares like the one he faced. And Flyte had been on the same mission and was still fighting the fight.

All she wanted to do was curl into a ball and give up, but she wouldn't shame Xavier's faith in her that way. She wouldn't fail the team.

She would complete her mission.

With the aid of a walking stick she'd picked up a half mile back, she reached the tree-covered ridgeline that was the upper boundary of the Lake Olympus drainage. She planted the stick with each step, using a piece of the wilderness she loved to pull her forward. She crested the ridge and began the descent into the new drainage. Here the air would be free of signal-jamming frequencies, protected by ridgeline and trees.

It was well past noon and darker on the east-facing slope. There were no gaps in the thick vegetation of the thriving forest.

This drainage transitioned from temperate rainforest to montane forest. Here she would find an abundance of silver fir trees that thrived in the moist, higher elevation. The shrubs were salal, Oregon grape, and devil's club and not the epiphyte and understory ferns and mosses of the rainforest.

She descended into the well of this new woodland, the ground slightly less saturated as the ridgeline deflected some of the rain clouds. The rain, which had reduced to a sprinkle before she crossed the ridge, was now just a vapory mist passing by.

She focused on these details, as they kept her from falling completely apart.

She checked her bearing and adjusted her trajectory. She should intersect with the Lost Goat Trail in a quarter mile. It didn't take long for her to reach the narrow trail, a strip of mostly cleared ground cutting through deep woods.

One end of this serpentine trail led to a trailhead just inside the park near Highway 101, and the other continued up and up on a twisted path to the top of Mount Olympus, the highest peak in the Olympic range.

She'd hiked the full trail in her early twenties with a group of college friends. They'd spent a full five days enjoying the long loop. It had been exhilarating.

She'd never imagined approaching the path by climbing overland from the lodge and wouldn't recommend it in her trail review. She could also do without the bloodshed and danger.

She swiped at another tear and kept moving. Another quarter mile or so and she'd reach the southern ridge, where there was a decent clearing at the top of the rise and a wide flat where one day an emergency shelter and cellular antenna would be constructed. The flat was wide enough for construction materials to be flown in by helicopter, and the antenna would rise above the trees—itself made to look like a large tree so as not to be a blight on the view—and hikers in this area would have the safety of calling for help and posting photos of their adventure on social media.

At last, she stepped into the clearing, her breathing heavy after another steep uphill climb—but at least this time it had been easier walking on a trail, and not a slog through heavy mud.

She looked up at the cloudy sky and hoped the cover was

thin enough. She had a military-grade satellite phone, the best of the best.

It had to be good enough.

She lowered her pack and pulled out the phone, while placing her other hand over the Glock loaded with paint pellets holstered at her hip. She could be ambushed again here, but she had no choice but to step out into the open. It was the best chance for a strong signal.

She powered on the phone and entered the pass code. She'd had a full tutorial, and the numbers she was to call were all programed in as well as written on a cheat sheet with the list of code words she'd need to get Naval Special Warfare Command to take her seriously.

She dialed the first number on her list, and it was answered immediately. She uttered the emergency password and issued her first mayday call. It took only moments for her to be on speakerphone with the top NSWC brass as she tearfully told them of the mercenary attack on Lake Olympus Lodge and the toll it had taken on a platoon of SEALs and their trainers.

Chapter Thirty-Six

*L*uke stripped down to his base layer, wishing he had a wet suit for this, but at least the compression shirt and long johns were skintight and wouldn't drag him down. He waded into the pool of mud. Cold, thick, and sometimes viscous. It was a rude, icy awakening for a body that hadn't expected to swim in mud today.

The cold was good for his hip, though, which had been burning from the long hike with endless elevation changes that crossed through lowland and montane forests before ending in temperate rainforest.

He used his arms to propel himself forward as he waded through the mud toward Rivera, who had given up on swimming and now desperately gripped a floating log with one arm thirty feet away.

There was a cracking sound from the hillside, and Luke held his breath. If the hillside hadn't finished collapsing, he was fucked.

The rope tied to his harness went taut, Jae ready to reel him in at the first sign.

On the far side of the slide, a tree tumbled down the slope and landed in the pool.

He waited, and there was no further earth movement. Thank you, Gaia.

He moved farther into the mud, fully swimming now as the pool deepened. Stroke by cautious stroke, he drew closer to Rivera, still a bit in awe that the man was alive and alert enough to cling to the log.

He would become a legend in the SEAL community. The guy who surfed a mudslide.

He reached the Laird Hamilton of mud and saw why the man held on to the log with only one arm. His left arm hung slack, dislocated.

Damn. Fucking legend.

"You still breathing, Rivera?"

The man's mud-coated eyes opened a slit. "Barely." He wheezed out the word.

"I'm going to hook this rope to you. You're going to need to let go of the log so Jae can pull you in."

"Can't…can't move my arm. Doubt I'll be able to keep my head up."

The guy probably sported a few broken bones too.

"That's okay. I'll be your float. But you'll have to let go of the log for me to get into position. Just like BUD/S."

Rivera nodded.

None of his military or even NOAA water rescue and survival trainings had ever offered a landslide mud rescue challenge, but this was a basic lifeguarding technique, upgraded for degree of danger and difficulty with the thick, frigid mud pool and ever-present threat of another slide.

BUD/S and SERE had nothing on this.

He quickly snapped a roped carabiner to Rivera's tactical vest, tethering them together, then gave the order for the man to let go of his float, allowing Luke to move into position behind him.

The log bobbled when released, and Rivera's head went under, but Luke caught him and managed to wedge his chest under Rivera's right side, unable to have the man lie flat against Luke's chest because he still wore his bulky backpack.

"Pull!" he yelled, and the rope went taut as the ranger reeled them in.

Luke kicked and used one arm to ease the load for Jae as much as possible.

It was slow going with Jae hauling in at least four hundred pounds of men and gear through thick mud that resisted their movement while dodging logs that floated into their path. But finally, they reached the shallow edge of the slide zone, and Luke got to his feet and dragged Rivera out of the frigid muck.

They couldn't pause to rest, as another slide could happen at any moment, so he dragged Rivera as far as he could in sock-covered feet, then stopped to don his boots and slip on his pack after cramming his discarded clothing inside.

Together, he and Jae carried Rivera upslope and away from the slide zone, finally stopping when they couldn't see the wrecked hillside through the thick trees. They should be safe from additional slides here.

Luke flopped down on the mossy ground next to where they'd placed Rivera and caught his breath. "Damn, and I thought the water in the strait was cold."

Rivera let out a wheezing sound. "Everything about this place is cold and wet and gray. How do you tolerate living here?"

Jae shrugged. "Generally, I avoid swimming in the strait or in mudslides."

"Easier said than done," Rivera said.

Luke smiled. Maybe he could like this guy. He hoped so, given what he'd just risked to save him.

Jae swore he was a good guy, but Luke was reserving judgment until he found out what happened to Audrey.

Rivera unclipped his water bottle from his pack and poured water over his face, rinsing away mud from his eyes and nose and running his hand over his mouth.

"Let's get that shoulder put back," Jae said.

Rivera must be in agony, but he hadn't said a word as Luke and Jay hauled him over uneven ground without bothering to pop his arm back first.

The guy got bonus points for that.

Badass surfer. Not a whiner. Undine would say this could be the start of a bromance, but she was also Team Audrey.

Rivera nodded and forced himself to sit up, gripping his ribs with his good arm. He grimaced but again didn't say a word.

Jae moved to his side and quickly popped the shoulder joint back into place. Rivera let out a hissing breath, then made a sound that could be relief. "Thanks, man." He turned to Luke and offered his good hand. "Chief Warrant Officer Xavier Rivera."

Luke took his hand. He'd forgotten that Rivera probably had no clue who the hell he was. "Lieutenant Commander Luke Sevick."

"SEAL team? You mentioned BUD/S."

"Was. Not anymore. I'm in NOAA's Commissioned Officer Corps now."

Rivera nodded. "Uniformed, but not armed service. Quite a switch."

"Injured on an op. Active duty on the teams was out. Returned to my first love, marine biology."

"Wait. You're Audrey's friend's husband. She never mentioned your name."

Luke nodded. So Rivera had been with Audrey, because they sure as hell hadn't talked about him and Undine last November, before Audrey had known Rivera was in the Navy. "Where is Audrey?" he asked.

Rivera's gaze turned toward the hillside he'd just surfed down. "Hopefully on the other side of that ridge, calling NSWC."

"What the hell happened here, Xave?" Jae asked. Then he shook his head. "Wait. We need to get moving. You can talk then. Can you walk?"

Rivera shook his head.

Damn. Hauling the guy and his pack down the mountain was going to suck. He studied the man's legs. "Sprain or broken?"

Rivera shook his head again, then slowly climbed to his feet, bracing his good arm on a log as he did so. "Sorry. I think I can walk. But I'm not going anywhere."

Jae frowned. "The hillside can give way again at any moment. We've got to get out of here and onto stable ground."

"Audrey's going to come back for me. Even though it's illogical for her to think I survived, she's going to come back here. So here is where I need to be."

Luke couldn't argue with that. They were here to find Audrey, after all. "We should climb up. Meet her halfway, then."

Rivera shook his head. "What if our paths don't cross? And besides, I don't know if I can climb upward. Down, I think I can handle. Up is a different story."

Luke's hip wasn't all that excited about going up again either.

A chill began to take Luke as they sat on the cold, wet ground, him still wearing nothing but mud-soaked skivvies.

"I'm going to change. You got something you can change into in your pack?"

Xavier nodded.

"Good, after we change, you're going to spill everything that's going on. And don't you dare try to claim classified after I just pulled your ass out of a pool of mud."

Xavier nodded. "We're way past worrying about classified now."

Chapter Thirty-Seven

*A*udrey sat in the clearing, hanging her head between her knees, breathing deeply. NSWC had wanted her to wait here, where a helicopter would be able to land and extract her, but she'd refused. How could she sit here for the hour or two it took to get a helicopter, when Xavier was on the other side of the ridge at the bottom of a mudslide?

Was he dead?

She didn't want to think it. Denial was her friend, but deep down, she knew the odds he'd survived were pretty much nil.

Even if he'd made it down without being crushed by logs or boulders, how would he get out of the pool the slide created?

He'd probably lost consciousness and drowned if he hadn't been crushed to death.

NO.

She rejected the thought.

Just no. Not her Xavier. Not now.

He was going to be a father.

She thought of how many men had gone off to war,

never to meet their offspring. It was foolish to think he'd escaped that fate.

But she had to. Until she laid her eyes on his body, she'd believe he was alive.

She rose to her feet and took a step toward the trail. She should probably eat, but didn't think she could stomach food right now.

Damned if she ate, damned if she didn't.

It had taken nearly an hour for her to get here from when she last saw Xavier, but the hike had been more uphill than down.

This was the reverse, and there was new urgency in her pace.

Help was coming.

Now to find Xavier.

She placed her hand on her belly. "Let's go get your daddy, Fig."

*A*udrey stepped wrong on a rock, and it rolled from under her feet. Her ankle twisted, and she went down, landing on the hard ground and sliding down the slope a few feet.

She stifled a sob as her spine let her know how happy it was to be jammed.

Fuck. Fuck. Fuck. Fuckity. *Fuck.*

She'd made good time, but that was because she was moving too fast. Being careless.

Plus, she was light-headed. Probably with hunger.

She was being foolish, something she'd sworn never to do while hiking alone. She knew a thousand horror stories of hikers being careless. She'd been involved in search parties for several.

She took a deep breath and dug in her heels to stop her downward slide.

She had to eat. Not eating was her first mistake.

She pulled out a strip of beef jerky and gnawed on it. Her body flushed with the first swallow. It was a wild sensation, to be so intensely in need of food without feeling even a pang of hunger. The opposite, in fact, as the thought of eating had triggered nausea.

But the baby knew what it needed and was demanding she pay the toll.

Okay. She knew who the boss was now. And she would listen to the little beast.

She finished the jerky, then ate several bites of cheese, not even bothering to slice it off the brick. Boss baby needed food.

After several moments, the shaking of her hands subsided.

When did my hands start shaking?

She thought back over the last half mile of terrain and realized she remembered none of it. It had been like driving a car down a familiar highway with no other vehicles in sight. She'd been so deep in her thoughts, she couldn't remember taking bearings and adjusting her trajectory, but she knew she had. Knew she was on the right course. She was almost to the flat where she'd watched Xavier tumble down the slope.

She took another bite, then put the brick of cheddar back in her pack.

It was time to find her lover.

Chapter Thirty-Eight

*X*avier's head swam, and he guessed he might have a concussion in addition to broken ribs.

Good times.

But fuck. He was *alive*, and that was more than he'd had a right to expect. The moment the merc threw the grenade at him was frozen in his mind. It was like he saw every moment through a disjointed strobe effect.

The grenade in the air, closer. Closer.

Batting at it with the empty Glock, trying to send it back downslope, toward the merc.

But he'd swung too hard, and the projectile went to the left, heading for third base. And it hit that rock and tumbled into the crevasse that snaked across the hillside, a split caused by the heavy rainfall of the last few days.

The shock of the explosion, the rocking of the hillside. He'd stood for a moment on the precipice, knowing the slightest movement would collapse the ground beneath his feet.

But then the ground dissolved anyway, and the next thing

he knew, he was gripping roots, hanging on with his one good arm as the other had been torqued when he grabbed at the collapsing hillside. Then the tree he gripped came down, with him clinging to the side.

It was a jumble from there. A blur of pain and motion. He and his tree plummeted into the pool. He lost his grip on the trunk and slipped underwater—or rather, undermud—and had grappled for the surface with his one good arm, the other hanging limp and useless.

He caught a branch and tried to surface, but couldn't through the leaves and twigs. He was going to suffocate in draping moss that grabbed on to his face.

He'd been forced to release the branch, dive under and kick for a new gap in the debris. He'd finally surfaced, face clear of moss, and found air and gray sky. Grappling between logs, he latched on to one and caught his breath. He tried to clear the mud from his eyes by rubbing his face on his shoulder. One arm was useless, the other gripped the log that kept him from sinking.

The world remained a muddy blur.

He'd had no idea how he was going to make it out of the mud pit until he heard Jae's shout. His friend's voice was like a dream. So unexpected. So necessary. He'd feared he was hallucinating.

But Jae had been real, and he'd brought along a friend, to whom Xavier now owed his life.

And both men had come here to find Audrey. In a way, his beautiful, amazing Audrey had saved him yet again.

His eyes burned at what she must be going through. She had to believe he was dead.

Hell, *he'd* believed he was dead. But he was gloriously alive. In a crap ton of pain, but breathing. He closed his eyes against the throbbing of his head.

"Stay with us, X-man," Jae said.

He nodded. "Not going anywhere."

"No sleeping. We need to get you back to the lodge so a medic can check you out."

He didn't need Smith to tell him he had a concussion, so they would stay right here. His future was on her way to find him.

※

*a*udrey scanned the wreckage where the hillside had given way, adjusting the binoculars as she searched the mud for signs of Xavier.

His camouflaged clothing would blend right in with the debris pool, it was a useless endeavor. She lowered the binoculars and left the rise that had offered a narrow view of the wreckage.

She would skirt along the slope, giving the weak hillside wide berth.

At last, she reached the bottom of the slide zone, where a pool had formed at the base of the hill. They were still well above the lake, on a shelf carved by a glacier thousands of years ago.

If not for this shelf, the mudslide would have continued downward. In its descent, it would have gained steam, like an avalanche, and taken out a massive swath of forest before wiping out several cabins and pushing into the lake, filling it with mud and trees.

But the shelf was stable, and the lower, less steep hillside remained intact.

She cautiously approached the debris field, aware that mercenaries could have made their way up here in her absence, in addition to the fact that the ground adjacent to the mudflow could be compromised.

But there was no way to search for Xavier without exposing herself to both the dangerous ground and the dangerous men who'd been hunting them for days.

She darted between trees, finding energy reserves that had been kindled by the hope she would find Xavier. She paused on the edge of the forest, looking over the cleared swath, when she heard a birdcall that sounded familiar.

She jolted and turned, searching the woods for the source of the sound.

She wasn't skilled enough to make the return call, wasn't even sure she remembered exactly the sound.

She raised her walking stick and hit it against the tree. Once. Pause. Two in a row. Pause. Then once again. The wood knocks carried through the woods, and a moment later, she heard the return knock: one, one, two.

The SEAL team knew the birdcall, and they even knew the first knock pattern, but only Xavier knew the reply.

Her vision blurred as she headed in the direction of the knocks and tweets.

She wanted to shout his name, but feared others might be in the vicinity. It would explain his caution in not calling out to her.

She raised her binoculars to her eyes and scanned the trees. Movement caught her attention. She adjusted the zoom. Three men. One seated, two standing.

Xavier slowly rose from the ground. His hair was thick with mud, but his clothes were not.

She dropped the binocs and ran toward him as he opened his arms. She stumbled slightly when her brain registered that the men with him were Jae and Luke. She'd figure out that part later.

She would have thrown herself into his arms, but she stopped short, seeing his battered face and pained expression even as his eyes burned with emotion.

"Is this real?" she asked as tears tracked down her face.

He closed the distance between them, and his arms encircled her. "It's real, sweetheart. I'm here."

Chapter Thirty-Nine

They debated heading down the hillside versus staying put, but in the end, Xavier passed out, making the decision for them. Audrey sat with her back to a log and Xavier's head in her lap, as Jae attempted to reassure her that Xavier would be okay.

His face was ashen and his skin chilled. She guessed he was running a fever, which was a bad sign with a concussion.

The whir of helicopter blades cut through the air, and her heart leapt as it became clear rescue was at hand.

Audrey's signal panel—the waterproof sheet with a forest-camouflage pattern that they'd used twice when taking shelter in tree roots—was put into use again, but this time, it was flipped over, revealing a neon-orange side. Jay secured it with rocks at the corners, laying it in a small clearing well away from the unstable mudslide perimeter. The clearing wasn't large enough for the helicopter to land, but Luke assured her the Navy would be ready with a stretcher to be lowered down on a cable.

He proved correct, and she watched anxiously as two

paramedics rapidly descended down a line that swayed in the wind.

The roar of the whirling rotors made only the barest of communication possible. In minutes, the paramedics had Xavier loaded on the stretcher and pulled up inside the aircraft.

Next, Audrey donned a harness so she could be hauled up into the bird. Ordinarily, being rigged to a hovering helicopter and winched upward while wind whipped at her skin might terrify her, but she'd lost the capacity for that type of fear at this point, and she watched the ground with Luke and Jae retreat without so much as a flutter in her belly.

Jae was lifted next, followed by Luke, who was a pro at this sort of thing from his SEAL days.

Her seat location made it impossible for her to hold Xavier's hand, so she gazed out the window as they banked and rose. First the lake came into view, then the lodge. She spotted another helicopter on the front lawn, between the lodge and the exploded dock.

The injured SEALs were being airlifted out, but she knew Lieutenant Flyte and the others intended to stay with reinforcements to find their missing teammates, assuming they hadn't been found already.

They would have all the firepower they needed, and as ONP archaeologist, they had her full permission—and for the record, George's blessing too—to let loose as needed, even if archaeological sites and historic lodges would be destroyed.

It was less than a forty-five minute flight to the Naval hospital in Bremerton. She knew that if Xavier's condition were dire, they'd have gone to Port Angeles, but he was in stable condition, so he went to the larger, better-equipped Naval facility.

At the hospital, she, Jae, and Luke were quickly routed

from the general emergency room to the waiting area for patients undergoing a full CT scan, as the staff was ready and waiting for Xavier and Collins. Paul Cohen had flown in with Collins, but he was in a different treatment area.

Even on the fast track, it was a long wait. Audrey was grateful Xavier had only lost consciousness for a few moments after they'd walked several feet. While blacking out was a bad sign with a concussion, a short incident could indicate it wasn't severe.

She paced the waiting room while Jae and Luke made phone calls, Jae to the park superintendent, and Luke to the Navy. Audrey had people she should be making calls to herself, but she could barely think, let alone try to explain to anyone what she'd just been through.

After they had word on Xavier, she'd call her parents.

And Xavier's parents, if he was unable to make the call himself.

At last, a doctor entered the waiting room. Xavier had given his permission for the doctor to share his medical information with Audrey, Jae, and Luke, so the doctor wasted no time and got right to the good news: "There's no sign of a brain bleed. While concussions should always be taken seriously and have long-term effects, it's possible he'll heal quickly without lingering issues. Quite a feat considering what he's been through."

Audrey burst into tears, and Jae put an arm around her. She noticed he was wiping his eyes too.

"What about the rest of him?" Luke asked.

"Again, considering what he went through, it's astonishing he's not in worse condition. Four cracked ribs. Contusions all over. His left shoulder is worrisome—he's likely to need another round of surgery to repair the new damage to the joint. His left clavicle is fractured. Like the ribs, there's not much we can do for it beyond pain management. We're going to wrap his ribs and immobilize his arm for two, three days max. Surgery—if he ends up needing it—can wait until he's in better shape and the concussion is no longer an issue."

"Can I see him?" Audrey asked.

The doctor nodded. "We're keeping him overnight for observation. He's being moved to his room now. He's taken a pain medication that will help him sleep, so it may be a while before he's up for talking, but you can make yourselves comfortable in his room." His gaze scanned the three of them and he gave a faint smile. "I can tell the nurses it's okay to bend the rules about only patients using the shower in the rooms."

They all looked a wreck, but Luke might take the prize with mud caked in his hair, streaking his face, and down his arms. The former SEAL laughed. "Thank you, Doctor."

After the doctor left the room, Audrey collapsed onto a chair and buried her face in her hands, letting out the full-body sob she hadn't permitted herself when she saw him caught in the slide.

The only difference between then and now was these were tears of joy.

*T*he last time Xavier had been hospitalized after a failed op, he'd woken to find his girlfriend had visited and left while he was sleeping, asking Chris to let him know that she'd been by to see him and wouldn't be back. Now here he was again, and his shoulder—and pretty much every other part of his body—was on fire with pain. So much pain, he hadn't even noticed the broken clavicle, but it did explain the extra misery on his left side.

His best escape from the agony was sleep, so he'd grudgingly agreed to the medication that would knock him out.

His mind swam with thoughts of yet another surgery. More rehab and recovery. But none of that worried him. Not when he'd survived the impossible.

No, the only thing that made him wary was the thought of going to sleep and waking up alone. He knew his concern was more superstitious than logical, which was why he'd taken the drugs, doing the right thing for his body. And now, regardless of his feelings on the matter, sleep won, and he slipped into blessed, pain-free oblivion.

He had no idea how long he'd been under when his mind slowly surfaced. The pain was back, but muted, a dull ache in key places.

Manageable.

His eyelids were too heavy to open right away, so he listened, letting his other senses do the heavy lifting. He wasn't hooked up to a heart monitor or IV. There was nothing tying him down. That was a good sign.

He tried to remember why he was here. It came to him quickly, slicing through groggy barriers. The slide. Battered by logs and rocks and a deluge of mud.

Audrey's face when she saw him afterward.

With that memory came the fear of opening his eyes and finding history repeating itself. Would she be here? Or was the thought of being with a broken former SEAL too much for her too?

Surely the world couldn't be so cruel as to spare him twice and then punish him for his mistakes in the same way.

Punishment. He'd never realized that was how he'd viewed Lynn's rejection. A deserved action for a man who'd been part of a disastrous op in which two SEALs died.

It was part survivor's guilt, but there was more to it. He'd been slow to react.

Now his mistakes were the same. His training. His plan. Slow to react when things went south. And this time, Audrey had reason to want to punish him.

If she walked away from him now, he'd be getting nothing less than what he deserved.

He heard a rustling sound and realized he wasn't alone. He dared to raise heavy eyelids. The room was dark. No light leaked around the pulled shade, so he guessed it was night.

He tilted his head to see the woman sleeping in the chair on his right side.

His heart pounded. His Audrey. Here. She hadn't left him.

In fact, she looked like she'd done little more than wash her face since escaping the forest.

Well versed in the buttons of hospital beds, he hit the one that would raise the head to a comfortable angle.

Her eyes popped open at the sound of the hydraulic lift. "Xavier." She said his name with excitement, but her voice remained soft and low.

"Hey, sweetheart."

She unfolded herself from the visitor's chair and was by his side, running a gentle hand over his jaw. "How do you feel?"

"I think the only correct answer is 'like I surfed a mudslide,' but thanks to the drugs, a bit better than that."

She smiled and pressed her lips to his. "No more surfing for you."

"I swear, I will never surf mud or water again. My body can't take this abuse anymore."

Even exhausted and grubby, she was achingly beautiful as she looked down at him. He needed to hold her, feel her heartbeat as she pressed against him. He moved ever so slightly to the side, his body protesting as each shift sent rivers of pain to all his extremities. But it would be worth it.

"What are you doing? You look—"

"Shh. I'm fine." He patted the bed beside him. "Join me."

"I can't do that. This is a hospital, and you're bruised from head to toe."

"I'm not asking for sex. I just need to feel you by my side."

"We'll get in trouble."

He grinned. "Maybe the hospital police will arrest us. C'mon. Live on the wild side." He scooted again, painfully making more room.

She let out a heavy sigh. "You're going to keep hurting yourself until I agree, aren't you?"

He hadn't planned to, but now that he knew it would work, he said, "Yep."

She climbed onto the bed, hanging off the edge, barely touching him.

"Closer," he said.

"But your ribs—"

"The fractures are all on the left side. Left clavicle. Left shoulder. The left got all the major damage."

"How very sinister."

He laughed and nudged her closer with his right arm. Once she was fully on the mattress, he pulled up the rail, locking her in with him.

She settled against his side as he lowered the head of the bed until it was just slightly raised. He wanted her to slide under the blanket with him, but he figured that would push her too far. At least he could feel her breath on his skin.

Somehow, miraculously, we survived.

"What've I missed?" he asked.

"A captain and some general came to see you a few hours ago. They'll be back in the morning."

"General?"

"Oh. Yeah. Maybe it was an admiral?"

"Probably. Although I'm sure the Army is involved in what's happening in the park now. They've probably got Green Berets and Rangers from Fort Lewis searching the forest."

"They wouldn't give me an update. Said we'd both be debriefed tomorrow. After being treated, Cohen was taken to NSWC, and my understanding is George was taken there directly. Between the two of them, they're giving the Navy all the intel they need to figure out who was in the forest with us and why."

He nodded. First priority was finding the missing teammates, second was figuring out who the mercenaries were.

"Did Jae tell them about the unruly Russian campers who waylaid him that first night?" Jae had given him the rundown while they waited for Audrey to find them after the mudslide, and they'd all figured it was too much of a coincidence for the campers to not have a connection.

"He said he would. He and Luke were both debriefed once it was clear you were going to be out for a while."

"Good." It was likely the RV full of Russian campers was long gone, but if they were still in Forks, they might be able to provide information on the third priority: finding the motive behind the attack.

On one level, it was obvious—an attack on an unarmed group of SEALs on American soil was a power play among enemies and would be useful as a recruiting tool for terrorist organizations. Like the bombing of USS *Cole*, this story would make headlines around the world if—*when*—the media got wind of it.

And, like the *Cole* bombing, it was less important to know

who the big players were in the conspiracy than who the ultimate mastermind was. USS *Cole* had been attacked by al Qaeda under the direction of Osama bin Laden.

This time, the mastermind was undoubtedly a Russian oligarch, but which one, and was this part of a bigger game plan?

And why had the mercenary leader—Mikhail—wanted Xavier, Chris, and Audrey specifically?

Was this about the op to extract the Russian chemist and her son? Or was this a target of convenience, knowing that SEALs were going to be isolated and essentially unarmed in the forest for a week?

"How's your head?" she asked.

"Better, actually. I think I passed out as much from the pain of my other injuries as from the concussion."

"Have you had a concussion before?"

He nodded. "Got too close to an explosion once and was tossed through the air. Can't say I recommend the experience."

"And yet you went back for more."

He did. And even after he'd been shot and out of commission, he'd never considered quitting. It was all ingrained in who he was. His life's calling.

What would he do now?

It wasn't a question he needed to decide right away. He had savings and, after twenty-two years in the Navy, would be able to retire with full benefits. Between re-signing bonuses he'd never touched and living cheaply on base for more years than not, he had a lot of money in the bank.

If need be, he could put off trying to find a job until six months after the baby was born. Maybe longer.

He could use that time to figure out the best ways to use his unique skill set. Hell, he could even go to college and learn something entirely new. If there wasn't a school that fit his needs on the peninsula, he could take online classes.

The whole world was open to him and all that mattered was he would find a way to be a full-time dad and, hopefully sooner rather than later, husband.

He had zero doubt that this was love for him. It had happened fast and under extreme circumstances, but his feelings were real, and there was no denying the chemistry that had been there from the start. Now he just needed to hope it was the same for her, or at least that it could be in the future.

Deep down, he knew that if they'd met under normal circumstances, they'd have begun dating and within weeks would have been just as serious as he felt now. But he also knew she didn't trust his feelings—and probably didn't trust her own—because they could be clouded by the baby and the nightmare she'd just survived.

So he'd be patient. He could be content just holding her for now.

A nurse entered the room and snickered at seeing them snuggled together on the narrow bed. "Well, it looks like someone is feeling better."

He smiled at the woman, whom he remembered from when he'd been installed in this room hours ago.

"Sleeping drugs did the trick, just like you promised."

"And look, Ms. Kendrick is still here." She winked at him.

Oh Lord. He'd been loopy when the painkiller took effect before he fell asleep. He must've told the nurse he was concerned he'd wake up alone, just like last time.

He supposed finding Audrey sharing his hospital bed made it clear his drug-induced fears had been completely unfounded and warranted a bit of teasing. He wondered what else he'd said in his loopy state.

"I need to check your vitals now that you're awake. I should probably ask Ms. Kendrick to get up…"

Audrey started to scoot back, but he tightened his arm around her. "No can do. She's twelve weeks pregnant and can't be expected to sleep in that miserable chair. She stays."

The nurse gave a knowing smile, and he realized he'd probably shared that detail with her too.

"Yes. I am aware. And I was going to add that I'm going to look the other way for now given that you both are VIPs and all."

"VIPs?" Audrey asked, her body relaxing against him now that it was clear the hospital police weren't going to be called in.

"Well, no one has told us *what* happened to you both except for Mr. Rivera surviving a mudslide, but it's been made pretty clear by the admiral and captain who visited and the calls that have come in from NSWC that you did *something* special that warrants preferential treatment. This is why you have a private room and we aren't enforcing visiting hours."

He smiled. "Audrey's the hero, not me."

"Hardly," she objected.

He kissed the top of her head. "You absolutely are, and I have a traumatic brain injury, so you aren't allowed to argue with me."

The nurse unhooked the sling that held his left arm in place and slid the blood pressure cuff around his upper arm. "Not optimal to do it this way, but you wanted Ms. Kendrick to stay."

"It's fine," he said. His arm itself didn't hurt; it was the shoulder joint and clavicle.

After she was done, she read out the numbers and said, "A little high, but that's expected under the circumstances."

To Audrey, she said, "Don't let him play the traumatic-brain-injury card too much, but give him that one."

She then ran a thermometer over his forehead and announced the slight fever he'd had when he'd first arrived was gone.

"You missed dinner, but I can order a meal for you or get you a yogurt smoothie if you're hungry."

He accepted the offer of the smoothie mostly because he could eat it without Audrey being forced to leave his side.

The nurse returned a few minutes later with the snack, and they were alone again. He ate his smoothie, offering to share it with her, but she declined. She said she'd eaten while he slept and had plenty of snacks to see her through the night should boss baby demand food.

He smiled at that and wondered when she'd taken to calling Fig *boss baby*, but they had time for that later. The second dose of pain meds was kicking in, and he was getting drowsy. His eyes slipped closed without permission.

"I should let you sleep."

"Don't you dare leave me."

"I'm not going anywhere, Xavier. I'll be right in the chair."

"No. Don't leave my bed. Please?" It was irrational, he knew, but he needed her there. It was one way to combat the fear that he'd wake up and find himself broken and alone in a hospital bed once again.

Chapter Forty

It wasn't the most comfortable night's sleep, but Audrey didn't care. Hearing Xavier's steady heartbeat all night long was exactly what she needed.

Undine arrived early the following morning with clothes and toiletries for Audrey. Xavier insisted that she break another hospital law and use the shower in his room rather than leaving to get cleaned up. After all, she had a history of making good use of his shower.

Clean and changed at last, she left Xavier's room while his doctor checked in on him during the morning rounds.

She and Undine went to the cafeteria, where Audrey filled a paper cup with decaf coffee for herself and bought a bran muffin for boss baby. They settled at a small table in the corner.

She let out a long breath. This was all so normal—coffee and muffins with a friend—and yet all so surreal.

"So, it appears you and Xavier have reconciled."

She smiled. "That's one word for it."

"I'm glad. Luke said he's a good guy. I mean…he rode a mudslide for you."

"For everyone. But yeah. For me too." She lowered her voice to the merest whisper. "I can't tell you why he did what he did…but I get it. It's okay." This was her first time saying this aloud, and as she said the words, she knew they were true with her full heart. She could let all the anger and pain go. More important, she trusted him again in a way she'd never thought she'd be able to.

Undine nodded. "Yeah. Luke said that too."

"I can't believe he and Jae were there. They saved Xavier's life. He'd have drowned in the mud if he was on his own." She placed her hand over her friend's. "They saved the life of the father of my unborn child."

Undine's eyes widened and her mouth dropped open. "Get out!"

Audrey laughed. "I guess Luke didn't tell you."

"Nope."

"I'm surprised you didn't guess when I got my coffee from the decaf carafe."

Undine took a sip of her tea. "I didn't notice. I'm sure Luke thought it would be more fun if you told me yourself. Especially since, if *you'd* been paying attention, you'd have seen that I skipped my usual Earl Grey and am drinking a caffeine-free beverage myself."

Now it was Audrey's turn to let out an excited squeal. "No way! When?"

"Mid-August. You?"

"End of July. Holy crap, we're just two weeks apart."

Audrey thoroughly enjoyed the conversation that followed. Not only was it not about mercenaries, explosives, or violent acts of nature, it was also the first time since she'd learned she was pregnant that she simply got to share the excitement and joy and talk about the wonders of it all, and that it was with a friend who was on the same wild, yet oh-so-common journey made it all the sweeter.

She walked Undine to the front of the hospital and hugged her tight as she thanked her again for bringing clothes and toiletries.

As she headed to Xavier's hospital room, she felt different. More herself now that she was in her own clothes and clean and relatively rested. But also, she touched the waist of her jeans, which were now snug, and thought about the fact that soon, she and Undine would be shopping for maternity clothes together.

For the first time since she'd learned she was pregnant, she knew she'd be able to enjoy sharing each milestone with not just her friends and family, but with Xavier's as well.

There was so very much joy and excitement ahead of them.

She reached Xavier's room, and the door was closed. Knowing the doctor would have finished at least twenty minutes ago, she knocked. The door was opened by the Navy captain she'd met last night. "Oh. I'm sorry. I'll go to the waiting room."

The man pulled the door wide. "Please, join us, Dr. Kendrick. This involves you too."

She stepped into the room and saw the solemn expression on the admiral's and Xavier's faces. She braced herself for whatever they had to say.

The captain cleared his throat. "Petty Officer Third Class Collins had surgery yesterday afternoon. It went well and his prognosis is good, in spite of the delays. Medic Smith is to be commended for managing to keep infection at bay under difficult conditions."

"I'm so glad to hear it," she said, seeing the same relief in Xavier's eyes.

The captain nodded. "Collins woke for the first time late last night. By early this morning, he was coherent enough to answer questions. He was able to share what happened to him and the three missing SEALs. We haven't yet been able to confirm his account, but Lieutenant Flyte is leading the search, now that we know where to begin looking."

"That's as far as they got before you arrived," Xavier said. He nodded toward the visitor's chair. "I have a feeling you'll want to sit for this."

She nodded and skirted the bed and dropped into the chair. She felt flushed and had cold chills at the same time. Her body was going into overtime stress reaction after a brief respite from the nightmare.

She met the admiral's gaze. It wasn't lost on her that two high-ranking Naval officers were delivering this news personally to the man who bore the weight of the entire disastrous training.

It was a kindness. A show of support. But it also meant the news was very, very bad.

The admiral picked up the story. "Collins said his team extracted from the lake in the location they'd selected during the planning session on Whidbey. Less than fifteen minutes after they entered the forest, they were engaged by an enemy combatant. Thinking it was part of the training, they took cover and returned fire. They had direct hits on their target and expected the man to lay down his arms and play dead, as expected given the shots landed in areas not protected by body armor. He should at least have presented as injured when the Simunition round hit an extremity. But the trainer —as that is who they believed they were engaging—didn't surrender. Instead, he approached Commander Odent and shot him point blank in the face."

Audrey covered her mouth with her hand and gasped, imagining the horror of the moment.

"Master Chief Petty Officer Mueller was shot next. Also point blank to the head. Seaman Hobbs and Petty Officer Collins both took cover and tried to escape. Knowing their weapons were useless, they had no other option. Collins was shot in the shoulder. He was left to bleed out while the shooter chased Hobbs. Collins isn't sure of the exact time-line, but he knows he lay in the forest for some time, possibly hours, before the initial shooter returned. Finding him alive, the shooter decided to take him to the lodge as another hostage. Collins lost consciousness while being dragged through the woods. He doesn't remember being in the lodge at all. Waking up in the hospital was quite a shock.

Audrey couldn't even begin to imagine how disorienting that would be.

"He said he has no idea what happened to Hobbs. He has provided their location in the woods as best he could esti-mate. We have a dozen men including Army Rangers, Special Forces, SEALs, and federal officers searching that area of the forest and expect to receive news soon."

She swiped at her eyes, fully able to imagine the horror of the night. She could see the trees, feel the rain, hear the shots, smell the gunpowder and blood.

The captain resumed. "Communication continues to be a problem, but we've restored cable and landlines and located three signal blockers so far and suspect there are only one or two more. The signal blockers are highly advanced. Technology we've never seen before." He cleared his throat, and his gaze flicked to Audrey, but he addressed Xavier. "We believe the mercenaries were hired by Grigory Laskin."

Xavier gave a slow nod. "I was going to suggest the same thing. I've been thinking along those lines since we knew the mercenary leader—Mikhail—was after both Chris and me. The merc who died in the mudslide mentioned Belarus and a woman."

Audrey had been the one to share what they'd learned from the mercenary on the hillside, as Xavier had been out of commission, first as he was being examined, then he'd been asleep, which was probably the only reason she was still in the room right now, because she had a feeling they were wading into the ultra-top-secret realm.

The admiral gave a sharp nod. Not surprisingly, he turned to her and said, "I'm sorry, but we're now in territory that we cannot share with you."

She nodded. "I understand." She even knew Xavier wouldn't spill the details later and had to respect that. There would be no blowback from what he'd revealed to her and George, but the military wouldn't offer more information than absolutely necessary.

To Xavier, the admiral said, "We'll discuss this further during your official debriefing."

"Have any of the mercenaries been detained?" he asked.

"Yes. Three were captured by the SEAL team not long after the mudslide. Jonas and Phelps had set out to attempt the same hike you and Audrey had made in case you both had died in the slide. They came across three mercenaries who were trying to flee—much as the mercenary you met on the hillside said he was doing. It appears Mikhail was no longer rational. He killed one of his own men in anger after losing the lodge and hostages."

"Do any of the mercs have a wound to the neck or shoulder—above the collarbone?"

"I'm not sure," the captain responded. "Why?"

"I shot one with one of Corporal Shaw's match guns—hit him with a nail—during the raid on the lodge. He got away when I went after Audrey."

She hadn't known about that, but then, in the aftermath of the fight behind the post office, she'd been too obsessed with getting the dead man's blood off her face to really remember anything else. It had all been a blur.

"The merc I shot… He was masked," Xavier said.

Audrey jolted as his words sank in. "But…Cohen said the

mercenary leader, Mikhail, was the only one who was masked."

He nodded. "I figured you should check, in case Mikhail is trying to pass himself off as a minion."

The blood drained from her face. Xavier had been on the verge of taking down the mercenary leader, but he'd abandoned him in order to save her.

"We'll check on that," the captain said. "We're still trying to get an accurate count of the number of mercenaries. To that end, we'd like you both to come to headquarters for a full debriefing as soon as you're released from the hospital, Mr. Rivera."

"The doctor said I'm clear to leave this morning. Keeping me overnight for observation was just a precaution."

"Good. We'll give you time alone first—I know this morning's news is a blow, as it is to all of us. When you're ready, tell the nurse, and we'll have a car pick you up."

The men left, and they were alone again. The silence was a heavy weight as Audrey thought about the three SEALs. Two known to be dead and the third unlikely to have survived.

Audrey rose from her seat and moved to his bedside. She took his hand. "I'm so sorry, Xavier."

She remembered those first minutes after they found the empty pit, and his desperate need to stop the training. She'd wanted to check on George and he'd wanted to go to the yurt. They both knew now that even if they'd gone to the yurt, it was too late. Jeb was dead and all wired communication destroyed. They couldn't have stopped it.

But even so, this had been Xavier's fear at that time, that the team would engage with tangos and assume they were actors. They'd expect the enemy to shoot paint pellets. His greatest fear had happened within the first fifteen minutes of the op.

He tugged at her hand, and she climbed onto the bed. She wrapped her arms around him as he let out a gut-wrenching sob.

She did the only thing she could and cried with him, deeply grieving three men she would never get to know.

Chapter Forty-One

They received word midmorning that two bodies—those of Odent and Mueller—had been recovered. The search for Hobbs remained ongoing.

Hours after that, the final update confirmed Xavier's greatest fear. Hobbs had been found in the lake.

With all three men accounted for, the focus on the search for Mikhail and any remaining mercenaries continued. The estimates for the number of mercenaries ranged from George's count that first night when he identified a dozen, up to eighteen, as claimed by one of the men captured, while the other two men said there had been only ten or eleven. Given that George had been accurate in everything else, it was clear the mercenaries gave unreliable information.

The number of dead mercenaries was easier to calculate. The body of the man Xavier had encountered on the cliff-side trail had turned up in the lake. That had been the first kill. Then there was the one he'd killed by snapping his neck, two. George had shot one with a match gun and taken out two with the explosive on the fishing boat, three, four, five. Add to that the one who died in the mudslide—six—and the one who'd attacked Audrey—seven—and the two killed in the lodge firefight—eight and nine. They'd also recovered the body of the man the captured mercs had claimed Mikhail killed, for an even ten dead.

Three captured.

Mikhail was the only one they were certain had escaped, as none of the three detained mercenaries had a wound to the shoulder. A balaclava had been found in a puddle next to Lake Olympus Road near Jeb's cabin. The mask would be tested for DNA, but after being soaked in mud, it was unlikely to yield actionable evidence.

The forest was searched by law enforcement from every walk of life—federal, state, city, military, park, and tribal—on the assumption that up to five mercenaries could remain, but no other trace was found of anyone in the days immediately following.

Audrey was sent home after a full day of debriefing, but Xavier had to stay on the base to go over again and again every detail of the planning for the training, as they searched for the pieces that would reveal the mole who'd compromised the exercise.

Chris was pulled from the forest to join the debriefing, and the more they compared notes, the more they were both certain that the entire plot had been executed as revenge for the failed mission in Belarus.

The days were long and emotionally grueling. He and Chris were put up in a house on the base, and he ended each night with a long FaceTime call with Audrey.

She was back in her house in Port Angeles. Her SUV had been transported to a body shop to repair the damage from the bullets. She had a rental car in the interim, but preferred to stay home as much as possible. Jae and Undine took turns sleeping in her guest bedroom because she didn't want to be alone.

Mikhail was still out there, and she'd been named as one of his targets.

The unruly campers Jae had dealt with the first night were long gone from Forks by the time investigators showed up, but that didn't mean they'd left the country. The police had her house on their regular drive-by schedule, she was the proud owner of a high-end alarm system, and she sported a new smartwatch, so she would never be without a phone.

Xavier ached to be with her, but the work he was doing was important, and they both knew it.

The nightly calls drew them closer together even as they were apart. They spent entire conversations talking about nothing related to the lodge events, just sharing their history and dreams for the future, and that, more than anything, healed pieces of Xavier's shattered heart.

He knew he faced a long road to finding a way to forgive himself. Right now, it didn't feel possible to take that leap as guilt weighed on him. But he also knew on an external, logical level, that it wasn't his fault.

Someday, he'd get his heart to believe it.

Fig had grown to the size of a peapod—he found it a little odd that fruits and vegetables appeared to be the standard base measurement for fetus size—when Xavier was finally cut loose for two days' leave.

A quick online search gave him the name of a peapod flower that could be found year-round, but he was disappointed when none of the florists nearby had bouquets on hand. Instead, he got Audrey two dozen roses and went to the grocery store and made a second bouquet of peapods.

He showed up on her doorstep with a bouquet in each hand, and the look on her face when she opened the door might have been the most perfect thing he'd ever seen.

Inside, she'd squealed when he set down the flowers and

peas on the nearest flat surface and scooped her up, draping her over his right shoulder. "Where's the bedroom?"

"Xavier, you're injured! Put me down."

"It's been a week. I'm fine."

"Hey, Xave," Jae said from the archway to what he assumed was the living room.

"Hey, Jae. Tell me where the bedroom is, then you can leave. Set the alarm behind you."

Jae laughed and pointed to a hallway, then headed for the front door. "Let me know when you need me, Aud."

They were halfway down the hall when Xavier heard the door close and the ping of the alarm. Audrey's bedroom was small, like the rest of her house. Her bed was queen-sized, filling two-thirds of the room.

He set her on the mattress and said, "When we move in together, we're going to need a bigger bed."

She laughed. "And a bigger house. This one is only a two-bedroom. What if we have guests, or want more children?"

The idea that she'd just agreed to move in with him and was pondering more than their one accidental baby made his heart leap.

🌲

*A*udrey studied his face as she waited for his response, and her belly did a small somersault at the spark that lit him up.

"You want more than one child?"

"If I can. I'm already in the advanced maternal age category, so we'll have to see. But as an only child who always wanted siblings, I would be happy if we had more than one little peapod."

"Do you want to learn the baby's sex before they're born?"

"No. I want the mystery. I don't care if we have a boy or a girl—I just want them healthy, and they may end up being a different gender than what they're assigned at birth anyway."

He nodded. "Works for me. Mystery it is."

She rose from the bed and reached for the top button of his shirt. "Okay, I need to see the damage for myself." He'd refused to show her his bruises during their video chats this week, leaving her to assume they were gruesome.

She opened his collar and gently pressed her lips to his healing clavicle. "I can't believe you picked me up and carried me."

"There weren't stairs involved, and it was a short distance. Worth the pain."

She gave him a stern look. "No more hurting yourself for me."

"I'm fine, Aud. I wore the sling until the doctor said I should start using my arm. It's even possible I might not need another surgery."

She knew that was because the doctors weren't confident another surgery would help and not because he was in better condition than they'd estimated a week ago. But she'd let him take it as good news. Either way, the surgery wouldn't happen for a few months, and he'd been relieved by that.

She slowly unbuttoned his shirt, revealing his muscular chest and the tight white wrapping around his rib cage.

Above and below the wrapping, his usually golden-brown skin was a mottled yellowish brown. Many of the contusions had probably been purple a day or two ago, as the bruises on his face had been.

His right eye had been swollen for days, and the skin

around it had been a deep dark purple—so dark it was almost black on his cheekbone.

Now his cheek was yellow with pale purple in the center, and his left jaw showed a similar impact point. She could only imagine how his scalp must have looked, as they believed the concussion had been caused by a blow to the back of his head, behind his left ear.

A week later and the bruises were impressive, but past their peak. She pressed her lips to each mark, placing at least a dozen gentle kisses on his face, shoulders, chest, and arms before circling him to inspect his back and seeing the same patchwork of marks marring his muscular perfection.

As she had with his front, she kissed each healing contusion, tracing a particularly long—and still purple—slash mark on his lower back below the tight wrapping that supported his ribs.

She returned to his front and reached for his fly, quickly popping open the top button on his dark slacks. She moved to the zipper, and his hand covered hers. "You unzip me and start kissing below the waist, and I'm not going to have a lot of patience for you to finish your inspection. I've missed you and am hard as a rock."

She grinned. "I'm counting on that."

She'd been wanting this moment for the last week, when she could give him pleasure that would make him forget his sorrow, if only for a few moments.

He'd made love to her in the lodge. Now it was her turn to make love to him. To transport him from his aches and pains and heartache.

She lowered the zipper and dropped to her knees before him, pulling down his pants. She frowned at his shoes, seeing her miscalculation.

She quickly untied them so he could toe them off. He then stepped out of his pants. She pulled off his socks, then looked up at the gloriously naked and very erect man who stood before her.

She'd never seen a more beautiful male body and she wanted to lick every inch of him. She smiled because that was exactly what she was about to do.

She started by kissing the bruises on his upper thighs, moving upward. When she reached his hips she grinned wickedly up at him and said, "Turn."

His nostrils flared, but he followed orders without complaint. Heat spread through her; he was enjoying the anticipation as much as she was.

His butt and upper thighs were as mottled as the rest of him, meaning there was much kissing to be done. She finished by taking a gentle nip of his left ass cheek, and enjoyed the sound he made at the back of his throat.

"Turn," she said again, and again he complied, faster this time.

She let out a soft chuckle, then resumed her kisses of his upper thighs and hips. "Tell me," she said in a husky voice, "where else does it hurt?"

His eyes narrowed to sexy slits. "Sweetheart, I think you know exactly where I ache the most right now."

"Poor baby," she said, then stroked the underside of his cock with her tongue, from base to tip.

He let out a low groan—more of a growl, really—and said, "More."

She rolled her tongue around his thick head, tasting precum, breathing in the scent of him. She loved this, the teasing and the sensory overload of scent, taste, the velvety feel of his cock on her tongue, the sight of his beautiful erection, and the sound of his pleasure.

She took him fully into her mouth, the better to taste and feel him. He added to her pleasure with more sound—a low groan as she took him deep into the back of her throat and sucked.

She'd gone down on him during their first night together, and it had been pleasurable for them both in a purely physical way. This was better. Intense in a way she hadn't expected. Infused with all the emotion that had brought them here.

She released him from her mouth, then nudged him toward the bed. "You're going to want to sit down for this."

With a laugh, he dropped onto the mattress and spread his legs. She slipped between his thighs and reached for his cock.

"Lose the shirt," he ordered.

Since he'd been so good at following her commands, she did the same and pulled her top over her head, revealing a simple beige satin bra that overflowed with cleavage. She'd been surprised to realize when she donned it this morning that her breasts were slightly fuller and the tenderness she'd been feeling for the last few weeks was subsiding.

The look on Xavier's face as he took in her overflowing bra while his cock jutted out above her cleavage was belly-flippingly smoldery.

He groaned again when she wrapped her hands around the base and took him into her mouth and swirled her tongue around the tip. She bobbed down, taking him deep, then came up again, sucking both ways while her hand kept pace with her mouth along his shaft. She found her rhythm and closed her eyes, the feel of him in her mouth, his cock growing thicker as she stroked him, was all the pleasure she needed.

His large hands cupped her head, his fingers grazing her scalp as she moved, adding to her pleasure. Soft sounds emitted from her throat as she sucked. This was everything she wanted.

She forced her eyes open so she could see his face. His eyes were slitted as he watched her go down on him. She felt the heat in his gaze to her core. Since he'd stripped, he'd touched no part of her body but her hair, but she was so aroused, she needed to feel him inside her. *Now.*

She released him from her mouth and rose to her feet, then quickly yanked off her yoga pants and underwear.

"Scoot to the middle of the bed and lie on your back," she ordered.

He complied without hesitation. She climbed on the bed, then crawled across the mattress and straddled him, taking his cock in hand and lining it up with her opening. She slid down onto his shaft, seating him deep inside her body in one motion.

Her nerves shot with pleasure at the fast penetration, a thick, hot intrusion into her tight body.

"There is something so fucking hot about you being slick and ready for me when I never even touched you."

She let out a soft groan, the feeling so intense, she couldn't even say the words to agree with him.

His hands found her breasts as she used her knees to push herself up and down on his shaft. When one hand dropped down to stroke her clit with his thumb, she threw her head back and moved in a primal rhythm that brought her closer and closer to the crest of the wave.

His hips bucked upward, and she moved in unison. His thumb worked magic, and she shattered, pleasure rippling through her from both the friction of his cock and the stroke of his thumb. His hips moved in an urgent rhythm, and he crested too, his body pulsing with his ejaculation.

Fast, intense, explosive, it was everything she'd needed from him. Everything she'd needed to give.

She gazed down at him and saw the burn of emotion in his eyes. He opened his mouth to speak, and she pressed a finger to his lips. She knew what he was about to say, and she didn't want his words in the air, lest he think she was giving him an echo, saying merely what she believed he wanted to hear.

She leaned down and pressed her lips to his, opening her mouth to kiss him. She realized they hadn't even kissed today. Not really.

Her tongue slid against his, adding another flavor to her sensory pleasure. Then she raised her head and met his gaze. "I love you, Chief Warrant Officer Xavier Rivera, and I want us to raise our baby together as a family."

Chapter Forty-Two

$\mathcal{I}$t was one thing to believe Audrey wanted him in her life as a lover and partner, and quite another to actually hear her say the words. The warmth in his chest expanded until he thought he might explode. He pulled her head down for another deep kiss. When he released her, he whispered, "I'm going to do everything in my power to make you as happy as being with you makes me."

She stroked his cheek. "You already do."

He rolled to his right side, moving her with him so they remained chest to chest. "Not even close." He kissed her neck, taking a deep breath and breathing in her scent.

It was probably wrong to feel this much joy right now, but he'd promised Chris—and himself—he would savor this break with Audrey.

Chris had told him about Pam's affair and their pending divorce. He'd admitted that deep down, he knew part of the reason she'd found a lover and wanted out was because he'd cut himself off after the way things went down in Belarus. It didn't excuse her actions, but it was there, a crack in the foundation.

He told Xavier not to make the same mistake, reminding him he had a right to live and love and find happiness, even now. *Especially now.*

Chris, more than anyone, understood and felt the same guilt that hounded Xavier. Three dead in Belarus including the hostage. Three dead at Lake Olympus.

Of course, Chris hadn't been part of the planning, and his teammates had died before any of the SEALs even knew the forest was filled with mercenaries, but Xavier knew the guilt clung to him just the same.

Especially because the targeting of the exercise was connected to Belarus. Revenge for the death of the hostage, paid for by the girl's oligarch father.

But right now, he had Audrey in his arms, and she'd just told him she loved him. He'd enjoy this feeling and keep his heart open when he was with Audrey.

"How long can you stay?" she asked.

"Two days. Then I need to go to Coronado. Among other things, there's going to be a service for the three fallen SEALs. You're invited, but it's the same day as Jeb's service."

"Oh, damn. That's a tough one. But I need to be here for Jeb. George is going to give the eulogy." She stroked his cheek again. "I'm sorry. I wish I could be there for you."

"I understand. Your community here needs you, and mine will need me there. It's the right choice for both of us."

She nodded.

"There's a lot to sort through, but while I'm there, I'm going to start the retirement process. Given the circumstances, my departure from the Navy is likely to be expedited. It's possible I'll be able to move up here before the end of March."

"You're really doing this. No hesitation."

"I'm really doing this." He threaded his fingers through hers and brought her hand to his lips. "No hesitation."

She smiled. "I feel like I should tell you, moving to Port Angeles was the deal breaker for my ex. He broke up with me when I landed the ONP archaeologist position, because he knew I would never move south, and he didn't want to move north. So...I get how big this is for you, to leave the Navy *and* move to a remote part of Washington."

"Well, it's only fair I should mention...the deal breaker for *my* ex was standing by me when I was in the hospital. I don't know what bothered her more, taking care of me as I recovered from surgery, or knowing I was going to be dealing with PTSD. Yet I don't see you running scared, and that means more than *I* can say."

She kissed him. "I think I would leave the Olympic Peninsula for you, Xavier Rivera."

His heart jolted. "Wow. You must really love me."

She brushed her lips over his. "I really, really do."

*T*he weekend passed far too quickly, but they both made sure not to waste a precious moment. Monday morning, a car arrived, sent by the Navy to deliver Xavier to the base for a transport to Coronado.

He kissed Audrey goodbye, absorbing this moment to give him something to hold on to while he was away and burying sailors who'd met an unfathomable end during what should have been a safe exercise.

"I love you," he whispered against her lips.

"I love you too."

With one more deep kiss, he left her and climbed inside the vehicle. Hours later, he was landing on the base that had been the closest thing he had to home for nearly eighteen years.

He was pulled straight into another debriefing, finding Chris, who'd flown back two days ago, already in the room.

He took a seat next to Flyte. They had a few minutes before the meeting would officially begin.

"How's Audrey?"

"Amazing."

Chris grinned, showing off deep dimples in both cheeks. "Excellent. You took my advice."

He nodded. "You're a wise man." He glanced at Chris's hand, noting his ring was still absent. "Pam?"

Chris gave a sharp shake of his head. "It's over."

"I'm sorry, man."

His nostrils flared. "Me too."

Cohen entered the room, the bandage on his hand much smaller now than the last time Xavier had seen him. Paul dropped into the empty chair on Xavier's other side.

"How's Carly?" Xavier asked.

"Thankful."

Both Xavier and Chris nodded.

"Thankful" was the word of the day, week, and month.

Thankful for George Shaw. Audrey's cameras and timely arrival. Thankful for Luke and Jae's concern putting them in the right place at the right time.

If not for those things, they all might be being honored in the memorial service scheduled for tomorrow.

The officers and military investigators who'd called the meeting entered the room, and everyone came to attention.

They began with an update on the investigation…and then things got interesting.

Captain Jane Harlow launched right in. "From the beginning, one of our analysts examined the intersection between the Belarus op and the Lake Olympus Lodge Exercise. Obviously, Mr. Rivera's and Lieutenant Flyte's participation in both activities was key, but the odds that both men would be assigned on opposite sides of the LOLE training was a coincidence that couldn't be ignored. The number of individuals who knew details of both ops was limited. The number who had the power to influence the assignment of which trainers would plan the exercise and which SEAL platoon would participate in the training even smaller. A deep search of the financial data and communications of everyone at the center of that Venn diagram led us to interesting results."

Harlow paused and met Xavier's gaze before moving on to meet Flyte's. "Mr. Rivera and Lieutenant Flyte were cleared immediately. I'm sorry, gentlemen, but it was necessary."

Xavier nodded. He knew he would be investigated and wasn't offended. The fact that he was still in the room was a testament to the fact that he and Flyte were innocent.

"Three days ago, our investigators discovered the wife of an officer integral to ops training and planning has large sums of money in foreign bank accounts. Far more than could be justified or explained."

Xavier studied the room, trying to think of who was missing at the table, and came on the answer a moment before Captain Harlow identified the missing man: Commander Pearson.

"Commander Pearson was taken in for questioning. We have a confession. We are waiting for confirmation of certain details, but it does look like we've got the right man."

Silence settled in the room as they all took this in. Selling military secrets to a Russian oligarch was treason. Directing operations to fit said oligarch's desires—actions that led to the deaths of three SEALs—was another level of betrayal.

Revulsion spread through Xavier. It was a good thing the man was already in a cell, because Xavier and a number of SEALs would happily tear him limb from limb.

"Pearson confirmed that Russian oligarch Grigory Laskin wanted revenge for the death of his daughter, who died in the rescue op led by Flyte and Rivera. It is worth noting that Katerina Laskin was kidnapped by men believed to be working for the president of Russia when the president was told Laskin intended to betray him and provide intel to the US."

"Was it true? Was Laskin turning against the president?" a captain near the head of the table asked.

"Yes. Laskin was in negotiations with the US when his daughter was taken. After her abduction, a deal was made that if his daughter was safely extracted, he would turn on the president. He also promised several other oligarchs would join him. But the Fire Team was betrayed. Katerina and two SEALs died."

Even now, in this room, the true circumstances of Katerina's death were left out. Those in the room who didn't know already didn't need to know the details.

Xavier had no idea if Laskin had been told the truth or not. The man would never have believed it anyway. They'd still be here, debriefing after the oligarch's revenge.

"Analysis of the failed op has determined that, given the level of betrayal, it was an impossible mission. The Fire Team had no chance of success, and Lieutenant Flyte is to be commended for his actions in saving himself and Rivera and bringing Forsythe and Adams home."

Flyte shifted in his seat, and Xavier knew the man was uncomfortable. There was no commendation for what happened in Belarus. No exoneration.

Captain Harlow resumed her seat. An admiral took over. "With this information, we've determined that the assault on the LOLE was unrelated to the attached operational mission. It appears the oligarch and mercenaries he hired knew nothing about the plan to extract the Russian scientist and her son."

"Pearson didn't know the purpose of the exercise?" Flyte asked, his voice showing the same surprise Xavier felt.

"He did not. His knowledge was limited to need to know for the LOLE, as is protocol, and he did not need to know the actual purpose of the training, just who was assigned and various parameters to make sure the proper equipment was available." The admiral cleared his throat. "An analysis of the satellite phones and radios provided to the trainers and SEALs shows that the team was given substandard equipment. The combination of poor-quality phones and radios and advanced signal-blocking technology ensured that no one working the exercise would be able to make a call within the lake basin area. A better phone might have been able to make the call from a clearing on the hillside."

Xavier let out a deep breath. They'd been sabotaged from every angle.

"Of note," the admiral continued, "it's clear that Russia's signal-blocking technology is far ahead of ours, but with the blockers we recovered from the forest, we have already developed a device that we believe can reduce the efficacy of the blockers currently in place in the target property where the scientist and her son are being held."

Xavier jolted.

The mission is a go?

The admiral addressed him directly. "Yes, Mr. Rivera. Between what we learned inadvertently in the disastrous training and the technology we've reverse engineered, we have learned what we need to extract the doctor and her son from Primorsky Krai. In that sense, the LOLE was a success. We're watching the weather forecasts for heavy rain to provide cover. As soon as one rolls in, we have a team ready to do a HALO jump into the storm."

en days later, the op went off without a hitch. The team had been prepared to hike out with the scientist, her son, and the data needed to halt the coming attack, but with the signal-blocker technology they'd recovered from the forest, they were able to disable the system and call for helicopter extraction in addition to being able to upload the scientist's vast data collection directly onto US military servers before they left the woodland mansion.

Xavier called Audrey with the good news as soon as he was cleared. "They want me here for a few more days to debrief with the team, then I'll be on leave." He was taking two weeks leave to sort things out. While he planned to spend as much of it in bed with Audrey as possible, they'd also agreed to a trip to the Bay Area to introduce her to his family and possibly a trip to Arizona so he could meet her father.

"I can't wait."

He knew she'd been going stir-crazy. She'd been on leave herself from work while investigations continued in the lodge, but a few days ago, Mikhail's body had been found inside an RV that had been abandoned in the woods near Sequim, a town fifteen miles east of Port Angeles.

The merc leader had hanged himself in the same RV that had been the home of the unruly campers who'd kept Jae busy the first night.

Three other dead bodies were piled in the rear bedroom, all shot in the head. Jae identified them as the campers he'd encountered in Mora Campground and ejected from the park.

The hanged man had a nasty wound to the shoulder that matched what they'd expect from a shot with a nail. If DNA could be gleaned from the balaclava, they would check for a match, but until then, the wound served to identify him as the missing merc leader.

The three mercenaries in custody refused to make an identification one way or another, and all three men only identified their leader as Mikhail, no last name.

Given that there had been no sign of anyone in the forest and there was no proof any other mercenaries remained at large, the search of the Lake Olympus basin and beyond came to an end. The op was over. It was time for cleanup to begin.

Yesterday, inholding landowners had been permitted to reenter their cabins. Repairs on the lodge would begin next week.

With the success of the SEAL mission, Mikhail's suicide, and the Russian oligarch's assets being seized as he now topped the FBI Most Wanted list, the nightmare was over.

"I'd like to meet with your boss when I'm in Port Angeles," he said. "To explain."

"You don't need to. I've talked to him. He doesn't know the details, obviously, but with everything that happened, he's ready to accept you had your reasons. He acknowledged that if I can forgive you, he certainly wouldn't make waves or do anything to jeopardize your retirement."

Xavier's brain stopped working the moment she uttered the words *"I can forgive you"*.

"You…forgive me? But what I did was unforgivable."

"Apparently not, because I do forgive you. I think I stopped hurting over it that night in the lodge, when you explained about the…*thing*."

He smiled at her way of avoiding revealing Top Secret information on an unsecure cell phone. "Thank you. I—I'm speechless." He picked up the ring box from his dresser top. Last week, his mother had shipped her mother's rings to him. He was more eager than ever to fly north and see Audrey, but their planned two week vacation wasn't nearly enough.

It was fast, but it was right. If Audrey wanted to wait until after the baby was born to get married, that was fine with him. He didn't care when they actually did the deed so long as it was a settled matter that they planned to be together forever. In sickness and in health, until the end of their days.

"You don't need to say anything. Just come back to me as soon as you can."

"I will. I promise. Who's staying with you tonight?" he asked.

"Undine. Jae's working today. Honestly, it feels weird having babysitters now, but I'm not ready to be alone."

"And I'm glad you don't have to be. Just a few more days and I'll be there. In the meantime, have fun with your pregnant girls' time."

She laughed. "We're already sick of the subject. This much time together is too much of a good thing. We're now binge-watching *Leverage* and planning our own con games."

"Isn't the point of the show to use cons to help the good guys?"

"Oh, naturally, we'll use our cons for good."

"Phew."

"When you get home, will you be able to tell me what all this was really about?"

The fact that she was already referring to her house as his home was an unexpected pleasure that almost eclipsed the second part of her question. "What do you mean?"

"It's pretty obvious that if you were able to run the op to rescue the chemist, then halting that mission wasn't the motive. No way in hell would a team of SEALs HALO jump into a compromised op two weeks after…everything we went through."

Audrey knew the limitations of what they could say on FaceTime. They were always careful in their conversations.

"I'll check with the brass and make sure I have clear parameters on what I can tell you. I'll push for full disclosure, but can't make promises."

"Fair enough."

He loved that he could trust she wouldn't push for more than he could tell. But then, she knew in his heart of hearts, he'd give her every ugly detail.

Someday, he'd have to share the full truth about what had happened in Belarus.

Maybe if Chris had been able to tell his wife everything, they'd still be together.

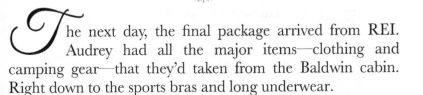

*T*he next day, the final package arrived from REI. Audrey had all the major items—clothing and camping gear—that they'd taken from the Baldwin cabin. Right down to the sports bras and long underwear.

She'd already spoken to Danielle, who'd been far more concerned about being reported for running a vacation rental when the easement with the park didn't allow for that than with Audrey taking items they'd needed to survive.

But given that she couldn't even tell Danielle the full story of why it had been so important, after assuring her she didn't give a damn about the vacation rental setup, she'd been determined to replace each item.

She had everything—right down to a brick of gourmet cheddar cheese. She would admit to being a bit surprised at the cost, but it did explain why the cheese had been so damn good. She'd ordered a brick for herself and figured she had a new obsession.

Along with returning Danielle's things, now that the lodge area had been cleared, she could finish recording the damage to the archaeological site and document the damage to the historic structures. Lake Olympus Lodge had survived a battle, but not without injury.

In addition to ordering replacements for the Baldwins, Audrey had put together a new dig go bag, having lost hers somewhere between the helicopter, hospital, and base.

The one item she didn't replace in her dig kit was condoms. One way or another, she wouldn't need those in her dig kit in the future. Although the last box had served her well in the strangest way.

"You sure you want to deliver this stuff today?" Undine asked as she surveyed the pile of gear in Audrey's living room.

"No time like the present. The locks haven't been fixed yet at the Baldwin cabin, so I can slip them inside, no problem. And I might as well record the site damage while I'm there. It'll nag at me while I'm on leave if I don't."

Undine sighed. "I hear that. Luke and I were on vacation

in New Zealand, and I woke up in the middle of the night because of an unfinished project—and it wasn't even my responsibility."

She nodded. "Been there. I want every piece of this behind me, and since Xavier won't be here for a few more days, I might as well get this done. Besides, it'll be good for me to go back and face the place. Get it over with."

"Will you be alone?"

She shook her head. "There'll be others around at the lodge—contractors are putting together bids for repairs, and some of the inholding landowners are returning."

"Will George be there?"

"Possibly. He was planning to move back to his cabin as soon as the all clear came."

"I'm sure it won't be the same for him with Jeb gone."

"Yeah. I think he wants to get back in the woodshop. To create again. He told me after Jeb's memorial that art was how he learned to cope with what he'd had to do in Vietnam." Jeb's coping mechanism had been more...defensive. "I can't even imagine what he's processing right now."

Undine gave her a squeeze.

"I don't grieve for a single mercenary who died during the op, but I feel for George and Xavier and everyone who played a part in the killing, even in self-defense. And it feels worse for George. Xavier—and Luke—they joined the SEALs intentionally. They fought to get on the teams and worked hard to stay there. They went on ops in which they knew they'd have to kill. George was nineteen when he was drafted into the army. He didn't choose the job, it was forced on him. He then spent fifty years moving on and building a life that centered on a love of art and nature, and then all at once, his most sacred places—his forest and his workshop— were under attack, and he had to kill again to protect his world. I'm in awe of what he did for us. Thankful. I hope the shop helps him heal and doesn't trigger remorse or pain."

"I hope you see him there today." Undine picked up a sleeping bag and backpack. "Let's get these loaded in your SUV. Maybe you can get to the park in time for tea with George."

$\mathcal{I}$t was strange to be driving back to the park. It had only been three weeks, and she used to do this drive often, but now it felt unreal.

She had four new tires, a new side panel and gas tank, but otherwise, her SUV was the same.

She itched for the day when life would feel normal again.

She felt a fluttering in her belly, and not for the first time, she wondered if that was the baby wiggling inside her. At fifteen weeks, it was still too early to feel movement for a first child, but not completely impossible. The fetus was now the size of an apple, and she was definitely starting to show.

This was a good reminder that there would never be a return to normal for her. And she wouldn't have it any other way.

She opened the gate. After a moment's hesitation, she pulled out her phone and dialed Jae. When he didn't answer, she left a message. "Hey. I just wanted to give you the heads-up that I'm heading to the lodge. First to drop off things in the Baldwin cabin, then I'm heading up to the site to record the damage. I guess I'm feeling superstitious because I had the urge to call you at the gate. I promise, I won't do that every time moving forward...but maybe for the next little while."

She set her phone back on the console and drove through the gate, then closed it behind her again.

She felt silly making the call, but also, it was like a phantom that would haunt her if she hadn't. An OCD tick.

She needed a successful number of trips down Lake Olympus Road before it would feel normal to not check in at the gate.

Jae had been her fairy godfather before. Best to keep him in the loop.

It had been at least three days since the last rain, and the air was unseasonably warm, alleviating any black ice fears she might have.

But still, tension knotted her shoulders as she drove. It was impossible to escape thoughts of the last time she'd been on this road and what had awaited her at the end of the drive.

She needed to get over this fear. She loved this lodge and forest and refused to give it up. Besides, she had to work here.

She'd learned a few days ago that Jeb's heir planned to sell his lakeside cabin, and George had asked her if she was interested in buying it. It was extremely rare for inholding parcels to come on the market, and when they did, the park tried to purchase them if possible. Jeb, however, had specifically stated in his will that the property was not to be sold to any government agency. Audrey had no idea if such a directive could be upheld, but there was no reason to believe his niece wouldn't follow it.

A lakeside cabin on Lake Olympus would be out of her price range, but Xavier said he had savings and wanted to think about it. The idea of owning a cabin as old as the lodge had a certain appeal, but it still seemed wild to consider it.

At last, she reached the lakeside, and instead of turning right at the fork and going straight to the Baldwins' cabin, she took a left and went all the way to the end of the road to take a look at Jeb's property.

She got out of her vehicle and approached the cabin, noting again all the "NO TRESPASSING" signs and feeling like she was doing something wrong here, even though Jeb was gone and the niece who inherited knew people would be viewing the property.

She circled the cabin to the lakefront side and climbed up the porch steps to look out at the water.

It was sunny and chilly, with patches of blue sky amid white and gray clouds. The calm water offered a near-mirror reflection of green tree-covered hillside with blue sky and clouds. An upside-down vision of the world.

It was serene and achingly beautiful, and she knew exactly why Jeb had loved his small sanctuary on the water so much.

She pulled out her phone and snapped a photo of the water and hillside, then texted it to Xavier.

He responded almost immediately.

Xavier: *Beautiful. Where are you?*
Audrey: *On Jeb's porch.*
Xavier: *Wish I was there with you. You okay?*
Audrey: *I think so. It was weird driving here, but I felt like I needed to do it alone. I'm going to have to return to my job at some point.*
Xavier: *I get that. You returning the camping gear to the Baldwins?*
Audrey: *Yeah. Then I'm going to record the damage to the*

site. Get it over with so I can enjoy my leave when you get home.

Xavier: *On that note… They released me early, and I'm on Highway 101 right now. I was heading to your place to surprise you. I'll keep going. Meet me at the gate?*

She felt a thrill at knowing he was back on the peninsula and was disappointed she wasn't home to greet him properly. The last time he'd shown up at her door unannounced had been rather spectacular.

Audrey: *The gate is closed but unlocked. There are contractors coming and going in the lodge.*

Xavier: *Great. Meet you at the site, then. Should be there in ninety minutes or so.*

That would be fast, but Lake Olympus Road was free of ice, so not unreasonable.

Audrey: *Don't speed. And I really hope you aren't texting and driving.*

Xavier: *Pulled over to look at the photo. Now using voice text. And I won't speed…much.*

She rolled her eyes.

Xavier: *I promise I'll be careful. How is Apple today?*

Audrey: *Snug as a bug. I'll let you focus on the road. Can't wait to see you.*

Xavier: *Soon. Love you.*

Audrey: *Love you.*

She tucked her phone away and circled back to her SUV, a happy buzz filling her.

Ninety minutes. She was giddy with excitement.

And so very glad she'd come here today to document the damage to the site. The moment that was done, she wouldn't think about her job again for two weeks.

She hadn't worked the last three weeks, but it hadn't been a vacation. She'd been recovering emotionally and providing long-distance support for Xavier. She'd been terrified of being alone at night knowing the unaccounted-for mercenary could find her name in the heavily redacted news accounts of what had happened in the lodge.

It had been a huge relief when Mikhail's body had been found, but she still hadn't been ready to be alone. Jae and Undine were the best friends in the world to agree to continue splitting babysitting duty until Xavier's return.

They would appreciate her vacation with Xavier as much as she would, and by the time Xavier had to return to Coronado, she'd be ready to be alone again.

She drove to the Baldwin cabin and took her time placing each item where the original had been located. She'd had to guess on a few items and wondered if she'd forgotten anything, but the REI gift card should cover anything she'd missed.

She wrote a note to Danielle, again thanking her for her forced generosity, then added a note about wanting to book the rental for a few days if possible. If the rental request didn't set Danielle's fears to rest, nothing would.

From there, she drove north to the lodge, passing the main structure and continuing on the gravel track that ran behind the complex, finally parking not far from where this same vehicle had sat for several days during the siege.

The lights were on in George's shop, and she popped in to say hello.

Stretched out between supports was a large log. It appeared George was embarking on making a new totem pole. He hadn't made one of those in a long time, and she couldn't wait to see what animals he would carve into the massive work of art.

He beamed at her as he took in her reaction to seeing the log being prepped for carving. "I've been saving this wood for a long time. Waiting for the right inspiration."

"I can't wait to see what you have planned."

"It's going to be my greatest work." Then he winked at her. "Well, until the one I make after it."

She laughed. "Of that there is no doubt." She nodded toward the rear door of the shop. "I'm heading up to record the damage to the site. Xavier should be arriving in"—she glanced at her watch—"about forty minutes." She'd spent more time at the Baldwins' than she'd realized and was pleased he'd be here soon.

"Maybe I'll take a break later and join you."

She nodded. "I have a thermos of tea."

"If I don't make it up, stop by on your way back."

"Will do."

She set out, stopping at her SUV to grab her backpack, reminded of the argument she'd had with Xavier about stopping for it on that fateful afternoon.

She climbed the hillside slowly, as befitting a fifteen-week-pregnant woman who'd gotten very little exercise in the last three weeks.

Even still, she slipped in a few places, as the ground remained saturated and slick. Life in a temperate rainforest.

She reached the site and set to work. The walls had slumped under the pressure of the rain, and investigators had been all through here, doing their own damage to the open pit.

She pulled out her notebook and wrote a description of the disturbance. Thankfully, it was confined to a small area.

Notes complete, she walked transects across the entire

site—forest and meadow—noting the condition of the ground everywhere and taking pictures with her phone.

Her back was to the forested portion of the site when she heard the crack of a stick, as if it had been stepped on. She paused, her heart surging. Xavier was here.

She turned, but no one was behind her.

She scanned the woods, but Xavier or George would call out to her, knowing how much it would freak her out to be sneaked up upon here of all places.

Her gaze dipped to her pack, on the ground in the forest near the pit.

Too far for her to reach quickly.

She'd purchased a new gun, as her previous one was now evidence in the investigation of the siege and they were matching fired bullets and casings to weapons.

She could have requested it back, but it had felt simpler to purchase a new one of the same type.

It was useless in her pack, however.

She walked sideways, toward the trail, keeping her front facing the forest where she'd heard the footstep.

It hadn't been a deer or a mountain lion.

Someone was in those woods. Watching her.

She could make a run for the trail.

She inched ever closer to the path in the woods. When she reached the hillside, her shouts might carry across the water. George might hear her.

But first, she had to make it through the woods to the open hillside.

Movement caught her eye as a man emerged from behind a tree. Without hesitation, she turned and ran for the path.

But the man was faster than she'd imagined possible, and he was on her in seconds.

She screamed as loud as she could as he overtook her and slammed her to the ground.

She landed on her belly and fear shot through her. The fetus was larger now. She was ever so slightly showing. Had it been hurt by the impact with the ground?

She screamed until a hand slammed over her mouth.

"Shut up," the man said in a heavy Russian accent, confirming her worst fear.

She bit his hand as hard as she could, determined to take a finger off if possible.

This wasn't a time for squeamishness. Not if she wanted to live.

He howled with pain and pulled his hand away. She felt a blow to the back of her head—a backhanded slap. He cursed and said, "Cooperate, bitch, or I'll make this more painful."

She bucked against him and he backhanded her again. Harder this time.

Her head swam.

She stopped fighting. She needed to think. Needed time.

Xavier would be here soon.

She cleared her throat and said, "Mikhail, I presume." She tried to sound confident, but her voice came out shaky.

"Good. You know who I am." He stood and yanked her to her feet, twisting her around to face him. "But do you know why I plan to kill you?"

Her head swam again at being forced to her feet so quickly. Her knees wobbled. "Because you're a mercenary and are being paid?"

"Oh no. I kill you for free."

"Oh goody. I'm flattered. Usually, mercenaries are so discriminating."

He slapped her, but she didn't care. Slapping wasn't shooting. Slapping her face didn't hurt the baby.

"At the start of the siege, I told my men to let you live. Women weren't to be part of our conflict. We never kill women or children."

"How moral of you." Her voice dripped with sarcasm.

"But then I read your letter and realized you were the answer to my prayers. I was hired by Katerina's father to exact revenge on the SEALs who botched her rescue. Your letter told me I could exact revenge of my own. You see, Katerina was pregnant with my child when your lover killed her. Shot her in the belly."

Another wave of dizziness hit her, and this time, she wasn't even sure why.

She gathered her wits and asked the crucial question. "How could you even know that?"

Behind her, she heard Xavier say, "Because he was there."

Mikhail yanked her to his chest, turning her so she was a shield in front of him. He placed his hand at her throat and squeezed lightly.

"That's why you wore a mask. You knew Flyte and I saw your face in Belarus."

The hand at her throat tightened, and she struggled to breathe, clawing at his hand.

After a long moment, his grip relaxed, and he said. "I was hoping you would come. I was hoping you would watch as I do to your lover and child what you did to mine."

She studied Xavier's face as he inched closer through the forest, his gun drawn but not pointed at Mikhail, as that would mean pointing it at her.

He avoided looking at her. His face was stone-cold operator. Deadly intent on the man who threatened to crush her windpipe.

"You hurt her and there is nothing stopping me from tearing you apart."

"So be it. I've already died once. Hanged myself."

"You shot your minion with a nail gun days before you hung him, so it would have time to heal, as your wound did. How did you get him to agree to that?"

"I paid him for the initial wound. Told him I wanted him to be photographed with the wound visible after taking the ferry to Victoria. Once he was in Canada, I promised to get him on a private boat and smuggle him out of the country."

"Then, after the puncture wound healed enough, you killed him and the other mercenaries in the RV," Xavier said.

"I still don't understand," Audrey said. "Why were you in Belarus? Were you trying to rescue Katerina too?"

"No," Xavier answered. "He was her captor. The one who abducted her."

"Her father hired his daughter's abductor to get his revenge against the SEALs who tried to rescue her?"

"I was an employee of Grigory Laskin already," Mikhail said.

He was clearly pleased to get to share this. But then, he wanted Xavier to know exactly why he was here. Wanted to draw out Audrey's pain as Xavier watched.

"She and I fell in love, but we knew her father would never allow it, so she came up with a plan that she would be abducted. Eventually, her father would pay the demanded ransom, and she and I would disappear together. But instead, her father was turning traitor against Russia and used a potential alliance with the US to pressure your government to rescue her."

"Katerina didn't want to be rescued," Xavier said. "She wanted the ransom money. When I told you we were betrayed, Audrey, I didn't say the full truth. It was Katerina who betrayed us. She shot Forsythe and Adams before we knew what was happening. She turned her gun on me. Chris and I fired at the same time. We both killed her. Her bullet landed in my shoulder at the same time she took one in the chest and one in the head." He glared at Mikhail. "Not in the belly. From the look of her, she was at least six months pregnant. Also worth noting, Katerina was only fifteen years old. She was a fucking child."

Oh good lord. No wonder Xavier was tormented by that op. He'd had to kill a pregnant girl to survive. *Fifteen.*

Mikhail was slowly dragging her backward, deeper into the woods.

Her heart ached at the nightmare Xavier and Chris had been through, watching the hostage they were trying to rescue kill two team members. Being forced to kill her.

Katerina would have killed Xavier next if they hadn't.

The truth had probably been buried. Did her oligarch father even know? Would he believe his daughter—a fifteen-year-old child—had planned her own abduction so she could demand a ransom and run off with her lover?

Did he know a man in his own employ was the one who'd taken her?

She assumed not, given that when he'd sent his henchman to exact revenge, he'd sent the true villain who'd seduced, then abducted his daughter.

"This is why the three mercs who were captured said you were unstable. You were more obsessed with taking Xavier and me than in getting out of the forest alive."

"I wanted Flyte too," the man said.

"You left the forest immediately, didn't you?" Audrey said. "You were hiking toward Forks before the helicopters were even in the air."

"I needed to call my men in the RV to pick me up before the idiots who let men with paint pellets take the lodge reached them first."

"But there were only three men in the RV," Xavier said. "Who was the hanged man?"

"He's the one who stole the master gate key from the camp host and changed the lock while the other three kept the cop busy. He had his own car and met the team in Forks after they'd been kicked out of Mora Campground. They then caused a mudslide to keep the local police busy."

That was the final piece. After Mikhail killed the rest of his team, he'd had a car no one knew about to move freely about the peninsula.

"And then you waited for 'your' body to be found so you could return to the forest and wait for me here?"

"Yes. I knew you'd be back. When your car was in the shop, I put a tracker on it. I knew the moment you drove through the gate. All I needed was to get into position."

Mikhail continued to pull her backward up the path, stumbling here and there on roots. His grip was on her throat, so she couldn't let him drag her, or she'd end up strangled.

She looked for an opening, a way to slip from his grasp so Xavier could take a shot.

"Did you know I'm the one who shot you with the nail?"

The hand at her throat tightened. "I suspected."

Audrey tried to keep her focus, even as her air was constricted. Her brain searched for ways to escape. He'd taken her bare-handed, which meant the hard object at the small of her back was probably a gun.

One of his hands left her neck, and she realized he might be reaching for it. She elbowed him in the ribs, a hard jab that triggered a surprised grunt.

The hand on her throat squeezed again, harder now. She went all in, elbows, heels, and a sharp head butt. She had four unrestrained limbs, and he was distracted by Xavier and his gun. Mikhail said something in Russian that she was certain was an insult.

She struggled to breathe while flailing, kicking, jabbing.

He caught one arm, but couldn't contain the other without releasing her throat. She worked her hand between their bodies and grabbed his balls and squeezed.

He released her neck, and she used the leverage from her hand on his junk to push off him, attempting to fling herself away, but he grabbed at her, pulling her back. She kicked him in the knee and dove to the side.

Mikhail caught her foot and shifted, crouching low to keep her between him and Xavier. She was on hands and knees, trying to get away while he dragged her back by the ankle.

She hung her head down, looking between her arms, trying to figure out how to kick with her free leg, when she saw him pull his gun.

His weapon had just cleared the holster when a shot rang out. He released her ankle, and she flopped flat on the ground while Mikhail stumbled backward.

A second shot sounded, and he dropped.

It was then that she'd noticed they'd backed all the way up to the storage pit. When he'd staggered back, he'd been on the cusp of the pit. The second shot had dropped him into the meter-deep hole.

She took in a ragged breath through her battered windpipe and glared at the body with a bullet to the heart and a second in the head. "Dammit," she wheezed. "He collapsed another sidewall. More damage to the site."

She wanted to laugh at her own terrible joke, but instead, she burst into tears.

*

Xavier was worried Audrey was going into shock. She was shaking and alarmingly pale.

George had appeared not long after the

gunshots. He took one look at Audrey and said, "Be right back," and ran in the direction of his cabin.

Minutes later, he returned with a blanket and a wheel-barrow, and Xavier wrapped her tight—even as she complained and said she was fine—and deposited her in the barrow and pushed it down the path.

"I can walk, Xavier," she complained, and her voice did sound better. Color was returning to her face.

"I'm sure you can, but why do that when you can ride?"

It was a quick, albeit bumpy trek down the trail, which had a groove from all the trips George made along the same path with his trusty wheelbarrow.

When they reached George's shop, Audrey insisted they take her SUV and not Xavier's rental the short distance to the lodge. "I refuse to leave my car here again. Call me superstitious, but I'm not taking chances."

Relieved she was sounding better by the minute, he tucked her into the passenger seat, ignoring his shoulder's complaints at the required lift.

At the lodge, she climbed out herself. They entered the building, finding it empty of contractors. George remained up at the site, guarding the body, so they were alone in the vast room.

He'd made an initial call to NSWC immediately after the shooting. He'd wanted a medic flight for Audrey, but she'd insisted she just needed to get warm. They'd compro-mised by requesting an ambulance so she could be checked out by a medic. It would take investigators time to get here. In all likelihood the ambulance would arrive first, and she could be cleared healthwise before being debriefed yet again.

He sat her in front of the great hearth and turned on the gas to start a fire. The fireplace had a gas line to get the fire going without kindling, but burned real wood. The result was a wood fire that put out instant heat, which was just what she needed.

Once the fire was going, he dropped on the sofa next to her, pulled her into his arms, and faced the flame.

"I assume what he said was true. You and Chris both shot Katerina?"

He nodded, that nightmare moment playing again in his mind. The unfathomable sight of a very young pregnant girl —the victim they'd been sent to save—shooting Forsythe before anyone could grasp what was happening. A heartbeat later, she shot Adams before turning her gun on him.

"Mikhail looks like he's in his forties. She was *fifteen*. He'd probably groomed her starting when she was thirteen or fourteen. Planning to use her to get to her father's money. She was a victim. I'm sure she was terrified of being returned to her father. He'd realize she was in cahoots with Mikhail and had been for a long time given how far along she was in her pregnancy. I gathered she hadn't been showing yet at the time of her abduction."

She'd been a victim, and he'd had to shoot her to save himself. But it had been too late to save the others. "When I think of what Mikhail did to her, I'd like to go shoot him again."

"And I wish I'd taken a shot too." She cupped his face in her hands and kissed him. Her voice was low and raspy when she spoke, and again, he wanted to mangle a corpse. "I'm sorry I worried you. I just…had a moment there. But I'm fine now."

"Sweetheart, you don't need to apologize for that."

"Okay. But really, I want you to know I'm fine now." She leaned back. "It's over now. All of it." She threaded her fingers through his. "Over. Really and truly over. I don't need to worry about sleeping alone anymore."

"Too bad you won't be alone."

She smiled. "No. Not too bad at all."

Xavier extracted himself from her and tossed another log on the fire. He glanced around the room. It was a bit the worse for wear, but they were all alone in the very room where they'd first met. When he'd first fallen under her spell.

He reached into his pocket as he lowered himself to one knee before her. "I doubt we'll ever have a chance to be alone in this room again, so I'm not going to waste my shot."

She looked at him in confusion as he reached for her hand and pulled it to his lips.

"Dr. Audrey Kendrick, you are the most amazing woman I know, and from the first moment we met, you pretty much stole my heart. I want to be with you for the rest of my days. Will you marry me?"

Tears tracked down her cheeks. She leaned forward and kissed him, then said, "Yes. Yes. Yes. I love you."

He presented the ring box. "This was my grandmother's ring. If you don't like it, we'll get you something you *do* like. I want you to love your ring because it's yours, and not settle for something because it's mine."

She opened the box and let out a gasp. It wasn't a traditional engagement ring—it had a sapphire in the center of six small diamonds—he knew it might not be to her taste. "Oh, Xavier. It's beautiful. I love it."

"It'll probably have to be resized." He slipped it on her finger, and thankfully, it was a little big. Resizing would be easy.

He returned to her side on the couch and held her as they gazed into the flames.

"Do you know what the first thing I ever heard you say was?"

"I asked Jae if I could use his shower."

"Yes, but do you remember your actual words?"

"No."

"You said you'd name your firstborn child after him if he let you use his shower."

She laughed. "Oh my goodness! That's right. And then you offered me yours and said I didn't even have to name my baby after you."

"Good thing too."

"Why's that?"

"Because I think I know the perfect name for Apple, and it's not after me."

Epilogue

*T*hey married a month later in a small ceremony in the gazebo not far from the new dock in front of the lodge. They went to Hawai'i for a two-week honeymoon and returned in time to pack up Audrey's small house for the bigger one they'd purchased down the road from Undine and Luke's acreage.

Xavier retired from the Navy in early July and spent his time preparing the baby's room while Audrey worked through the last week of the month.

When she reached her due date with no baby, she decided to start her maternity leave anyway. She was exhausted and cranky and had reached the point where she no longer was concerned about labor, she just wanted the baby out.

Early in the first week of August, she got her wish when her water broke with a rush all over their kitchen floor. Contractions started immediately, and they definitely weren't the Braxton-Hicks kind she'd been having for weeks.

She practiced her breathing exercises on the car ride to the hospital, and by the time she arrived, she was convinced they were a hoax designed to make pregnant women believe they were prepared for something for which there was no preparation. But once she was able to walk around again and breathe, she decided perhaps they offered some merit.

Still, labor lasted twenty hours, some of which raced by and some of which dragged. But through it all, Xavier was there, holding her hand, feeding her ice chips, and providing indefatigable support.

Her rock.

Her husband.

Her life.

Their daughter was born in the early afternoon, and Audrey found she also wasn't prepared for how beautiful her child would be, how amazing it would feel to have her tiny body, with umbilical cord still attached, placed on her chest.

She was so enamored of her perfect little wonder, she barely registered the passing-the-placenta part of the process.

Xavier was equally in awe, and the look on his face as he held their baby for the first time was yet another high.

At some point during their hazy first hours of parent-hood, they learned Undine had gone into labor. She and Luke were down the hall.

Labor, delivery, and aftercare rooms were all one at the medical center, and Xavier spent the night in a large reclining chair next to her bed while she slept—or, at least, tried to sleep—with their daughter in her arms.

The next day, they learned Undine also had a girl in the wee hours of the morning. Their daughters' birthdays were just a day apart.

Jae arrived with George to meet the baby at the start of visiting hours. They'd requested these two men be the first guests for a reason. Audrey was sitting up in the bed holding the baby when George entered the room, a wooden seal carved and painted in the Coast Salish style in his hands. "For the baby's room."

"Oh, George, that's beautiful. Thank you so much."

Xavier took the carving, freeing George's hands.

"Do you want to hold her?" Audrey asked the elder.

"I'm a bit out of practice when it comes to babies. Never had any of my own kids. Just nieces and nephews."

She placed her daughter in his hands, and he held her out, his large palm supporting her head, her swaddled body resting on the length of his arm. "Well, aren't you a little beauty," he whispered in the softest, cooiest voice she'd ever heard him use. His gaze flicked from Audrey's to Xavier's. "What's her name?"

Xavier squeezed her hand as she said, "Georgina Jae Rivera."

Both men looked up sharply, and George said, "Georgina?"

At the same time, Jae said, "Jae?"

"Yes. Because she wouldn't be here if not for either of you."

"Luke is gonna be pissed," Jae quipped.

"He's got his own daughter to name now," Xavier said with a laugh.

George pulled Georgina to cradle her against his chest. "Georgina Jae," he murmured, and she could swear she saw a tear in his eye. He looked up. "I'm honored."

Jae reached for the baby. "My turn, old man." He took the sleeping baby and held her against his chest and whispered, "Someday, I'm going to tell you all the ways your dad got in trouble when he was a kid."

"Crap," Xavier muttered. "Sorry, Aud, we're doomed. Maybe we should move after all."

She chuckled. "Not a chance. If Jae has kids, you can

threaten him with the same thing. You know, like that time you both got arrested for grand theft auto…"

"Damn, he told you?"

"That and soooo much more."

After their visitors left, Audrey stared at her beautiful daughter some more, marveling at her perfection of nose, lips, and rounded cheeks.

She then looked at her husband, who also had a beautiful face she could spend hours adoring, and felt a glow of warmth and love. She took his hand and pulled it to her lips. "You know what I want to do today?"

"Sleep?"

"Well, yeah, that, but also, I want to go down the hall and introduce Gina to her first friend, and then I want to go home and start our next adventure of raising our baby together as a family."

Author's Note

For much of the last seven years, my husband's job as an archaeologist for the US Navy has involved the process of assessing the potential for effects that Navy SEAL trainings in Washington State Parks could have on historical and cultural resources. Giving Audrey final approval over the Lake Olympus Lodge Exercise was no exaggeration on my part. My husband met with SEAL teams more than once to discuss their protocols for engaging with the environment when they train. They demonstrated their use of Simunition and other equipment. In one instance, my husband conducted a sensitivity training to alert SEALs how best to avoid harming cultural and historic resources. I laugh every time I think of my husband leading a SEAL sensitivity training.

Naturally, my husband's work in this area led me to wonder what would happen if you had a top-secret training with unarmed SEALs in a remote area and the wrong people got wind of the exercise, and INTO THE STORM was born.

My fictional Lake Olympus Lodge is modeled after Lake Quinault Lodge in the Quinault Rainforest. It is truly a spectacular place to visit—even in January (the lodge is open year-round)—if you get a chance.

About the Author

USA Today bestselling author Rachel Grant worked for over a decade as a professional archaeologist and mines her experiences for storylines and settings, which are as diverse as excavating a cemetery underneath an historic art museum in San Francisco, survey and excavation of many prehistoric Native American sites in the Pacific Northwest, researching an historic concrete house in Virginia, and mapping a seventeenth century Spanish and Dutch fort on the island of Sint Maarten in the Netherlands Antilles.

She lives in the Pacific Northwest with her husband and children.

For more information:
www.Rachel-Grant.net
contact@rachel-grant.net

CPSIA information can be obtained
at www.ICGtesting.com
Printed in the USA
LVHW041345040123
736362LV00001B/90

9 781944 571528